A Liz Higgins Mystery

FRONT PAGE TEASER

By Rosemary Herbert

Down East

This book is a work of fiction. While some of the landscapes, businesses, and other venues may be recogniz **3 1712 01347 4823** be based on actual places— all of the action that oc~~~~~~~~~~~~~~~~~~ ~~~~~~ ~~ ~~~~~~~ a work of the imagination. The author does not recommend that readers assume they may have access to any properties shown herein, especially including university libraries or private landscapes. Similarly, with the exception of the cat Prudence and mystery writer Mary Higgins Clark, the characters portrayed within the pages of this book are entirely fictional, although a few friends and family members have graciously allowed the author to borrow their names or create variations upon them. While a former mayor of the City of Newton reportedly gave Fig Newton cookies to visitors, the Newton mayor depicted here is not that man. The author would also like to emphasize that the names of the fictional characters in these pages who are shown as associated with terrorism are chosen randomly. The author neither possesses knowledge of terrorist networks nor of individuals who are involved in such activities, nor does anyone who advised her about any aspect of this book. While sometimes the characters in this book refer to the *Beantown Banner* simply as "the *Banner*," this is not to be confused with the *Bay State Banner* newspaper, of which this author has no experience.

Copyright © 2010 by Rosemary Herbert
Cover photograph © iStockphoto.com/4971695

ISBN: 978-0-89272-852-7

Library of Congress Cataloging-in-Publication Data
Herbert, Rosemary.
 Front page teaser : a Liz Higgins mystery / by Rosemary Herbert.
    p. cm.
 ISBN 978-0-89272-852-7 (trade pbk. : alk. paper)
1. Women journalists--Fiction. 2. Boston (Mass.)--Fiction. I. Title.
 PS3608.E7296F76 2010
 813'.6--dc22

                                        2010012133

Designed by Lynda Chilton
Printed at Versa Press, East Peoria, Illinois

5 4 3 2

Down East
BOOKS·MAGAZINE·ONLINE
www.downeast.com

Distributed to the trade by National Book Network

For Bill Wyman
—who truly knows how to celebrate Christmas—
with love and gratitude

And to the worlds of the newsroom
and public and academic libraries.
May newspaper journalism find its way and thrive again
even as technology changes, because a free press
staffed by professional reporters and editors
is nothing short of fundamental to a democratic society.
Similarly, another foundation of democracy
may be found in libraries, where staff members
protect patron privacy while they also dedicate their
efforts to ensuring freedom of access
to information.
∽

Books by Rosemary Herbert

Acknowledgments

I would like to extend my thanks to the following people who provided everything from professional expertise and practical help to friendship and encouragement: Pamela Ackerknecht, Catherine Aird, Alfred Alcorn, Tony Alcorn, Cindy Atoji, Peter Alden, Father Joseph Bagetta and the DYS crocheting group, Jean and Jim Behnke, Dana Bisbee, Paula Blanchard, Henri Bourneuf, Gerry Boyle, Margaret Byer, Mark Chapman, Rochelle Cohen, Neil Cote, Guy Darst, Nancy Day, Renée DeKona, Dick Donahue, Paul Doiron, Jane Gelfman, Dr. Herbert Gross, Bonni Hamilton, Jeremiah Healy, Barbara Herbert, Janice Herbert, P.D. James, Sande Kent, Linda Kincaid, Cara Nissman Kraft, Jeffrey Levine, Tom Libby, Reuben Mahar, Kevin McNamara, Janet Mendelsohn, Jenny Miller, Susan and Steve Moody, Elaine M. Ober, Diana O'Neill, Richard Olken, Eliza Partington, Juliet Partington, Mike Pingree, Arthur Pollock, Jeanne and Darrell Ray, John M. (Tim) Reilly, Chris Rippen, Eileen Tomaney Robinson, Tenley Rooney, Daisy and Jeremy Ruggiero, Todd Sawyer, Stephanie Schorow, Michael Seamans, John Sgammato, Al Silverstein, Clara Silverstein, Peter Skagestad, Barbara Sloane, Curtis C. Smith, JP Smith, Katy Snow, Richard Stomberg, Brian Sylvester, Sonya Turek, Cathy Weider, Karin Womer, Wayne Woodlief, and Bill Wyman. I also would like to remember the following people who always believed in me: my father, Robert D. Herbert; my grandparents, Mary and Harry Fransen; my creative writing teacher, Alfred E. Haulenbeek; and to these masters of mystery—Tony Hillerman, John Mortimer, Robert B. Parker, and Julian Symons.

With special thanks to Mary Higgins Clark, for her encouragement, and for consenting to be a character in my mystery.

And with profound appreciation to Dick Sloane, for his generosity and belief in me as a writer, and to his mother, the late Vera Sloane, simply for being herself.

Rosemary Herbert

"Let nothing you dismay."

Christmas Muzak was playing over the loudspeakers in Penn Station as Ellen Johansson strode to the escalator leading from the AMTRAK train waiting area to the taxi stand. So eager was she to make her date that she walked up the escalator steps even as they rose.

There was little to burden her. She carried only a purse and a small briefcase filled with correspondence, much of it written on onion-skin paper, postmarked from one of the world's hotspots.

In the briefcase, she carried something else. A surprise she longed to present to her foreign correspondent.

Pushing through the glass doors with the crowd, Ellen buttoned up her dressy winter coat and arranged the scarf she chose especially for the occasion. It would help the person she planned to meet to recognize her. She only hoped that person would also remember to wear something similarly recognizable.

If there had been room to do it, Ellen would have paced with impatience as she waited with passengers from Boston and elsewhere who swelled the snaking line of people seeking taxis. Instead, she found herself wringing her hands, a gesture that was quite uncharacteristic.

When, at last, it was her turn for a taxi, Ellen leaned forward toward the driver's rolled-down window and said, "Can you take me to the World Trade Center?" As she made her request, a gust of wind tossed her strawberry-blonde hair across her freckled face.

She brushed it out of her eyes as the driver barked, "Get in, lady," in a heavily accented voice.

Ellen unbuttoned her coat in the overheated cab as it made its way out of the station and turned a corner. At the tail end of the Christmas rush, the area was thronged with shoppers. Ellen knew she looked like the out-of-towner she was, and wondered if the cabbie would try to take a circuitous route all the way to the Twin Towers. Then she would have to deal with the unpleasantness of telling him she knew better

"Mind if I smoke, lady?" the cabbie said, lighting up a cigarette before she could reply.

"Yes, I do," she wanted to say, but decided to pick her battle instead, asking, "Are you heading for Seventh Avenue?"

"Of course, lady," he said, assessing her through the rearview mirror.

"You think I take you for a ride?" he added, chuckling at his own joke.

But his eyes seemed mirthless in the small rectangle of reflective glass.

"Alhamdulillah," he mumbled in Arabic. By the grace of Allah.

"By the grace of any god, I'll get to my destination," Ellen mused inwardly while matching the man's face, as reflected in the mirror, with his identification picture posted on the seatback in front of her. *"Same man, all right,"* she thought. *"Samir Hasan,"* his card read.

The traffic remained jammed, but Hasan demonstrated skill in crawling through it, sometimes squeezing so close to other cabs that Ellen was sure their sides would scrape or the mirrors jutting out would slam together. Looking at her watch, Ellen's anxiety grew, but she had to admit, no driver could have improved upon Hasan's effort. And while he wove among other vehicles, around double-parked delivery vans, and stopped on a dime to let a man push a rack of garments across the taxi's path, he kept up an animated conversation in Arabic with another male voice on his two-way radio.

Animated, yes. But also very earnest.

Once, Ellen caught him casting his eyes back at her through the rear-view mirror with a kind of intense scrutiny. But then he shook his head as if laughing at himself.

The radio conversation might have been about anything unpleasant. Marital problems. A nasty cab dispatcher. A business deal gone bad.

Then it took on a new tone. Might they be discussing a woman in intimate detail?

As, at last, the cab turned onto Seventh Avenue, Ellen found Hasan's eyes on her again. Paired with the tone of the conversation, his gaze instilled in her a sense of real dismay. Was he describing Ellen herself to his radio pal? But no, it must be someone else, she realized, as she heard him mention more than once a woman named Tina. Ellen indulged in a good-natured mental shrug, and asked herself if she would have been similarly uneasy if the driver were of something other than Middle Eastern extraction. Silently, she scolded herself for almost entertaining the prejudice that so many embraced after the towers she was about to visit were the targets of terrorist truck bombers in 1993. And, after all, wasn't she on her way to make contact with a Palestinian who held major importance in her life?

The Twin Towers loomed ahead. She was almost there.

The cabbie pulled the taxi to a stop. "Here you are, lady," he said, and collected his fare.

Ellen stepped out of the cab. *"Shukran,"* she said, on impulse, thanking *the cabbie in his own language.*

Looking over her shoulder to gauge his reaction, Ellen had to wonder if she was imagining what she saw.

The color seemed to drain completely out of the man's swarthy complexion.

Chapter 1

Boston, December 18, 2000

Liz Higgins sat on the city editor's desk and surveyed the sea of desks extending around her in the *Beantown Banner* newsroom. Unlike the tabloid's competitor, the broadsheet *Boston World*—whose newsroom packed with cubicles was rumored to have all the ambience of an insurance office—the *Banner*'s digs were like something out of an old-time movie, minus the cigarette smoke and clatter of typewriters. There were no dividers between the many desks where reporters worked on outdated word processors. To maintain their trains of thought, newsroom hacks had to tune out their co-workers' telephone conversations, ignore the voices of announcers on radios constantly monitored by lowly editorial assistants, resist listening to the engaging banter between editors at the city and photo desks, and overcome the urge to strangle political columnist Fred Constanzo, who read his work-in-progress aloud to himself, so as to better appreciate the flow of his golden words.

This was a place of bold headlines—in typeface and attitude. The *Banner* took pride in calling a spade a spade—or any term that took a dig at its subject. When a toymaker killed his wife and buried her in his backyard at Christmas, the headline read, "HOE, HOE, HOE!"

In short, the home of the *Beantown Banner* was a red-blooded, American newsroom.

And it was the place where Liz Higgins wanted to be taken as seriously as the breaking news she wished to cover. To that end, she spun around on her city desk perch and looked city editor Dermott McCann straight in the eye. That movement represented a calculated risk. The U-shaped desktop was littered with coffee cups damp with dregs of caffeine fixes past, a cardboard Chinese take-out box exuding a greasy odor, and waxy red china marking pencils, which the editors used to mark up copy. Since none of this detritus landed in McCann's lap, he appeared to tolerate Liz's in-your-face eye contact.

"What now?" he said, returning her gaze.

"Look, Dermott," she said forcefully while running her hand through her wavy mane of auburn hair. "You know I'm a good sport about these soft news stories, but do I have to go to the mall *again?* Can't you send the traffic reporter to write about the aggressive SUV drivers in the parking lot there? I'd say that's his beat, not mine."

"We've got him covering guys who don't dig out the snow around their fire hydrants, Liz. You've gotta agree, his story's got priority after that kid was killed in the house fire because firemen couldn't get to the hydrants quick enough."

"I agree the hydrant piece is more important, of course," Liz said. "But I don't agree that I should always get the assignment that's bound to get less play in the paper."

"Whaddaya mean?" Dermott demanded. "Didn't you get a front-pager on that piece you wrote about the cute kid who rated the Santas? 'Best white beard. Most jolly ho, ho, ho. Most believable.' There's a mall story that made waves."

"That was only a front-page teaser, Dermott, and you know you only put that minuscule photo on Page One because the Santa she rated 'Best' worked for one of our major advertisers. The story itself ran on page thirty. You buried it as deep as a fire hydrant in a blizzard."

"Bah, humbug!" Dermott said. "Now who's the cynic? I seem to recall running the teaser because the Santa looked classic and the kid in his lap had a strawberry-blonde mop and the face of an angel."

"*If* you could make out their features," Liz interjected. "The photo was so small, the U.S. Postal Service should consider it for next year's Christmas stamp."

"Don't give me attitude," Dermott warned. "It might take the edge off your success. That story was a heart-warmer; I gotta hand it to you. You picked the perfect kid: polite, funny, cute as a button, and full of amusing requests for the seven Santas."

"Yeah," Liz said. "That was a bonus. We knew she was just at the age where it was safe to let her know a department store Santa is not the one who comes down your chimney. But she believed just enough to hedge her bets and ask for a different gift from each one."

"Just in case they brought it on The Big Day," Dermott said, warming to the subject. "What a hoot she was, asking the last Kris Kringle to bring her new wallpaper for her bedroom!"

"I guess she'd run out of big toy ideas after sitting in the laps of six Saint Nicks. I was impressed when she was hesitant to diss the skinny Santa at the South Shore Plaza."

"Come to think of it, she did go easy on him. Considering she said the Bargain Bin's Santa 'didn't have a clue about Ho, Ho, Ho-ing,' and the Chestnut Hill guy was 'as snobby as that mall.' I'd have expected her to say more about a Santa with no gut."

"She did have something to say, but she asked me to keep it off the record."

"That kid has observed too many politicians."

"Actually, it was more a question of political correctness. Or, I should say, some pretty great sensitivity for a young kid. She said he was 'totally unbelievable,' but added, 'That isn't nice to say because he comes from another country and his feelings would be hurt.' She even said, 'If they have Santas in Palestine, kids there might think he was real.'"

"That would have been a great quote," Dermott said. "Too bad you didn't use it."

"Yes, and no," Liz said.

The city editor chose to ignore that remark. "That kid's a deep one," he said. "What was the kid's name again? How old is she?" Dermott asked.

"Veronica Johansson," Liz said. "She's eight years old. No nickname. Just Veronica."

"Great kid. Like I said, great feature."

Liz pressed her advantage. Leaning forward and crossing her legs she inquired, "Since I proved myself there, how about giving me a more exciting assignment this time around?"

"Shapely," Dermott mused aloud. "Now that's a word you don't hear often these days."

"What?" Liz asked, perplexed. Then she noticed Dermott ogling her legs.

"Maybe I'll take pity on you and have you do a hosiery feature," he laughed. "In a mall, of course."

Before Liz could make a retort, editorial assistant Jared Conneely sidled over to Dermott. Simpering and oddly prim for his twenty-some years, Jared possessed an air of being up to no good. Behind his back he was known as the Uriah Heep of the newsroom.

"It seems there might be a bit of a to-do at Newton City Hall's Hanukkah fête this afternoon," Jared said, using the old-fashioned vocabulary of which he was so fond. "The Italian-American mayor thinks he'll win Jewish voters if he dances the hora with them on the frozen lawn there. But I fear the poor fellow just might meet his Waterloo," Jared added, pausing for effect.

"You mean he'll slip on the skating pond there? For Chrissake, spit it out, Conneely," the city editor said, looking pointedly at the clock. "I've got a paper to get out."

"Someone has set up a crèche on the lawn there, complete with holy infant, wise men, and shepherds. Mayor Ficarelli will have to step smartly to dance around that one," Jared opined.

"OK, kiddo," Dermott said to Liz. "Thanks to that hot tip, you've won your reprieve. Forget the SUV parkers at the mall and get yourself out to Newton. Grab a photographer and make sure he gets the crèche in the shot. Put on your dancing shoes. And step lively," he said with a glance at Jared.

"All right, Chief," Liz said. "I'll cover another earth-shaking assignment in feature territory. Just promise me one thing."

Slowly, she recrossed her legs.

"What's that?" Dermott asked.

"If a big story ever breaks on my beat, you'll let me run with it."

"Yeah, sure. Now, get outta here and run on over to Newton City Hall."

Uncrossing her legs in a leisurely manner, Liz stepped down from the city editor's desk. It was not for nothing that her newsroom nickname was "Legs." She picked up her reporter's notebook and put on her coat.

"Shameless hussy," Jared said in a stage whisper.

The city editor winked.

Chapter 2

Liz was no stranger to the common at Newton City Hall. Composed of a spreading lawn, duck pond, and handsome oaks, it was just the kind of suburban site Dermott had made her news beat. Located at the start of the Boston Marathon's infamous uphill stretch known as Heartbreak Hill, it was the ideal place to interview spectators and faltering runners for marathon-related human-interest stories. Runners know Heartbreak Hill is the place where the race is won or lost, but, even so, it was miles from the finish line where front-page stories are made. In the summer, the common was also the site of farmers' markets and crafts fairs that, for Liz, promised more features than hard news.

"Still," Liz reminded herself, "you never know where you'll find breaking news."

The last time she set her eyes on this property, Newton's Mayor Giancarlo Ficarelli made news by dancing with a man dressed as the Nabisco fig. It was the 110th anniversary of the creation of the Fig Newton cookie, a confection that had been named for the well-heeled Boston suburb.

"Come to think of it," Liz recalled, as she parked her green Mercury Tracer on Commonwealth Avenue, "the story was a front-pager." That was thanks to a hilarious photo of Ficarelli and the fig in free-fall from the dance platform, a tumble that occurred when the over-enthusiastic mayor stepped too lively to a rendition of "New York, New York" by the Newton North High School's Northern Heights singing group. The lyrics, slightly altered for the occasion, went, "If I can make it there, I'll make it anywhere, so here's to you New-ton, New-TON!"

Recalling the headline, "NEWTON BIGWIG FELLS FIG NEWTON," Liz smiled and scanned the scene for any sign of the fleet-footed Ficarelli. He was nowhere to be seen, but the loudspeakers, blaring the tune to *Hava*

Nagila," were impossible to ignore. Liz wondered what self-respecting citizen would participate in the mayor's quirky notion of celebrating the Jewish holiday. Rounding some shrubs, she received her answer. Led by the mayor, some thirty preschoolers dutifully attempted to imitate the mayor's dance steps as the line of snow-boot–clad dancers wound its way through the property. Ficarelli only needed a flute to complete his image as the Pied Piper of Newton.

As carried away by the music as he was during the fig fiasco, the mayor seemed oblivious to the fact that he was leading the diminutive dancers straight toward the controversial crèche. But everyone else, including the preschoolers' parents, assorted dog walkers, and the *Banner* photographer René DeZona, could see the mayor's mistake. DeZona zoomed in eagerly as the mayor, who was looking over his shoulder at dancing preschoolers, slid on some dog droppings and ploughed straight into the Holy Family, scattering them all over the slippery scene.

"You have to hand it to the guy," Liz thought as she watched Ficarelli's feet fly out from under him and point straight up at the sky. "When he falls, it's picture perfect."

This time he outdid himself and delivered a quote, too.

"Holy shit!" the mayor declared.

Picture and quote might have made Page One—if the commotion on Newton City Hall Common had ended then and there.

But it didn't.

Before Ficarelli could stand up and dust the snow off his coat, before the preschoolers' parents could suppress their laughter long enough to round up their children, a kind of keening sound rent the atmosphere. Dogs on leashes howled in response and strained at their collars as a coatless, small child ran straight to the center of the common, looked frantically around her, and then threw herself into Liz's arms.

"Somebody bleeded all over my kitchen," the girl said, shivering. "Where's my mommy?' she cried.

"Veronica!" Liz exclaimed. And she hugged the child close. Taking off her own coat and wrapping it around the frantic youngster, she added, "Don't worry, Veronica. We'll find your mom. I promise."

Briskly crossing the common, a policeman approached.

"Dan Atwood," the officer said, naming himself. "What seems to be the problem here?" he demanded. "Where do you think you're going with that girl?"

"I'm taking her home. She lives on the side street there, just across Commonwealth Avenue. I'm acquainted with her family."

"I can't authorize you to do that," the officer said.

"Well, that's too bad," Liz replied, "because I plan to do it anyway. Can't you see she's ill-dressed and in shock?"

Taking in Liz's own coatless state, Atwood softened. "All right, take my jacket," he said. "Let's take her back to her house together."

"Thanks," Liz said, gratefully taking the proffered jacket. "It's okay, honey, we're taking you home," she said to Veronica, as Atwood took the child in his arms.

But Veronica wailed.

The child's evident terror at returning to her house erased any doubts Liz might have held when Veronica first spoke of her bloodied kitchen. But there was nothing to do but see the scene for herself.

"We won't make you go in the kitchen," she promised as the trio set off across the wide avenue, with photographer DeZona following at a discreet distance. "We're just going to look for your mom and dad," she explained.

"How do you know this family?" Atwood asked Liz. "I need you to identify yourself."

Liz hesitated. Should she let on that she was a *Banner* reporter so soon? He might then bar her entry to the Johanssons' house.

Veronica spoke up. "She's my friend. She took me to see Santa!" she said.

"My name is Liz Higgins," the reporter added and scanned Atwood's face to see if her name rang a bell. Apparently he did not read the *Beantown Banner* deeply enough to recognize the byline. When they came to the unlocked door of the Johanssons' house, he flung it open for Liz, then he carried Veronica over the threshold.

"Please don't make me go in there!" the child cried.

"We won't, Veronica. We won't," said Liz as Atwood handed the child over to her. "We'll just get warm in the living room."

Liz patted Veronica's head as the policeman barged through the dining room toward the back of the house. A minute later she heard him radio Newton Police headquarters. He gave the address and added, "Apparent B&E here. Blood all over. Send the crime scene unit right away."

DeZona stepped in and snapped reporter and child. "Sorry for startling you," he said as Veronica renewed her crying.

"Get outta here!" Atwood snarled when DeZona stepped into the kitchen.

DeZona did, but not before taking the shot that was bound to push the mayor's spectacular fall far off the *Beantown Banner*'s front page.

"I want my mommy," Veronica insisted.

"Let's see what we can do to find her," Liz said. "While Officer Atwood looks around the house, why don't we do some detective work? We'll write down our clues in my notebook, OK?"

Veronica nodded as Liz began to take notes. Liz knew she had just minutes to spare before Atwood discovered she was a reporter or brought in a youth officer to take charge of the child. Then, too, although the *Boston World* had not thought the Newton City Hall hora worthy of their reporters' time, no doubt they'd be onto the breaking news soon. Liz hoped the youth officer would take Veronica in hand before the *World*'s best and brightest darkened the door.

Avoiding direct mention of the kitchen, Liz asked, "When did you come home to the house, sweetie?"

"After school," Veronica said. "I'm allowed to walk home on Tuesdays because that's our afternoon."

Liz recalled Ellen Johansson's readiness to accompany her and Veronica to visit the first of seven Santas on a Tuesday afternoon. Ellen had said that was her "mother-and-daughter afternoon." A librarian, Ellen worked one evening per week, while her husband, Erik, took over childcare, so she could have an afternoon each week to devote to her child. A protective mother, Ellen told Liz she only allowed her daughter to serve as the *Banner*'s Santa rater because the child dreamed of becoming a reporter, and because Liz was known to the after-school teacher whose program Veronica attended four afternoons a week. But even so, Ellen had insisted on tagging along on the first Santa visit.

Liz recalled how Ellen had paused as soon as the trio entered the mall and asked her daughter to look up at a sleigh and reindeer suspended from the ceiling.

"Do you notice how you can see that from almost anywhere in the mall?" Ellen had asked Veronica. "And do you see that there is a desk right underneath it where the mall lady is selling gift certificates? If we become separated, I want you to look for the sleigh and go there. You could also ask a lady with children to take you to the gift certificate desk. Remember, always ask for help from a lady who has children with her, okay?"

At the time, Liz complimented Ellen on the levelheaded advice and promised she would provide similar advice at every mall she visited with

Veronica. Now, in the family's living room, she returned her attention to the safety-conscious mom's very bewildered daughter.

Still avoiding direct mention of Ellen, Liz asked, "Did you walk to school today, too? And what were you planning to do this afternoon?"

"No, my mom drove me," Veronica said. "She says there's too much traffic in the morning for me to walk. We were going to bake Christmas cookies after school. The kind you squish through the tube and decorate with chocolate."

"Spritz cookies. My favorite!" Liz said, certain that rushing the child would be a big mistake. "Did your mom seem the same as usual this morning?"

Veronica wrinkled her brow. "What do you mean, Liz?"

Liz did not want to plant thoughts of any kind in the child's mind.

"Just think carefully," she said. "It will help us with our detective work if you noticed anything different about your mom today."

Veronica rubbed her freckled nose in concentration. "I remember something! She didn't wash her hair this morning. And she didn't put on lipstick. My mom always takes a shower in the morning. And she always puts on lipstick. Every single day."

When Liz wrote the information in the notebook, Veronica looked encouraged.

"Is that a clue? Will it help you find my mommy?"

"Everything you remember is a clue, Veronica," Liz assured her. "Now, can you tell me if your mom did anything special lately?"

"Yeah, she was so happy to meet Nadia in New York City. They had lunch on the top of the tallest building in the world! I wanted to go there, too. But I couldn't. I had school. But she took pictures!"

"Did you see the pictures?" Liz asked.

"No. She was gonna take the film to the camera store today. There it is!" Veronica said, pointing to a plastic film can on the telephone table. "Do you think there's a clue in it? Would you take it to the camera store so we can see?"

Liz hesitated.

"Please?" Veronica begged.

"Okay, honey," she said, and pocketed the film.

Hearing Atwood—who had been rummaging around upstairs—approach the room, Liz also pocketed her reporter's notebook.

"Let's call your dad," she said, although she doubted she'd get the call through before Atwood entered the room. Fortunately, the policeman passed by and headed down the basement stairs instead. "How about you remind me of his number?" Liz asked. She had a record of Erik Johansson's work number in her newsroom ATEX machine. Ellen had given it to her in case she could not be reached if something went wrong during the Santa visits. But Liz did not have the information with her.

"I can dial it!" Veronica said proudly. And she punched in the numbers with painstaking care, at a speed that made it easy for Liz to commit it to memory.

"I'd better talk to your dad first," Liz said, hastening to take the receiver.

"Oh, yeah," Veronica said, as the call went through. "I remember something else. The phone rang a lot last night. Over and over again."

"Environmental Solutions. Erik Johansson here," Veronica's dad said over the phone.

"Mr. Johansson, this is Liz Higgins, the woman who took Veronica to visit the Santas," Liz said, carefully avoiding any mention of the *Banner* as she heard Atwood come up the stairs.

"You can call me Erik," Johansson said in a friendly tone. "What's up? Do you need Veronica to rate New Year's Eve noisemakers now?"

"I'm so sorry that's not the case," Liz said. "Veronica is okay, don't worry. I'm with her at your house. But I have to tell you Ellen's not home and there are signs of violence in your kitchen. Do you have any idea where Ellen might be?"

At the mention of the kitchen, Veronica let out a wail. "Daddy, Daddy, I want to talk to my daddy!"

"What?" Erik said. "I should have stayed home. I knew something wasn't right. I'd better call the police."

"They're already here."

"I'm coming home," Erik said, hanging up before Veronica could say a word to him.

And before anyone else could, either. That included Atwood, youth officer Grace Houghton, and two crime scene officers who all burst into the Johanssons' living room at the same time.

"Who were you talking to?" Atwood demanded.

"The husband," Liz said. "He's on his way from Lexington."

"This is Liz Higgins, a family friend," Atwood told the youth officer.

"The *Banner* reporter?" the officer asked. Apparently, she read the features about malls and dancing figs. But she was not amused. "Some coincidence that you're a 'family friend,'" she said cynically. "Why'd you let her in, Dan?" she asked Atwood.

"I had no idea she was a reporter," he said, chagrined. "What do you think you're up to?" he demanded, turning to Liz.

Again, Veronica saved the day. "She's my friend," she said. "We went to see the Santas!"

And then Veronica blew it.

"We're going to solve the case. We wrote clues on the pad. We're gonna find my mom."

"Outta here!" Atwood barked at Liz. "And you, too!" he added, to the *World*'s whippersnapper reporter Mick Lichen, who poked his head through the door at that moment.

"I really do know this family," Liz said. "Please let me stay with Veronica until her dad arrives."

"No way," Atwood said, taking her arm.

"Don't take Liz away!" Veronica said, clinging to her.

"I have to go for now, honey," Liz said, without hurrying to extricate herself.

Wondering when she would gain entrée again, Liz scanned the room. She'd been there eight times before, once to have tea with Ellen, once to pick up mother and daughter for the first Santa-seeking foray, and six times more to collect Veronica at the door. Now, while dawdling on the sofa with Veronica clinging to her for comfort, Liz examined her surroundings. Much remained as she remembered it. Numerous bookshelves were packed with women's fiction, books about explorers and naturalists, some mystery novels, and several memoirs about women who live "under the veil" in the Middle East. Liz remembered making conversation with Ellen about a shelf of older books including Charles Lindbergh's *The Spirit of St. Louis*, Beryl Markham's *West with the Night,* Virginia Woolf's *Mrs. Dalloway*, and Susan Glaspell's *A Jury of Her Peers*. Ellen had said these volumes were her treasures, since they were signed first editions.

"I've read some of these books over and over again," Ellen had said. "Here I am, a suburban wife and mom. You might expect me to be more interested in Martha Stewart's decorating books or novels about suburban angst, all of which are hot with our Newton Free Library patrons. But I guess my house is as decorated as it ever will be and I'm too in love with my husband to have a taste for tales of adultery in the suburbs. Picking up *The Spirit of St. Louis*, she had mused, "I suppose I'm an adventurer at heart, but too comfortable with my husband and daughter to indulge that part of me. Still, did you know, when Charles Lindbergh feared he'd fall asleep at the controls of his plane, he dipped *The Spirit of St. Louis* so close to the waves of the Atlantic that he could feel sea spray on his face? Now that's living on the edge!"

"What about the Virginia Woolf?" Liz recalled inquiring.

"On the surface, the Woolf doesn't seem like it's in the same category, does it?" Ellen had said. "Mrs. Dalloway is a kind of stay-at-home, isn't she? But the world comes to her, and when she crosses the road to buy flowers for a dinner party, she's as intensely alive as Lindbergh was with the sea spray in his face. As for the Susan Glaspell, she has real insight into…"

Thanks to Veronica spilling tea, Ellen never completed her thought on that unfamiliar author. Now Veronica's current distress allowed Liz to look around the Johanssons' living room just a little bit longer. Were there any signs of struggle here? No. Nothing seemed to be in disarray. The open book splayed pages-down on an armchair did suggest a reader had been interrupted, especially since there was a bookmark and a half-empty cup of tea on the nearby side table. But this was the house of readers where books were no doubt often left ready to pick up again. Was it fair to assume it was Ellen's book? The bone china teacup with its delicate pattern looked likely to be chosen by a woman for her drink. What was the title of the open book?

Standing up at the urging of Atwood, Liz could see the book's title plainly. But Liz could not tell what it said, since it was spelled out in Arabic.

Assuring Veronica she would see her later, Liz crossed the room in the direction of the kitchen. Atwood need not have been on the alert, because as soon as she headed that way, Veronica cried out, "Don't go in the kitchen!"

As a result, Liz only got as far as the doorway to the dining room, where she noticed the glass door to the built-in china cabinet was slightly ajar. Inside, a set of perfectly lined-up teacups and saucers lacked not just the cup and saucer she saw in the living room but another cup, too. Perhaps if and when Ellen was interrupted in her reading, she had invited her visitor to join her in a cup of tea.

At Atwood's urging, Liz made her way to the vestibule where she pulled gloves out of her pocket and purposely dropped her keys on the floor. This gave her the chance to stoop down and examine something metallic on the floor next to the umbrella stand. It was a woman's lipstick. Beside the lipstick lay a dime and an elastic hair band. Liz picked them up. Rising slowly, she looked into the up-ended umbrella in the stand. Sure enough, something had fallen into it, too. Snapping up the scrap of paper, Liz took the coat the youth officer handed her, and made her exit into a suburban front yard that was alive with reporters.

There, *World* reporter Mick Lichen was reduced to taking down low crime statistics rattled off by a flustered Ficarelli, while television crews zoomed in on neighbors who echoed each other's sentiments:

"Such a wonderful mother."

"Great neighbors."

"How could this happen here?"

Liz hurried as quickly as the icy conditions would allow back to her green Mercury Tracer. As she neared her car, she saw *Banner* colleague Dick Manning draw up in his retro-fitted Mustang.

"I've got this one, Dick," Liz said, surprising the guy who was as well known for his front-page bylines as he was for his sexual conquests. "If DeZona's still here, you might get some quotes from neighbors and have René shoot their photos. But don't delay him too much, please. I need to see his kitchen pix."

As Liz waved goodbye, Dick appeared dumbfounded. Knowing this could not last, Liz could not help gloating as she made the six-mile drive back to *Banner* Square. It was an unfamiliar and welcome experience.

Chapter 3

Liz fairly flew down the ink-stained hall that led from the reporters' parking lot to the lobby. While riding the escalator to the newsroom, she peeled off her coat and gloves.

"There you are," Dermott McCann said, "We were wondering when you'd mosey in."

"René said you gained entrée to the premises," Conneely volunteered.

"How'd you pull that off?" Dermott demanded.

"The girl is the same one who evaluated the Santas for us: Veronica Johansson. When she got scared at home, she must have heard the music from the mayor's event. When she ran over to get help, I was a familiar face," Liz explained. "That's great news René's back. I've gotta see his kitchen shots before I write my story. How many inches do I get?"

"Whoa, there, Higgins," Dermott said. "We've gotta wait for Manning to call in before we decide where we're going with this one."

"That's easy," Liz said. "He'll need a sidebar. By the time Dick got there, the police had sealed off the house. He'll have comments from the neighbors and the mayor."

"We'll see about that when we hear from Manning. And don't forget, I'm the guy who decides what goes into a sidebar and what goes into the main here," Dermott warned. "Meanwhile, show me your stuff in ten inches."

"Just ten?"

"All right, you can have thirteen. Slug it 10NEWT1 and send it to city-news," he said, referring to the code that identified stories filed for publication. "Now get a move on."

Liz hurried across the newsroom to the photo department, where DeZona was cutting negatives on the light box. The *Banner*'s photographers worked with a combination of old and new equipment, using single-lens reflex cameras that produced negatives for less urgent work and digital cameras for hard news assignments that were likely to require the quickest processing. Never guessing the Newton event would have front-page possibilities, DeZona had shot it with his standard Nikon SLR.

"I can see the headline now," the photographer said, "'BLOODY MESS.'"

It was not easy to pick out details in the tiny negatives.

"How soon can you print some of these?" Liz asked, looking at the clock. She had about a half hour to complete her story, less time if she wanted to get a hop on Manning. "Give me twenty minutes. Here, mark the negs you want me to print first. I'll let you know when I have something."

"Thanks, René," Liz said, looking through a magnifier at the negatives on the light box and marking a wide view and a close-up of the kitchen counter. "Tell me, did you happen to notice a woman's handbag in the kitchen?"

"No, but that doesn't mean it wasn't there. My lens often sees things the eyes miss."

"Thanks, too, for acting like you didn't know me there."

"No problem. My shot doesn't have a chance in hell of getting front page unless there's a story to go with it."

"Or at least a juicy caption."

"You'd better run, so we both get Page One."

"Right," Liz said.

Liz stayed in the *Banner* newsroom until 11:10 p.m., when the first newspapers, wet with ink, sped on clips along the ceiling of the pressroom and up to the second-floor mailroom. Although the men who bundled papers to place on the delivery trucks did not send the papers through the mail, the job title they all held was "mailer." Once, when Liz asked about the job title, the foreman had explained, writing with a marker on a blank sheet of newsprint, "The job title says it all: We're 'male-er' than the average guy. Isn't it obvious?"

Now, a worker handed Liz a damp copy of the *Banner*. "You're new here?" the alpha-male shouted over the din of machinery.

"No. Just rather new to Page One," she said.

"That your piece about the mom gone AWOL? Sad, huh? Looks like the mother had everything. What would make her want to throw it all away like that?"

Not for the first time Liz reflected on how the attitudes that readers bring to the news cause them to interpret it in surprising ways. The press-man was all too ready to fault Ellen, even in the face of reported evidence that suggested she was the victim of foul play.

DeZona's color photo had made the front page. It showed a marble countertop laden with softening sticks of butter, paper-wrapped squares of chocolate, canisters of flour and sugar, and glass custard dishes filled with sprinkles, chopped walnuts, and shredded coconut—all of which were splattered with blood.

The story also made Page One. "COOKIE MONSTER" was the headline. The byline read, "By Liz Higgins and Dick Manning."

"My commiserations," DeZona said, as Liz stepped out of the pressroom. "They had to give Dick his kudos again. At least you got first billing."

"Dick did get a quote from the husband," Liz admitted. "So he got the byline, too."

"Not much of a quote," DeZona said, reading it aloud from the paper. "'I can't believe it. She was such a devoted wife and mother.' Don't they all say that?"

"Dermott nixed the quote the husband gave me on the phone."

"What was that?"

"'I knew something was wrong. I should have stayed home.'"

"They used it, all right," DeZona said. "Look at the related story on Page Nine."

Headlined "HORA HORROR," the article was accompanied by a photo of a coatless Veronica clinging to Liz as the snow-covered mayor looked on. That picture was captioned, "Traumatized Veronica Johansson seeks comfort from *Banner* features writer Liz Higgins."

"Wouldn't you know they'd peg me as a features writer rather than a news reporter?" Liz said.

On the same page was DeZona's photo of Ficarelli's spectacular fall. Its caption suggested Newton's mayor was bowled over by Veronica's news: "Crime crashes party: Ficarelli flips as child's outcry halts hora."

Buried in the article, which bore the Manning byline, was the first hint of what Erik Johansson was in for from the police and from hotshot reporters. Only partially quoted, the hapless husband was made to look dismayed at not having a better alibi. Following his explanation that he had left a board meeting early to work alone in his office for most of the morning in question, Johansson was quoted as saying, "I should have stayed there."

"Oh, God," Liz groaned as she read to the bottom of the piece, where she received unwelcome credit: "*Banner* features writer Liz Higgins contributed to this piece."

"Credit where credit is due," she heard Manning say over her shoulder. "Couldn't wait to see the edition?" he asked. "It's a thrill to be on Page One, huh?"

"I see you're not waiting for the papers to get delivered to the newsroom any more than I am."

"I'm not sure I'd agree with you there," Manning said, looking pointedly at Liz's ink-smeared fingers. "At least my copy of the rag is dry," he said as the pressman handed him a fresh newspaper. "I'd like to linger at this little tête-à-tête, Miss Lizzie, but I'm afraid I've got to get going. McCann wants me on the Johanssons' doorstep at dawn tomorrow."

Hoping this did not mean what it sounded like—that she'd been taken off the story—Liz returned to the city desk.

"Dermott has made his exit," Conneely announced in answer to Liz's unspoken question. "You'll have to take it up with Esther," he said, referring to the humorless night editor now ensconced at the city desk. She was using a copy of the early edition as a placemat for a take-out meal of General Gao's chicken.

Known for being as tough as the toughest male reporter, Esther O'Faolin had fought tooth and nail for her newsroom position—losing her marriage and custody of her kids in the process. Feminism might once have spurred her on, but she was no friend to other women. "I climbed the ladder without advantages," she said often and with pride. "You can do the same," was the unmistakable implication.

"Hey, Liz," she said. "You still here? Go home and get some rest. We're sending you to the Worcester Public Library tomorrow for that mystery writers' conference."

"Gee, Esther, I'd hoped to follow up on some leads I have on the missing mom case," Liz said, impulsively running her fingers through her auburn curls so that they were swept back from her forehead. "You know I reported on that today." She loosed her locks so they spilled over her forehead again.

The anger in Liz's tone was lost on the night editor. "Oh, yeah?" Esther said, using a chopstick to push a gummy piece of chicken off the lead story. "Nice initiative, backing Manning like that."

"With all due respect, Dick came on the scene after it was closed off to reporters. I was the one inside the Johansson house for more than half an hour."

Esther opened the paper to Page Nine. "What's this?" she demanded of Bert Garamond at the copy desk. "You know it's not our policy to print photos of our own reporters."

"That wasn't my call," Bert said. "Dermott insisted on it."

"He probably liked the leg shot," Esther said under her breath, scanning the photo disapprovingly. The night editor's own unremarkable legs were just one of many testimonies to the fact that Esther had "climbed the ladder without advantages."

"Tricks like that make us look self-promotional, not professional," Esther added.

"You've got a point, Esther," Bert said, "But Dermott said, 'That picture speaks five words: You can trust *Banner* reporters.'"

"Not after Manning misleads with partial quotes," Liz thought to herself. "How will I ever get Erik Johansson to talk with me again?"

"I see Manning got the husband on the record," Esther said approvingly. "Watch these pages. I'll bet you dollars to donuts the husband is guilty as all hell."

"You can't assume that, Esther," Liz said. "He told me he was worried about his wife when he left for work that morning. He blamed himself for leaving anyway."

"That's not what it says in here," Esther said, pointing to the Page-Nine article.

"That's not my doing. Someone cut the quote I reported," Liz said, looking at Manning's empty desk. Unlike her own, it was situated in easy reach of the city desk.

"Dizzy Miss Lizzie," Manning said from over Liz's shoulder again. "It's easy to talk about Tricky Dick when you think he's not around, huh? Yeah, I know you guys call me that behind my back. I make it my business to know everything that goes on around here. Just make sure your head isn't spinning with dreams of Page One when you hand over the rest of your reporting."

"Are you implying I didn't give you everything Erik said?"

"Oh, it's 'Erik,' now, is it? A word to the wise, Liz: If you get too chummy with your sources, you'll find it hard to tell it like it is when it turns out they're scum. Anyway, kid," he said, switching to a magnanimous tone, "thanks for helping me out on this one. Here's looking at you," he added, as he made his exit.

"The answer is no," Esther said before Liz could say a word. "It's the mystery writers' conference for you tomorrow. Here's the press release."

"OK, Chief," Liz said, trying to sound like a good loser.

"Look," Esther said, softening, "you'll get more lucky breaks. Just spell out every fact."

"Thanks, Esther," Liz said, both surprised to see the night editor express encouragement and peeved that Esther seemed to buy Manning's lie about the incomplete quote.

As Liz crossed the room to her distant desk, Esther used her password to get into Manning's ATEX materials. Like his presidential namesake, the *Banner*'s Tricky Dick suffered from overconfidence. Never thinking anyone would check up on him, he hadn't killed the material Liz had shared with him. There it was. Erik Johansson's entire statement.

"Hey Liz," Esther called out. She had to make it loud to carry across the big newsroom.

Liz looked up from her desk, where she was retrieving a fresh reporter's notebook from amid the clutter.

"I can't speak for Dermott," Esther said, "but I'm sure I wouldn't reject any hard facts you can turn up about the missing mom. It won't be a breeze to score any Newton news from Worcester, but who knows? Good night."

Liz still felt wired as she wound her way through silent streets to her digs on Gravesend Street. It was a dead-end street, but not the kind of cul-de-sac that offered respite from traffic. Perched on an embankment bordering the Massachusetts Turnpike, even in the dead of the night the place pulsed with the soundtrack of fast-moving vehicles, syncopated irregularly with the deep backbeat of trucks slamming over potholes.

Liz pulled into the parking space alongside her building, angling the Tracer carefully between a bare lilac bush and the iron stanchion that stood straight beside the two-room house she called home. Another stanchion, wrapped with the thorny stems of climbing roses, stood just beyond the far end of her house. By any standard the abode was small, but a massive billboard placed directly over it added to that impression. Supported by those stanchions, the billboard made the house appear tiny, since the advertisement space was wider and taller than the building itself.

Not for the first time, Liz regretted that she had no say over what was advertised in her air space. Still, she did not dare jeopardize the flow of money she received from renting it to an advertising firm. Those funds allowed her to indulge her love of a career that offered little in the way of medical benefits. The overhead ads not only paid for her medical and dental insurance, but it covered the lion's share of her monthly mortgage payments on the quirky property.

Craning her head to read the current ad's suggestive warning, "Don't be caught without one!" Liz told herself for the hundredth time, "When I get rich, I'll hire them to advertise Dr. Ecklenbergh's eyeglasses, like that billboard in *The Great Gatsby*. I wonder how many Pike drivers would get a chuckle out of that!"

The billboard of the moment was not so bad. It showed a heel-kicking Gene Kelly singing in the rain, umbrella held high. It might have been an ad for umbrellas, but, judging by the bottle of vodka in the dancer's other hand, this was a pitch for drink.

"Not a bad idea," Liz said aloud, indulging the habit of talking to herself when on her own turf. Her gray cat, Prudence, rubbed at Liz's ankles as the reporter placed her keys in her coat pocket. She kept the keys there in the thus-far vain hope that she would have to grab her coat and rush out to cover breaking news. "Blast!" Liz said as she felt the film can in her pocket. "I should've asked René to process this."

René would have left the newsroom long ago, and there was no way Liz would trust Ellen's film to the other photographers. They were all too eager to stay in the good graces of Manning. Figuring she could put the film in DeZona's hands in the morning, Liz poured herself a glass of Chardonnay and put together a meal she'd dubbed "Cask of Amontillado Chicken," in honor of the famous story by Edgar Allan Poe. Made with chicken, mushrooms, shallots, slivered pecans, and, of course, amontillado sherry, it was one of those dishes that took little time and fuss to make but tasted like it was the result of a professional chef's labor. She spooned some onto her plate and sat, feet up, in front of one of her luxuries, a gas fireplace that came to life with the flick of a switch.

After eating, she covered herself with her favorite purple and white crocheted afghan. It clashed with her home's peach and rust color scheme. Its edges were uneven, too. But these characteristics only added to the afghan's value in Liz's eyes. Made from donated wool in unfashionable colors, it had been crocheted for Liz by six incarcerated adolescent girls who had opened their hearts to her on the topic of body piercing as self-expression for a *Banner* feature. Usually, their chaplain had said, they crocheted bedcovers for themselves, but they took a liking to Liz and decided to make one for her, too. Along the way, they proved they could stick with, cooperate, and complete a generous and time-consuming gift.

As one of the girls put it, "A hole in your tongue says as much as words do, sometimes."

Pulling the afghan up to her chin, Liz decided those words of wisdom were worthy of billboard space, too. "When I'm rich . . . ," she mused, as she dropped off to sleep, lulled by the sound of passing traffic.

She awoke to the scream of sirens. An accident on the Mass. Pike. Too bad for the people in the fender bender, but terrific for Liz, since she had forgotten to set her alarm. Looking at her watch, Liz saw it was too late to zip over to the *Banner* to give René the film for processing. The city of Worcester and its public library were in the opposite direction.

Shaking off the afghan and Prudence, who was sleeping on it, Liz removed her slacks and crossed the room towards her shower stall and bathroom area. It was located between the main room and kitchen area, behind a custom-designed, curved partition built by a budding architect whom Liz met while writing an article on design solutions for small spaces. After her article about the architect's transformation of a studio apartment on Boston's Beacon Hill was published, his career took off. Meanwhile, Liz hired him to help her improve her then-new-to-her digs. When she rejected his offer to do the work without charge, he surprised her by producing the curved, polished cherry partition instead of the boxy divider of painted pine she had hired him to install. He also installed built-in cherry bookcases.

Semi-dressed, Liz made her way to the kitchen to start some coffee brewing before she took her shower. Without her eyeglasses, she saw little. But she was not so blind that she could not see the pair of legs, visible from the knees down, which filled the small window over her kitchen sink. She had not thought to close the blinds on the previous evening.

"You startled me, Tom!" she said at the top of her lungs. But the man whose legs she saw did not hear her through the double-glazed windows she'd had installed to cut down on the traffic noise.

She rapped on the window and then lifted it a few inches.

"What are you doing here?" she asked, startling Tom in turn.

"Jeez! You scared me!" Tom said as his long-waisted torso, chest, shoulders, and head came into sight in that order.

"You startled me, too. It's not billboard day," Liz said, opening the coffee canister. Tom regularly changed the billboard advertisements beginning on the first Tuesday of the month, spending an average three days per billboard change. This was the third Tuesday of December.

"I know, but a car dealer wants to make end-of-the-year sales, so I'm putting up a new ad before the month ends. The dealer must have money to burn. I don't think this ad will be up as long as two weeks. Don't get me wrong," Tom said, grinning at Liz's bare legs. "I'm not complaining."

Liz shut the blinds on his smile, pulled on some slacks, and then opened the blinds again.

"Tom Horton at your service!" he grinned.

"Cup of coffee?" she said.

"Sure thing!"

"It'll have to be quick," Liz said, giving up on taking a shower. "I'm on assignment this morning. I've gotta get out to Worcester."

Tom cleaned his boots on the doormat with care before entering.

"I can really use that coffee," he said. "It's cold enough to . . ."

". . . freeze the balls off a brass monkey," they said in unison, laughing. Over the year that Liz had lived below the billboard, she and Tom had enjoyed quite a few cups of coffee. The first time, she'd invited him in out of pity. Hanging an ad in below-freezing temperatures, he had muttered that same line only to look down and see Liz gazing up at him.

"It sure is!" she had said. "Don't be embarrassed," she'd added, when she saw his sheepish expression. "The phrase doesn't mean what you think it does, so I'm not offended. Come on in and have a cup of coffee and I'll tell you where it comes from."

He'd wiped his boots thoroughly then, too. And he'd said, "I can sure use this coffee."

And when Liz told him the crude-sounding expression was actually a sailor's turn of phrase, he said, "That doesn't surprise me. Sailors can turn the air blue with their cussing."

"No, no! It's not what you think," Liz had said. "Sailors didn't say that to be foul. On old warships, the 'monkey' was the platform that held the stack of cannon balls. It was made of brass. When the temperature was low enough, the brass monkey contracted, allowing the cannonballs to roll off it."

"Yeah, sure!"

"No, really. Look, I'll show you," she had insisted, opening a well-worn copy of Brewer's *Dictionary of Phrase and Fable*.

"Well, I'll be! Are you some kind of professor?"

"No, I'm a reporter for the *Beantown Banner*. And I'm a word nut. That's why I have all these dictionaries."

Now, as the reporter and the billboard hanger laughed over the expression again, Tom said, "I'm sorry to tell you that expression about the brass monkey is just an urban legend. Cannonballs were never stored on deck like that. I saw it on the Internet."

"I always believe a published reference book over the Internet," Liz said. "In my line of work, I have seen too much misleading material on the Web. By the way, whose ad are you hanging over my head this time?"

"Maksoud's," he said. "The car dealership over on Needham Street. I hear they've got such an overstock, they're practically giving cars away. I guess old man Maksoud wants to drum up some business quick. Hey, look, you'd better get going. Didn't you say you had to get over to Worcester this morning?"

"That's right," Liz said, tucking a fresh reporter's notebook into her purse. "I'll see you out."

Chapter 4

Liz made the fifty-minute drive without incident and arrived at the Worcester Public Library with time to spare. That meant she could take a look at the *Boston World*. Passing through the etched-glass sliding doors that formed a pleasing entry to the large building, she went straight to the Periodicals Room. Fortunately, the library stocked several copies of both the *Banner* and the *World*. While every copy of the *Banner* had been snatched up by readers, three copies of the competing paper remained on the rack.

The *World* was a well-named publication, since it prided itself on its international coverage. Its lead story's headline read, "No Room at the Inn for Bosnian Refugees." Apparently, the *World*'s editors did not even think their lead story deserved full upper-case type. The article at the bottom of their front page bore an even more reserved headline, "Newton Police Mull Missing Mother Case."

The *Banner*'s big, bold "COOKIE MONSTER" headline had done a better job of grabbing readers. Still, Mick Lichen had reported a fact that Liz and Manning had missed.

"Ellen was not the only thing missing from the Johansson household. Her newly purchased Honda Civic was also gone from the drive of the family home in this low-crime neighborhood," Lichen had written.

"Hey, aren't you the gal in this picture?" an elderly reader asked, looking at Liz over the edge of the *Banner*.

"That would be me," Liz admitted.

"How come you're way out here in Worcester?" the old man inquired. "Do you think you'll find a body in the library?" he chuckled.

"Maybe not a body, but information about it," Liz said, looking at the line-up of conference guests that was posted on the Periodical Room's bulletin board. Apparently, mystery writers used more than their imaginations to turn out their thrillers. On the roster were Mary Higgins Clark, mystery writer; Dr. Cormac Kinnaird, M.D., forensic pathologist; Pamela Nesnarf, private investigator; and Maurice E. Bouvard, *Boston World* literary editor. Not for the first time, Liz wondered whether it was *World* muckety-mucks or Maurice himself who decided to term Bouvard "literary editor," instead of endowing him with the more prosaic title "book review editor."

"Ah, the lovely Liz Higgins," Bouvard said as she entered the reception room where the Friends of the Worcester Public Library were serving coffee and homemade cookies to conference participants. "I see the *Banner*'s bookworm Rose Morgan is not here to dazzle us with her literary insights. Such a pity."

"Alas!" Liz said, playing along. "Our book review editor is not among the speakers. But I have no doubt you will wow the crowd, Maurice."

"Too bad your editors will eschew using any reports you might wish to make upon my words of wisdom."

"Verily, they may. But surely the *World* will quote you at generous length."

"Ah, there's the rub. They've got everyone working on that breaking news in Newton. The missing mom, you know."

"May I have your attention!" library director Vickie Nichols said. After some words of welcome, she led a bevy of bookworms, aspiring authors, and mystery writers into the assembly hall. There a well-dressed smiling Mary Higgins Clark recounted the story of her many rejections when she began to try her hand at writing short stories to her incredible multi-million dollar contract for her most recent books. The author's caution to beginning writers was to never give up, and her freely given advice about how to write variations of the woman-in-jeopardy situation won a standing ovation.

"Always, always look for the overlooked domestic detail," Clark advised, before adding, "I'd love to stay and hang out with you for the rest of the day, but I'm scheduled for a reading in Hingham at noon. Great to be with you. Cheers and may the cash registers jingle for all of you one of these days."

Liz followed the author out of the assembly hall. "Ms. Clark," she said. "Have you read about the missing persons case in Newton?"

"Yes, I have. It's very sad."

"Allow me to introduce myself. I'm Liz Higgins, reporting on the case for the *Beantown Banner*."

"I read your report, and I thought a number of things in it were suggestive."

"Yes?"

"I do have to get on to my next reading. But why don't you walk me to my car?"

The two put on coats and left the library.

"What is your read on the mystery, Ms. Clark?"

"Oh, for heaven's sake, call me Mary,"

"All right. If you'll call me Liz."

"I'd take a long look at that front-page photo, Liz," Clark said as she got into her car. "Good luck to you."

Liz returned to the library, hung up her coat, and returned to the Periodicals Room. Fortunately, a copy of the *Banner* had been left on a table there. Scrutinizing DeZona's Page-One photo of Ellen Johansson's kitchen, she saw again the blood-splattered baking ingredients lined up on the countertop. Above the counter was a blackboard. On it, written in chalk, was a list. The first three items were spelled out neatly. They were also crossed out.

~~MMs~~
~~Choc. chips~~
~~Coconut~~

The fourth item was written in a hastier hand. And it was not yet lined out.

"FORGET ME NOT," it read.

Back in the assembly hall, Dr. Kinnaird was sending shivers through the mostly female audience with a slide show of horrors—and perhaps with his good looks, too. The adjective "distinguished" seemed made for him. When Liz re-entered the overheated room, he was removing a suit jacket that had to have been hand-tailored, revealing a shirt ornamented with cuff links. Draping the jacket over a chair and turning back to the assembly in one smooth motion, he enlightened the crowd: "Bite marks, like fingerprints, are very individual markers that help us identify, with a fine degree of certainty, the animal or person who made the marks." He went on to display slides of distinctive teeth-filled jaws and some grisly bite marks that had been made by those teeth.

The library director turned in her chair and surveyed the room with concern. Probably, she had expected the good doctor to focus on assault with blunt instruments and other less blood-curdling acts of bodily harm. She needn't have worried. Only two ladies left the room in apparent distress. The others hung in for the whole horrific presentation, paying rapt attention. Dr. Kinnaird only succeeded in drawing a collective groan from them when he spoke of the likelihood that a victim might urinate under stress or in the throes of dying.

It was difficult to get Kinnaird's attention after his talk, since his audience looked ready to make his book, *Signs of Struggle*, into a bestseller. They lined up eagerly to buy pre-signed copies of Mary Higgins Clark's memoir and personally inscribed copies of Kinnaird's book. Liz shook her head as she heard a woman ask Kinnaird to inscribe a book, "Happy Birthday, Matt. May this bring you many hours of enjoyment." Neither amused nor nonplussed, Kinnaird carried out the request and signed his name with a flourish.

The forensics man only became free when it was Pamela Nesnarf's turn to speak. The blowsy blonde looked more like a hooker than a private eye. And that, Liz heard her say, was the secret of her success.

"You've heard of the equal playing field. Well, that's how I like my turf," she said. "I figure, the cheating husband is gonna be pretty good at hiding who he really is—a suburban spouse with kids. So when I track him down with his lady friend in a bar or wherever, I don't want to look like what I am, either. If he looks at me, he *might* think I'm a working girl," Nesnarf said with a wink, "but I'm not the kind of working girl he imagines."

In the library's lobby, Liz turned her attention from Nesnarf's talk, which could be easily heard, thanks to loudspeakers in the assembly room, and focused her attention on Dr. Kinnaird.

"I wonder if you could help me?" she said. "I've been covering the missing persons case in Newton. Have you read about it?"

"Indeed, I have. I commend your editors on having you consult me."

Liz smiled. "We always seek the top experts," she said.

The doctor's ice-blue eyes flashed. "Of course, I'm handcuffed, so to speak, by not having visited the scene of the crime. All I have seen is your paper's front-page photo. That's very little, indeed, to work with."

"Does it tell you anything at all?"

"It tells me the missing woman was trying her darnedest to outdo Martha Stewart. A custard dish for every sprinkle and flake of coconut. She hardly seems like the kind of person to leave such a bloody mess."

"What about the blood? Does it give you any hints as to what must have happened?"

"Blood stains always have much to tell a knowledgeable forensics man. But when they're only seen in a photo, let's just say their communication would be rather more like a timid whisper than a definite shout. I would need considerably more to go on before I could hope to make any useful comment."

"If I were able to supply you with more photos of the scene, do you think it's possible you could draw any further conclusions?"

"It's hard to say if there would be anything I'd be willing to state for the record. But I'd be willing to take a look at your pictures, on the condition that you don't quote me unless I okay it."

"Agreed! I'll be going back to the newsroom this afternoon. I should be able to get copies of the photos then. What's your schedule like? Could I show them to you by around 4:00 p.m.?"

"I'm afraid that won't work for me. I'm scheduled to testify in Cambridge this afternoon." Although his accent was American without any regional edge, Kinnaird pronounced "scheduled" in the British manner—"sheduled"—adding to the pompous impression his choice of words had already given. "It's impossible to predict how late that will run," he went on, and then surprised Liz by adding, "and I'm playing at the Green Briar after that."

Liz knew the Green Briar was an Irish pub in Brighton, a working-class Boston neighborhood located on the Newton line. But it seemed strange for a distinguished forensics expert to admit he "played" there at night.

Reading the expression on her face he said, "The banjo. I play the Irish tenor banjo."

"I didn't know such a thing existed. What makes it different than the 'Oh, Susannah!' kind? Are you in a band?"

"So many questions! I don't have time to explain it now. Look, if you're interested, why don't you meet me at the Green Briar at around seven tonight? You can bring the photos and I'll take a look at them."

Liz thought quickly. If she couldn't get information from Kinnaird before the six o'clock deadline for first edition, she might still have a chance of getting something into a later printing.

"You're on!" she said. "See you at seven."

Taking a seat on a bench in the lobby, Liz gave some attention to the last half of Nesnarf's talk. It seemed to be based on the private eye's specialty, rounding up straying spouses. The sobering statistics she delivered about unfaithful mates seemed to upset this mostly female audience more than did Kinnaird's bite marks presentation. Despite this, Nesnarf managed to make the mystery mavens laugh, as she enlivened her talk with anecdotes about men whose foolish infidelity to clever wives landed them in hilarious fixes.

"Sometimes I wonder why these wives hire me," Nesnarf said. "Forget the old evidence of lipstick on the collar. I had a case in which an errant husband came home from a rendezvous with custard on his cravat. Yes, a cravat! That's how uncool this dude was. The problem was, he was one of those extreme vegans who won't eat any animal products. And his wife was a food sciences professor at the culinary institute. A quick analysis in her lab proved this guy truly had egg on his cravat, if not his face."

The mention of cooking ingredients made Liz recall the bloody scene in Ellen's kitchen, captured in DeZona's photo. She found a pay phone and called the *Banner*'s photo department.

"Photo. DeZona here."

"René! I'm glad you answered. It's Liz. How long are you on tonight?"

"Another few hours unless they send me out on assignment."

"Listen, could you do me a favor?"

"Depends on what it is and on what The Powers That Be need me to do."

"Could you print the rest of your pictures from the Johansson kitchen?"

"I only took two shots before the police kicked me out, but I have some I took outside and in the living room with you and the kid, too."

"Print as many as you can, please. I need them to show to a forensics guy tonight. And could you enlarge any sections that show blood or other forensic evidence?"

"Yeah, sure. You know Dick has already been interviewing the medical examiner. What's his name? Barney Williams. I know because I took a head-shot for the paper."

"Were you with Dick all day?"

"Part of the time. Look, where are you calling from?"

"Worcester."

"Well, why don't you let me get on with this? We can talk when you get to the newsroom."

"Okay. One more thing, René."

"What's that?"

"I've got a film Ellen Johansson took when she was out of town, I think. Could you print it on the sly for me?"

"I'll try," DeZona said, hanging up.

Liz made her way to the reference desk.

"I have a Boston Public Library card," she said. "Would I be able to use that card to take out books here?"

"I'm afraid not," the librarian said. "We're in a different network. And you'd have to be a resident of greater Worcester in order to apply for a library card here. You can certainly use our books within the building, however."

"That won't work for me. I really need to look at some books for an article I'm writing for the *Beantown Banner*. I'm working under a tight deadline and need to take the books home with me to examine later."

"There is something I can do to save you time at the Boston Public Library," the librarian offered. "I can look online to see which branches of the BPL hold the books you need. I can even tell you if they are listed as checked out."

"That's much better than nothing. Thank you."

"What titles are you looking for?"

"Charles Lindbergh's *The Spirit of St. Louis* and Susan Glaspell's *A Jury of Her Peers*."

The librarian rapidly typed in the first title.

"Lindbergh's book is in at the BPL main branch and in Jamaica Plain. Now, let's see about the Susan Glaspell. Hmm. Nothing under the title. Let me try the author's name."

"What Glaspell work are you looking for?" said a man wearing a "WORCESTER READS!" T-shirt. Below that exclamation, his shirt was emblazoned with the words, "Friends of the Worcester Public Library."

"Oh, hello, John," the librarian said. "I'm not seeing the title *A Jury of Her Peers* under the name Susan Glaspell."

"That's because it's a short story, not a novel," John said. "It should show up in something like *The Oxford Book of American Detective Stories*. The story is based on a murder she covered when she was a reporter for some Midwest newspaper. She actually first wrote a play based on the incident, and titled it *Trifles*."

"You're in luck," the librarian told Liz. "John's a book dealer and detective fiction buff."

"Would you have a copy of the play in your store?" Liz asked him.

"I wish I did. It would be worth a pretty penny."

"Too bad. I want to get my hands on a copy of the book urgently."

"I've been looking for it in the BPL system," the librarian said, "but it's not there. Now I see it's not in our catalogue, either. And I also don't see it in the Minuteman Library Network."

"As you can see," John said, "copies of the play are hard to come by. I could probably get you one through another book dealer, but that could take weeks or more. But if you're just interested in knowing what the play is about, the short story will be adequate."

"Our copy of *The Oxford Book of American Detective Stories* is out," the librarian said. "Let me look in the short story index to see where else it might be anthologized."

"Don't bother," said John. "I've got a copy of the *Oxford Book* in my store. It's pretty dog-eared, so it'll go cheap."

"I'm afraid I don't have time to travel far," Liz said.

"My shop is just across the street."

"Fantastic!" Liz said, putting on her coat and following the book dealer to his shop.

Except for a single high-school student holding the fort, the Worcester Hills Book Shop was completely deserted. Apparently the bibliophiles who usually frequented it were all clustered at the feet of Maurice E. Bouvard, who was holding forth at the Worcester library at the moment.

John found the *Oxford Book* without much ado, and then made his way to a section of bookshelves labeled "Aviation History." He returned to Liz with a wide smile on his face.

"Yup, just as I hoped," he said. "Here's the *Oxford Book* with the Glaspell story in it. And here's an anthology that excerpts Lucky Lindy's *The Spirit of St. Louis*. I realize it's not Lindbergh's full account, but it may be adequate if you're working under a deadline. That's an odd combination of topics. Do you mind if I ask you what the connection is?"

Liz was usually loath to reveal what she was working on, but the man had been so helpful that she told him, "A missing woman loved both of these books, and some others, too."

"The combination is a bit suggestive, but I wonder if I think so only because you've told me the reader's circumstances. If she had treasured those two books but never went missing, would the same thought come to mind?" the book dealer mused aloud.

"What thought?"

"This woman flies from home but knows any loose ends she leaves will be seen as significant—*if* a woman gets the chance to look things over. That'll be eleven dollars for the two books."

"They're worth much more than that to me," Liz said, waving away change from a twenty-dollar bill. "Thank you."

Chapter 5

It was mid-afternoon when Liz left the bookshop. She'd lost count of how many times she wished the *Banner* supplied her with a cell phone. Now, without one, it was a question of taking time to return to the library's phone booth or waiting until she was in the newsroom to contact Laura Winters, Veronica's aftercare program teacher. Looking at her watch, Liz figured the aftercare provider would presently be welcoming her charges. She'd wait to phone her and get on the road immediately.

Seated in the Tracer, Liz wished she'd returned to the library after all, since it would have been the source of brownies and coffee served by the library's friends. Having eaten neither breakfast nor lunch, Liz was ravenous. Once she was moving steadily along Route 290, en route to the Mass Pike, she took a granola bar from her glove compartment and turned on the radio.

The former was inadequate to appease her hunger. The latter only whetted her appetite for finding out what happened to Ellen Johansson.

"Turning to local news," the announcer intoned, "Erik Johansson has been detained by police for questioning again today, in the case of the missing Newton wife and mother. Johansson's remarks, reported this morning in the *Beantown Banner*, indicate he wished he had a better alibi for the hours during which his wife, Ellen Johansson, seems likely to have disappeared."

Newton Police Chief Anthony Warner's voice came on the air. "More troubling than that is the guy's apparent belief that his wife is dead," he said. "You can see in the *Banner*, the guy's talking about his wife in the past tense."

Hearing this, Liz stepped a little harder on the accelerator and made her way to the Mass Pike. This took her straight past her house and the billboard above it. The latter formed an amusing tableau, since half of the billboard still showed a rain-splashed scene and the words "DON'T BE CAUGHT," while the other half showed a flashy red sports car zooming down a snaking road straight for the vodka bottle.

"At least the dealership name is not on that half of the billboard," Liz thought. "Old Man Maksoud would be fit to be tied if he saw this combination of ads."

The next few billboards along the pike advertised the Museum of Science—"IT'S ALIVE!"—and the *Boston World*—"The sun never sets on our coverage."

"They don't even give their own ad uppercase type," Liz laughed to herself.

There was no billboard in sight for her newspaper. The *Banner* made up for that with huge advertisements for itself on the sides of their newspaper delivery trucks. With circulation done for the day, these vehicles were packed into the parking lot, making it harder for Liz to find a space for the Tracer. Backed by an image of the American flag unfurling in a wind, the ads on the trucks proclaimed the *Banner*'s well-known slogan—"STAR-SPANGLED REPORTING!"—in uppercase type.

Under icy gray clouds that looked loaded with snow, Liz hurried from her car to the *Banner*'s brick edifice. Liz rushed down the ink-stained hall that led past the huge room filled with printing presses, only stopping to grab a can of orange juice from the vending machine before heading to the photo department. She flung open the door to see René working on the Mac on photos of a fire.

In a rare move, Dermott entered the photo department at that moment. Usually, the photographers came to him.

"How you doin' on those fire shots?" he demanded.

"They're coming along. What's the hurry?"

"We've got a goner, now, so the story may go front page. Especially if you've got a wham-o shot. Hey, is that a figure behind the flames there?" he asked, scrutinizing the photo now displayed on the computer screen.

"Could be. I think it is."

"That does it! Print that one pronto. I want it in time for the news meeting."

"Sure, Dermott. I'll have it for you ASAP."

"Have it sooner!" Dermot said, rushing out of the room.

"Yeah, I did get a chance to print the photos—not all of them but enough to get you started, I hope," René said, anticipating Liz's question. "As you can see, they sent me to a fire scene. Your prints are in my cubbyhole there, in a manila envelope. You won't find any enlargements of details. There just wasn't time. I'll get to the rest as soon as I can."

"Thanks, René. I owe you," Liz said, and handed him Ellen Johansson's film.

"That's true enough!"

"Looks like a woman in the flames there. That's a great shot, René. Upsetting, though."

"Another case of the camera seeing more than the eye. I just kept shooting. It was only when it came up on the machine that I knew what I had."

"I'll let you get to it," Liz said, collecting the manila envelope from DeZona's cubby.

"Just so you know, Manning's hounding the hubby in your Newton case. And the medical examiner thinks the mom may have manipulated the scene."

"You mean in the kitchen?"

"That's right."

"What makes him think that?"

"Manning will explain in tomorrow's *Banner*," Dermott said, standing in the door. "For Chrissake, let DeZona get on with his work! Now what have you got for me on the mystery mavens? Whatever it is, you'd better be able to spell it out in six inches. Between the freakin' fire and the missing mom case, there's a squeeze on for space."

"Six it is!" Liz said. For once, she was relieved to have little space. It would allow her to file her story and head out again. "I've got Mary Higgins Clark and a private eye telling mystery fans how they go about their work. You could head it, 'HOWDUNIT?'"

"We'll see about that," the city editor said.

At her desk, Liz took out another granola bar and opened her orange juice. Then she scanned her contact list on ATEX and dialed the Children's Enrichment Aftercare Program.

"Laura left for the day," a receptionist informed her. "May I take a message?"

"Isn't it early for her to leave?"

"It is, actually. But she's helping out with a child who's been traumatized."

"Veronica Johansson?"

"How did you know? And whose mom are you?"

Liz hung up without answering. Then she wrote an unremarkable, six-inch story about the mystery conference. While she was writing, the message "File and fly rule in effect" flashed at the top of her screen. She looked out the window. Heavy snow. Marvelous! This meant she could send the story into the system and split. Liz pulled a file photo of Mary Higgins Clark from the *Banner*'s photo library, turned it in at the city desk, and returned to her desk.

She looked in the *West Suburban Boston* phone book for Laura Winters in Newton. No Laura there, so she turned to the *Boston* book. A "Winters, L." was listed at a Brighton address. Liz noted the address on Summit Street, took down the phone number, then dialed the latter. A perky voice on the phone answering machine invited her to leave a message. It sounded like the daycare provider. Again cursing her lack of a cell phone, Liz left a message with her work and home phone numbers. On impulse, she said she'd be at the Green Briar around 7:00 p.m., and invited Laura to call her there. Then she phoned Veronica's home. If she didn't catch Laura Winters there, perhaps Erik Johansson would pick up.

"Hello there! You've reached the Johanssons' voice-mail box. If you'd like to leave a message for Erik, Ellen, or Veronica, go right ahead after the beep," announced Ellen Johnasson's recorded voice. Just as though nothing had happened to her.

The cheerful ordinariness of the message stopped Liz cold. She had sipped tea with this woman, even held Ellen's traumatized child in her arms. But in her quest to grab the front page, she'd offered only cold comfort. Now, miles from their home, she did the best she could to embrace Ellen's shattered family more warmly.

"I'll find you, Ellen," she said after the beep. "I'll bring you home."

As she pulled on her coat, she saw a copy of the front page that had been prepared earlier. "A PINCH OF BLOOD," its headline read. It would never run, since the story had been bumped off Page One by the fire fatality. On an inside page there'd be smaller type and less hype.

And because it would never run, the rejected page was fair game. Liz snatched it up and made a swift exit into a driving snowstorm.

The *Banner*'s parking lot was normally a litter-strewn expanse of concrete, old-model cars, and newspaper delivery trucks. But now the fast-falling snow softened every angle, transferring this urban eyesore into a winter wonderland. If there had not been a missing mom or fire fatality, *Banner* headline writers might have been playing with words like "GUARANTEED WHITE," since this snow would surely stay on the ground until Christmas. Unless Ellen Johansson showed up in the six days remaining before the holiday, the little girl who started out the season finding the area's best Santa would not find her Christmas to be merry and bright.

Shivering, Liz approached the snow-covered Tracer, unlocked it, and took out her combination windshield scraper and brush. As she pushed snow off the spoiler designed to improve the aerodynamics of her car, she shook her head at the silliness of it. The accessory only made the vehicle look like a clunker that aimed—and failed—at looking sporty.

"Not unlike this reporter," she thought. "I'd like to be the *Banner*'s hottest writer, but . . ."

Still, the car made up for its uncool appearance with compact size and reliability. In a city where parking spaces were at a premium, Liz could park the car on a dime. Now, it started up immediately when she turned it on. On the snowbound city streets, it performed just as well as the much more expensive, four-wheel-drive vehicles that shared the roads with her. But, in this snow, would it make it up the hills in Brighton? And when she arrived at the Green Briar, would Kinnaird be there after all? Would the good doctor be so keen on Irish music that he'd brave a blizzard for a chance to play his banjo?

The weather dictated Liz's next decisions. Traffic was too slow to allow time for a quick stop at home before her Green Briar meeting. So she steered the Tracer to Brighton. The Beatles belted out "You're Going To Lose That Girl" on her radio as Liz passed Saint Elizabeth's Hospital. It made a welcome change from the Christmas carols jamming the airwaves. Until Liz thought about the song's title, that is. Feeling sure Veronica's mother would not voluntarily abandon her daughter, Liz looked up at the hundreds of illuminated windows and large electrified cross that glowed through the falling snow on the massive hospital complex set high on a hilltop.

Below, traffic was snarled in the complicated intersections of Brighton Center. A Christmas tree lit with multicolored bulbs shared a small traffic island with an antique clock topping a pole like a lollipop. Liz passed the Green Briar, traveling about a half-mile farther west to the base of Summit Street. Finding the road ran one way in the wrong direction, she drove around in the intensifying storm until she found a road that wound around the hill to what she thought was the other end of the one-way street. But it was the wrong road after all, Liz realized, as she pulled out of a skid in time to read "Tip Top Street" on a snowy street sign. Liz recognized the street name but, distracted by the storm, couldn't recall why. It turned out the well-named street went up one side and down the other of a hill cluttered with quirky houses. With many of the houses lit up in Christmas lights, the effect was like an illustration in a child's picture book. Descending the hill, and ascending another, Liz at last found Summit Street.

The street was neither plowed nor sanded, so Liz drove at a steady pace to a house on the hillside where, thanks to a porch light, she could make out Laura's house number. Reasoning that if a snowplow came by, it would be preferable to dig out the tail of her car than the full length of it, she pulled into the tiny driveway.

The doorbell of the hillside house was labeled with three names: Winters, Smythe, and Jacobson. It was just a one-in-three chance that Veronica's aftercare provider was at home. But Liz was in luck. Although another young woman answered the door, she invited Liz inside and called for Laura. The bungalow was fragrant with the smell of Indian food. To a reporter who had dined on nothing but granola bars all day, it smelled heavenly.

"Have some," Laura said, leading Liz into a kitchen fitted with a breakfast nook. "We've got plenty," she added, taking down an extra dish.

Laura introduced Liz to her two twenty-something roommates, Sue Smythe, a student nurse at Saint Elizabeth's Hospital, and Becca Jacobson, who had answered the door. An aspiring actress, Becca said she was supporting herself by walking dogs. Clearly excited to be talking with a reporter, the young women needed no nudging to talk about the Johansson case.

"It's totally shocking," said Sue, spooning raita and chutney onto her plate. "Laura says Veronica is a mess."

"I gather you helped out with Veronica today," Liz said to Laura.

"Not for long. Her grandmother was coming in from Wellesley. I just kept Veronica occupied while her father took phone calls. Veronica would have been much better off following her normal routine and attending aftercare, but Mr. Johansson didn't want to let her out of his sight. I guess I can understand that."

"Was he screening his phone calls?"

"Yeah, that's what the police told him to do. He had to keep the volume up on the answering machine so he could hear who was calling in. We kept hearing Mrs. Johansson's voice on the answering machine message. Over and over again. It was eerie, I can tell you, and I know it upset Veronica. I was glad when Mrs. Swenson arrived."

"Is that the grandmother? Do you know where she lives?"

"Yes. And no. Mrs. Swenson is the grandmother but I don't have her address."

"What about at work?" Becca offered. "I bet you have it on Veronica's emergency card."

"It's possible. I could look tomorrow."

"What was it like at the Johansson house?" Liz asked.

"Weird. Mr. Johansson was totally tense. I could see he was really upset about it, but he did bring in the Christmas tree and set it up when Veronica asked him to. She said she wanted to decorate it and surprise her mommy when she comes back. I could see he was having trouble staying cheerful, so I offered to put the lights on the tree. I didn't get very far before Mrs. Swenson arrived."

"Tell her about the weird calls," Becca urged.

"Some woman called sounding like she thought she was some kind of hero. 'I'll find you, Ellen,' she said. 'I'll bring you home.' Go figure!"

Liz used her napkin to hide a sheepish expression.

"Tell her about the other call," Becca put in.

"Some guy with an accent called saying she forgot to pick up some book. Mrs. Johansson's a librarian, you know. Imagine a library patron calling someone's home at a time like this! And some foreign woman called in saying, "Ellen, I'm so sorry. It's all my fault, but I will make it up to you."

"I'm surprised the husband wasn't instructed to keep callers on the phone so the calls could be traced," Liz said.

"I think he was supposed to do that if the call seemed suspicious. The idea was to screen the calls, I think, and pick up ASAP when one seemed significant."

"It sounds like he didn't see these calls as significant."

"I think he might have tried to pick up that foreign woman's call but she hung up too quick. At least, I heard him curse when, I guess, the call ended. I wasn't in the room with him, so it's hard to be sure. I know he picked up real quick on the call after that one and talked to someone. That seemed odd because you could hardly tell who it was before he picked up."

"Did you hear what he said?"

"It was hard to hear. Remember, I was putting lights on the tree and trying to talk to Veronica so she wouldn't get upset hearing her mom's voice again and again. I did think it was strange when one caller on the answering machine started humming, though. Weird time to be singing, huh?"

A loud scraping noise sounded from outdoors.

"Must be the plow," Sue volunteered. "If you're parked on the street, your car'll be buried."

"Fortunately, I'm in the driveway, but I'll still need to borrow a shovel to get out. I'd better get digging," she said, looking at the clock. It was 6:50.

"I'll help you," Sue said. "I've got to get over to the hospital."

Liz offered Sue a ride, thanked the young women for sharing their dinner, got assurances from Laura that she'd check on Mrs. Swenson's address, and hurried to the door. In her haste, she dropped the envelope of René's photos from her purse. Sue picked them up.

"Omigod!" Sue cried. "How awful! Is that the Johanssons' kitchen? We knew from news reports the kitchen was bloody, but it's a different matter to see it." Sue paused. "You know, an expert can tell a lot from blood like that."

"Like what, Sue?"

"Well, there are genetic tests, of course, to prove whose blood it is. But you can also tell if the person was anemic, for instance."

"I'm on my way to meet a forensics man now."

"Cool!"

With Sue's help, Liz cleared boulder-like hunks of snow that had been pushed and compacted by the plow and then she backed the Tracer onto Summit Street. With Sue in the passenger seat, she rode the brake down the hill and turned toward Brighton Center. Now the snow was coming down so hard that the lights of Saint Elizabeth's Hospital seemed veiled. Sue pointed out a parking lot and urged Liz to let her out there to avoid struggling along the sloping hospital driveway. Located next to a police station, the parking lot across the street from the Green Briar seemed to have priority on plowing. It was cleared of snow for the moment at least. Liz parked there and crossed the street to the bar, full of doubt that Kinnaird would show up.

The Green Briar's unremarkable exterior offered little hint of the atmosphere within. And the latter arose less from the décor than from the sound of some thirty musicians who filled the place with traditional Irish music. Liz passed through a barroom to a brick-walled room hung here and there with photos of Irish scenes. Under a weathered pub sign from Dublin, the players were clustered around a large table. It was difficult at first for Liz to tell whether it was the fiddler or the pennywhistle player who served as leader here, but it was clear that the rest of the musicians were taking their cues from one or both of them. It was immediately obvious that the more confident players were seated closest to this pair while those who sat farther from this inner circle included some who seemed to lean in toward their instruments while playing lightly on them, as if they were trying to learn the music by ear.

The players were remarkably mixed. Septuagenarians and teens, working men and yuppies, ruddy-faced Irish-Americans, and a twenty-something Asian Indian all lost themselves in the music that went on and on, gaining momentum and spirit along the way. Liz marveled to think this world existed a few miles from Gravesend Street without her having enjoyed it until now.

She scanned the group more than once before picking out Dr. Kinnaird. He was sitting behind a man who was playing an instrument Liz had never seen before, which required squeezing a bagpipe-type inflated bag repeatedly with his elbow. There was no doubt the unusual instrument was enough to distract Liz's attention. But there were other reasons she did not recognize Kinnaird at first. He was dressed far more casually than he'd been during his bite-marks presentation. Along with his suit, tie, and cuff links, he'd left behind his know-it-all demeanor. The expression on his face as he bent over his banjo was positively boyish.

Liz noticed he was seated far from the leader. Here, he was not the top of the heap. And he didn't seem to care.

The tune went on and on. To Liz's untutored ear, it was repetitious, but highly pleasing. While the musicians played on, she took off her coat, and removed from its pocket the crumpled front page she had taken from the *Banner* newsroom. The "PINCH OF BLOOD" headline played on Dick Manning's report of his conversation with Medical Examiner Barney Williams: "'The distribution of the blood over the countertop and baking ingredients, but not on the floor or elsewhere, suggests the scene was manipulated,' Williams said. 'One has to wonder if the blood was sprinkled there intentionally, rather than spilled as the result of an injury.'"

As Liz read, the Irish tune came to an end and Kinnaird noticed Liz. He set his banjo down on his chair and joined her.

"So you braved the storm?" he said.

"I'm so glad I did. This is terrific."

"You brought the photos, I suppose," Kinnaird said, looking longingly at his banjo as the music started up again. "I know this tune."

"Do you want to join in? I can wait," Liz said, hoping he would not take her up on the offer. "Or you can let me buy you a beer. You're my research assistant after all."

"I wouldn't hear of it. I'll take care of it," he said and ordered a lager for

Liz and a tall glass of water for himself. "I usually don't take alcohol until much later in the evening if I'm playing," he explained.

No table was particularly well lit, so they chose one for privacy rather than illumination. Kinnaird's lighthearted expression vanished as he looked over the prints. His eyes lingered over them for a long time.

"Most interesting," he said. "Of course, without being privy to accurate measurements of the spaces between the blood droplets, the precise shape of them, and the chemistry of them, I can't draw any detailed conclusions. But I can tell you what someone with that information should be able to glean from this scene."

"Please do."

"First, look at the big picture. There's blood on the countertop and ingredients but apparently not on the floor."

"Does that suggest the blood may have been intentionally sprinkled there?"

"Possibly. It would be odd for blood flowing from an injury sustained in a violent attack to confine itself to one surface area. That's why it would be important to study the shape of the drops. If they fell straight down from a wound, they would be fairly circular with a spreading pattern around the perimeter of each. That doesn't look to be the case from these photos. If they were strewn there, say, with someone's fingers, they would likely lay out in an arched pattern like a sunrise, with no blood underneath a kind of horizon line," Kinnaird said. He demonstrated by bringing his fingertips together, dipping them into his water, and opening his fingers quickly to fling water on the table.

"The problem at the Johanssons' house is most of the blood drops have fallen into the sprinkles and shredded coconut. That seriously undercuts any conclusions about how the blood fell there."

"If the blood did come from a wound, what kind of injury might account for it?"

"Impossible to say. Could be a facial wound. They flow freely and, given that the blood is confined to a rather high surface area, it would make sense for it to come from the upper body. The wound might have been stanched before the injured person crossed the floor. That would account for the lack of blood anywhere else. But I wouldn't bet my life on that. The droplets here don't scream 'head wound' to me. They're small. The few I can make out on the countertop appear teardrop-shaped and too evenly distributed to suggest that."

Rosemary Herbert

"What about the chemistry you mentioned? What might be learned from that?"

"The amount of drying would suggest how long the blood had been there. Analysis of the blood would reveal blood group, whether or not the person was anemic or suffered from certain diseases, and, of course, DNA analysis would pretty much nail the bleeder's identity. *If* you had a sample to match it to."

"Those are all things that show up in mystery novels these days, aren't they?"

"I suppose so. Less often mentioned in mystery novels is luminol, a chemical that would be sprayed around such a scene to reveal traces of blood that someone tried to clean up. If and when the police release what they learn from that, the reporter whom they inform first will have a huge advantage."

Across the room, the musicians had started up another tune.

"That's a hornpipe. Do you hear the syncopation in it?" Kinnaird said, brightening measurably and looking longingly at his banjo. "If you'd like to stay on, you can pull up a chair over there. The musicians tend to sit as close together as they can, near the leader."

"Maybe another time. It's been a long day. But thank you for sharing your expertise."

"Bring me a drop of blood from the scene, and I'll tell you more."

Chapter 6

"Yeah, sure," Liz thought but did not say aloud. Instead, she thanked Kinnaird warmly and headed into the still-falling snow. Thanks to its proximity to the police station, the parking lot had been plowed again. The Tracer's tires made it through the small mound the plow had pushed against them. It was a greater challenge to drive through the light industry and warehouse area that stood between Brighton and Gravesend Street in Allston, where no municipal snowplow had passed through since the storm's start. Fortunately, Sal Mione of Mione's Towing and Plow Services had cleared not just the driveway at Liz's place, but—as he often did when the city plow neglected the area—a single lane of Gravesend Street to her place.

He'd never accept a monetary tip, but Liz made a mental note to give him the box of PG Tips tea and chocolate digestive biscuits she'd bought for him a few days previously. She knew they were comfort foods reminiscent of his boyhood. Although he bore an Italian name, he spoke in an appealing Cockney accent, having grown up near the Angel Tube Station in London. Corny as it was, she meant it when she told him he was an angel. Without him, she'd probably lose her job waiting for plows that cleared school, retail, and residential areas in order of priority.

Prudence seemed bound to trip Liz as the reporter entered the little house under the huge billboard. Her dish was half-filled with dry food, but the cat loved her evening treat of gravy-laden canned meat. Liz fed the cat and poured herself a glass of Chardonnay. Then she sat down in her green chair facing the flaming gas fireplace, put her feet up on her hassock, pulled the purple and white afghan over her knees, and spread open *The Oxford Book of American Detective Stories* she'd acquired in Worcester. Turning on a CD of Erik Satie's *Gymnopédies*, she read Susan Glaspell's story "A Jury of Her Peers" from start to finish.

The story was as melancholy as Satie's first *Gymnopédie*. A woman has murdered her husband. But while the police blunder around looking at big, obvious clues, such as the rope he has been strangled with, the farmers' wives see the significance of unfinished work in their friend's kitchen. They recognize that an open sugar bag beside a dish means the woman was interrupted in her work. And they find heartrending evidence that their friend was driven to kill her husband. The men see the women's concerns as "trifles," but these trifles turn out to be the keys to the mystery.

Liz turned off the third *Gymnopédie*—a dissonant, jarring piece—and leaned back in her chair, pondering what she'd read. The Glaspell story was a favorite of Ellen Johansson. Had it come to mind for her during the incident in her kitchen?

Liz didn't like to entertain the notion, but suppose Ellen had perpetrated a crime, as Millie Wright in Glaspell's story had done? How would the insights from the story help her to hide it? Would she slash her own face and fling blood from it onto the countertop? This would go far toward suggesting she was a victim of someone else. And what if Ellen had been attacked by an assailant? How would the Glaspell story help her in that case? She might try to shed her attacker's blood to leave evidence for those who sought to help her. Much rested on the analysis of the blood, information that had not yet been released. But perhaps the scene of the crime would hold additional clues.

Liz got up from her chair, picked up her envelope of photos, turned on the bright light over her own kitchen counter, and spread out DeZona's prints there. For Glaspell, it was an open bag of sugar beside a partly filled sugar bowl that started the wheels turning toward an understanding of the crime. But in Ellen's kitchen everything looked so well organized that the only thing out of place was the blood splattered over the ingredients.

The blackboard in the photo caught Liz's eye again. "FORGET ME NOT," Ellen had written in apparent haste. But the hastiness of the writing could have been feigned. It was hard to imagine an assailant standing by while she wrote a note to her loved ones, even a three-word message. Did those words suggest Ellen intended to leave? Could they indicate she was contemplating taking her own life?

Liz matched the ingredients listed on the blackboard with those in the dishes. There were the chocolate chips and the coconut and other, unlisted ingredients, too. Only the M&Ms were not poured out into a custard dish. But then, Liz thought, no one would decorate delicate spritz cookies with

M&Ms. No doubt the M&Ms were stored away for another baking project or to serve in a candy dish at the holidays.

What else was in the photographs? Three poinsettia plants, dolled up with big bows and labeled with tags, stood to one side on the counter. Whose names were on them? Liz took a magnifying glass out of her desk to examine the photos more closely. One tag was out of sight. Another read "Margaret." And the last read "Ms. Winters." *Laura.*

Liz picked up the phone and dialed. Laura answered.

"Yes, Veronica gave me the plant before I left. She would have given it to me at the aftercare holiday party, but she was being taken to her grand-mother's early."

"Could you set the plant aside where no one will handle it? And if you have the tag that was on it, please save that, too. I'll call you back in a few minutes."

"I don't have the tag, Liz. I guess it got lost in the shuffle. With every-thing that was going on, I was surprised Veronica thought to give me a gift at all."

"Never mind. The plant is the main thing."

Liz looked up the Green Briar in the telephone book and called the bar. She could hear Irish music still being played there. The bartender told her to hold on while he fetched Cormac.

"Kinnaird here. May I help you?"

"It's Liz Higgins again. I may have something useful—a poinsettia plant that was on the counter at the crime scene. It was given as a gift to the babysitter who took it home to Brighton. Not very far from the Green Briar."

"It's strange that it was not sprayed with luminol. You're in luck. I've got my car. If she's willing, I could stop by and collect it."

Liz provided Kinnaird with the address, phoned Laura to have her wait up for him, and decided it was time for her to get some rest. She changed into a long T-shirt and snuggled under the covers, recalling, as she dozed off, the Worcester book dealer's words: "This woman flies from home but knows any loose ends she leaves will be seen as significant—*if* a woman gets the chance to look things over."

The sound of snowplows scraping along the Massachusetts Turnpike awoke Liz more than once in the night. Each time, she turned over and returned to sleep until one pre-dawn noisemaker was just too much for

Prudence, who dashed around the small abode in a frenzy, making Liz laugh herself awake. In her mad movements, the cat had skittered across DeZona's photos, causing one to drop to the floor. Flipping her fireplace switch to fill the room with flickering light, Liz crossed the room to pick up the photo. Turning on her kitchen counter light and the stove burner under her kettle, she measured some coffee into a filter and took another look at the photo.

This one was a shot of the Johanssons' living room. In it could be seen part of the book bearing an Arabic title. The kitchen crime scene had naturally become the focus of investigators' and reporters' attention. Had anyone taken a hard look at the living room, too?

The kettle whistled in concert with a scraping sound in her driveway. Sal Mione had arrived to plow away the last of the snowfall. Pulling on jeans and a sweater, Liz rushed to her front door.

Opening the door, she called out, "Got a minute?" to the plow driver.

"For you, of course!" he replied.

"I've got something for you," Liz said. "Hold on, I'll bring it out to you."

Grabbing the plastic bag of PG Tips tea and chocolate digestive biscuits, she stepped into her boots and put on a coat before wading out into some nine inches of snow. Handing the package in through the plow driver's rolled-down window, she saw copies of the *World* and *Banner* on the seat beside him.

"Some fire," Sal Mione said. "Bloody shame," he added, nodding at DeZona's grim front-page photo. As Liz had expected, the *Banner*'s front page was entirely consumed with the fire story, headed "INFERNO" in bold caps.

The broadsheet *World* had room for more Page One articles. She could only see below the fold of the front page. It contained an article about the fire, which *World* editors had not chosen as their lead story; a photo of an exhausted-looking fire chief; and an article headed, "Blackboard Message Muddles Missing Mother Inquiry."

"Don't you get enough of the news?" Sal Mione said to Liz.

"Never! I've been reporting on that missing mom, so I'm interested in what the *World* reporter turned up."

"It's all yours. I've already read it," Sal said, handing her the paper. "And thanks for the tea and biscuits. Much obliged."

Back in her house, Liz read Nancy Knight's coverage of the Johansson case. Apparently the *World* had put Mick Lichen on the fire story, handing Knight the Johansson assignment.

"Forensic evidence and a crime scene message leave investigators puzzled in the case of missing Newton mother, Ellen Johansson, 34." Knight wrote. "'We have to consider the possibility that Mrs. Johansson planned to leave home,' said Newton police chief Anthony Warner yesterday.

"According to Medical Examiner Barney Williams, tests on blood found in the upscale kitchen reveal two people were injured there. And a message written on Johansson's kitchen memo board suggests she was saying goodbye to her husband, Erik Johansson, 37, and eight-year-old daughter, Veronica.

"'FORGET ME NOT,' the message reads. Warner said the words, spelled out in chalk under a grocery list, are currently under examination by a handwriting expert."

"I can't believe she would walk out on Veronica," Liz exclaimed aloud, making Prudence's ears perk up. "There must be another explanation."

Liz dug the crumpled *Banner* page out of her purse and smoothed it out on her kitchen counter next to DeZona's photos. Under the "PINCH OF BLOOD" headline and Dick Manning's byline, she read, "Newton cops can't fathom why a well-heeled wife and mother would scrawl an exit line on her kitchen blackboard before leaving her family in the dark about her whereabouts. 'Seems weird to me,' said Newton police officer Dan Atwood, who was first on the scene after Ellen Johansson, 34, disappeared from the $640,000 home she shared with her husband Erik, 37, and the couple's daughter Veronica, age 8.

"'It's hard to believe any perp forcing a woman from her home would wait for her to write a message to her hubby and kid,' Atwood added.

"The three-word plea, 'FORGET ME NOT,' appeared at the bottom of a grocery list written on a blackboard in the Johanssons' state-of-the-art kitchen where, two days ago, the couple's third-grader came home from school to find flaked coconut and other baking ingredients splashed with blood on the Italian marble countertop.

"The missing woman's husband, an environmental consultant, has been questioned several times by police. 'If she wanted to leave us, why would she set up a baking project?' the distraught husband reportedly asked police. 'It just doesn't make sense.'"

Setting aside the *Banner* page, Liz realized Dick Manning had failed to contact the Newton police chief. He was also scooped by the *World* on the blood typing. No doubt he dropped the Johansson story like a hot potato when the fire broke out, knowing the blaze would have first priority in the eyes of *Banner* editors—particularly if the fire produced fatalities.

Liz turned to her phone to leave a message for DeZona and found the message light blinking. A call must have come in while she was outside delivering treats to the plow driver. She pressed the incoming message button.

"I've got those snapshots for you," DeZona's voice said. "That's all they are. Tourist pix of New York City. And pretty lousy, too. Only one of them shows any eye for a decent camera angle. I'll put them in my cubby so you can pick them up whenever you're in. I'm beat. The bucks are good but the hours aren't when you do too much overtime. I'm heading home before I drop dead on my feet."

Liz looked at the clock. Six a.m. DeZona must have been called in early. While her head swam with questions and avenues she might pursue to answer them, Liz took a shower. Afterward, she sat in front of her fire wrapped in a terrycloth robe, waiting for her shoulder-length auburn curls to dry in the flickering heat.

Half an hour later, the phone rang.

"Liz? This is Laura. I couldn't sleep last night so I went to work early. Plus, I thought it would be a good idea if I looked up Veronica's emergency information card before my boss comes in. I've got Mrs. Swenson's information for you."

Liz took down the Wellesley address and telephone number and asked who else was listed on the card as authorized to take care of the eight-year-old in an emergency.

"It says, 'Elizabeth Seaport, friend'," Laura said, giving Liz the phone number. "Actually, I recognize that name. She's the parent of another after-care kid, Rhoda Seaport. Rhoda is a year younger than Veronica. There's one more thing," Laura added. "In the 'Additional Information' section of the card it says, 'Under no circumstances to be picked up by taxi or hired vehicle.' That's dated December 18, this year."

"That's the day Ellen disappeared. I wonder what that's all about?"

"Me, too. I hope this was helpful. By the way, that forensics guy did pick up the poinsettia. Before he left, he looked the whole thing over with a magnifying glass, just like Sherlock Holmes. I kid you not! It was all Becca, Sue, and I could *do* to keep ourselves from bursting out laughing. He asked us for a dry cleaning bag to put it in, but we didn't have one so we gave him a garbage bag instead. He said you'd hear from him soon."

"Thanks, Laura. You've been extremely helpful."

"No problem. Would you let me know what develops, though? It's all such a mystery and I'm really worried about Veronica."

"Sure thing. I'm worried about her, and about Ellen, too."

Hanging up the phone, Liz took another look at her countertop. Picking up the Ziploc bag containing Ellen's lipstick, the hair band, and taxi receipt, she dialed the number for Cormac Kinnaird.

"You have reached the office of Dr. Cormac Kinnaird. This is December twentieth. This morning, I will be testifying in Concord District Court. Please leave your message and I will get back to you at the first opportunity."

Surprised that Kinnaird would reveal his schedule in a phone message, Liz recorded her own message for him, letting him know she had more materials relating to the Johansson case.

Next, she phoned Elizabeth Seaport, reaching yet another answering machine. This one had a message with a child's voice advising callers, "You have reached the Seaport family. Please leave us a message!" as a dog barked in the background.

As Liz began to leave a message, a woman picked up the Seaport line. "Just screening my calls, ever since I had a friend disappear," she volunteered.

"That's just what I wanted to discuss with you," Liz explained. "I'm a *Banner* reporter who's working on the case. . ."

"I don't want to talk with reporters!"

"No! Please wait. I'm also acquainted with the family, and I'm truly concerned about Ellen and particularly Veronica."

"Oh, you're the one who took her around to the malls, aren't you? Veronica was so proud when her Santa ratings made the paper."

"That's right. I was at the Johanssons' soon after Ellen disappeared and I promised Veronica I'd find her mom. To do that, I need your help."

"Look, I'm just about to take Rhoda—that's my daughter—to school. Then I was going to wrap presents while Rhoda is out of the house."

"I'm great at wrapping. How about I save you some time? We'll wrap gifts together while you share some insights about Ellen?"

"Well, it does seem sort of callous to go on with Christmas preparations while she's missing. And Ellen spoke so highly of you. All right. Come on over in about a half an hour. I live two doors down from Ellen, in the center-entrance colonial. Our shrubs are covered with white Christmas lights and there's a reindeer loaded with lights on the lawn. Kinda kitschy, I admit, especially for this neighborhood, but the kids love it."

"See you then. Thank you!"

Liz lingered near the phone, tempted to place a call to Olga Swenson. But she decided to put that off until she'd spoken with Elizabeth Seaport. Very possibly,

Ellen's friend and neighbor would have insights or information that would smooth the way toward an interview with Veronica's grandmother. Instead, Liz phoned the *Banner* and asked to be connected with the city desk."

When Jared Conneely answered, Liz dared to hope Esther O'Faolin was still in charge at this early hour. She was in luck.

"Listen, Esther," Liz said. "I've got some lines of inquiry I'd like to follow on the missing mom case."

"You know, Dick has the contacts for that story."

"Let him chase his. But I've got some promising community contacts I'd like to pursue. I've also got fewer assumptions than Dick and, for that matter, the *World* reporters who are covering this case."

"Let's be clear on this. What do you mean by 'assumptions'?"

"They look at her kitchen memo and see it as a goodbye message. They look at the blood and think she put it there on purpose. I'm not ready to draw conclusions so early in the game."

"I'm the first to admit that the reporter who works without blinders will see the most in a story. But you may be wearing blinders without knowing it, Liz. Have you considered the possibility that you may be looking for a way to exonerate a person who deserted her husband and child, just because you knew and liked her? Or maybe you bonded with her daughter so well that you are hoping against hope you can save the day for her."

"You're on target on both counts, Esther. Sure, I'd like to save the day, as you put it. But more important than that, I'd like to tell the truth here—even if it *is* ugly. I have some avenues that might lead me toward that truth, and I'd like to have a day to pursue them."

"Well, you know it's really up to Dermott to decide where to send you when he gets in at ten. But if you're already engaged in some reporting that can't wait until then, I guess I can authorize it. What's up?"

Liz paused. Then she said, "I plan to help Ellen Johansson's neighbor wrap Christmas gifts while she shares insights about her friend. I have an appointment to arrive at her house in a half-hour."

Esther groaned. "That hardly sounds urgent enough for me to pull strings with Dermott on your behalf when he gets in."

"My thought is that she'll give me enough insight about the family to smooth my way to an interview with Veronica's grandmother."

"OK, I'll give you an inch, but you've got to win your mile. You go play Santa's elf for a short while. Then, if you get an appointment with the grand-mother, you can have the rest of the day on this. That would free up Dick for the fire story follow-up. If you don't nail an interview with the grandma, I expect you to cover whatever Dermott has in mind for you. I'll authorize overtime for your early start today with the expectation that you'll put in a full day for Dermott—on the Johansson story or something else."

"You won't regret this, Esther. Thanks."

New York City, December 16, 2000

"Stereotypes!" Ellen thought as she stood on the curbside by the World Trade Center. "Here I am feeling bad about any prejudice I might be feeling and, all the while, that cabbie is making assumptions about me. Just because I'm a blonde, it doesn't mean I'm stupid. Well, I showed him!" she thought to herself, smiling.

Looking at her watch, she realized the cabbie had been a good one. She was early for her date. There was enough time to document the occasion in photographs. Taking out her camera, she pointed it at the towers, only to realize immediately that they were too large to frame in her lens. In the hope of getting a slightly better perspective, Ellen crossed the street where she joined a Japanese tour group that was also attempting to capture the scene on film.

Even from this perspective, it remained impossible to capture the full buildings in a single photo, but Ellen could get a sense of their size by having pedestrians and traffic in the foreground, looking dwarfed by a fraction of one tower. Seeing her with a camera, the Japanese tourists asked if she would photograph their group in the scene. When she assented, they provided her with five cameras. Using one camera after another—all but one equipped with much better wide-angle lenses than she had on her camera—she shot five photos of the patiently smiling group. As a thank-you gesture, one of the tourists offered to photograph Ellen, using her camera. When he recognized the limitations of her lens, he made the effort of walking half a block down a side street in order to capture more of the scene. Ellen walked with him so that she would be in the photograph's foreground.

On her way back toward the towers, she shot another photo of her own, this one with a street-corner vendor of roasted chestnuts shown in the foreground. This shot particularly pleased her, since she saw it as a scene that brought together timeless and contemporary New York.

Snapping the lens cap onto her camera, she reached the corner as the WALK light invited her to cross. She stepped off the curb with a crowd and strode across the street toward her long-awaited rendezvous.

Chapter 7

Newton, Massachusetts, December 20, 2000

The plastic reindeer in the Seaport family's front yard was an eyesore during daylight, at least. But it made the house easy to identify. When the mom who ruled the roost opened the door, it was immediately obvious that the Seaport home had a more lived-in atmosphere than did the Johanssons' house. A plastic mat covering the carpet in the vestibule was cluttered with shoes, boots, and a dog bone, all of which were rapidly becoming more disordered as a good-natured golden retriever danced around in excitement at Liz's arrival.

"It's so wonderful of you to help out," the lady of the house said as she led Liz into her dining room. "I'll just get you some coffee. Cream? Sugar?"

"Just cream, please, Elizabeth," Liz said, thinking how rare it was to be thought of as helpful to others in the course of reporting.

"Oh, please, call me Betsy. Everyone does."

The dining table was covered with rolls of wrapping paper. And the floor was piled high with presents.

"Are all of these for Rhoda?"

"Not quite. A few are for her cousins. I know we overdo it, but it's so much fun to buy for her."

Liz rolled out some paper and placed a box on it to gauge the amount of paper needed to wrap it. Then, as she cut the wrap, she said, "You know, Betsy, some people are speculating that Ellen left her family of her own free will."

"That's impossible. I know Ellen, and I know she would never leave Veronica and Erik. Veronica is the joy of her life. And the marriage looks good to me, too. I know they say the husband is always a suspect when a wife goes missing, but I just know there's no weirdness with them. They're solid."

"Is it possible they're *too* 'solid'? Could Ellen have been restless?"

"God knows, she and I have kvetched about the predictability of our lives, but that doesn't mean either of us would take off and leave our family. I'd be more worried about a friend who never vented than I would be about a person who can complain and laugh about it later. Ellen was open about this stuff. And we often had a good laugh about our kids and parenting."

Betsy paused in the struggle to wrap a stuffed orangutan. Liz tore off some tape to help her with the process.

"Thanks. It's amazing how often you need three hands in the course of a day of mothering."

"As neighbors, you and Ellen often gave each other a hand?"

"We spent a lot more time together when our girls were infants and toddlers than we have recently. Ellen took two years off to be a full-time mother after Veronica was born. She went back to work full-time, let's see, about six years ago. We're not strangers to one another even now, but the librarians see more of her on a day-to-day basis than I do. You'll probably want to talk with them. If you decide to do that, steer clear of Monica Phillips. She's the kind of biddy who gives librarians a bad name. You know, finger to her lips and 'Shhh!' every time my Rhoda makes a peep. But Lucy Gray's a different story. She and Ellen attended Simmons together—you know, the library college in Boston—and they're great friends. And book lovers, too. Tell Lucy I said to talk to you and she'll tell you a lot about Ellen, I guarantee it."

"Thanks. Would it be too much trouble for you to give Lucy a ring yourself and smooth the way?'

"No problem."

"What do you know about somebody called 'Nadia'? Apparently, Ellen met Nadia in New York City the other day."

"I don't have a clue. Never heard of anyone by that name."

"Did Ellen talk with you about the trip?"

"No. Not a word. I'm trying to remember the last time we spoke." Betsy tied a bow while wrinkling her brow. "I know! It was when my husband was setting up the reindeer out front. I came out to bring him some hot chocolate and Ellen was pulling into her drive with her new car. One of those fuel-efficient models. Erik Johansson's an environmentalist, you know.

"She was all excited about the deal she got on it. Something about bargaining with an Arab. But I only had a sweater on and it was freezing out, so I didn't stay to talk. I remember the sweater because it matched hers. We both had on thick cardigans with Christmas reindeer and presents knitted into the pattern. We both laughed and said we'd either have to look like twins or make a decision about who gets to wear the sweater at the school holiday gathering. As it turned out, I said I'd wear my holly sweater. But I needn't have worried. She never made it to that party after all, did she? She went missing and her mother whisked Veronica off to Wellesley before the party day anyway."

"What about Mrs. Swenson? Do you have the impression Ellen and her mother are close?"

"Much closer than she was with her late father. He died when she was still in elementary school."

Betsy paused to measure another sheet of wrapping paper.

"You know," she said, "the more we're talking, the more I realize how much I've lost touch with Ellen over the last several years. Things like that scene in her kitchen make everything different, don't they? They make you wonder."

Opening her scissors slightly and positioning the sheet of paper between the blades, Betsy leaned forward into her task, neatly shearing the paper along an unseen line. Her expression formed a sharp contrast with the beaming Santas pictured on the wrap.

"I'll let myself out," Liz said, leaving Betsy to compose her face and her thoughts.

It was a short walk to the Newton Free Library—just across the City Hall Common. Kicking herself for failing to get a description of Lucy Gray, Liz walked between tall piles of plowed snow on the drive that crossed the City Hall property to the new and impressive library building. The last time she'd seen it, the statuary there—including a brass Eeyore beloved by children— was eye-catching. After the snowstorm of the night before, such landscape ornaments were only suggested by mounds of snow.

Fortunately, the library's circulation desk was staffed by two men and a woman who had to be in her early twenties. Monica Phillips might be avoided.

Or maybe not. When Liz asked for Lucy Gray, the young circulation librarian directed her to the reference desk. Arriving there, Liz saw two names listed on the "ON DUTY" sign: Monica Phillips and Lucy Gray. The librarians wore name tags, too, so Liz posed her question to Lucy.

"I'm looking for a mixed bag of books," she said, and listed the four books that she knew were Ellen Johansson's favorites.

Automatically, Lucy began to input title and author of the first. She typed "trifles susan glasp" and then broke off her work. She glanced at Monica Phillips.

"Actually, I have another author I'm seeking. Would you see what comes up under 'Liz Higgins'?"

Lucy looked at Liz. Then she seemed to make up her mind.

"I happen to know that first book you requested is on a book truck waiting to be reshelved," she said. "If you'll join me, we may be able to retrieve it."

As the two reached the lobby near the circulation desk, Lucy said, "You're the reporter Betsy called about, aren't you?"

"That's right. Betsy told me Ms. Phillips is difficult, so I decided not to announce myself as a reporter. I'm glad you realized who I am."

"I wanted to get away from the desk. It's not that I particularly care what she thinks in the ordinary course of things, but I've really been on edge since Ellen went missing. I want to help Ellen, but I've been debating what to do about some information I have about her."

"Do you think it's germane to the case?"

"Absolutely. But I shouldn't be sharing it. With a boss like mine, I could even lose my job if I do."

The two reached the circulation area where Lucy made a show of looking over volumes on a book truck.

"Not here, I'm afraid. Perhaps it's already been shelved," Lucy said. "Not here," she said again, pointedly.

The pair walked away from the truck.

"When's your coffee break?"

"In twenty minutes."

"How do you take your coffee? I'll be waiting for you in the parking lot. Green Mercury Tracer."

Liz drove down the long hill known as Walnut Street into the heart of Newtonville, one of the city's seventeen village centers. Standing in shin-deep snow at an outdoor phone booth, she called the city desk and had the good luck of reaching Jared's morning equivalent, an editorial assistant named E.A. Tenley. Liz said she was following a lead on the missing mom case and hung up the ice-cold phone before E.A. could ask for details. Then she purchased two tall cups of coffee at a place called Café Appassionata before driving the mile back to the library parking lot.

Lucy Gray was waiting for her. After the librarian got into the car, Liz drove over Heartbreak Hill and onto a residential side street, where she parked the car.

"I only have fifteen minutes," Lucy said. "And I'm still debating whether I should tell you what I have on my mind."

"I know. And I'm a complete stranger."

"Well, not completely, fortunately. You see, Ellen and Veronica both spoke so highly of you. Veronica's my goddaughter, you know. I promised her I'd do everything I could to find her mom. She told me someone else made the same promise: you."

"If we work together, maybe we can both keep our promises. Look, I'm willing to take the heat for anything that might be against library policy. But you'll have to tell me the nature of the information so we can find a way for me to be the culprit here."

"It's not just a problem with my boss. I see eye-to-eye with Monica Phillips on just about nothing else, but I share her views on this issue. All I can say is it has to do with the right of privacy, and our duty as librarians to protect that right for our patrons."

"Am I correct in assuming you have access to information about Ellen's reading, about the books she has taken out recently?"

Lucy turned her head and gazed out the window at the suburban scene. The view fogged over as she sighed and her breath reached the window glass.

In matching movements, each woman opened her car door and stepped into the cold air. Liz walked around the car and joined Lucy on the sidewalk.

"I'm sorry. I can't answer that right now. You can't imagine how sorry I am."

"Maybe you can supply some other information instead. Do you know anything about your friend's trip to New York? And do you have any idea who someone called Nadia is?"

"I thought I knew about the nature of the trip, but now I'm not so sure. Ellen could hardly talk about anything else. She was going to the city to meet Nadia for the first time. Ellen and Nadia have been writing to each other for twenty-one years, since they were thirteen years old. They were going to treat themselves to lunch in the Windows on the World restaurant at the top of the World Trade Center. Ellen kept saying the view would be so great, they could almost see both of their homes from there."

"Where is Nadia from? Do you know her last name?"

Rosemary Herbert

"She is from Jerusalem. No, I don't know her last name, but I know her first language is Arabic. Although I gather Nadia's English was good and the two wrote to each other in English, Ellen said she was learning some Arabic so that she could greet her friend in Nadia's own language."

"How conversant do you think she was in Arabic?"

Lucy stopped in her tracks.

"Shouldn't we be saying 'she *is*' instead of 'she *was*'? It's not as if we know she's dead."

Liz flinched. "How fluent do you think she is?"

"I wish I knew," she said. "I thought I knew. But now I'm not so sure."

"Because of her library records?"

Lucy pulled her hood up, obscuring part of her face. "I shouldn't have let on as much as I did. It's not only that I'm such a staunch believer in this right to privacy," Lucy explained, "but I don't like what Ellen's reading list suggests about her—and about her possible plans. It's heartbreaking. And it makes me wonder if I knew my friend at all."

Lucy's chest and shoulders shook as she took in two quick breaths, like a child on the verge of sobbing. But she steadied herself.

Sometimes time and silence can serve as handmaidens to revelation. But neither moves at a lively pace. With her unvoiced question hanging in the air as tangibly as the breath she exhaled into the cold winter morning, Liz took Lucy's arm and led her back to the car.

"Your coffee break is almost over," Liz said. "When you're ready to tell me more, let me know."

Chapter 8

More snow was falling as Liz dropped Lucy off at the library. She trudged through it to use the phone booth on the premises.

"So, did you nab an interview with the grandmother?" Dermott asked her over the phone.

"No, Dermott, I didn't, but I've been pursuing some other leads that came up."

"Have they led to a story you can file tonight?"

"Not yet."

"Then take this one and run with it," Dermott said. "Seems some jogger called in from Newton and said he saw a couple of Arab guys at the Johansson door about an hour before the kid came home. Take this down. Guy's a hairdresser. Calls himself P.D. Cue but his real name's Paddy McCuddy. He's probably a fuckin' fairy."

"Hey!"

"Ah jeez, don't get all PC on me. Be glad you're back on the missing mom story with a real lead after chasing shadows all day. Or was it playing elf? I hear you were wrapping presents with some gal all morning, on company time, no less! And you wanted to step out of features territory!"

"You have a number for the hairdresser?"

"Yeah, but I got better than that. He's at his shop now. On Cue Hair Design, in Newton Upper Falls."

"Say no more. That's part of features territory. I know where it is."

The hairdresser was no fairy, although he could charm the socks off every one of his mixed bag of customers. When Liz walked into his shop, he had two clients' coiffures well under control.

"Just sit here for a few minutes, Miss Monroe," he said to an elderly woman whose head was covered with old-fashioned rollers. Leading her to a seat under a hair dryer, he inquired, "Or may I call you Marilyn?"

"You can call me Norma Jean," the woman replied, smiling broadly. "I reserve that name for my intimates."

"I'm honored, Norma Jean," the hairdresser said, bowing slightly. "OK, buddy," he said, changing tone as he spoke to a mailman who had apparently shown up for a haircut during a lunch break. "Do you think the Celtics have a chance in hell of winning tonight?" he asked, as he fitted a plastic sheet around the mailman's neck. "Do you have an appointment?" he said, turning to Liz. "I'm not sure if I have time to take a walk-in at the moment."

"Actually, I'm here in response to your call to the *Beantown Banner*." Liz held out her hand. "Liz Higgins" she said.

"Paddy McCuddy. I had to change the name for the shop. McCuddy's Hair Design might make it in Dublin but it doesn't cut it in this suburb."

"Shame about that mother running out on her kid," the mailman offered.

"What makes you think she ran out on her family?" Liz asked.

"They're on my route. A mailman sees more than most people think."

"Like what?"

"Well, there's the deliveries we make, for one thing. There's one household on my route keeps receiving pink envelopes. I'm not surprised to see the house went up for sale recently. They're up to their ears in debt."

"What about the Johanssons? Anything unusual there?"

"You bet. Lots of letters from the Middle East. All for the missus. She's been receiving them for years. And he receives all kinds of insects. I don't deliver them. UPS does. But I see them sitting on the stoop. Trusting household. Has a little card on the mailbox that says, 'If we're not home, please leave deliveries.'"

"What are the bugs for?" Paddy asked.

"Guy's an eco-nut. I guess he releases them into the garden to eat other bugs. Seems like a waste to me. You open a box of ladybugs and who's gonna tell 'em you paid for them so they better stay in your yard?"

"You got a point there," Paddy agreed.

"I think it's wonderful," said "Miss Monroe." "We need people like that to keep down the use of pesticides. Let some of the ladybugs fly into my garden anytime. They bring good luck, you know."

"Ladybug, ladybug, fly away home. Your house is on fire, your children will burn," the hairdresser said as he turned on the electric razor to trim the mailman's neck hair.

"Name's Len Fenster," the mailman said loudly over the razor's buzz.

"May I quote you about the Johanssons?" Liz asked.

"Yeah, sure. Don't quote me on the dunning slips, though, will ya?"

"No problem."

"That's it, buddy," Paddy said.

"What do I owe ya?"

"The usual."

Paddy turned to his curler-covered customer and told her, "You need another ten, fifteen minutes, Norma Jean." He turned the drier to high.

Over its airy hum, Liz asked him, "Have you spoken to anybody else about what you saw at the Johanssons' house?"

"Sure. My wife. She's the one who told me to call the *Banner* after they found blood in the house."

"How about the *World*?"

"That rag! Nah."

"I'd appreciate it if you'd keep this exclusive."

"No problem. It was weird, though, to see two guys on the Johanssons' doorstep on the day in question," the hairdresser said, sounding like he fancied himself to be an actor in a TV-courtroom drama.

"Why?"

"They just didn't fit in."

"In what regard?"

"Well, they were Arabs, for one thing."

"Surely some people of Middle Eastern extraction live in Newton."

"Sure they do. I have one or two families who bring their kids for haircuts in my shop. But they *live* here. They don't drive up to houses in big, jazzy cars without license plates and then stand around at people's doors."

"Are you saying there was no license plate on the car they arrived in?"

"That's right. They drove up in a Crown Victoria with no plates. They looked pretty put out when nobody answered the door, I can tell you."

"What do you mean by 'put out'?"

"They were talking to each other a mile a minute. I couldn't understand a word that they said. It must have been Arabic they were speaking. They were shaking their heads and talking away. Finally, they got in their car and drove off."

"If you hadn't heard about the apparent crime scene at the Johanssons', do you think you would have thought their behavior was significant?"

"I think so. Like I said, they were out of place."

Liz left the hairdresser and drove straight to the Johanssons' street. She wasn't keen on running herself but she knew enough joggers to be aware that exercise nuts are creatures of habit. Chances were good that one or more of the two o'clock joggers would pass by at the same time today.

It was 1:50 when Liz introduced herself to the first jogger on Fenwick Street.

"I *would* have been passing by then," said a woman dressed in Olympic-quality running gear, "but I'd stopped to see the events on the City Hall Common. It was hilarious, I tell you! Until the little girl ran into the scene. Hey, haven't I seen you somewhere before?"

Liz interviewed six more runners before a pair of women had information to add.

"No plates on the car? I didn't notice that," the taller of the two said.

"But it would make sense!" her running partner exclaimed. "They probably forgot to put dealer plates on the car when they took it out."

"Dealer plates?"

"Yeah, it was Sam Maksoud and his son at the Johansson house. I know them because I bought my car from them."

"'We always go the extra mile,'" the two women said in unison.

"Not us as runners," the tall gal laughed in response to the puzzled look on Liz's face. "The Maksouds. That's the dealership's motto."

"Is that the dealership on Needham Street?" Liz inquired.

After the joggers nodded confirmation, Liz drove her Tracer straight to it.

"Yeah, I remember the lady," Sam Maksoud said, waving Liz into a chair in his glassed-in office with a view of the car showroom. "After the deal I gave to her, I'll never forget her!"

"I've heard you're doing some great price cutting for end of the season sales," Liz said, remembering Tom Horton's tip.

"That is true, but in Mrs. Johansson's case it was a different story."

"I'd love to hear it."

"You have met the lady, yes?"

Liz nodded.

"An attractive lady, with the berry-blonde hair. I would never have imagined she would know the niceties of our language, our Arabic ways. Nor did

I think such a polite lady had it in her to bargain like that. She so charmed me that I took some big dollars off the price of her car."

"How did she do that?"

"She arrived here in her husband's car, not the one she wished to trade in. When I asked her about the other vehicle, she said it needed a repair and she didn't want to put any more money into it. When the customer says that, we know the car is rather iffy, but, of course, our mechanics can fix most anything. It's often a different story if the vehicle is not running. So I asked the lady, 'Does it run?'"

"What did she tell you?"

"That's when she surprised me. '*Hamdu-lillah*,' she said."

"What does that mean?"

"Thanks to God. For those words, I took another two thousand dollars off the price of her car," he grinned. "That's not all the story. It turned out the trade-in was truly on its last legs. That delightfully devious lady had it towed up the steep hill of Walnut Street and then drove it the last few blocks to my dealership, on the level road! I know, because she hired my cousin to do the deed!"

"You're smiling! Didn't that make you angry?"

"Not at all! I have respect for such a woman. And I made up my losses by the end of the same day by bargaining hard with some customers who could afford it. Of course, she was much less comfortable when it came time to pick up her new car. So amusing it was! She hurried off without picking up the title. That piece of paper proves you own it, of course. I phoned her more than once about it. And when she was never in, I decided to deliver it myself. My son and I tried to drop it off at her house, it turns out, on the very day she disappeared. By the way, you need a new vehicle, you let old man Maksoud know, OK?" the car dealer said, pressing his business card into Liz's hand.

That eliminates one of the 'foreign' phone callers, Liz thought to herself as she returned to her car. The guy who called about "some title" was not a library patron, after all. It was the car dealer. Placing the business card on her dashboard, Liz noticed the pair of boldfaced Ms. Could the two Ms on Ellen's blackboard have referred to Maksoud Motors rather than the colorful candies that "melt in your mouth, not in your hand?"

Still, positive news was a hard sell at the *Banner*. Back in the newsroom, Liz's satisfaction in tying up some loose ends was short-lived under the city editor's scrutiny.

"OK, five inches," he told her. And play up the mailman's reaction."

It turned out that Dermott McCann made an excellent, if reluctant, decision. When Maksoud and son were taken in for questioning an hour after Liz left them, the *World* was onto the story—their only source an oil delivery man and Gulf War veteran who had seen men he took to be "Iraqi thugs."

Liz did mention the mailman's take on things in her story's lead, but only to make him look as suspicious of airmail letters as he was of insects. Fortunately for the *Banner*, Dermott McCann had other fish to fry that night, so he didn't edit Liz's piece. He was occupied overseeing coverage of a basketball player who was hauled in and then released by police for attempted rape of a nightclub "date." While the papers that came off the *Banner*'s press splashed the headline "BOUNCER BOUNCED," the *World*'s front page broke the news, "Father & Son Car Dealers Implicated in Missing Mother Case."

In the early hours of the morning, after the first copies of the *World* reached the *Banner*'s newsroom, night editor Esther O'Faolin saw to it that in late editions, Liz's story got a front-page teaser headed: "TITLED GENTS: Do-Good Dealers Slammed Unjustly."

New York City, December 16, 2000

Ellen waited at the elevator bay to ascend to the Windows on the World restaurant. Excitement about meeting Nadia was foremost in her mind, but it did not prevent her from noticing that the small crowd with whom she stood waiting for elevators was also a melting pot of peoples. While many were well dressed businessmen and women sporting corporate duds, they possessed complexions and facial characteristics from every corner of the world. Others in the crowd were an international mix, too, whether they wore the camera gear and belly packs marking them as tourists, casual dress and envelopes that identified them as couriers, the uniforms and clipboards that announced them as UPS or FEDEX delivery staff, or the garb of other workers, including telephone, copy machine, and computer repairmen. Ellen scanned every face she could see in case she and Nadia were already keeping company, but she did not recognize her pen pal among the elevator crowd.

The experience made her call to mind an arrival at a large international airport, where, after fetching baggage and going through customs, you step through double doors into a huge lobby to find yourself suddenly surrounded by a crowd of expectant faces. If you're looking for someone from whom you've been long separated, you feel pressured to recognize the person first, so you scrutinize the crowd in earnest haste. But if you know no one is among the crowd to greet you, you nevertheless feel the full weight of the crowd's attention and experience the urge to do something—a casual soft-shoe, perhaps, or quick juggling act—to merit it.

But Ellen was not the center of attention here. Except in the eyes of one Middle Easterner. And it was not Nadia.

Finally, the elevator doors opened. After some thirty people exited the single car, Ellen pushed forward to board it for its return trip. Then someone grabbed her shoulder firmly and spun her around.

"Ellen, Ellen!" Nadia cried out with delight. "I am giving thanks to Allah that it's you. Only my pen friend could be wearing the scarf I sent to her twenty years ago."

"You sent it to me for my fourteenth birthday, when you said I had become a woman. Oh Nadia, how wonderful to see you after all these years! And look, you are wearing the leather belt I tooled for you when I was thirteen!"

"Not, I am afraid, as easy to see as that scarf. I wonder, would you have recognized me if I hadn't seen you first?"

Rosemary Herbert

Ellen paused. Then she said, "Ya sadiqati al habibah aa rifuki kull al-awqat."

Nadia smiled and shook her head in pleased amazement, swinging her chicly bobbed brown hair from side to side. And then she pressed her cheek against Ellen's and held it there for a good few seconds.

After opening their hearts to one another in letters for decades without laying eyes on anything but photographs of one another, the two women only had eyes for each other. Arm-in-arm, they joined the crowd entering an elevator.

Chapter 9

Boston, Massachusetts, December 21, 2000

W hen Erik Johansson discovered the title to his wife's car in his mailbox the following day, he shared the information with Ramona Hobart, host of the nationally broadcast morning television program, *Wake Up USA*. Erik had consented to an interview in order to spread the word about his missing wife to millions of American households.

Liz arrived in the newsroom to find a message from editor-in-chief James Conrad glowing in green letters on her ATEX terminal. "SEE ME ASAP," it read.

Liz hardly knew what to expect when she arrived at the editor's office. Certainly, it wasn't the instruction, "Smile pretty and show your smarts." But that was the advice Conrad gave her.

She'd seen similar happenings in the newsroom before but had never been the focus of them. Now, as *Wake Up USA*'s production team arrived and set up lights in the newsroom, she knew those lights would shine on her. The idea was to show the journalist at work amid the sea of desks. Since Liz's workstation was not near the city desk and large *Beantown Banner* sign, she was seated for the occasion at political columnist Fred Constanzo's desk. When Constanzo walked away muttering, no one could be sure if he was voicing complaint about being bumped from his desk or mouthing lines from his latest column.

Liz was glad she'd chosen to dress in a reasonably respectable teal sweater and black skirt that day. She took off her snow boots and put on the pair of heels she kept under her desk. Then, wired with a microphone, and with no other preparation, she crossed her legs as the bright lights came on. Through an earphone hidden under her auburn curls, Liz heard the disembodied voice of Hobart herself.

"Now we turn to Liz Higgins, features reporter for the tabloid *Beantown Banner*," Hobart announced. "Good morning, Liz," Hobart said familiarly. "Would you say the police action in hauling in the car dealers was another case of racial profiling?"

Liz looked straight into the camera. "That's a possibility, Ramona. Certainly everyone was ready to leap on the characterization of the men as Arabic or foreign. Our competing paper reported the police were contacted by an oil deliveryman. He told police he'd seen two men on the missing woman's doorstep in the hour before the bloody scene in the kitchen was discovered. According to their report, the oilman called the men 'foreign.' My first sources, a mailman and a jogger in the neighborhood, called the car dealers 'out of place' in the neighborhood."

"The neighborhood seems to have been full of people."

"Certainly there were several. In addition to the father-and-son car dealers, there were the oilman, the mailman, and some joggers. While all of these people were in the vicinity around the time of the disappearance, police did not take the non-Arabs in for questioning."

"Why didn't you fall for the assumptions made by your first sources?"

"I try to look at facts, not skin color or accent. When I learned the car had no plates, I went back to the neighborhood and interviewed joggers until I found two who guessed the truth. When they pointed me to Maksoud Motors, I learned the nature of the car dealers' errand. The men just wanted to do a favor for their customer."

Now Hobart changed her friendly tone to one that was much more challenging. "And you believed them, just like that? Isn't it true, proof of their good deed didn't surface until this morning, after your article went to press? Couldn't that have been just dumb luck?"

Liz saw James Conrad and Dick Manning through the bright lights. They were watching the interview on the technician's monitor. The editor looked worried. The reporter looked pleased.

"I believed Sam Maksoud because he told me an anecdote about the car deal that jibed with information I had from Ellen Johansson's neighbor. He also admitted he phoned Mrs. Johansson about the car's title. I knew from another household insider that he'd done that. I filed that report because I knew—not just believed—it was true."

Liz blinked as the lights went off and the commotion of packing the equipment away ensued.

"Nice job, Higgins," Conrad said, as if he hadn't doubted her for a moment.

Manning was nowhere to be seen.

Thanks to the television spot—and to ongoing problems for the basketball star—Liz was granted another day to work on the missing mom case while Dick set his sights on the hoop star's lawyer. Although she had not succeeded in having anyone else smooth the way toward an interview with Ellen's mother, she made a call to the Wellesley telephone number Laura Winters had provided to her. A male voice answered and repeated her name aloud. Was it a police officer or male relative screening calls for Mrs. Swenson?

Apparently, Veronica was within ear range. "Liz! Liz! I want to talk to her. She said she would find Mommy. I want to know if she found her! I want to talk to Liz!"

Olga Swenson came on the line.

"What do you want with us?" she asked. "I'm not talking to the press."

"It's my hope you will consider talking with me, off the record if you insist. The more I know about your daughter, the more I can do to find her."

"My son-in-law talked to your paper and they made him appear to be a man looking for an alibi. In fact, wasn't your name on that piece?"

"My colleague wrote that piece, using some quotes I supplied. But he cut short your son's remark about wishing he had stayed home. I know that made Erik look suspicious. I apologize."

"It's bad enough that they always think the husband did it, without the newspapers adding fuel to the fire. But I saw in the paper today that you got the whole story about those car salesmen. You were more thorough than the *World*'s reporter."

"Thank you, Mrs. Swenson. I have an advantage: I know Ellen and Veronica enough to care about finding the whole truth."

Olga Swenson said nothing.

Liz waited out the silence.

"Please, Grandma!" Veronica said at a distance.

"Let's go find Hershey," a voice in the background said, apparently succeeding in leading Veronica away.

"I always walk my dog along the shores of Lake Waban at around one-thirty p.m. If you park at the Wellesley College Faculty Club and walk west around the lakeshore, you'll see me. If you bring anyone else, I won't talk. No notebook. No recorder, either. I caution you, my dog can be protective."

Liz wanted desperately to ask Olga Swenson to bring a hairbrush or personal item of Ellen's to their rendezvous. But, fearing the request for a source of DNA would turn off the woman altogether, she said only, "Thank you, Mrs. Swenson. You can count on me."

Next, Liz dialed up her voice mail. It was full of messages from public relations people trying to get attention for authors coming to town, community group events, and the like. Nothing useful. Liz's ATEX machine held only internal messages. Nonetheless, she looked them over. Again, nothing germane to the Johansson case.

It was a thorn in the side of most *Banner* staffers that they did not have PCs at their desks. Consequently, they also did not have e-mail access unless they worked on a PC in the *Banner*'s photo library. It was a place filled with battered filing cabinets—topped with brave and dusty philodendrons and filled with photos—arranged in a backward, right-to-left alphabetical order around the room. Some of the file drawers were made more noticeable by cutouts of notables—ranging from dead presidents to Miss Piggy—pasted or taped on them.

Since the PC was in demand more often than not, staffers had to take turns using it. Such was the case this time, too, as an editorial assistant from the sports department was using the machine to call up statistics—and perhaps look for former faux pas—regarding the troubled basketball star. Probably, he was compiling the information for Manning. Liz stormed out of the library and headed for the photo department. There she picked up the manila envelope DeZona had left for her in his cubbyhole.

Liz retraced her steps to the library, where the PC was unoccupied at last. She put in her password and called up a long list of e-mail messages. Like her voice mail, most of the messages were from PR people. She ignored all but a few. Beginning with addresses she did not recognize, she opened a message that turned out to be an ad for printer cartridges, then one from a self-proclaimed expert on astrology, and finally a one-word message from an e-mail address she did not recognize. "Blister," it read.

Perplexed, Liz moved on to the next message from kinnarddoc@north-eastern.edu: "Poinsettia productive. Need sample for comparison. Tir Na Nog tonite at 7?—CK"

It was clear the message was from Cormac Kinnaird. But what was 'Tir Na Nog'? Liz returned to her desk and picked up the Boston Area phone book. Sure enough, Tir Na Nog was listed at an address in Somerville. She dialed the number. It was not yet open at eleven in the morning, but a recorded message revealed it was an Irish pub. "Why didn't I think of inputting the pub name on the Internet?" Liz scolded herself. Without ready access to the system, such Internet use simply didn't occur to her.

Liz returned to the library to reply to Cormac Kinnaird's e-mail message. The PC was occupied.

"What else is new?" she asked herself as she sat down at a small table and opened the envelope of photos. The first few pictures were of Veronica and Erik selecting, sawing down, and dragging away a tree at a Christmas tree farm. The next handful were of New York City street scenes, including a shot of traffic passing by a large building, a photo of a chestnut vendor and newsstand, a much better-framed shot of Ellen standing in a city street with a skyscraper completely filling the background. Then there was an indoor shot showing a restaurant table with a chic woman seated at it and another shot of the same woman and Ellen raising their glasses in a toast. Finally, there was a photo of the two women dwarfed by a large, globe-shaped sculpture, and another of the two carrying shopping bags, standing before one of the lion statues at the New York Public Library.

There was also an enlargement from one of René's photos taken in the Johanssons' kitchen. What Liz saw in it caused her to ask the editorial assistant using the PC if she'd be done with the machine soon. This was a break in protocol. By unspoken agreement, reporters did not hound one another here, since they all could appreciate how much time had been spent—and wasted—in waiting for a turn to look at e-mail or to use the Internet.

But even inconveniences can sometimes turn out to be opportunities in disguise. Liz took the time to make a Xerox copy of Ellen's taxi receipt. Placing the original in one of the *Banner*'s business envelopes and placing that in her purse, she used scissors to trim down the copy to the same size as the original. Then she crumpled it a little bit and flattened it out again, and stored it in the manila envelope with the photos.

Fortunately, Liz soon had her chance to reply to Kinnaird's message. "Tir Na Nog at 7 looks fine," she wrote. Then she stopped by the city desk, let Jared Conneely know she would be out on assignment, and made her way downstairs, along the inky hall and into the snow-heaped parking lot.

The snow there was filthy, but once Liz was out of town driving west along Route 16, the white stuff did a great deal to beautify the roadside landscape. It also became deeper as Liz put more miles between herself and Boston. After passing through part of the Wellesley business area, she saw children sledding down large hills on her left. The timeless scene made her think of Veronica, who had asked one of the Santas she had evaluated to bring her a toboggan. Then the Wellesley College campus entrance appeared on her right. Turning in at the gate, she noticed that the faculty club was immediately on her left. She was so early for her appointment that she went inside, looking for lunch. When it became clear Liz had no faculty I.D. card, the maitre d' made his disapproval evident, but when Liz showed her press card and she said she was on assignment on campus, she was shown to a seat near the kitchen.

After enjoying the best meal she had consumed in many days—lobster bisque, crab cakes, and spinach salad—Liz changed into sports leggings in the ladies' room. They were at least a little bit warmer than her skirt. Back at her car, she traded fashionable boots for a pair that was insulated. Then she set out to find and follow the lakeshore.

Even in the harsh winter conditions, the Wellesley College campus could only be described as the lap of luxury. Wrought-iron pole lamps, curved over at their tops and holding glass-paned lanterns like dangling gems at their ends, added grace and contrast to a landscape where every tree and shrub was blanketed in snow. The lake, too, was white with ice, except for a slate-gray segment of open water where some swans swam so gracefully that they might have been placed there by central casting to add elegance to the scene.

Wading through eighteen-inch-deep snow, Liz crossed a small stone footbridge that arched over a frozen stream. Then she walked over a meadow until she reached the lakeshore path. It was clear from footprints that others had gone before her—people and dogs on foot, and one skier, too—but not very many of them. Liz wondered if Olga Swenson was among them.

But Liz remained a solitary figure in the landscape. After about a quarter of an hour, she came to an open fence with a large sign on it: PRIVATE PROPERTY BEYOND THIS POINT. NO TRESPASSING AFTER SUNSET. PLEASE KEEP ALL DOGS ON LEASHES.

Reminded of Olga Swenson's warning, "My dog can be protective," she earnestly hoped the animal would not be loose in this remote spot. Passing through the fence, she saw hundreds of conifers planted on the undulating landscape to her left. They took many shapes and sizes, from classic Christmas tree contours to weeping and prostrate forms. Fascinated, Liz realized this was a collection of trees.

Then the landscape opened up on a visual surprise. Fronted by a lakeside marble balustrade ornamented at each end with a marble urn, a hillside sloping up to the left was graced with perhaps a hundred carefully pruned topiary trees and shrubs. Some towered more than thirty-five–feet high, trimmed like fat bullets pointing skyward, with cutaway sections adding whimsy to their disciplined silhouettes. Others looked like lopsided lozenges resting on the hillside. Still more had the appearance of sugared gumdrops, bowler hats, or fantastically large chess pawns. As Liz stopped in her tracks and gazed at the topiary, the sun broke through the clouds and caused the ice and snow that frosted them to sparkle.

Dazzled, Liz stood transfixed, until she was startled by a panting sound behind her.

A dog, straining at his leash.

The owner appeared to be more tentative about the encounter. If her carefully coiffed silver chignon was any indication, she looked to be in her late sixties.

"Wesley Hightower's Pinetum and topiary garden," the woman said, pulling hard at her dog's leash. "Is this your first visit, or do you find, as I do, that each time you come upon this place, it takes your breath away?"

"It's my first visit. But I'm sure this is not the only time this sight will leave me breathless."

"Then you don't know the story behind the landscape?"

"I'm afraid not. But before coming upon this group of sculpted trees, I passed through a collection of conifers in their natural forms."

"You know something about trees, then. Most people just think of those trees as 'pines.'"

"I would call them 'pines,' too, but I can see that there are many varieties here. I'd love it if you'd tell me a little bit more about this place, if you have the time."

"Liz Higgins, I presume?"

"Yes."

"Olga Swenson. And this is Hershey. Silly name, I know, but Veronica insisted on it."

Liz couldn't help noticing that, for all his straining at his leash, the chocolate-brown Labrador retriever was wagging his tail to beat the band. His breathlessness, at least, was occasioned by friendliness.

"How is Veronica?"

"Sad. Then excited, despite herself, about Santa. And then sad. Very mixed." Veronica's grandmother looked about her and seemed to gather strength from an environment she evidently knew well.

Certain Olga Swenson would tell her more about Ellen if she could first talk about her passion for this place, Liz bent down and patted Hershey while looking at the older woman expectantly.

"You know, four generations of Hightowers marked their wedding anniversaries by pruning this topiary. Wesley Hightower told me he could always remember how many years he had been married by counting the times he had pruned these trees. He died just a year ago, but not before adding and labeling hundreds of trees to the collection started by R.T. Hightower, Wesley's great grandfather. R.T. made his fortune in shipping and used it to build the mansion on this property and to indulge his passion for conifers. R.T. took his own collecting trips to China and other eastern climes that are remarkably similar to our own, and he sent men to collect conifers for him. And by allowing us access to the property, Wesley—and now his widow—are sharing their remarkable legacy."

"How long have you known this place, Mrs. Swenson?"

"Since we moved here, shortly after Ellen was born." She gulped in a breath and paused to compose herself. "We have a house on this lake, farther along the shoreline. When Ellen was a girl, I was not quite a stay-at-home mother, since I was active in a number of charities and my garden club. We had a nanny helping us out. But Ellen and I always had our Thursday afternoons together, just the two of us. We called it 'Our Afternoon.' And more often than not, no matter what the season, we'd stroll along here with our dog. Wesley discouraged public picnicking here, but he made an exception for Ellen and me. He allowed us to sit in the summerhouse you see there, with our sandwiches. When the weather was fine, we sometimes took along books and I read to Ellen. As she got older, we read our own novels side-by-side. I always think it's no mistake Ellen became a librarian and married an environmentalist."

"And became such a good mother, too. Now I know where she got the idea of spending a mother-and-daughter afternoon on a regular basis with Veronica. Has there been any word at all from Ellen?"

"Not a one. And I hope that goes for any words I share with you. Not one will be printed in the paper. I'm talking to you strictly to give you background information. I hope I may have your word on that."

"Yes, of course. Any insights you can provide may be invaluable. May I ask, what made you consider talking with me? Was it because I know Veronica?"

"She did press me to see you. But that didn't decide me. It was because you spoke of Ellen in the present tense. You wouldn't believe how many people—officials and even close friends—talk of her as if she is not just missing but gone. Gone forever."

"Not her friend Lucy Gray, surely. And not me. From what you are telling me, it seems Ellen enjoyed an idyllic girlhood. And her home and family life certainly present a good impression. Was this the whole story, Mrs. Swenson?"

"I feared it would come to this. You want me to dig up some dirt on Ellen or her husband, just like the rest of the media."

"You're a gardener, Mrs. Swenson. You know you can't cultivate anything without getting your hands dirty. The result itself doesn't have to be filth, however. It might be something quite beautiful, in fact—like the truth."

"That's very prettily put. Your talents are wasted in a tabloid. But where will your pretty words lead me, and Erik, too?"

"I hope they will take us to Ellen."

Olga Swenson shivered. She turned and began to walk to the far side of the topiary garden, making no objection as Liz stayed by her side. She remained mum as the pair passed masses of rhododendrons, their leaves curled as tightly as profiteroles against the cold. Liz imagined the mother and daughter laden with picnic basket and picture book, rejoicing in the flowers that would bloom here each June. Was the scenario too good to be true?

With footfalls softened by the snow, only the sound of the dog's panting disturbed the peace as the women followed the wooded lakeshore. When Ellen's mother picked up her pace, Liz was grateful, for the increased speed helped warm her. A quarter of an hour passed in this manner before Liz sensed the silence had become a companionable one. Then the older woman struck away from the shoreline up a small rise to the basement door of a stone and wood-shingled house. Nodding an invitation to Liz, she stepped inside to wipe Hershey down with an old towel.

"Would you mind waiting in the mudroom?" she asked, and disappeared up a stairway before Liz could reply.

There was nowhere to sit, so Liz stood as she surveyed the large workspace. While the New Englanders of her acquaintance tended to term an unheated porch or perhaps a vestibule "the mudroom," this one existed on a much grander scale. It contained a large potting bench stocked underneath with bags of potting soil, vermiculite, sand, and peat moss. Another potting bench stood nearby, apparently used for flower arranging. Beside it were shelves packed with unusual vases. On the floor nearby, even in the dead of winter, stood a half-dozen French florist containers made of dust-colored aluminum, holding cut flowers fading on their stems. It seemed likely they were purchased before—and had not been touched since—Ellen's disappearance.

"Coast clear," Olga Swenson said from the top of the stairs. "I wanted to be sure Erik had not returned with Veronica yet. Thank you for waiting. Come on upstairs and warm yourself."

Following her hostess' lead, Liz removed her boots and padded, in her stocking feet, up the steps. Mrs. Swenson looked on approvingly and pulled a pair of terrycloth slippers from behind her back, offering them to Liz when she reached the landing.

It was the sort of house in which one "retired" to a sitting room where a fire was laid ready to blaze at the flick of a match. The matches were some ten inches long, and they were kept in a brass match holder permanently attached to the stone fireplace. Kindling and extra logs stood end-up in brass containers, too. These objects spoke more of comfort than money. While a professional no doubt laid the fires and cleaned the room, the brass wore the patina of age and usefulness. "Not a bad goal for any one of us to aspire to," Liz reflected.

"My husband always prided himself on laying the perfect fire," Olga Swenson said. "He'd never have been able to admit our housekeeper can do as well."

"Where is your husband now?"

"He may be safely spoken of in the past tense. He drowned in the lake twenty-six years ago. It was the beginning of the end."

"Oh, how awful! How old would Ellen have been at the time?"

"She was just eight years old.

"The same age as Veronica is this year."

"Of course I'm haunted by that coincidence. I can't bear the thought of Veronica suffering as my Ellen did. That's why I've decided to talk with you. In confidence. I beg you, in confidence."

Liz nodded.

"You're an unusual woman," Mrs. Swenson said.

"How is that?"

"You don't ask the obvious. Yet I feel drawn to answer your unvoiced questions."

Liz held her peace.

The widowed woman crossed the room to a sideboard.

"Madeira?" she asked. "Or, have you got beyond that?"

It sounded like a line in a drawing room comedy. But the seriousness of Olga Swenson's expression erased that impression immediately.

"Madeira sounds lovely."

"Yes, the word is melodious. But you're thinking, 'The drink may loosen her tongue.'"

Liz only smiled and took the small glass from her hostess' hand.

"I thought I'd go to my grave with the information I'm about to share with you."

"Now you won't do that alone. I will take it to my grave, too."

Mrs. Swenson considered her glass. Then she set the drink down, untasted, on the table beside her chair.

"My husband's drowning was ruled accidental, and it may have been. But that does not mean it was not complicated."

Liz resisted the urge to lean forward.

"It so often seems to me the English language lacks the capacity for shades of meaning that you find, for instance, in French. No, I'm not going to break into another language. Don't worry. English suffices to describe Karl's state on the day he died. He was beside himself. Pure and simple. Beside himself."

"May I assume that was unusual for him?"

"Not entirely. I'd seen him that way when Ellen was born. When the night-blooming cerius came into flower. When our whippet died after lapping up antifreeze in the garage. When Ellen shot her first skeet into smithereens. At times of great emotion."

"What caused him to be beside himself that day?"

"It was Ellen. He had to know it wasn't her fault. She was only eight years old. I kept telling him, she's only eight years old!" Olga Swenson said. "But he was so sure she'd sought to tease. Ellen was an early bloomer. Some girls are these days, you know? But within her generation she was very early. She was at that stage my generation reached at around thirteen years old. You know, more than prepubescent."

"If she caught the eye of some man, she would not have been the first to do that at a younger than expected age. Why was your husband so distraught?"

"Karl came upon them in the Pinetum. Under a weeping cypress."

"He came upon whom?"

"Ellen and Al, one of the young men from across the way."

"'Across the way?'"

"The school for delinquents, near the property where the Massachusetts Horticultural Society is headquartered now."

"Ellen and this young man were under a tree together?"

"No. Karl was under the tree. He was spying on them."

"They were not aware of your husband's presence?"

"Not at first. I had the impression Karl caught the boy ogling Ellen. When she heard Karl and Al arguing, she ran and got me. That's how I know how she was dressed. She'd been running along the shore, like a little bird. She seemed to have no idea of the nature of the argument. I calmed her down, helped her change her clothes, and sent her off to her skeet-shooting lesson before I went over to the Pinetum. By then, Karl had his hands around the young man's neck. If I hadn't been there, he'd have killed the fellow, I have no doubt."

"I'm sorry to have to ask you. . ."

"No, you aren't. Not really. You hope it will solve the case, make your career, if you know what they were up to. Well, if you keep your promise, it won't do the latter, since you will never put this in print." Olga Swenson took a swig from her glass at last. Then she continued speaking. "From when she was much younger, Ellen liked to imagine she could fly. She'd run among the trees in the Pinetum, arms out, trailing some of my scarves. She called it 'flitting and flying.' Well, on this occasion, it was swelteringly hot, so she took off her blouse and ran around in her little undershirt. The effect was—just too stimulating."

She rose from her chair and added a log to the fire.

"Karl was disgusted with Al, and not just because, as he put it, 'the bastard got off on watching.' He was furious at Al's reticence. The young man was tongue-tied. I don't know whether it was from shock and embarrassment at being caught with his pants down, as it were, or because he was learning disabled, or both. Anyway, he kept humming tunelessly and mumbling something like 'Rah, rah shock. Rah, rah shock,' like a cheerleader gone crazy.

"It absolutely infuriated Karl, I can tell you.

"Anyway, I urged—I insisted—that Karl get out in the kayak to cool down. I was afraid he'd be arrested. He wouldn't have taken my advice, except Al's absence had been noticed at the school and a teacher came looking for him. My husband didn't bother with the kayak. He stripped off his polo shirt and jumped straight into the lake while I explained to the teacher that there had been an unfortunate misunderstanding. The school was on its last legs financially then, so the administration wasn't looking for any bad publicity. The boy was transferred to another school. Nothing about the boy ever made the press."

"Even though there was a drowning?"

"That happened six months later. And it was ruled accidental. After a deep freeze, Karl walked out on the ice. But he misjudged the ice's thickness. We were all devastated, of course."

"You said the summertime incident was the beginning of the end. Do you feel it was related in some way to the drowning?"

"Did I? Then I misspoke. What I mean is that was the first shattering incident in a terrible year."

"If it was so neatly stored away, why are you opening the door on this skeleton in the closet now?"

"Because every year, on the anniversary of his death, I receive a strange phone call. Every year except this one, that is."

"The calls seemed connected with the incident?"

"Let's just say, they brought the incident to mind."

"How come?"

"The caller hummed tunelessly, just like that boy Al did. But they were just phone calls, nothing more. No letters, no other contact. I tried to put them out of my mind. But now that my daughter's disappeared, I wonder if the caller found her this time. Could the caller have abducted her? Was it that boy, all grown up now?"

"Do you remember the boy's last name?"

"It was Leigh."

"How would you spell that?"

"I always assumed it was 'L-E-I-G-H'. He was foreign but not Chinese. But I thought you weren't going to put this in the paper."

"I'll keep my word. What about his age at the time?"

"Fifteen."

"Do you know if Al had any prior record of violent behavior or run-ins with the law?"

"He had struck out at his mother. She used the incident to get him some special education in that disciplined school environment, but she did not press charges against her son. Karl looked into it. If he had anything else in his record, I'm sure my husband would have moved heaven and earth to have the boy put away for life."

"How certain are you that Ellen was unaware of the sexual nature of the incident? Do you think if Al confronted her recently, he might have stirred up memories that would have caused her to strike out at him?"

"I hope she has no memory of it. Frankly, I think it's more likely she'd strike out at a perfect stranger who surprised her in her kitchen." Ellen's mother gazed out the window. "It's getting dark. Are you parked at the faculty club? Perhaps I should drive you around to it."

"That's all right. I think there's enough light for me to make the walk. I could use the time to digest what you've told me."

"That's good. Then I won't have to leave the house while the fire is still burning. And I'll be here when Veronica returns."

The two women walked downstairs to the mudroom, where Liz handed her hostess the pair of slippers and donned her boots and coat. As she stepped out into the snow, she turned and said, "I am assuming your demand that I do not print what you have told me does not extend to any information it might lead to."

"That's right. If you discover Al has threatened or taken my daughter, you'll have the scoop. You can say the young man was fixated on her. But there's no need to mention my husband's involvement. On the other hand, if you discover Al's whereabouts and there's no connection, the incident need never be publicized."

Pulling on her gloves, Liz asked one more question.

"What was the date of your husband's death?"

"December 18, 1974."

Twenty-six years to the day before Ellen exited her own family circle.

Chapter 10

Perhaps because clouds had rolled in as the sun advanced to the horizon, daylight was fading faster than Liz had expected. After the comfort of the warm sitting room, the atmosphere felt raw, too. Those two factors meant Liz would have to adjust her expectations of a leisurely, contemplative stroll. Still, Liz reasoned, without the need to proceed delicately with Mrs. Swenson—conversationally or otherwise—she should be able to retrace her steps before the sun went down entirely.

As the cold easily penetrated her sports leggings, Liz also felt chilled at the prospect of calling in to Dermott to say she had no story to file. Although the day was productive, nothing printable had come of it. And the city editor was bound to think she was not hard-nosed enough when she would have to admit the information she had gathered was confidential.

"No use thinking about that," Liz decided, picking up her pace. She might as well take this time of forced speed walking and use it as best she could. As she strode on briskly, her eyes naturally traveled to the open surface of the lake, where the scene was best lit.

How did Karl Swenson's drowning there change Olga's and Ellen's enjoyment of their Thursday afternoons? she asked herself. *Did it put a damper on their walks, after the incident with Al? Or, since the boy was transferred from the school across the way, did they continue their perambulations and picnics there untroubled in the months before Karl went through the ice?*

Perhaps they'd never stopped enjoying the landscape here. To this day, Olga Swenson seemed fond of the Pinetum and topiary garden. What gave her the strength to continue residing on the shore of a body of water that had taken her husband's life?

If deepening dusk endows rhetorical questions with significance, it serves even better to clothe those who pose them with an air of wisdom. Or so it was for Liz Higgins, walking through the snow along Lake Waban that cold December evening. The farther her feet and her thoughts carried her, the more convinced she became that Olga Swenson had chosen well when the widow decided to confide in Liz.

But Liz's confidence was in for a blow.

Night fell as Liz came to the edge of the woodland and approached the western gate leading into the topiary garden. Relieved the gate was not chained shut, Liz took comfort in knowing that beyond the rhododendrons, the scene would open up until she reached the Pinetum. Then, even when the walk darkened amid the collection of conifers, she would be closer to the well-lit college pathways and her car.

Rounding the rhododendrons, she looked ahead eagerly towards the balustrade-bounded walkway.

Much brighter.

Bright enough to reveal the silhouette of a Doberman pinscher, posed in an unmistakably challenging stance.

Liz froze in her tracks. Then, very slowly, she turned to retrace her steps.

The Doberman advanced.

She halted.

So did the dog.

With her back to the watchdog, Liz listened for its approach. The only sound in the moonless night was that made by the reporter's own rapid breathing.

Wasn't it always said dogs can sense your fear? And that attack dogs were more likely to strike if they smelled your cowardice?

Liz took in a few long breaths through her nose, exhaling each from her mouth. Perhaps she'd slowed her breathing. But her heart did not stop pounding. Surely she must be broadcasting her terror.

Liz felt a breeze on her face. It was blowing from the direction of the open space. Good. Her scent would not be reaching the dog. But that was small comfort when she had no idea if the dog had continued to approach her.

She had to know if the Doberman had gotten closer. Slowly, she turned her head and then her shoulders, too.

She saw the dog had held its place, but now that she moved, he did, too. Straight toward her.

Haunches forward, the dog took several steps. The movements were slow, precise, light-footed.

Liz took a few leaden steps away from the animal.

The hound halved the distance between them.

There was nothing to do but test one remaining hope. The dog might stop following her if she crossed the property line. Steadily and slowly, Liz covered the remaining few yards to the gate and passed through it.

Then Liz's breath was not the only noise in the night. She heard the short pants of the Doberman, too.

Liz knew it would be madness to strike out into the dark woods with the dog on her heels. At least on the Hightower Estate there was the hope of someone hearing her if she screamed. So, slowly bringing her forearm across her chest in case she had to protect her face, Liz turned and, to steady herself, softly muttered the first song that came to mind.

"God rest ye merry gentleman, let nothing you dismay. . . "

Then, one snow-muffled step at a time, she rounded the rhododendrons.

At first, the dog was nowhere to be seen. Then she spotted him in the fantastic landscape, standing, ears pointed toward her, in front of a corkscrew-shaped topiary. Placing front paws lightly on the snow, he advanced, sniffing. In his new location, the breeze would blow Liz's odor of fear straight to him.

The dog made a sudden change in posture.

Was he teasing her before attacking? The damnable beast seemed to romp in her direction, circling a gumdrop-shaped conifer before flying down the hillside straight towards Liz.

Liz lifted her arm in front of her throat. But the dog did not leap at her. Instead he circled round and round Liz's statue-still form and finally sat down in front of her. Louder than her heaving breathing, more steady than her throbbing heartbeat, there was another sound.

Flop, flop, flop, flop.

A stubbed tail beating against the tightly trimmed branches of a topiary shrub.

Amazed, Liz did not question the change in her circumstances. As she walked along the balustrade through the Pinetum and out the eastern gate of the Hightower property, the Doberman trotted at her side like her own protector. At the gate, the dog halted and sat watching her protectively until Liz crossed the arched stone bridge that led, at last, to the lamp-lit campus walkway.

In her car, Liz turned up her heater until the windows steamed over and her teeth stopped chattering. Then she removed her jacket. Pulling her arm out of a sleeve, she found a thin, nearly threadbare scarf that was not her own. It must have gotten caught there when her jacket was hung on a hook in the Swenson mudroom. Holding it to her face, she breathed in the subtle scent of another human, an odor that must have saved her life.

Liz turned on the defroster and, when the windshield cleared, pulled her car out of the faculty club parking lot. It felt as though an entire evening had passed, but it was only 5:50 p.m. She should have called in to the newsroom much earlier to report what she was up to, and now it looked like she would be late for her meeting with Cormac Kinnaird, too. With the faculty club closed, she drove to Wellesley Center to find a phone booth.

"Pissed."

That was how Dermott McCann described himself at learning Liz had no story for him. When he gave her a piece of his mind about the late call-in, she gave him a piece of hers.

"Why don't you arm your reporters with up-to-date technology? Have you heard of a cell phone?"

"Some reporters take pride in being up to date for their own sakes. Christ, how do you have a personal life without owning a cell phone these days? You know we'd pay for calls you make for us, if you submit the receipt."

"But not for the basic bill or the phone itself. Thanks a lot!"

"You got a chip on your shoulder?"

"More than that. If I'd had a cell phone an hour ago, I might have been spared a threatening encounter with a Doberman!"

"Yeah, yeah. A likely story."

Hoping he'd be lingering over his banjo at Tir Na Nog, Liz left Kinnaird a phone message. Saying she'd been unavoidably delayed, she asked the doctor to phone her at Gravesend Street, where she planned to stop and change her clothes before heading to the Somerville pub.

By the time she arrived in her Pike-side abode, Liz was so beat that she would have greeted with relief a message from Kinnaird postponing their encounter. She wanted nothing more than a very hot shower and an equally steaming bowl of soup. She treated herself to one after the other, and then fell into bed. It was just 7:10.

At 9:30, the ringing telephone startled her awake. It was her mother calling from Mexico, where she and her partner were spending the winter in his Airstream trailer.

"I was gearing up to leave you a voice-mail message, Liz," she said. "I thought you'd be out on the town or with friends the Friday before Christmas."

Liz gave her a nutshell account of the story she was covering and told her mother how frustrated she was about the weekend falling just when she needed a business day to follow a great lead.

"You don't need a business day to take a ride in a New York City taxi. Why don't you go down to the city and follow up on that taxi receipt you found? You could stay with Aunt Janice and have a good laugh while you're at it."

"I thought she was in England this time of year."

"Not this Christmas. She had to stay in town to play an extra on a soap opera."

"At Christmas? Couldn't she turn it down?"

"Normally she would. But she couldn't resist playing the role of a jaded ballerina-turned-dance critic, after spending so many years in the Radio City Music Hall corps de ballet herself. Of course, she'll be missing your cousin and the grandchildren. It will do you both good to spend the week-end together."

"It's true the *Banner* will never send me to New York to follow up on that taxi receipt."

"Then go for it! In fact, I'll fund the train fare as an extra Christmas present. What does it cost, eighty-some dollars each way? Charge it and I'll send a check you can pay the bill with. Where will you be on Christmas? Are you scheduled to work? Or has a special someone entered your life?"

"I volunteered to work the holiday. I figured, when a special someone *does* come along, the *Banner*'ll owe me the day off. As it turns out, it may give me the edge on the Johansson story. After all, Mom, this isn't a story about aggressive people stealing parking spots from one another at the mall. A woman's life may hang in the balance here."

"You're too good. The paper's lucky to have you. Don't work too hard, OK? I'll give you a call on Christmas."

Enlivened by the nap and, after she phoned her, by Janice's delight at the idea of having a pre-Christmas guest, Liz arranged for train tickets and packed her bags. She also wrapped up a bottle of Pol Roger to present to her aunt and hand-washed a few pieces of clothing. Recalling Cormac Kinnaird's appealingly boyish appearance while banjo playing, Liz changed into black velvet pants and a forest-green velvet tunic. The outfit seemed a bit dressier than others she had observed in Irish pubs, but it was one of the few clothing combinations she had neither packed for New York City nor left dripping on her clothes drying rack. And the truth was, she didn't mind standing out just a little bit in the eyes of Dr. Kinnaird. So, Liz applied some make-up with care, threw on a hooded jacket and dry boots, and went out into the night again to make her way to Tir Na Nog.

At the door of her Mercury Tracer, in the chill of the December night, Liz remembered to return to her house to pick up the Ziploc bag containing the lipstick and hair elastic. At the same time, she remembered Dr. Kinnaird's self-important posturing at the Worcester Public Library, and the gravity of her investigation, and revised her hopes for the evening.

It was a good thing Liz had downsized her expectations, since the tiny Tir Na Nog pub did not have music on the menu that night. While his banjo lay unplayed on one end of his table, Kinnaird looked ill at ease as Liz greeted him. Feeling overdressed, she hesitated to remove her coat. When she did, Kinnaird studiously registered no reaction.

"It's charming," she said of the bar's interior decorating, which blended Irish and Bostonian elements into one harmonious whole. The atmosphere of the small pub was intimate, too, but that dimension seemed lost on Kinnaird. She ordered Chardonnay and sat in silence until her drink was delivered.

Liz took the opportunity to study her surroundings further. The brick walls were hung with an eclectic mix of items, including a blackboard listing bands scheduled to perform there, a circular ship's life preserver, and a vanity license plate bearing the word FIDDLE.

"Usually, this place oozes music," Kinnaird said morosely. Presumably because he was not playing that night, he was drinking a pint of Harp.

"Maybe you should play something for us. You have your banjo."

"I'm not at a level to perform solo. I'm a rank beginner," Kinnaird admitted, killing that idea.

Fortunately, there was business to attend to. Liz pulled out her Ziploc bag and turned it over to her companion, if "companion" he could be called.

"Ellen's," she said.

"Ah, indeed," he replied. "At last, one is privy to some physical evidence."

"To be sure," Liz heard herself say. "I wonder if his formality is contagious?" she asked herself.

"Of course, I already have the poinsettias."

"Have they revealed anything helpful?"

"Two different blood types. Hers, as reported in the press. And that of another person, as yet unidentified, of course."

"Blood type?"

"B-negative. Uncommon."

"Uncommonly good."

"Let us hope. But it's useless without additional evidence with which to match it."

"I hope we've got that here," Liz said, glancing at the Ziploc bag.

Kinnaird made no comment.

"And how shall you be spending the holidays?" she said, noting as she did so that it was unlike her to use the word *shall*.

"That remains to be seen," Kinnaird replied cryptically. "And you? How shall you spend your time off?"

"Not 'off.' I shall have to echo you," Liz said. "'That remains to be seen.'"

"You've no plans? I'm surprised."

"Oh, I've got plans, all right. I just don't know the specifics. I'll be on assignment for the *Banner*, covering whatever comes up: incendiary Christmas trees, kids choking on small toy parts, that sort of thing, I suppose. I hope there will be time to find fruitful developments in the Johansson case."

"Ah, there we are in accord," Kinnaird said.

Accordingly, shall we relax our vocabulary a bit? Liz thought but did not say aloud. Instead, she laid her right hand palm-up on the table and said nothing.

Cormac Kinnaird picked up her hand and pressed his lips to it.

Since he said nothing at all after that gesture, Liz dearly wished—as probably he did, too—that there had been some music playing. But there was no tune to be heard. So Liz picked up her new friend's left hand and gently kissed the calluses on the tips of each finger.

"Tir Na Nog is a kind of Celtic paradise, you know," he said.

"I know it now," she replied. When he wouldn't meet her eyes, she added, "I'm off to Manhattan before dawn tomorrow, so I must get some rest. You had better find yourself a pub where music is playing."

Looking over her shoulder as she left Tir Na Nog, Liz saw the man who had kissed her palm pick up the plastic bag of evidence and his Irish tenor banjo with equal enthusiasm, without allowing his striking blue eyes to follow her out the door.

Rosemary Herbert

Remembering her encounter with the Doberman, simple joy at being alive and unscathed almost overcame Liz's perplexity at the doctor's behavior and her own impulsiveness. As soon as she reached Gravesend Street, she settled in for a short winter's nap, knowing she would have to rise at 4:45 a.m. in order to catch her train.

Chapter 11

L iz closed her eyes and dozed in the Amtrak train until it reached the Connecticut coast. Then she purchased a cup of coffee from the café car and enjoyed the view of Long Island Sound over the reeded shoreline. It always amazed her how unspoiled some of the landscape appeared to be, considering the densely populated nature of the nearby New York metropolitan area.

Taking her eyes away from the view, she took out the copy of the taxi receipt. It measured only one and a half by two inches, but the small slip of paper carried a considerable amount of information. Headed by the words, "I ♥ NEW YORK," the receipt recorded the cab's medallion number, the date of the trip, start and end times, trip number, rate, miles, fare, and a telephone number for the "Consumer Hotline." As insurance against losing the receipt, Liz copied the information into her reporter's notebook. Then she sat back until the train arrived in Penn Station.

After exiting the train, Liz made her way up the escalator to the taxi stand, took her place in line, and finally secured a yellow cab. Once inside, she told the driver her aunt's address. Then she said, "I wonder if you could answer a few questions for me? I'm a reporter working on a missing person's case and I'd like to know how to identify who was driving a certain cab at a particular time."

It was unclear if the cabbie's heavy accent was affected or if he genuinely had trouble understanding her. What was certain was that he would not answer her question.

Arriving at her aunt's address, Liz requested a receipt before getting out of the cab. The driver took out a pad of receipts and filled one out by hand.

"Why aren't you printing one from the meter?" Liz demanded.

"Not working," he said, driving off as soon as Liz was clear of the cab.

The hand-written receipt delivered far less information than did the printed one.

After an evening of laughter and delicious dining with Janice, Liz rose early and phoned the telephone number on the taxi receipt. It seemed the "Consumer Hotline" was hot indeed, since it was constantly busy. When half an hour of calling kept producing a busy signal, Liz decided to seek out another cabdriver.

At Janice's street corner, she hailed a cab. Once inside, she began with a less honest conversational gambit.

Giving the driver an address located far downtown, Liz turned her smile on him and said, "I wonder if you could help me? I'm writing a book with a taxi driver as the hero. Just one of his good qualities is his helpfulness when a woman leaves a diamond ring in his car. I'm trying to find out what a driver like you would do if he found something valuable in his car."

"I would turn it in, of course."

"Where would you turn it in, I wonder?"

"At the nearest precinct."

"Do you mean a police station?"

"If it was valuable, yes. Sometimes I also have called people on the phone, you know, when they drop something like a wallet that has an address in it. Then I meet them in a coffee shop and return it myself."

"What a nice thing to do!" Liz enthused.

"Well, honestly, I sometimes get a reward if I do it in person. So it pays to be nice. Of course, it isn't always a happy ending like that. It all depends on the next rider. After someone loses something in the cab, it is usually the next passenger who finds it, not the cabdriver. We can't check the backseat every time someone gets out of our cab."

"Of course not. Do you ever take things back to the dispatcher's office?"

"We're hail-only in New York."

"What?"

"We don't need dispatchers in Manhattan. People flag us down in the street."

"What about your garage?"

"I don't have one. I'm independent. I got my own vehicle. I park this at my place at night, not at some garage. That's why I take valuables to the precinct. I guess drivers that work from garages might take valuables to their bosses."

The cab came to a halt in traffic.

"If I gave you a printed receipt, could you tell me which garage the cab came from?" Liz asked. She handed the driver the copy of Ellen's receipt.

"For that, you have to call the number on the receipt."

"It's always busy. Could you radio in and get the information for me?"

The driver hesitated.

"I'll pay double for this ride."

That decided it. The driver pulled over, and with the cab idling and the meter running, he took his time gathering the information.

"Do you know where that taxi garage is located?" Liz asked.

"You should'da asked me that when you got in my cab. It's a block from where you got in."

"Would you mind turning around and taking me there?"

"The things people will do for a story!" the driver said. "You realize it's quite a few blocks, in traffic? And at double the fare, it'll cost ya."

"No problem. With this receipt, should I be able to find out who was driving a certain cab during a particular trip?"

"If it was my cab, they could. Like I told you, this is my vehicle. Unless I'm on vacation and I rent it to another driver when I'm away, I'm the one driving it. If you called the number on the receipt, they'd ask you the medallion number. That's my cab. The taxi commission would point you to me. But, like I said, it isn't always up to me to find your valuables. You're outta luck when you lose something if the next rider doesn't turn it in."

"I see. I'm not too worried about valuables. What if you drove a cab from a garage? Then how would I know if you were the driver at a particular time?"

"You can ask at the garage. Here it is," he said pulling up to the curb.

The taxi garage was located next door to a red-painted building that looked like it had been custom built as the subject for an Edward Hopper painting. A lone customer sat absorbed in the *New York Post* behind the plate glass window, which was painted with a salmon-pink image of a minaret and the words "Fabulous Falafel" in bright blue lettering.

Liz passed by the felafel shop and made her way into the garage. There, two mechanics, supine under a battered taxi, leered at Liz, behaving far more like alpha males than did the *Banner*'s mailers. One of them directed Liz to an office at the far end of the work area. On her way past the men,

Liz tried, with difficulty, to feign interest in the surroundings. There wasn't much to catch the eye: a few out-of-date license plates, a vending machine offering "Salted Peanuts: 25 cents," and a girlie calendar.

The office held more to look at, as Liz soon learned. As she entered the room, its sole occupant signaled her to wait while he carried on a heated telephone conversation with a taxi driver.

"I'm telling you, my friend, that's how it is," he said. "You either get in here with that cab this minute and turn it over to the guy on the next shift, or I consider you on duty and earning. Don't give me a song and dance about being in the boroughs. I don't care if you're at Montauk Point," he added, referring to the easternmost point of 118-mile-long Long Island. "You're due in *now*, pal. And make sure your cab's clean. I've had two complaints in the last three weeks about your filthy trunk."

Liz took the opportunity to look around the office and found it to be well organized. Keys to cabs were hung on numbered cup hooks screwed into one wall. Below the keys was a system of open cubbyholes, each one labeled with a driver's last name. Another wall was hung with fan belts, numerous family photos of the man in the office and his brood, and an oil painting of Mount Fuji, done in flaming hues that suggested either a violent sunset or an ongoing eruption of this symbol of Japan.

Slamming down the phone, and shrugging his shoulder in the direction of the painting, the garage manager said, "One of our drivers painted that."

"It's pretty good."

"Yeah? Maybe for a guy from Canarsie who's never been east of Queens. Frankly, I think he got the Jap mountain mixed up with the Eye-talian one. You know, Mount Vesuvius. The thing looks ready to blow."

"Or like it's already flowing with lava," Liz laughed.

"You didn't come in here to discuss art. What's on your mind?"

"I'm here because I'm writing a mystery novel. . ."

"I don't want anything to do with that."

"Please, hear me out. I've got a taxi driver in my book—who saves the day. But before he does, he gets in some hot water. I don't want him to be too goody-goody, you know, because then it won't be surprising if he's the hero."

"Yeah?"

"I was hoping you'd let me know some things a driver could do that would jeopardize his career, like keeping his vehicle messy."

"That'll do it. Or smoking without the passenger's permission. Or keeping the cab out beyond your hours so the next guy can't drive it, like the clown I was just talking to is doing, as we speak."

"That's really helpful," Liz gushed. "I was thinking about having a character lose something in a cab. Then she tries to find it by using her receipt. I probably have a receipt here," Liz said, digging in her pocket. "Here's one. What would happen if she followed up on this receipt?"

Her companion examined the receipt and narrowed his eyes.

"By the way, my name is Liz," she said, turning a big smile on him. "What's yours?"

"It's Jake. Hey, listen, if you're trying to get one of my guys in trouble, you've come to the wrong garage. This cab isn't one of ours."

"Let's try another one," Liz said, pulling out the hand-written receipt.

"This one'll tell you jack-shit," Jake said. "It's not legal."

"What do you mean?"

"See here," Jake said, pointing to the printed receipt. "This one has the medallion number. It I.D.s the cab and much more. This other one here doesn't tell you a thing. You lose something in that cab and it's gone—for*evah*."

"I gather your drivers use the right kind of receipt."

"You bet!"

"And they return found articles to you?"

"Right again."

"So, if my character loses something in one of your cabs, you'd be able to tell if it was turned in."

"Assuming it *was* turned in and not taken by the next rider in the cab. Listen, what *is* it you're looking for? I don't believe you're a mystery writer. You're looking for something for yourself, aren't you?"

"You ought to be a detective yourself, Jake. You're right. The missing item I'm looking for is the cab itself. And here's the receipt that identifies it."

Jake scrutinized the receipt. Then he looked Liz over slowly.

"You a cop?" he demanded.

Liz remained silent until Jake realized his mistake. Obviously, the cab was one of his. And there was something questionable about it.

"This isn't a real receipt. The paper's too good and the edges aren't torn. Who are you and what are you after?"

"A reporter. *Beantown Banner*. A woman called Ellen rode in that cab before she went missing from a Boston suburb a few days ago. She's just a librarian and housewife and mother of an eight-year-old daughter," Liz said, moving her gaze to the Jake's family photos. "I'm trying to find her."

"Cut the violins," Jake said. "*And* the appeal to my fatherly instincts. If I help you, it's more a question of this," he said patting his pants.

Liz looked away and stood up from the stool.

"Not *that*! My pockets," Jake said. "That guy brought in the bucks. And now he's not showing up for work. I want my driver but I don't want to call the cops on him. I've got a lot of foreigners working for me. Cops make them nervous."

"I can't promise the police will never be involved, but I can tell you that at this point, my interest in your cab and driver is a question of grasping at straws. Is the cab here?"

"No, it's with the jerk-off I was just trying to haul back from the boroughs. What use would the cab be to you, anyway?"

"Honestly, I'm not sure. I know the missing woman rode in this cab. And it's just about the only lead I have. I thought I'd see if she left anything behind in the cab, or maybe retrace where she'd been by looking at cab records. Now there's the stunner that the cabdriver's unaccounted for."

"Not only that. . . " Jake broke off. "The hell with the other foreigners. I wanna know what Hasan's up to."

"That his name?"

"Yeah, Hasan. Sonofabitch calls himself Samir Hasan. OK, how about you go to the corner felafel place and get us a couple o' coffees? I take mine black. Then I'll see what I can do."

As Liz left the office, she heard Jake radio a cabbie.

"Shit!" he shouted. "Why did you have to pick today of all days to follow my orders for the first time? Get your ass in here!"

When Liz returned with the coffee, Jake was standing outside the garage beside an idling cab. "Here it is, spick-'n'-span for the first time in memory."

"Ah, no! He cleaned the cab?"

"Inside and out!" Jake said, opening the trunk. "What's this?" he demanded of the driver who could do nothing right.

"Just junk. No valuables."

Jake joined Liz as he opened the plastic shopping bag. Inside were a small child's Yankee-insignia sweatshirt, a couple of cardboard coffee cups, and a book of matches. While Jake angrily dismissed the driver, Liz got into the front seat and opened the ashtray. Butts galore. She dumped the contents into a Ziploc bag. Then she looked in the glove compartment. It contained the vehicle's registration and a grocery list. Nothing more. She pocketed the list.

"Hey, what are you taking from that glove compartment?"

"Just a grocery list. It might have been Ellen's."

"In the glove compartment? Why would a passenger's list be in the glove compartment?"

"Looks like one of your drivers used it to test a pen on." Liz turned the paper over and pointed to some squiggles. "Would you like to keep it?"

"Nah!" Jake said, tying up the plastic bag and setting it on top of the one untidy item in the room, an overfilled trash container.

"I've got just a few more questions."

"Yeah?"

"Hasan's home address."

"Not sure."

"What?"

"I have one on record, but when he went missing, I found out he doesn't live there. He's been feeding me a load of bull."

"You must be furious. Do you keep a log of trips made by your drivers?"

"Sure. It's required by law."

"Can you tell me anything about Hasan's remaining hours at work before he went missing?"

Jake paged through his log book.

"How do you like that?" he asked. "Right after he made that trip with your gal, he has more than forty-five minutes unaccounted for. Then again, throughout the day, more of the same. No metered rides after 3:00 p.m. on December 16."

Two days before Ellen went missing.

Jake's phone rang and he engaged in another adversarial conversation with a driver while Liz waited. "Look," he said, turning to Liz after hanging up the phone. "I know what you're going to ask me next. What kind of guy is he? Am I right?"

Liz nodded.

"Well, I don't know. These Arabs, they have a different language, a different cultcha. I know he smoked in the cab. We got complaints. I know he played Middle Eastern music in his vehicle, too. Hasan sometimes turned in valuables. We logged them in here." He opened a well-worn logbook to a page headed "December 16, 2000."

"No, he didn't turn in anything on his last day at work," Jake went on.

"I know he rarely turned down a fare. He kept that cab moving. Beyond that, the guy was a closed book. Didn't talk about a wife, kids, sports, anything."

"What's this?" Liz asked, pointing to some wiring on the dashboard that seemed to lead nowhere.

"That's the connection for his two-way."

"Radio?"

"Yeah. He was always yakking on that thing."

"Did he use it to communicate with you?"

"Nah. I told you, in the city we don't dispatch cabs via radio. He used it to talk with his buddies. We allow this, if it doesn't interfere with the driver's work. But you have to be licensed to operate a two-way from the cab. He had to remove his when he wasn't using it so the other drivers couldn't use it. I got the documentation filed here, don't worry."

Like the rest of the office, the filing cabinet was orderly. It held several original documents pertaining to the missing cabbie, and photocopies of each. Jake handed Liz an extra copy of the radio license.

"Take it," he said.

The document had the same false address that Liz had seen before. But the face in the photo was new to her.

"A dark horse," Jake concluded. "That Hasan was one dark horse."

December 16, 2000

The word Shukran *was astonishing enough coming from the mouth of that* whdah franjiyah, *that non-Arab. But the remark,* "Ya saqiqati al-habibah aa rifuki kull al-awqat," *was more alarming still.*

"My beloved friend, I know you always."

This is not the "How do you do?" greeting a foreigner might learn from a phrase book. Colloquially correct and properly, if slowly, pronounced, this was the statement of a person conversant in the Arabic language.

That shaqra, *that blonde. Help me, Allah, she can indeed speak the language.*

Such were the thoughts that drove Samir Hasan, cabdriver, to follow the pair of women into the elevator, even while his cab was idling at the curb. Making sure to turn around and face the elevator door as soon as he entered it, he heard the pale-haired woman ask someone to push the button for the top floor where the Windows on the World restaurant was located. When she awkwardly interjected the word mishmish *into some silly conversation about fashion, the cabdriver decided to get out the next time the elevator doors opened and take another one back down to the lobby.*

Hardly able to disguise his agitation, Hasan hurried back to his two-way radio to broadcast his panic to a compatriot he only knew as Fa'ud, the same man who had, while assuming the cabbie was alone, radioed a grocery list of highly secret code words.

"Ladhibhah teena is not enough. How tall is she? How is she dressed? Where is she at this moment?" Fa'ud demanded.

"Why are you asking this? I am telling you the words are no good now. The shaqra heard them but she doesn't know why we are using them. We must change them."

"It's too late. Allah save us. You must take care of her."

"You cannot be saying. . ."

Chapter 12

New York City, December 23, 2000

L'iz decided to lose no time in getting back to Boston. But there was
something she wanted to accomplish before leaving the city.

Hiring a cab from the garage, she got in the vehicle and opened her
envelope containing Ellen's photos. Squinting to read the print on the
shopping bags held by Ellen and Nadia in the photo taken at the New York
Public Library, she asked the driver to take her to Florissa's Gift Emporium
on 44th Street.

"Got a street number?" the cabbie asked.

"Sorry, no."

"East or west?" he asked.

"Not sure."

"Forty-fourth is one-way running west. Unless you hit it lucky, this'll
cost ya."

"Let's start near the New York Public Library and take our chances."

"You're the boss."

Liz was in luck. The gift shop was just two blocks west of the library.
She paid the cab and entered a shop that exuded a sickeningly sweet smell
of potpourri pillows and scented soaps. It hardly seemed the sort of place
a woman like Ellen would find attractive. Nor did it look like the kind of
shop a tourist would favor. Even the generous stock of crystal and china
sold here was largely imported from Ireland and the British Isles, making

it an unlikely choice for anyone wishing to bring home something made in America. There wasn't even a rack of postcards in the place.

Liz showed her photo of Ellen and Nadia to three clerks, but none would admit to recognizing the shoppers. Two volunteered that they'd worked on the days Ellen and Nadia spent in the city, but they said another clerk, who was presently taking a few days off for Christmas, had also worked afternoons during that time. Not surprisingly, they refused to give contact information for their colleague.

Disappointed, Liz took a business card and gave the shop girls one of her own. After leaving the shop, she hailed another cab. It was no use following up on the other shopping bag in the photo. It would be an impossible job to interview countless clerks in the massive department store, Saks Fifth Avenue. So Liz swung by Janice's apartment. After making apologies for cutting her visit short, she picked up her travel bag, hailed another cab, and paid a pretty penny to be driven to LaGuardia Airport. She had to wait for two fully booked flights of holiday travelers to take off before she finally got a shuttle to her city. But since the shuttle flights took off every half hour and the flight was only thirty-eight minutes long, Liz made her way to Boston in time to report her story.

When she told Dermott about the cabbie's disappearance, the city editor gave her twelve inches and the order, "Deliver the new stuff and then recap. Be sure to pull the heartstrings about the kid. Doesn't look like Mom's coming home anytime soon."

On her ATEX keyboard, Liz began to hammer out her article. Then, unzipping the coconut on her desk, Liz took out a chocolate. Voted "Most Unusual Freebie of the Year" by the editorial assistants, the oddball item had been sent to her some months ago by the Fijian Tourism Board on the mistaken assumption that "Misses Higgins" was a travel editor. Originally filled with a bar of coconut soap, a vial of coconut oil, and a press release about a Fijian spa, the hollowed-out shell with a red zipper running around it now served as a quirky stash for sweets.

Thanks to editorial assistant E.A. Tenley, the bizarre candy container also served as a paperweight for two articles from that day's papers. Liz picked them up. One was an article by Nancy Knight, headed: "Fingerprints Inconclusive in Missing Mother Case." The headline said it all, but nevertheless, the broadsheet *World* gave Knight plenty of space in which to elaborate.

"Newton Police reported yesterday that missing Newton librarian Ellen

Johansson's kitchen was remarkably free of fingerprint evidence," Knight wrote. "'The dearth of fingerprint evidence suggests that an attempt was made to wipe down surfaces,' said Newton police chief Anthony Warner, referring to the Fenwick Street home from which Johansson, 34, went missing five days ago."

In contrast to Knight's luxuriously long rehash, Dick Manning's shorter *Banner* piece telegraphed the essentials—and the Page-Five article offered a nugget of new information:

WIPE-OUT
By Dick Manning

Newton police chief Anthony Warner fingered what he called 'a dearth of fingerprint evidence' as stalling the wrap-up of a chilling pre-Christmas crime that has tony Newton suburbanites shivering.

Fingerprint evidence was just one thing that went missing five days ago, when well-heeled Newton mom Ellen Johansson, 34, made an unexplained exit from the home she shared with her husband, Erik Johansson, 37, and the couple's eight-year-old daughter, Veronica. The couple's new Honda Civic was gone, too, when the strawberry-blond third-grader came home from school to a kitchen stocked with bloodied Christmas-cookie-making ingredients.

Warner said he saw evidence of a "wipe down" of the Johanssons' top-of-the-line marble countertops. But the police chief could only speculate about why the cleanup job was left unfinished.

"It looks like someone was interrupted," Warner told the Banner. "It's like somebody wiped the place down before sprinkling blood on those ingredients. The only fingerprints we found in the countertop area were on the dinky dishes that held the ingredients, and those prints belong to Mrs. Johansson," the chief added.

"The only unaccounted-for fingerprints we found were on an empty teacup in the kitchen sink," Warner said. Other nonfamily fingerprints found on the scene belong to a handyman, Floyd Margate, 43, of Everett, who repaired the disposal last week, and the couple's babysitter, Laura Winters, 26, of Brighton.

At the time of this reporting, police had not yet verified the whereabouts of Margate and Winters on Dec 18, the day Ellen Johansson went missing. But the Banner learned Margate was on another job in Everett throughout that day. And Winters was at work at the Children's Enrichment Aftercare Program and later at the Johansson home on the day in question. The daycare provider stayed to help with Veronica until the child's grand-mother, Olga Swenson, 69, returned from her hairdresser's appointment on Boston's posh Newbury Street and was contacted to take the child to her Wellesley home.

"Hey, Dick," Liz called out, seeing the reporter crossing the room with a cup of coffee. "Nice follow-up on the handyman and daycare provider." It was nearly Christmas, after all.

"Just part of the job," he said, but smiled and added, "Thanks, Legs."

Liz turned her attention back to the ATEX terminal where the message "Lines are up!!" flashed across the top of the screen, alerting reporters they could find out how much space they had for their stories. This was a throw-back to a much earlier time in the news business when type was set line by line by compositors. Now, reporters were actually given their assignments in column inches, which were measured at the press of a button by the ATEX machine. Similarly, the term "slug," referring to the name for each story file, harked back to the days when type was set in trays for printing and lead slugs were used to identify them.

As Liz typed in her byline, another message flashed on her ATEX terminal. "Cut to 8 inches," it read.

Sighing, she made a quick phone call to Laura Winters. Fortunately, Laura was in.

"Listen, Laura, do you have the impression that Mrs. Johansson is a neat freak? I'm asking because my colleagues in the press are jumping to the conclusion that her fingerprint-free countertop is evidence that a criminal tried to wipe down the scene."

"Yeah, I saw those reports. But it doesn't surprise me at all that those countertops were so clean. She's the type to take a sponge to anything in reach—even doorway moldings—when she's talking on the phone. And I've seen her, on more than one occasion, wipe the counters off before starting a cooking project. Come to think of it, she usually did that while wearing rubber gloves. I wouldn't call her a neat freak. It's more like she is in the habit of being tidy."

"Do you have any idea why she would have an empty teacup with a stranger's fingerprints on it in her kitchen sink?"

"Sorry, I don't have a clue on that one."

"Any word from the Johanssons?"

"To me? 'Fraid not. With Veronica at her grandmother's, I wouldn't expect they'd need me to babysit. Maybe they'll call on me after Veronica comes back to aftercare."

Laura was eager to hear the latest news on the case, but Liz had to say good-bye in order to write it. After filing her story, she phoned her friend Molly Trowbridge at the reference desk at Harvard University's Harry Elkins Widener Memorial Library, the largest of the well-endowed institution's ninety-six libraries. When Molly informed Liz that their specialist in Middle Eastern languages and literature had gone home and would not be back until after Christmas, Liz pressed the librarian to help her find a faculty member who could help her translate the Arabic words she'd seen squiggled on the back of the cabbie's grocery list.

"I'll give you the phone number for the faculty office of the Middle Eastern department, but you should be aware that the university is closing for Christmas break as of this evening. Too bad, because normally it wouldn't be hard to find a grad student who could help you. If that doesn't pan out, you might try a book dealer the library buys from—he's originally from somewhere in the Middle East but has a shop in the vicinity of the Cambridge courthouse. Or, as a last resort, you could contact Finn Peter Translation Services in Central Square. I say 'last resort' because they mostly deal with Western or European languages, but they may be able to point you in the direction of an Arabic translator—*if* they haven't closed shop for the holidays."

Liz took down the librarian's information. Sure enough, both the faculty office and Finn Peter Translation Services were closed. But the phone answering machine message at Turkoman Books was somewhat more promising. On it, a pleasant male voice announced the shop's address, noted hours for the weeks of December 17 and 24, and invited inquiries. In case a mention of her newspaper would alarm the book dealer, Liz decided not to leave a message. Instead, regarding the blinking light on her own answering machine, she retrieved her messages.

Two of them grabbed her attention.

"Hello, Ms. Higgins," a female voice said. "My name is Nadia and I'd like to talk with you. Since you're not in, I will call you again."

Liz pressed *69 to find out where the call had come from, but a recorded message informed her that the caller's number could not be identified.

The other message was short but sweet. "It's Cormac. Call me. Please."

Liz dialed the doctor's number, only to receive a recorded message. This one gave no particulars of his whereabouts.

Before exiting the newsroom, Liz accomplished three more tasks. She photocopied both sides of the grocery list she'd found in the New York City cab. She retrieved another manila envelope bearing her name from René DeZona's cubby. And she read her e-mail messages. Amid a slew of public relations pitches and several holiday wishes from far-flung friends, Liz noticed five messages sent from as many different e-mail addresses, all bearing the same one-word message: "Blister."

"At least it's not another ad for Viagra," Liz thought, exiting the e-mail system. It was too late to take time for personal messages, except for perhaps one. Reentering her password, she replied to an old message she'd saved from Cormac Kinnaird.

"Tidings of comfort and joy," she wrote, and signed the message just "Liz."

Out in the *Banner*'s parking lot, the snow was heaped in discolored mounds. But the windows of Ho Tong Noodle Company, across the street, were illuminated later than usual. Perhaps the staff was enjoying a holiday party, or working late to produce products for the New Year.

"No, no," Liz chided herself. *After three years working in this neighborhood, how could I forget Chinese New Year does not fall on January 1st? I must be tired. And no wonder*, she thought as she drove past the *Banner*'s outdoor Christmas tree, strung with multicolored lights as if to compete with the bright hues of neon signs shining nearby in the windows of Asian restaurants.

In contrast, Liz had lost her glow. As she turned the Tracer onto the turnpike, she found herself peeved by Kinnaird's brief message. Or perhaps it would have been more accurate for her to admit annoyance at herself for how much it mattered to her. On the one hand, he'd referred to himself as Cormac. Surely it was a good sign that he'd dropped the last name and the title "Dr." But then the message was so uninformative. He could just as well be seeking her for personal reasons as for business. Here it was, the last night before Christmas Eve, and Liz hadn't acquired a gift for anyone other than her plow driver and her cat. Even she and Molly Trowbridge had failed to set up a time to exchange gifts, neglecting a tradition that went back many years for them.

Liz had to bypass her house and its billboard before reaching a turnpike exit that would take her in the direction of Gravesend Street. As she approached the billboard, she wondered for the umpteenth time why the company that handled renting it did not arrange for messages to be hung on both sides. Surely that would bring everyone involved double the income. But this was not the time to inquire.

As the structure came into sight, Liz was taken by surprise. The ad-free side of the billboard was strung with lights forming the letters, MERRY XMAS LIZ.

The message in Christmas lights was not the only thing Tom Horton had arranged to brighten Liz's holiday. Walking up to her house, Liz noticed a fresh-cut Christmas tree leaning against her front door. And beside her stoop, she found a cardboard box wrapped in a garbage bag. A note was taped to this package: "Tom Horton, at your service." A Christmas tree with a star on top was sketched beside the message.

Laughing with pleasure, Liz moved the tree aside and leaned it against her house. She and Tom had never celebrated any occasion before this one. Not only had they never been on a date, they'd not even shared coffee together anywhere but at Liz's house. Overcome with surprise at Tom's attention now, Liz picked up the box, unlocked her door, and entered her small abode. Even before taking off her coat, Liz tore open the box. It was packed with five strings of lights, a multisocket adapter to plug them into, and four more gift-wrapped items of varying shapes and sizes. Intrigued, Prudence climbed into the large box and purred contentedly while Liz looked up Tom's phone number. The address listed was Tip Top St., Brighton. Now Liz realized why that street name had seemed familiar to her. Tom must have mentioned it at some point. Smiling, she dialed his number.

"I'm on my way," he said, with unguarded warmth, when she invited him over.

"Wait!" she said, and heard herself giggling. "You have to wait an hour before setting out. There's something I need to do."

"Please, don't feel like you have to give me a present!" Tom said. "I know I surprised you with mine."

"Well, I want to surprise you, too," Liz said.

Hanging up the phone, she found a foil pie plate, some scissors, and an ice pick. Then she cut the plate into a star shape, used the ice pick to poke holes parallel with the star's edges, and, after a moment's hesitation, poked more holes in the shape of a heart at the center of the star. Then, she took out a bottle of champagne and set it in the snow pile beside her doorstep, tucked her travel bag under her bed, and changed into a bright green, tunic-length sweater and some black velvet leggings. Finally, she took out red tissue paper and used some to wrap the homemade gift.

Liz was rummaging in her freezer for something to cook when Tom rang her doorbell. Before opening the door to him, Liz turned on her fireplace switch and ran her fingers through her hair. Tom stood on the doorstep grinning, but even as he picked up the tree to carry it indoors, he remembered to wipe his feet on the mat.

As Tom carried the tree into the room, trunk end first, so as not to snap any of its branches against the doorjamb, Liz said, "Oh, but I don't have a tree stand."

"Maybe you do," Tom winked. "I think it's time to open the present wrapped in the reindeer paper."

Sure enough, the package contained a tree stand. While Tom cut off the bottom of the trunk with a saw he'd thought to bring, Liz went back to her freezer and examined it with disappointing results. But she did have the makings of crêpes, so she made up a batch of crêpe batter and set it in the refrigerator to settle. Then she steadied the tree while Tom locked it into the stand.

Crawling out from under the tree, Tom said, "I'll bet you're wondering what you'll use to decorate it, aren't you? Don't worry. If you put enough lights on the tree, you almost don't need any ornaments. But if you've got a needle and thread, I've got the makings of a garland. You'd better open present number two, in the snowman paper."

Rosemary Herbert

Liz opened the cylindrical package and found it was a jar of popcorn kernels.

"I'll be right back," Tom said, pulling on his jacket and running out to his truck.

By the time Tom returned with a perforated metal popping box on a long handle, Liz had set about peeling four apples, which she sprinkled with sugar and cinnamon and set to simmer in a pot on the stove.

"I could have brought microwaveable popcorn but I knew you had the fireplace and I thought this would be more fun," Tom said, pouring kernels into the boxy popper.

"Where did you get that thing?"

"Scouts. I bet I never told you I'm a Boy Scout leader. I got this to take on our Camporees. Here," Tom said, "you hold it over the heat while I get the lights on the tree."

"What's a 'Camporee'?"

"It's when a bunch of troops get together and camp in one place. We always have a big campfire with all the boys together."

While the aroma of apples mixed with the fragrance of fresh popcorn in the little house by the turnpike, Tom attached lights to the tree in a slapdash manner.

"Doesn't matter how evenly you place them if you've got enough of them," he explained.

Any doubts Liz might have had about the wisdom of his words were erased when he turned out the table lamps and the two stood together gazing at the illuminated tree.

"It's beautiful," Liz said, "and even more lovely for the surprise of it all," she said, placing her gift for him under the tree. "Maybe you'd better open the gift I made for you."

"Let's wait," Tom said. "If you don't mind, that is. I don't want this all to be over too soon."

"Neither do I," Liz agreed. Feeling slightly overwhelmed by Tom's smile, she returned to the stove to stir the apples and make the crêpes. Meanwhile, Tom arranged his two remaining gifts under the tree and then, opening the sewing box Liz pointed out to him, he set about stringing popcorn on thread.

When the crêpes were ready, Liz spread a tablecloth on the floor in front of the tree, set a votive candle in a glass globe between herself and her friend, and asked Tom to bring in the champagne. After he'd popped the cork and filled two glasses, Liz produced the plates of apple-filled crêpes. Sitting cross-legged on the old tablecloth, facing one another, the reporter and the billboard hanger raised their glasses in a toast.

"God bless us every one!" Tom said, smiling broadly. "The two of us in particular."

"If you haven't got a penny a ha'penny will do. When I haven't got a Christmas tree, I'll call on you!" Liz sang, laughing.

It was such a delicious experience, sitting in the glow of the Christmas tree, that Liz was loath to go to the door in answer to an unexpected knock. But she did get up and looked through the small windowpane to see who was on her doorstep. Partially hidden behind a lavish bouquet of white chrysanthemums, deep red roses, and holly, she saw Cormac Kinnaird.

Staggered, she nonetheless gathered together some vestige of poise and opened the door to him.

"I know I behaved appallingly the other night," the doctor said. "I'm like that sometimes. But I wanted you to have these."

"They're lovely," Liz said, taking the flowers. "Would you like to step in and meet my friend Tom?" she added, stepping back from the doorway.

"Oh, I'm so sorry. I had no idea you had a—a guest. I would never have barged in, had I known."

"Please, join us in some champagne," Tom said in a friendly tone that contrasted with the expression of sad perplexity on his face.

"I wouldn't think of it. I'm interrupting," the doctor said. "But thank you—both."

After Cormac Kinnaird left, Liz carried the bouquet to her kitchen counter, pulled out a large spaghetti pot, filled it with water and set the stems in it.

"Aren't you going to get a vase?" Tom asked. "It's a nice bouquet."

"I don't have a big enough vase for it. And, even if I did, I don't want to take the time away from our celebration to arrange them now. They're in water. They can wait."

Liz returned to her position across from Tom on the tablecloth.

"You're probably wondering who that was."

"That's your business."

"You're right in more ways than you think. He's someone I've met through my job—a forensics guy who's helping me on the missing mom case."

Tom made no reply.

"To return to more important things," Liz said, "it's time for you to open a present."

This time, Tom was ready for his gift. Opening it with care, he smiled widely when he saw the heart at the center of the homemade star. And when he reached out for Liz's hand and clasped it tightly she needed no words from him to realize how much it meant to him.

"Merry Xmas, Tom," Liz said, pronouncing the "X" in honor of the billboard display.

"Merry Xmas to you, too," he replied, handing her a small present in a jewelry box.

Liz was concerned. An expensive gift on top of providing an instant Christmas would be too much, she thought.

But Tom must have known that would be the case.

Slowly lifting the lid of the jewelry box, Liz looked inside and burst into gleeful laughter. The box contained a key ring and chain, on the end of which dangled a brass monkey.

If Tom had any concerns that his gift would be underwhelming after the arrival of Cormac Kinnaird's magnificent bouquet, those worries were wiped out when Liz stood up, pulled Tom to a standing position, too, and threw her arms around him in an enthusiastic hug.

"Something's missing! We need some music," she said, removing the Erik Satie CD from the CD player and replacing it with a Bing Crosby Christmas album. As Bing crooned "I'm Dreaming of a White Christmas," Liz sat down and began to string popcorn for the tree.

"Wouldn't you like to string some more, too?" she asked Tom, who remained standing.

"Not yet. There's something else missing, too, don't you think?"

"What do you mean?"

"You'll see," Tom said. And picking up the ice pick, scissors, and strips of pie plate Liz had forgotten to clear off her desk, he set about fashioning a ring of foil with holes punched in it. Borrowing an extra needle and thread from Liz, he sewed the ring to the back of the star, making use of the holes Liz had punched on one of the star's points. Then, he took Liz's hands and pulled her to a standing position. Standing on a chair, he slipped the tin ring over the topmost point of the tree.

"But that's *your* present!" Liz exclaimed. "You should take it home for your tree!"

"If it's my present, I get to decide where it belongs. And I think *your* tree needs *my* stah," he said in his winning Boston accent.

"You might just be right," Liz said, smiling at him.

As Bing changed his tune to "I'll Be Home for Christmas," Tom took Liz in his arms, kissed her tenderly on the lips, and led her in a slow dance on the popcorn-strewn tablecloth.

Chapter 13

The next morning, the thin winter sunlight that spilled through the window onto the Christmas tree could not hold a candle to the glow that had shone there the night before. Alone in her bed, regarding the tree from across the room, Liz saw this, and told herself it didn't matter. It was enough to enjoy the memory of Tom's surprise.

Nor was Liz disturbed by Tom's 3:00 a.m. exit. Picking up the brass monkey key chain on her night table, she turned it over in her hands and recalled how relieved she had been to find it, rather than an expensive gift, in the box. It was pleasant to discover Tom's evident affection, but she was also aware she had never before then considered him as a potential date. This line of thinking led her to wonder if her pleasure in remembering last evening stemmed from receiving unexpected attention and treats or if she would have been attracted to Tom without them.

Then, too, she mused, while regarding the large bouquet leaning at an angle in her spaghetti pot, *how differently the evening might have progressed had the enigmatic Dr. Kinnaird arrived at Gravesend Street before Tom did.*

Kicking off her covers at the thought of two men surprising her with Christmas attention she had not sought, Liz gave her body rather more attention than usual in the shower, and while her hair was drying, she set about arranging Cormac's bouquet in a hammered metal ice bucket. Clearing her desk of the pie-plate scraps, ice pick, and scissors, she set the bouquet upon it and stood back to study the effect.

But there was little time to linger. Although it was Christmas Eve day, Liz was scheduled to show up in the *Banner* newsroom, so she put on a snow-white angora sweater and doe-colored slacks, grabbed a plastic bag full of chocolate Santas, and donned her coat and gloves. Then, with a look over her shoulder at the tin star on the top of her Christmas tree, she smiled and left her house. As Liz crossed the short distance to her car, she noticed that the sunlight had fought and lost a battle with a sky full of clouds. The weather was unexpectedly mild, too. It looked like it would rain.

The raindrops that soon followed, splattering onto her windshield and soaking into the snow cover, might have dampened her spirits. But Liz was too intent on business to think along those trite lines. Instead, she pulled into an ugly strip mall made even less attractive by a huge sign with the words "EXTENDED SHOPPING HOURS!!" spelled out in large plastic letters set in slits on a vinyl signboard. The eyesore was also eye-catching, since it was elevated on the back of a flatbed truck.

Fortunately, the cellular phone shop was less mobbed than the toy store next door to it. If cell phones were in demand this year, those who shopped for them evidently did so at a more reasonable hour than did the last-minute toy crowd. Liz was disappointed to learn that although she could purchase a cell phone on the spot, thanks to the holiday, it would take forty-eight hours to activate it. Still, she made the purchase, and drove on to the *Banner* newsroom.

"How would you like to cover some hard news for a change?" Dermott McCann asked Liz as she handed him a chocolate Santa. "Mind you, you're not getting the assignment thanks to this big bribe," he added, unwrapping the candy and swallowing it in two bites.

"Where're you sending me?"

"Poultry place in East Cambridge. Seems some guy dressed in a Santa suit ripped off a ton of turkeys in the early hours of the morning."

Liz wrote down the address and, tossing holiday greetings and chocolate Santas to her co-workers as she passed by their desks, crossed the newsroom to her own desk. She used the phone book there to look up the address of the Arabic-speaking book dealer who had been recommended to her by Molly at Widener Library. As she had recalled, his shop was located in the same multi-ethnic neighborhood as the poultry place.

The neighborhood was alive with activity as Liz pulled the Tracer into a parking spot. While two Cambridge police officers decked the building and nearby parking meters with bright yellow plastic ribbon reading POLICE LINE—DO NOT CROSS, a harried-looking Portuguese butcher complained to a policeman in plain clothes, "It's criminal, no? To take-a my turkeys like that!" The butcher rubbed his hands on his bloodied apron and added, "I just-a killed them this morning for the Christmas dinners. My sign, it tells-a the truth. 'Fresh Killed,'" he read, pointing proudly to the bright yellow, hen-shaped sign jutting out from the building over his head.

"Good morning, Officer, and good morning to you, too, sir," Liz said, addressing the policeman and butcher in turn. "I'm Liz Higgins of the *Beantown Banner*. Do you mind telling me what happened here?"

"Mr. Torrentino here claims his shop assistant, Lucarno, gave some guy dressed in a Santa suit twenty-seven birds this morning."

"Fresh-killed! Put that in the pay-puh. Four and twenty fresh-killed turkeys, two ducks, and one goose," the butcher said.

"Where's Lucarno now? Why would he give away the turkeys?"

"It's turkeys, two ducks, and one goose. All fresh-killed. Not only the turkeys," Mr. Torrentino said. "He's a-went with the other policeman to the station. He's a-gonna look at the mugs shots, like-a they have on the television."

"To see if he can I.D. the thief," the police officer interjected. "Kid claimed the Santa told him he was there to pick up the birds for charity."

"Lucarno didn't check with you before he gave them away?" Liz asked the butcher.

"That's a-right. The idiot, he's a-never asked me."

"More a scam than a straightforward theft, then? Is that how you see it, Officer?" Liz asked.

"That about sums it up. Kid did chicken shit to prevent it, though. In fact, he helped load the birds into the van they were taken away in. He actually helped the birds fly the coop," the officer smiled, obviously proud of his own joke. "And here's the kicker—after all that, he couldn't describe the vehicle!"

"May I quote you? Sorry, Officer, I didn't get your name."

"Sure you can quote me. And it's Hurley. Detective Matt Hurley."

"What's with all the crime scene tape, then, Detective Hurley?" Liz inquired.

The policeman whispered in Liz's ear, "Makes Mr. Torrentino here feel like something's being done. Don't ever let anyone tell you the Cambridge Police don't have a heart."

"Thanks, Detective. Will you give me a call if anything else develops?" Liz asked, handing him her card. "And by the way, do you know where Turkoman Books is located?"

"That way, past the gravestone yard, cigar shop, and curtain place. It's upstairs, over a shop called Rosalita's Notions."

"Thanks, and Merry Christmas."

"Yeah. You, too."

After getting a few more details for her story, Liz retrieved an umbrella from her car and set out on foot to find Turkoman Books. With the raw drizzle intensifying into a pounding rain and the sodden snow banks oozing slush puddles, it might not have been a pleasant walk, but there was something oddly heartwarming about the plethora of Christmas lights and cheap decorations that ornamented the area. Even Empire Monument Works—a yard filled with shaped blocks of granite awaiting the names of the dearly departed to come—was strung with colored lights. Looking at one block carved in the shape of linked hearts with a cross—instead of Cupid's arrow—piercing the pair on an angle, Liz told herself even gravestone merchants deserve a little holiday cheer.

The cigar shop outdid the monument yard in ornamentation, with a pair of plastic candy canes, illuminated from within, on either side of the doorstep and bubbling Christmas lights strung around the door and in the shop window. Here, cigar boxes and humidors formed a semicircular backdrop around a crèche complete with figures of the Holy Family.

The curtain shop, too, was dolled up for the holidays. Behind its expansive plate glass windows was a gaudy array of heavily embroidered curtain panels in shades of red, green, and gold. But that wasn't all there was to see. Also packed into the display were a set of crisp white café curtains embroidered with poinsettias, shower curtains printed with a snowflake motif, and padded plastic toilet seat covers printed with Santas, snowmen, reindeer, and even an image of the Grinch from *How the Grinch Stole Christmas*.

Finally, Liz came to Rosalita's Notions, a tiny storefront with a window jammed with religious statuary, cut-glass candy dishes, gilt-edged tea sets, and silk flowers. All of the items were covered with a layer of dust so thick that it made the illuminated Madonna and Child look as if they were covered with volcanic ash. Now here was a home for that New York City cabdriver's painting!

Liz knocked on the door next to Rosalita's and, receiving no answer, looked around for a doorbell or buzzer. Before she found one, the door opened inward and she saw, standing in a dust-free, newly refurbished stairway, a small man with a warm smile.

"I'm looking for Turkoman Books and a man by the name of Faisal Al-Turkait," Liz said.

"Then you've come to the right place and the right man. Let me show you into the shop."

Although many of the books that lined the walls were old, the clean, well-lighted environment they were housed in formed a sharp contrast with the notions shop downstairs. Here, the odor of old leather bookbindings blended pleasingly with the aroma of recently brewed coffee. Motioning his visitor into a chair, the proprietor of Turkoman Books said, "Let me give you a cup of coffee. Then we can sit and you can tell me about the library you represent and discuss the books you're looking for."

"This is delicious," Liz said of the strong brew. "But I don't want to mislead you, Mr. Al-Turkait. I'm not a librarian and I'm not here to purchase numerous books."

"Ah, then I have the rare pleasure of welcoming a browser!" the book dealer said. "You see, the vast majority of my business consists of acquiring books on demand for academic and research libraries. I take it you are a scholar then?"

"I wish I were! As it happens, I would be incapable of browsing here, unless it were for an Arabic–English dictionary. I have familiarity with neither Arabic nor any other Middle Eastern language. I came here to ask if I might hire you to translate a book title and a list of words for me. I'm rather certain they're written in Arabic."

"Let's start with the list of words. How long is it?"

Liz pulled the Xeroxed copy of the list out of her bag and showed it to him.

"I cannot take your hard-earned money for such an easy task. This list and the title of one book? It's nothing."

"No, really, I'd be happy to reward you for your valuable time."

"I agree time is valuable, but the value of it is not always to be measured in money. Here it is, the beginning of the Christmas holiday, a day I fully expected to spend entirely on my own. Not because, as you may assume, I am Muslim. On the contrary, I am a Christian Arab. There are millions of us, you know. I'm alone because my only daughter is abroad on a work-study project. She is a college student," he added proudly, pointing to her photo on his desk. "I'm a widower, and the rest of my family is in Tikrit—that's in northern Iraq." Looking around his shop, the book dealer went on, "I kept the shop open today because it gives me something to do. There is always correspondence to catch up on. But I never thought I'd be welcoming a customer, and one who must have a story to tell, since it would only take something important, worrying, or complicated to bring a lovely lady like yourself into a hole in the wall like this the day before Christmas. Especially with a mere grocery list to consult me about."

"I realize there's a grocery list on one side of the paper, but it's the Arabic writing on the other side that I need you to translate for me," Liz said.

"That's just what I am telling you. The Arabic writing is also a grocery list, you see. It lists exactly the same things in Arabic, and in the same order, as it does in English. Look here: This word, *tuffahah*, it means 'apple.' One apple. For apples in general, we say *tuffah*. For two apples, we say *tuffahtayn*. This Arabic word, *mishmish*, means 'apricot.' This word *teen* means 'figs.' And, here, *tukki*, that means 'wild berry.' It looks like someone has a taste for fruits."

The grocery list might not have been very helpful, but at least something remained to be learned from the book dealer. "I still have the book title for you to translate, if you wouldn't mind," Liz said, taking out the photo of the Johanssons' living room with the open book splayed on the armchair.

The book dealer's demeanor changed. But he retained a polite tone as he said, "This is a strange way to inquire about a book title and, perhaps, a less honest approach than I would have expected from a polite lady like yourself, to involve me in something I should not involve myself in. This is a police photo, is it not?" he said, holding the eight-by-ten-inch picture at arm's length.

"You were correct, Mr. Al-Turkait, when you said it is a complicated, worrying story that brings me into your shop the day before Christmas. And you deserve to know the background of my inquiry. Will you please let me fill you in?"

Setting down the photo and fetching more coffee for them both, Faisel Al-Turkait sat without a word while Liz told him how the list had been found in a New York City cab, how the cab and a few photos were all she had to go on regarding Ellen Johansson's outing, and how the cabdriver had gone missing, too. "I've been grasping at straws," she concluded.

"But sometimes that's the only way to find the needle in the haystack," Faisal Al-Turkait said. "Perhaps you've found one such needle here," he added, picking up the photo. "The title of this book translates to *Slang and Common Arabic Expressions for Foreign Service Officers*. It's edited by Martin Holmesby."

"The British intelligence expert who's always commenting on problems in the Middle East!" Liz exclaimed, meeting the book dealer's eyes.

"Your taxi driver may be an average guy, but perhaps your lady is a spy," he said.

Chapter 14

Liz popped open her umbrella to walk back to her car, crossing the street this time to get a closer look at shop windows on the other side. They were just as varied and just as interesting. Here, a carpet shop loaded with the "Remnants and Mill Ends" its sign promised was neighbor to a Portuguese fish market and a toy emporium calling itself Godzilla Toyshop. A few doors down, Liz came upon the Globetrotter's Music Shop, with a window advertisement promising, "International Instruments Our Specialty."

Here was a case of truth in advertising. The walls reaching up to high ceilings were hung with drums of every description, many of them made of skins stretched over huge, hollowed-out gourds. There were also maraca-like gourds on handles, and guitars, balalaikas, lutes, ukuleles, and banjos.

"Do you carry strings for Irish tenor banjos?" Liz asked the clerk and was pleased when he pulled four cellophane packets, each containing a different string, from a well-organized drawer.

After paying the clerk, she returned to her car and drove through very sluggish shopping traffic to the newsroom. She arrived early enough to open a number of small gifts on her desk, adding several small chocolates she found there to her stash in the zipped coconut.

Then, after fetching a cup of coffee and sandwich from the cafeteria downstairs—egg salad, not chicken or turkey—she started to write her story about the turkey heist. Lines were not up, and she did not know how much space she'd be given, so she took special care to keep the essentials at the top of the story.

"It was a case of duck, duck, goose—and 24 turkeys, too—when a Santa-suit–clad scamster lifted 27 fresh-killed birds from Torrentino's Poultry Place in East Cambridge yesterday," Liz wrote.

"According to butcher and shop owner Luigi Torrentino, 68, his shop clerk Lucarno Fino, 15, was taken in by the Santa look-alike's story that he was picking up the fresh-killed fowl for charity. Torrentino said the teen did not verify with him that the poultry was intended as a charitable donation.

"Detective Matt Hurley characterized the Christmas Eve day chicken heist as a scam. 'The kid did chicken (expletive) to prevent it, though,' Hurley said, referring to Fino. 'In fact, he helped load the birds into the van they were taken away in. He actually helped the birds fly the coop,' Hurley added. 'And here's the kicker. After all that, he couldn't describe the vehicle!' Hurley said."

Liz pressed the H&J button on her keyboard and watched the machine lay out her story in a long column. The ATEX machine measured the piece, too. 3.6 inches. Probably just about right for the gravity of the crime.

Dermott McCann came by her desk, and said, "What have you got for me, Higgins? I need to know for the meeting."

Liz gave him a nutshell summary. Then she made her way to the library to read her e-mail while McCann determined story sizes and placement in the afternoon meeting. Besides more spam messages reading "Blister," there were Christmas messages from her mother, Aunt Janice, and several colleagues and friends. Nothing new from Cormac Kinnaird. Annoyed at how much it mattered to her, Liz knew she needed to separate her need for his professional expertise from her personal feelings for him. Although she would have preferred to phone him, in the hope that the tone of his voice would help her to read his mood, she knew she had to contact him regarding the Johansson case, so she tapped out an e-mail message on the keyboard: "Dear Cormac, I would very much like to connect with you regarding professional matters—and especially to deliver a little something to put under your Christmas tree. I hope you will get in touch with me as soon as it is convenient. With warm gratitude for the gorgeous bouquet, I wish you a Merry Christmas. Liz."

After replying to a few family messages, Liz returned to her desk and saw the light blinking on her phone. Before picking it up, she logged onto ATEX and found her chicken heist piece was just the right length. She also read, with gratitude, the words "File and fly rule in effect. Merry XMAS." After sending her story into the system, she dialed up her voice-mail messages and found she'd just missed a call from her mother and another one from Cormac.

"It's Cormac," the doctor said on her voice mail. "It's a business matter. You can catch me on this line until around six-thirty, when I'll be meeting some people at Tir Na Nog. Come to think of it, you can catch me there, too, in the evening."

Liz looked at the clock. It was 6:20. But when she phoned Cormac, he did not pick up. Unprepared for this, she left an awkward but honest message.

"I'm disappointed not to find you in, Cormac," she said. "And I feel unsure if I should take your time for business on Christmas Eve. Really, I don't know what to do. I'll give this all some thought during my drive and hope, whether I see you or not tonight, you have a wonderful Christmas."

It might be a toss-up as to whether Liz should go to the Irish bar, but she was certain of one thing. If she did go out, there was no way this bird would turn up at a Christmas Eve gathering in the same clothes she'd worn to cover the fresh-killed poultry scam. So she got on the Pike and headed back to Gravesend Street.

Along the way, she saw her name and the Christmas greeting in lights again on the dark side of her billboard. This made her remember she hadn't phoned Tom to thank him for his surprise. After turning on her Christmas tree lights, phoning him was the first thing she did when she arrived home.

But Tom was not in. And the message on his answering machine gave her pause. "We're out for Christmas Eve, but please leave a message," a woman's recorded voice said. "And Merry Christmas to all!" Tom's voice added.

"We?" Liz almost said aloud. She had been under the impression that Tom lived alone. Who was this woman? Surprised again by unexpected information in an answering machine message, she said only, "Merry Christmas to you, too," and hung up without adding the words she had expected to say: "And thank you for last night."

Then she sank into her chair, pulled up the purple and white afghan and gazed at her tree. There remained one more gift under it. Getting up to examine it, she saw that the paper on it was tattered and torn. And when she opened it, she realized why: It was a catnip mouse for Prudence. Apparently, the cat had tried and failed to open it.

What's a guy with a girlfriend doing providing treats to another woman and to her cat? Liz wondered. Throwing the mouse to Prudence, she decided not to spend Christmas Eve alone, even if it might mean awkwardness with Cormac. Using the remaining red tissue paper, she wrapped up the four guitar strings in separate pieces of paper, tied them together in a flat stack with gold ribbon, and poured herself a glass of Chardonnay.

Then she went through her closet and dresser in frustration. Even at age thirty-two, it was possible to be plunged into a high-school moment when challenged to pick out an outfit intended to make a good impression on a member of the opposite sex. Casual dress had been the norm at the Green Briar and Tir Na Nog, but Liz had no idea if this would be the case on Christmas Eve. Too bad she had already worn her forest green velvet tunic to one of her two meetings with Cormac. While its fabric was soft and luxurious, the color did not stand out as loud or dressy. Finally, Liz decided to forget about fitting into the crowd and to put on her mint-green, shot silk tunic-length jacket over black velvet leggings. It was her favorite outfit for festive occasions, and it was clean, so it would just have to do.

Liz needn't have worried about her fashion choice. When she wedged her way into the crowd that packed Tir Na Nog, she found it was impossible to stand back and get a full-figure look at anyone. In the small room, made warm with body heat and cigarette smoke, she was glad she had opted for the silk instead of a sweater.

It took some doing to find Cormac, but, predictably, he was seated at a table near the musicians. Less predictably, he was leaning forward in animated conversation with a red-headed woman. The eye contact he made with her beat any he'd ever made with Liz. The pair looked like a couple. Seeing this, Liz went to the bar and bought her own drink, another glass of Chardonnay. As she turned to find a seat, she found Cormac standing behind her.

"I would have bought you that," he said.

"Thank you, but I didn't want to interrupt your conversation."

"It's a reel," Cormac said, referring to a lively tune filling the air.

"Aren't you playing tonight?"

"Not with this group. They're so much more advanced than I am. I left my banjo at home. But I'll learn a little something by listening. Come on over, and I'll introduce you to Maggie," he added.

The redhead gave Liz as thorough a looking over as could be accomplished in the crowded place. Then, placing one hand proprietarily on Cormac's, she spread the fingers of the other and ran them through her gorgeous mane of straight, copper-colored hair, lifting her locks so that they fell fabulously again to her shoulders. The gesture—so reminiscent of Liz's own movement when she was stressed or excited—made the reporter feel intensely uncomfortable. So did the realization that Cormac apparently had a taste for women with red-toned hair. The effect of Maggie's movement seemed not to have been lost on Cormac, who could hardly take his eyes off her, even as she turned her back on him and stepped forward to speak to one of the musicians.

"I'm ready whenever you are," Liz heard her say.

The reel spun on for some minutes. But after it was through, Maggie turned and faced the crowd. The musicians lay down their instruments and gave her their attention as, closing her striking green eyes, Maggie lifted her voice to sing:

> It was down by the salley gardens
> my love and I did meet,
> She passed the Sally gardens
> with little snow-white feet.
> She bid me take life easy,
> as the leaves grow on the tree;
> But I, being young and foolish,
> with her would not agree.
> In a field by the river
> my love and I did stand,
> And on my leaning shoulder
> she laid her snow-white hand.
> She bid me take life easy,
> as the grass grows on the weirs;
> But I was young and foolish,
> and now am full of tears.

Slowly lifting her eyelids, Maggie accepted the applause her perfectly delicate singing deserved and, smiling at Cormac, returned to the table. It was impossible to hear what she said to him as the musicians struck up a syncopated tune. But Cormac replied by squeezing her hand across the small table and gazing intently into her eyes.

Certain she did not wish to witness any more of this, Liz made a hasty exit from Tir Na Nog, missing the chance to observe the redhead turn, a moment later, to give an open-mouthed kiss to a bearded musician who tapped her on the shoulder. Turning around, himself, to look for Liz, Cormac's face fell as he realized she was out of sight. As he wove through the crowd looking for her, his expression changed. Realizing his actions must matter to Liz, he began to smile. Returning to his table he said to Maggie and her man, "Congratulations on your engagement!"

There was still the question of forensic news, Liz realized as she drove to Gravesend Street in silence. It remained unclear if Cormac had planned to share more information with her. Well, her e-mail message to him would serve to remind the doctor of that. If it wasn't going to be a personally satisfying evening tonight, at least it would have been useful to have the forensics information to use on Christmas Day, when she was scheduled to work. Otherwise, she might be sent on another fresh-killed goose chase.

As she approached an all-night store lit up and open even on Christmas Eve, Liz pulled into the nearby parking lot and went in to purchase milk, eggs, and cheddar cheese. On the rack near the cash register, she saw new stacks of newspapers, delivered early for Christmas Day. Probably, the drivers had worked as fast as they could to get them delivered so they could get home to their families. Liz picked up copies of the *Banner* and the *World* and made haste to get home, too.

Back at Gravesend Street, she turned on her Christmas tree lights, lit her fireplace, and whipped up a soufflé. Relaxing in her chair with a glass of mead while Elizabethan lute music played on her CD player, she took a look at the newspapers while the dish baked.

The *Banner*'s front page was taken up with an old engraving of Santa Claus and a printing of the poem *The Night Before Christmas*. Headed "FAKE ST. NICK HAS KNACK FOR NICKING," Liz's story made Page Fifteen. It was accompanied by a photo of the hapless Lucarno, looking thoroughly perplexed, at the police station. The caption read, "BIRD-BRAINED poultry clerk admits aiding Santa look-a-like in Christmas Eve turkey heist."

On the same page, a small item ran under the headline, "TEACUP PUZZLER," and the Manning byline. "A teacup found in missing mom Ellen Johansson's kitchen sink may have held no liquid. But, according to Newton Police Chief Anthony Warner, it contained plenty of inconclusive evidence. 'The prints on it belong to Mrs. Johansson and two additional unidentified individuals,' Warner said. 'It's unusual to find numerous prints inside and out like this on a drinking cup. But without matches for the other prints, we can't draw any conclusions here.'

"When Johansson, 34, disappeared December 18, leaving her kitchen full of cookie ingredients splattered with blood, a matching teacup was left on a side table in the living room. The discovery of the teacup in the sink has led police to speculate Johansson was interrupted in serving tea to someone known to her on the afternoon she went missing. 'We found no evidence of forced entry,' Warner said, in a December 18 interview."

Rosemary Herbert

Setting down the *Banner*, Liz went to her desk and took out her envelopes of photos, leafing through them to find the extra photo DeZona had taken of the Johansson kitchen. Evidently, DeZona had climbed on something— perhaps a kitchen step stool—to fire his second kitchen shot, since this photo offered a view into the sink. Sitting in the perfectly clean, stainless steel sink was a delicately patterned, bone china teacup. Liz turned to the living room photo she had recently shown to Faisal Al-Turkait. There was the matching teacup, half-filled with liquid, resting on a saucer. Using a magnifying glass, Liz examined both teacups bearing a design of tiny blue blossoms.

Calling to mind her conversation over tea at Ellen's house, Liz remembered how Veronica had interrupted it by dropping the teacup. And she remembered, too, her quick glance into the Johansson dining room on the day Ellen disappeared.

Just then, the timer rang and she paused in her thinking to take a perfectly formed soufflé out of her oven. She sliced a tomato over a few spinach leaves, then cut into the soufflé, causing it to collapse with a small sigh, and placed some on her plate. Before taking her late-night dinner to her table, she put some of Prudence's favorite canned food into a clean dish and set it down for her.

Only then did Liz raise her glass to Prudence and say, "Forget-me-not!"

Liz knew the hastily written words on Ellen's blackboard were no farewell message. They were just the name of the china pattern. When Veronica dropped her cup, it must have cracked or chipped. That was why there was a saucer lacking a cup in Ellen's china cabinet. The replacement, which most likely was purchased in Florissa's Gift Emporium in New York, had been sitting in Ellen's sink. Any fingerprints inside it were less likely to belong to an intruder in the kitchen than to Ellen, a shop clerk, and perhaps Nadia.

The shop would never be open at this hour, and it would almost certainly be closed on Christmas, but Liz remained eager to know when it would open again so she could ask about the sale of a single teacup. She dialed the number on the gift emporium's business card and listened to the message—with a music box tune tinkling tinnily in the background—which informed her the shop would reopen December 26.

That meant she could not write a follow-up story about this on Christmas Day and would be stuck covering whatever struck the city editor's fancy. Unless she found another promising avenue of investigation.

While washing her dishes by hand, Liz let her thoughts flow freely. Just as the "FORGET ME NOT" message meant something different than it first suggested, so must some of the other evidence in this case have been misread. It was time to look at other pieces of information with fresh eyes.

It was nearly 1:00 a.m. when Liz stepped away from her sink and into her bathroom. Stepping out of her clothes, she showered and washed her hair. Then she took out her vial of Fijian coconut oil and slowly spread it all over her body. It would spot her sheets, but they were old anyway, and the pleasure of slicking her skin with oil from two hemispheres different from her own—the eastern and the southern—was too good to resist.

Slipping between her sheets, Liz turned out her lamp and let her gaze linger on the glowing Christmas tree. Finally, she got up and turned the tree lights out. Back in bed, she lay quietly, wondering, *Where in the world is Ellen Johansson?* while watching the flickering light reflected from her fireplace as it danced across her ceiling.

New York City, December 16, 2000

Samir Hasan was at a loss. Not dressed adequately for dining in the Windows on the World restaurant, he pondered how he could keep his eye on the women there. Then, noticing another man in the elevator holding a plastic bag from the Gap, he asked him if the shop was located nearby.

"Turn right, out of the elevators," the fellow said.

Fortunately, the sporty shop located on the World Trade Center's ground floor did carry navy blazers. Along with a pair of new slacks, a pale blue shirt and tie, and a pair of sunglasses, the blazer would make him look both presentable and unfamiliar to his former taxi passenger. Hasan tried on the outfit, then, cursing the time it took to remove and purchase it, he returned to the dressing room and put on the new clothes again. The whole process took some twenty-four minutes. It took another six for him to reach the restaurant.

Luck was with him as a single businessman gave up a table just as Hasan arrived. But the maitre d' was in no hurry to give him the uncleared table.

"I am in such a haste," Hasan explained. "I will be closing a business deal shortly, but with the jet lag and no good meal since I departed London, I am ravishing," he added earnestly, winning a smile at last from the maitre d'.

Shown to the seat, Hasan was asked if he preferred the buffet or the à la carte menu. Following the waiter's outstretched hand pointing in the direction of a large buffet spread, the cabbie hardly dared believe his luck. There he saw the pale-haired woman approach the sumptuous spread. A moment later, as her friend joined her, Hasan was also at her side, serving himself fruit salad while overhearing the pair's enthusiastic chatter.

"Isn't it something, after all these years of being pen pals, to find out how many tastes we share?" the Middle Eastern woman said.

"I can't get over it!" the fair woman enthused. "Now, tell me Nadia, what is the word for this?" She pointed to a coffee urn.

No speaker of the Arabic language would be at a loss for such a word. Riveted, Hasan had to remind himself to act interested in the buffet food while he listened for more. He picked up a roll and a pat of butter.

"I know that's mishmish, but how about these berries?" the fair woman said, pointing to a tray of fresh strawberries.

"I'm not sure of the word for them. We call a wild berry tukki but these look like they are cultivated."

"Tukki. What a cute word! And easy to remember, too. It sounds a little bit familiar, but I can't figure out where I've heard it."

Was it possible this shaqra *did not understand his language after all? That her knowledge of Arabic was limited to a few phrases she had learned to say when greeting a pen friend? Could it be she not only did not understand but had barely found memorable the code words he should never have discussed over his two-way radio?*

Shaken, the cabdriver spilled coffee down the front of his new trousers. When the shaqra *turned to help him, he made a little bow and begged her not to worry. When she realized the spill was in the groin and leg area, she seemed glad to move away while a male waiter stepped in to assist.*

Hasan was overcome with dismay. Once a mere messenger of code words in a larger scheme, the full implications of which he was not worthy to know, he now found himself asked to eliminate an innocent woman. He knew he had given out the woman's location. If he did not do the deed himself, it was only a matter of time until Fa'ud's associates came to help him "take care of" her. Almost paralyzed with panic, he cast about mentally for some solution. Then it came to him. The only thing to do was to empty the place urgently. That might be done by means of a minor fire. Playing up his recently established awkwardness, he managed to dump over a chafing dish full of hot rolls. As they rolled onto the floor, paper doilies running the length of the buffet table burst into fire, ignited by the blue flame of the Sterno can. It was hardly a major conflagration, but nonetheless, it was enough to set off shrieking fire alarms and sprinklers forcing diners to flee the room.

In the exodus, Hasan saw the fair woman become separated from her friend, as the latter was unable to get on the same elevator with her. The friend also did not make it onto the second elevator, which Hasan was able to catch. During the long descent to the lobby, Hasan could only hope he would arrive in time to find the lady. Meanwhile, he prayed to Allah to help him overcome the emasculating inclination to help the woman flee from the danger she was in.

When Hasan finally arrived in the lobby of the World Trade Center, he saw one of Fa'ud's protégés lurking beside a potted palm. But Hasan's trendy Gap outfit was not what the operative was looking for. In addition, the arrival of firemen on the scene added to the chaos.

A fireman had already taken Ellen firmly by the arm and maneuvered her away from the elevator bay. So when Hasan gripped her shoulder and, with a hand at the small of her back, urged her forward briskly, she was not entirely surprised.

"This way, ma'am, this way," he said keeping his face out of sight over

her shoulder, as emergency personnel handled other confused individuals similarly. Ellen cried out when he threw open a door and thrust her into a janitor's closet, but, in the confusion, no one seemed to notice. With the door shut, Hasan turned her to face him and said, "Allah help us. I have made a grievous mistake."

Chapter 15

Gravesend Street, Allston, Massachusetts,
Christmas Day, 2000

Christmas Day dawned silvery gray and glaring as the sunshine streaked intermittently through oyster-colored clouds. With her hair all haywire because she had gone to bed when it was still damp, Liz took some time to dampen and re-dry her auburn waves, while coffee brewed in her kitchen. After dressing in a black lamb's wool sweater, black slacks, and a festive gold and cream scarf, she phoned both her mother and Janice to leave them holiday messages. She knew they both kept their phones turned down overnight. It was better to leave one for each of them now than to get consumed in a day of reporting and miss sending her love on the holiday.

Hanging up after leaving her second message, Liz considered how sad Veronica must be feeling, wondering each time the phone rang if it would be her mother calling. And here it was Christmas, with no word of her.

Pouring coffee, Liz picked up the unread copy of the *World*. Amusingly, like the *Banner*, its front page also featured the poem *The Night Before Christmas*, but thanks to its larger format, it also contained articles on world and local news. Leading the paper's Western Suburbs section, Liz found a piece by Nancy Knight bearing the headline, "Tragedy Haunts Past of Missing Newton Woman."

Although the article revealed no more than could be found in news archives—the accidental drowning of Ellen Johansson's father—the unearthing of old news was apparently enough to raise the ire of Olga Swenson, who phoned Liz moments later.

"It was only a matter of time until those old press clippings would be dug up. You know that, Mrs. Swenson," Liz said. "They're a part of the public record, after all. This is what happens when there are no new leads on a case that has gripped the public's imagination."

"All right, all right," Olga Swenson said. "I understand what you're saying, but it's painful, nonetheless. Now that it's out there in big type again, I'm wondering if anything I told you is getting you any closer to bringing my daughter home to me."

"Not directly," Liz said. The desperate, pleading tone of Mrs. Swenson's voice caused the reporter to feel apologetic. Even though it had only been a few days since she'd learned about the boy from the school for troubled teens, she felt remiss in having no ready answers for Ellen's mother. "But you can help me put to rest one item."

"Oh, here's Veronica," Mrs. Swenson said. "It's Christmas morning, after all, and we must open gifts. Let me meet you a little bit later. I shall need to walk Hershey."

"Could we make it somewhere other than the topiary garden, please?" Liz asked.

"All right. I'll meet you in two hours at the Wellesley College faculty club parking lot. We can stroll around the campus."

"Assuming my editor okays this, I'll be there. I'll phone you only if the editor says no."

"And, Liz?" Olga Swenson said.

"Yes, Mrs. Swenson?"

"Thank you for devoting your Christmas to this."

"You're welcome. May your day be the best it can be, under the circumstances. Please give my love to Veronica."

"Yes, of course."

Olga Swenson's call gave Liz the opportunity she'd been looking for to design her own Christmas Day assignments. If she were given the okay by phone, she would not even have to drive in to the newsroom until the afternoon. Fortunately, Esther O'Faolin was ruling the roost. And she was in better spirits than usual.

"Gobble, gobble," Esther said. "Cute turkey piece in today's paper. Not that anyone will read it. Sales are close to zero on Christmas Day."

"I may be onto something that will give us some news for tomorrow's paper, when everyone picks it up for after-Christmas sales ads," Liz said, telling Esther she had an exclusive opportunity for a Christmas Day conversation with Mrs. Swenson.

"Go for it," Esther said.

Liz realized Esther must not yet have read the *World*, since she didn't point out how that paper had scooped the *Banner* on Karl Swenson's drowning death.

With more than an hour of free time before she would have to set out for the Wellesley rendezvous, Liz looked about for a way to enjoy the unexpected at-home stretch of Christmas morning. It was time to give Prudence her gift, a carpet-covered little cave that looked just the right size for the cat to cuddle up in. Hoping it would help attract the cat, Liz put the catnip mouse from Tom inside the structure. Standing up and stretching her front legs luxuriously, Prudence approached the gift as though it was the Trojan horse. After examining it for a good few minutes, she decided to ignore both the cozy interior and catnip mouse. Instead, purring loudly, she climbed on top of the structure and perched herself on it proudly, like a sentry.

Liz was laughing when she picked up the ringing phone.

"Merry Christmas to you, too," Tom said, sounding piqued. "You didn't even leave your name when you called."

"Well, I wasn't sure if you'd want your lady friend to know about me."

"What are you talking about?"

"The gal on your answering machine."

"I can explain that."

"You don't owe me an explanation."

"But—hey listen. I thought you said you'd be working today."

"I will be, in a little over an hour."

"Are you busy until then?"

"Very! Drinking coffee and playing with Prudence."

"Can I come over and play with you two, too?"

"Oh, all right. But make it snappy!"

"Bah, humbug! See you soon."

Liz applied a touch of make-up and lipstick and dressed in flannel-lined jeans, a heavy Irish-knit sweater, and thick wool socks. This time, she would be prepared to walk in wintry Wellesley. She was about to pull on her insulated boots when Tom arrived at her door. Still in stocking feet, she stood aside as he entered bearing two Styrofoam containers of coffee and a battered cookie tin.

"From my 'lady friend,'" Tom grinned, handing Liz the cookie tin. When she said nothing, he said, "Well, aren't you gonna open it?"

The tin contained two circular pastries, filled with currants.

"Eccles cakes," Tom said. "Mind if I sit down?"

Liz swept her hand in the direction of her armchair. "Be my guest," she said. But she remained standing.

"I gather you've never had Eccles cakes before. Well, they're always a treat, but these are better than most. My cousin Caroline makes them every year. Most of the time, my relatives in Swanage—that's on the south coast of England—get to eat them. But this year, she's with us for the holidays. I'd have brought her to meet you, but she's home with my folks."

"Is she living with you?"

"Just for a few weeks. She's a student at BU, lives in the dorms. She's with me while the dorm's closed for Christmas vacation."

Liz bit into the pastry and smiled. "Delicious," she said.

But Tom was quiet, looking at the ice bucket full of flowers.

"I guess there's a lot we don't know about each other," he said.

"That's for sure. But, oh my God, I've got to run! I'm supposed to be in Wellesley in under a half-hour," Liz said pulling on her boots and grabbing her reporter's notebook. She was glad the car keys were stowed in her jacket pocket, for once.

"That's cutting it close," Tom said, wrapping up her Eccles cake in a napkin and carrying it and the coffee containers to the door. Following Liz to her car, he handed a coffee and pastry to her before she slammed the door shut. Rolling down the window, Liz leaned out and said, "Thank you, Tom, for the treats. Merry Christmas!"

As she drove away, Liz took a sip from the coffee container and grimaced. It was loaded with sugar. Tom had handed her the wrong one.

By the time she reached the Wellesley College faculty club parking lot, it was almost twenty minutes later than the appointment time. And there was no sign of Olga Swenson. Cursing the cold and sickeningly sweet coffee, Liz got out of her car and scanned the scene. With the snow washed away by the rain, it was pointless to look for footprints. And, she reasoned, if she walked around the faculty club building to look for Mrs. Swenson and Hershey coming or going along the campus path to the lakeshore, she might miss their approach on foot—or by car if Mrs. Swenson was also late and had chosen to drive to the meeting place.

Deciding it was worth a quick look at the campus path in any case, Liz ran as fast as she could in her heavy boots and rounded the building. Olga Swenson could be seen, back bowed, returning along the path towards the lake. When Liz called out, Hershey bounded in her direction.

"I'm so sorry to be late, Mrs. Swenson," Liz shouted.

Turning to face Liz, Ellen Johansson's mother lifted her shoulders and straightened her posture, but her facial expression remained crestfallen.

"Still no word," Liz spoke for her.

"And it's Christmas," the older woman said.

She didn't have to say more. Both women shared the same thought. If Ellen Johansson were alive and well, she would not fail to be in touch on the holiday. The two women walked in step, side-by-side, along the campus path.

"It's not much, but I think I've got a piece of somewhat heartening news for you," Liz said, taking DeZona's photograph of the living room from her handbag.

The older woman scrutinized it, perplexed.

"Do you see the teacup there?" Liz asked.

"Of course."

"Look at the china pattern, please, Mrs. Swenson. Am I correct in concluding the pattern is called 'Forget-me-not?'"

"Yes. It is. Of course! 'Forget-me-not!'"

"When I first met your daughter and Veronica, Ellen served us tea. Veronica dropped her teacup. I think the cup must have cracked or chipped and Ellen wrote herself a blackboard memo noting the china pattern."

Olga Swenson's eyes brimmed with tears as, without a word, she embraced Liz. Then the two walked in tandem, with the older woman holding her companion's elbow. Perhaps, once again, the pair shared the same thought: At least Ellen did not choose to desert her family.

But if this was not a case of suicide, what was the truth of the matter?

Olga Swenson seemed to collect herself. Noticing another dog walker approaching, she called Hershey to her side and attached his leash. But as he pulled in excitement at seeing the other dog, she grimaced.

"Blister," she said. "It's nothing, just from the dog pulling."

"No, perhaps it's not nothing," Liz said, recalling the repeated e-mail messages.

"Hmm?" Olga Swenson said, pulling on her gloves.

"Do you have any idea what your daughter has been reading recently?" Liz asked.

"Why should I?"

"I must tell you this in strictest confidence."

"It seems I owe you that, at least."

"One of Ellen's library colleagues seemed to be worried about your daughter's choice of reading matter, which, I gather, she could see listed in the library's circulation records."

"It wouldn't surprise me if she refused to say what those records contain. Ellen's talked to me about it. She and her colleagues regard themselves as a kind of last bastion protecting readers' privacy. That seems reasonable to me when it's a question of one scholar repeating or getting a hop on another's research, but what could there be to hide in a housewife's reading list?"

"Apparently enough to worry your daughter's friend, Lucy Gray."

"I'll give Lucy a call right away."

"That would make it clear I'd betrayed her confidence."

"Well, we have to do something!" Olga Swenson said exasperatedly.

"I think there is something you can do, Mrs. Swenson. I have been repeatedly receiving a one-word e-mail message that might just be significant. It didn't occur to me until just now, but the word in the message, 'Blister,' contains the word 'list.'"

"And a *B* at the start of the word! That's precisely the kind of shorthand Ellen and her colleagues often use. 'Blown' for 'book on interlibrary loan' and that sort of thing. Ellen has said they try to select words starting with *b*—for 'book' or 'biblio'—that mean something in themselves."

"I hope we're onto something. Do you think you could get access to your daughter's computer terminal and personal items at the library?"

"I think I'd find it easier to collect her knickknacks than log onto her computer. Why do you ask?"

"I'd like you to try that word on the library system and see if it's a password to the circulation record. If it isn't, perhaps you could look around and see if she kept a list of passwords to be used at work."

"How would I guarantee that I'd have any privacy? I'm not very computer savvy, either, you know. Wouldn't it be better for you to get Erik to do this?"

"I don't think so. First of all, he hardly trusts me after he was misquoted in that article."

"I could convince him that you're working with us."

"Even if you could, he's under some suspicion in this case. I think the librarians would be much less likely to leave him alone in Ellen's workspace than they would you."

"But Ellen shares an office with Monica Phillips. If she's not lording it over the library patrons, she's at her desk impressing everyone with her efficiency."

"That could be an advantage, since it would be quicker and easier to input a potential password on an active machine than to start up Ellen's PC. And we have another advantage in predicting when Ms. Phillips would have to cover the reference desk. I happen to know when Lucy Gray's coffee breaks occur."

By the time the two had parted at the gate to the Pinetum, their scheme was complete, and scheduled for the next morning. As Olga Swenson walked off towards her home, she raised her blistered hand in a little salute to Liz. Both of the women held themselves taller as they strode purposefully in opposite directions.

New York City, December 16, 2000

"Of course it was a mistake," Ellen said to the man in the closet, whose coffee-stained pants identified him as the fellow who had accidentally started the fire. *"Anyone could see you didn't set the fire intentionally,"* Ellen added.

The poor fellow looked petrified.

Ellen was alarmed, too, to have been pushed into the closet by the stranger. But she saw his agitation as stemming from fear that he would be in deep trouble for the accident. After all, he appeared to be of Middle Eastern extraction, and wasn't it common knowledge that crimes were punished harshly there?

"I would vouch for you, sir, and I'm sure my friend would, too," Ellen said, hoping that he would relax enough to let her exit the closet without much ado. *"Please don't worry yourself so much."*

Samir Hasan was overwhelmed. One after the other, this woman had destroyed every assumption he had ever held about her. First, she looked like a spoiled American out-of-towner who knew nothing about New York traffic and less about his language. Then she seemed to know taxi routes and understand the radio communication she should never have heard. Now, it was clear that this assumption was a mistake, too. And last, the woman he had put into grievous danger turned out to be a person who would help him— Samir Hasan, a total stranger and an Arab, too—when he was in trouble. This was a good person, a kind woman.

Standing there, in the closet he'd thrust her into, this shaqra was a living and breathing contradiction to the kind of rhetoric that had won his cooperation in the code-passing operation. Large-eyed and clearly afraid, this woman who was putting his worries before her own proved all Americans are not cold-hearted infidels.

"Do you have children?" she asked him next, surprising Hasan with the question.

"A son, at home with his mother in Baghdad," he found himself replying.

"You must miss him terribly," the woman said. *"I have a daughter at home. She's just eight years old. How old is your son?"*

Hasan's head was spinning. Why in Allah's name was this woman making small talk? He had to get this shaqra out of here. But how? And where to? *"He's the same,"* he said. *"The same age."*

And then, the closet door was flung open by a firefighter. Before the fire-man could finish demanding, "Is everything all right in here?" Ellen flew past him and across the lobby, into the embrace of her pen pal.

"I thought I would protect the lady," Hasan explained before brushing past the incredulous fireman. Inspired, Hasan added, "I see she has found my sister."

Hasan hastened across the lobby as the women exited, arm-in-arm, crushed in one compartment of a revolving door. While Hasan followed, the pair crossed the plaza to the globe-shaped sculpture and asked a passerby to take their photo in front of it. While his head spun in the effort to find a way to warn her about her plight—or to somehow to be man enough to carry out his horrific order—he nevertheless found himself marveling, again, at the woman's faith in other people. He would never hand his camera over to a total stranger and leave, as she did, valuables such as a purse and briefcase lying on a bench while the photo was being taken. In fact, the woman never picked up her things. Instead, rapt in animated conversation with her friend, she simply walked away from them.

Now I am a thief, as well, Hasan told himself as he picked them up. Or, maybe not, he thought, more happily. Here was the excuse to approach the woman again as a Good Samaritan.

Waving the purse and calling out, "Lady, lady! I have found your hand-bags!" Hasan attempted to get Ellen's attention. But he was too late.

The women were already too far away to hear him, and before he could break into a run to catch them, they had entered an idling cab. To make things worse, Hasan's cab was nowhere to be seen.

Exasperated and frantic, Hasan was confused as to where he had left his cab. Nevertheless, he retained the presence of mind to repeat to himself the medallion number and cab company name emblazoned on the women's cab as it drove away, headed uptown. He could plant it in his memory.

At least in the eyes of one man, he didn't look suspicious carrying the woman's things.

"Nice try, buddy," a businessman said to him. "You're a rare bird."

Whatever that meant, it was said in friendly manner. Still, Hasan was uneasy to be seen with the bags. He wished he still had his Gap bag contain-ing his old clothes. But that had been left behind in the restaurant. Taking off his blazer, he wrapped the purse and slim briefcase in it and hailed a cab himself, asking the driver to follow the woman's cab. But such chases are far more difficult in real life than they are in films, and the cabbie soon lost sight *of the vehicle. Hasan ordered him to return to the World Trade Center and make a circuit of the building. Allah be praised, Hasan's cab had not been towed away, although it was parked in a tow zone. Perhaps the police had been too preoccupied with the fire emergency to take heed of it.*

Hasan's relief was short-lived. The two-way radio crackled to life as Faud's voice commanded, "You know what you have to do. The teena must go missing. For always."

"Hamdu-lillah," Hasan said, hoping his cohort would take it as assent, while in fact it was his prayer to Allah to help him have the manhood to do what he must.

Chapter 16

Newton, Massachusetts, December 26, 2000

I f Olga Swenson felt edgy as she entered the Newton Free Library, no one took notice at first. The day after Christmas, the place was little used by patrons, leaving the library staff free to take extended coffee breaks and tell one another about their holiday celebrations. It was also a day for Monica Phillips to shine by overseeing a "Boxing Day Cookie Fest" that she had made a tradition for several years. Apparently, the librarian had some English background and felt eager to acknowledge, with a little celebration of her own, the December 26 holiday that was celebrated with a day off from work in the British Isles. The event required librarians scheduled to work that day to bring leftover cookies from their family celebrations for all of the colleagues to share.

Although Olga Swenson had forgotten all about the occasion until she arrived at the library, she did have a tin of leftover cookies with her to present to the librarians. Little did she know how useful this icebreaker would become.

"Mrs. Swenson, how lovely to see you," Monica Phillips said, as Olga approached the reference desk. "And how kind of you to remember our Boxing Day Cookie Fest!"

"How could I forget it?" Olga fibbed. "It is one of Ellen's favorite library occasions. So lovely of you to have established the tradition."

"Perhaps you'd like to join us," the librarian said, looking at the clock. "We begin in about fifteen minutes in the conference room."

"It's kind of you to include me, but I fear I couldn't face all of Ellen's colleagues just now. It's all so very upsetting, as I'm sure you may appreciate, Miss Phillips."

"Of course, of course," Monica Phillips said with a small reassuring smile that masked her great pleasure in being the only person privy to a conversation with Ellen's mother. It would mean she would have gossip—or at least an impression of the woman's demeanor—to share at the cookie fest. "May I offer you a cup of tea in my office, at least?" she inquired, stepping away from the reference desk in the rare act of leaving it unattended.

Monica Phillips led the way to the modest office Olga knew the librarian shared with her daughter. Shrewdly, Olga decided to give the librarian something to talk about in the cookie party.

"That would be just wonderful," Olga said. "I find I need to stop and collect myself, off and on, all day. Ellen's absence has a kind of physical effect on me, you know. Mentally, I feel distracted, and profoundly worried, of course. But physically, I feel quite drained—exhausted without being sleepy."

"How strange that must be," Monica said. "How difficult for you! And Veronica? How is she bearing up?"

Olga bristled. It was awful enough to have to emote about herself to this woman, but she felt the others in her family—especially her granddaughter—were completely off limits. Still, it was important to feed Miss Phillips something more to talk about.

"At a time like this, the presence of a pet in the household is wonderful, don't you think?" she said, as the pair entered the small office. Pinned up all over Miss Phillips's bulletin board were photos of her three cats.

"I wasn't aware Veronica had a pet."

"Not in her home. But Veronica has grown up—during visits to my home in Wellesley—with Hershey. That's our chocolate Lab. In fact, Veronica is the one who named him."

"So, Veronica is staying with you then?"

"Oh, yes. But although the circumstances this time are—unusual—it's quite ordinary for her to stay with us on Boxing Day. Unless it fell on a weekend, Ellen always had to work then—*and* enjoy your cookie party—so it's become an annual treat for me to have Veronica overnight on Christmas and for the day on December 26th. Erik is looking after her and Hershey this morning so I could deliver the cookies."

Monica Phillips tore herself away from the conversation to fetch the tea. During the seven or so minutes she was gone, Olga noticed her daughter's PC was gone from her desk while the screen on the PC belonging to Monica Phillips was entirely black. It had not been turned on.

"Sorry about the delay, but I had to get someone to cover at the reference desk before I could fetch the tea."

"I'm sorry for the inconvenience."

"Not at all. I would have needed a substitute at the desk in a few minutes anyway."

"I suppose I will have to consult your reference desk colleague about my question before I leave."

"What question is that?"

"I wanted to see if I could borrow a copy of *Gone With the Wind* today. It's the book Ellen was reading, in paperback, when she—well, before she left. She must have taken her copy with her. I'd like to read the novel, too, if there's a copy here in the library. I think it would make me feel closer to my daughter at this time."

"Please, allow me to help you," the librarian said, turning on her PC and typing in her password with one finger, spelling out the word MEOW as Olga looked on.

In a minute, Monica had the call number and the information that the book was available on the second floor. She wrote the call number on a scrap of recycled paper and handed it to Olga. "I see you've noticed your daughter's PC is gone. The police removed it. But have no fear, Mrs. Swenson, she never overused the Internet for personal searches or anything like that. Her reputation is secure."

"Would it be all right if I took a look at the contents of her drawers? Perhaps there's a little something I can take home to Veronica to cheer her."

"I don't see why not. The police have already taken what they want."

When Olga Swenson looked shaken by this last remark, the librarian took the occasion to look pointedly at the clock and make her exit for the conference room. After a minute, Olga opened one of her daughter's drawers, pulled it out thoroughly, and allowed it to drop to the floor.

Stepping around the mess, she sat down at Miss Phillips's PC and moved the mouse. The screen saver photo of three cats seemed to melt away, revealing a screen cluttered with icons. One of them was labeled "Blister." Apparently, the word was not a password. It was the list itself. Olga's edginess turned to jubilation, until she moved the mouse to click on the icon. A box appeared on the screen demanding a password.

Congratulating herself on her powers of observation, she typed in the letters *M*, *E*, *O*, and *W*. But the blasted machine rejected the password. Suppressing a moan, she stood up to survey the room. Would there be a password list on hand somewhere?

Just then, Monica Phillips opened the door.

"You see, I am a butterfingers, too, in my current state of mind. I managed to dump the whole drawer!" Olga said.

"Perhaps it was because I startled you," the librarian said. "My colleagues always accuse me of creeping up on little cat feet," she said, slowly arranging her lips into a large smile. The action recalled the Cheshire cat in *Alice in Wonderland*. "I just came for the cake server. Ellen always kept it in her desk. Oh, I see it's on the floor."

"Allow me," Olga said, picking up the implement and handing it to the librarian. Fortunately, the PC screen did not face the door. "I've been noticing your photos of three lovely cats. What are their names?"

"They *are* dears, aren't they? The black-and-white "tuxedo" cat is Fred. The ginger cat is, of course, Ginger," the librarian smiled proudly.

"Of course! For Fred Astaire and Ginger Rogers! How clever!" Olga enthused. "And what about that handsome fellow? What's his name?"

"Actually, that's a female. I named her Judy, after Judy Garland."

It seemed a strange name choice for a Siamese cat.

"It's because of her voice," Miss Phillips went on. "Siamese cats often vocalize, you know. They actually speak—in their own language of course—as they go about their business. My Judy, though, does more than that. She seems to sing. I've got to admit, she's my favorite."

When Monica left the room with the cake server, Olga reseated herself at the PC; input the letters *J*, *U*, *D*, and *Y*, and was given instant access to the records under "Blister." Then she met another roadblock, apparently put there to make the records somewhat more secure. Another box appeared on the screen asking for a library card number. It was not possible to see records listed by name. Confidently, she typed in the numbers *1*, *9*, *9*, and *2*. Veronica's birth year.

A document headed with the name "Johansson, Ellen Swenson," and filled with dates and book titles spread itself out before her eyes. It was too much to take down—or to take in. Recalling Liz's instructions, Olga turned on the printer and used the PC's mouse to click on the print icon. After the page printed out, she followed more instructions from Liz and closed the document until the desktop of icons appeared. Slipping the printed page into her purse, she turned to tidy up the spilled drawer. Along with a few pens and some pads of Post-it Notes, she found a twelve-inch ruler, decorated by Veronica with a hand-painted crown and letters spelling out the statement, "MY MOM RULES!!!" Placing the ruler in her purse, she made a quick survey of the rest of her daughter's drawers. They contained some drawings by Veronica; a mug sporting a portrait of Virginia Woolf; some feminine supplies; a much-used, folded-up tote bag imprinted with the words, "So many books, so little time"; and a packet of Reese's Pieces.

The items were predictable, mundane. But the emotions they stirred were not.

Olga Swenson sat down heavily in her daughter's chair and sobbed.

When, at last, she made her way out of the office, she could hear one voice sounding from the conference room. "Ellen's mother is a wreck. She's so jittery, the poor woman can't open a drawer without pulling it out completely and spilling it all over the floor. She's so bereft, she's even going to read *Gone With the Wind* because it's the last book she thinks Ellen read. Pretty sad title in the circumstances, don't you think?"

"Really, Monica," another voice said. Olga recognized it as Lucy Gray's. "Surely it's too soon to speak of Ellen as if we'll never see her again. And as for *Gone With the Wind*, I hardly think that's Ellen's reading taste."

"Well, I have that from Mrs. Swenson herself," Monica said, rising to the conversational challenge. "And she told me Veronica is hopeless unless she's with her grandmother's dog, constantly eating chocolate. It's a wonder Mrs. Swenson had the presence of mind to bring us these cookies!"

Fed up with the whole charade, despite its success, Olga Swenson left the library without going to the trouble of finding and signing out a copy of *Gone With the Wind*. Only when she reached her car did she remember she'd forgotten to turn off Miss Phillips's printer. Unable to face hearing another word of gossip about her loved ones, she settled into her car. Turning her key in the ignition, she drove a short distance and parked her car on Fenwick Street. Then, using her key, she let herself into her daughter's house.

Taking off her coat, she made her first uncharacteristic move. Instead of carefully hanging the garment on a hanger in the hall closet, she draped it over the back of an armchair. Then, she did something else that was highly unusual for her. After taking a teacup and saucer into the kitchen with the intention of making tea, she filled the cup halfway with bourbon instead.

Whispering the words "Forget me not," she then settled into Ellen's favorite chair in the living room and unfolded the list of books that revealed her daughter's recent library borrowing habits. Studying the titles, she was glad her cup held bourbon.

Meanwhile, in the *Banner*'s newsroom, Liz began trying to locate Dr. Douglas Mayhew, former headmaster of the Wharton Alternative School.

Using old clips provided by the *Banner*'s ever-helpful librarian, Conan Forbes, Liz found Mayhew's name mentioned in connection with the opening of the school in 1960, in several stories about fundraising and about the philosophy of teaching troubled teens, and regarding the school's closing in 1975. Apparently, after his stint as headmaster, Mayhew was not a newsmaker since his name appeared neither in more Boston-area newspaper clips nor in Internet citations.

In her work, Liz often found the requirement of noting people's ages not just a thankless task but one that sometimes caused her sources to balk or clam up. Early on, she learned to ask for ages only after securing the quotes she needed from people. Now, she silently thanked the reporters who had done their duty and reported Mayhew's age at the time of their writing. On one Internet site, she was able to take the many Douglas Mayhews with listed telephone numbers in the Northeast and narrow the search by age. This left just five, including two in Maine (Douglas Mayhew, Junior and Senior), one in Worcester, one on Cape Cod, and one in Brookline, a city bordering Boston.

The Brookline number, which Liz dialed first, seemed the most promising. "You have reached the infernal machine of Dr. Douglas Mayhew. Please speak loudly after the beep," the voice-mail message announced. Liz left a message and went on to phone the others. Luck was with her. The first Mayhew of Boothbay Harbor, Maine, said he knew the other, in Port Clyde, since both were in the boat business. Neither of the Maine Mayhews, he said, had ever headed "any school, anywayuh." The Worcester Dr. Mayhew was a dentist. Finally, Douglas Mayhew of Cape Cod was not in. His message began with a segment of the rock group No Doubt's song, "Spiderwebs": "Sorry I'm not home right now / I'm walking into spiderwebs / So leave a message and I'll call you back." It finished with a young man's voice saying, "Hey, I'm not home. So leave a message." It was hardly the message of a retired headmaster, but Liz left a message anyway. The young man might have a relative of the same name who was the headmaster's age.

Waiting for replies, Liz looked in her purse for coffee money. She hadn't been to the bank in such a long time that she was down to a few dollars. Hoping to find change at the bottom of her bag, she dug deeper, only to have her fingers encounter a plastic bag filled with something soft: the cigarette butts she'd collected from the taxi. Scolding herself for forgetting about them, she immediately phoned Cormac Kinnaird.

The man might be unreadable when it came to personal interaction, but he was unreserved in his enthusiasm to get his hands on this evidence. As the two were about to arrange a meeting time and place, Jared Conneely stopped by Liz's desk. Noticing she was on the line, he wrote on a scrap of paper, "I regret to inform you that you are on the 'New Year's resolutions of the rich, famous, and infamous' beat today. Stop by the city desk at your first convenience." Liz silently mouthed "OK" and continued her conversation with Cormac

"I've just been assigned a story I can at least begin to work on in the newsroom," she told him. "And I'm hoping I can linger here to receive a return call from a potential source on the Johansson case."

"Say no more. I know where the *Banner*'s building is. If I can park in your lot, I shall stop by and pick up the stuff on my way to Northeastern. I've got to meet with a student at two-thirty, so I've got some flexibility. If you have a minute, we could have coffee. If you've got more time, I could take you out to lunch in Chinatown."

"By the time you get here, I'll know more about my schedule. If you don't mind winging it regarding my availability, that would be great."

After hanging up, Liz noticed the light flashing on the phone, indicating a call had come in while she was on the line. Actually, two calls had come in. One was from the young Cape Codder who said, "Hey, it's Doug Mayhew. Are you gonna put me in the pay-puh? Cool. Call me back." And he left his number.

The other was from the much more gentlemanly Dr. Mayhew of Brookline. "Hello, Miss Higgs. This is Dr. Douglas Mayhew, former headmaster of the Wharton Alternative School, responding to your message." He left his phone number.

Down at the city desk, Jared Conneely was making exaggerated waving signals, urging Liz to approach the desk. Liz raised one finger to indicate she'd be there in a minute. Then she dialed the Brookline telephone number.

After introducing herself, Liz quickly realized why the headmaster had referred to her as "Miss Higgs." He was hard of hearing. While Jared changed his wide-armed signal to a one-fingered, schoolmarmish scolding motion, Liz said loudly, "I'm writing an article about New Year's resolutions and whether they actually lead to a genuine kind of resolve in young people. I thought I'd call on you, hoping your years of experience with troubled young people would help to anchor my article."

"I'm flattered that you ask. I suppose I could make myself available, but

I'm not good on the phone. I'm going deaf, you see."

After arranging to meet Dr. Mayhew in two hours, Liz phoned Father James, Department of Youth Services chaplain, and set up an interview and photo shoot of the girls in his care for an hour after that. Then she rushed down to the city desk.

Before Jared could whine or Dermott could bark at her, she told the city editor, "Thanks to Jared, who gave me a heads-up about the New Year's resolution piece, I've already gotten a jump on the article. I've arranged to talk to a long-time teacher of troubled teens. Then, I'll interview a group of adolescent girls who are Department of Youth Services detainees to get their take on whether New Year's resolutions are a setup for failure or the occasion for truly resolving to take charge of some aspect of living."

"But we had in mind a celebrity piece. Didn't Conneely tell you?"

"Great idea for a sidebar!" Liz exclaimed. "And a byline for Jared, if he can afford the time," she smiled, knowing how difficult it was to get celebrities to respond to such questions on short notice. "I'm sure the 'Here's the Buzz' gals or the society editor would be glad to give him some contact info."

Like every editorial assistant in the newsroom, Jared lived for such opportunities. While he might have been the first to admit celebrity chasing was not his cup of tea, a byline was not a thing to turn one's back on, and he knew it. Even his customary pallor disappeared as, smiling broadly, he piped up, "I'm on it!" and made a beeline for the Buzz gals' office before Dermott could object.

Returning to her desk to write up photo assignment sheets, Liz found her phone ringing. The caller was Olga Swenson. "I've gotten my hands on Ellen's book list," she said. She sounded shaken. "There's something else I should tell you, too. The police have had the walls in Veronica's room stripped."

"Stripped?"

"They've taken down the wallpaper."

"Did Erik tell you when they did this?"

"No. I haven't spoken to him since yesterday morning. I'm sure he would have mentioned it if it had occurred before then."

"Then, how do you know it was done?"

"I'm here at the house now."

"May I meet you there in about three quarters of an hour? I'd come sooner but I'm waiting for another person to help me with the case."

"I don't like to sit here alone. It gives me the willies. I feel so useless, Liz!'

"Don't be silly. Think about all you've accomplished today. I have an idea. You know where the copy shop is in Newtonville?"

"Yes."

"Take that list there and make a couple of copies of it. Then I'll meet you back at Ellen's. You could wait in the car if you like and we could go back in together."

Olga agreed and ended the conversation just in time for Liz to turn and see Cormac Kinnaird, sporting a visitor's badge, enter the newsroom. He was carrying a ribbon-wrapped vase filled with red tulips.

"I didn't know if the newsroom ran to vases," he said, giving Liz a peck on the cheek. He picked up the plastic bag of cigarette butts.

"Not a very fair exchange," Liz said, smiling. "I'm afraid I can't take you up on the lunch offer," she said, and told the doctor about her appointments with Olga and Dr. Mayhew. "But I could offer you a very quick cup of coffee in our cafeteria."

"You have too much on your plate. You go take care of those appointments and tell me about them this evening at dinner. We'll make it on the late side, so you have time to dress up. I'm taking you to a rather nice place, if that's all right with you. Do you know the restaurant, Upstairs at the Pudding? Shall we meet there at eight?"

Riding the escalator to the newsroom's lobby, side-by-side with the doctor, Liz remembered the redhead in the bar.

Apparently, Cormac was not put off by Liz's perplexed expression.

"Deadlines become you," he said.

Chapter 17

Olga Swenson was sitting in her car when Liz startled her by tapping on the older woman's steamy window. Without a word, Olga led Liz into the house on Fenwick Street. Standing aside to let Liz enter first, she let out a sigh. With some surprise, Liz noticed the smell of alcohol on Olga's breath.

Olga did not take off her coat but led Liz straight up to Veronica's bedroom. A scrap of yellow "CRIME SCENE" tape provided the answer to Liz's unasked question: "How did Mrs. Swenson know the stripped wallpaper was the work of the police?"

Inside the room, everything was in disarray. Plastic sheeting covered a bed heaped with stuffed animals and dolls, while trash bags appeared to be stuffed with other trinkets and toys.

"Veronica loved her Madeline wallpaper," Olga said. "We purchased it for her when she was five. I'm not sure we could find it again if we tried. Hasn't she suffered enough without having her room vandalized by the authorities?" She sat down heavily on the only available piece of furniture in the room, a child-sized wooden chair. "Why would they do this?" she nearly sobbed.

As Liz moved to crouch down beside Olga, she realized she must have set this destruction in motion by reporting Veronica's unusual request: "Please, Santa, bring me new wallpaper." The police must be grasping at straws to regard that report as significant.

Crouching, with tears in her eyes, Liz took Mrs. Swenson's hands in her own but could not admit she knew the answer to the question. "I will do everything I can to find more of that wallpaper for you," she promised. Standing, she pulled the older woman to her feet, then picked up a sizeable scrap of the paper from the floor. "Let's make some tea and look over that book list," she suggested.

In the kitchen, Olga seemed to gather herself together, as she prepared coffee rather than tea. "I just can't think of using those teacups," she said. She did not take off her coat.

Meanwhile, Liz studied the list, which recorded three months of Ellen's borrowing records. Most titles were followed by the author's name, a call number, and two dates, presumably indicating the date borrowed and date returned. In four cases, there was no return date. And, in the case of the children's book, there were three renewals. Liz turned her attention to the titles and authors:

The Friends of the Environment New Car Buying Guide by Harold Gold
The Consumer Guide to New Car Ratings 2000
Silent Knights by Josephine Henshaw
Private Schools in Massachusetts: 1974 by the Private Schools Consortium
How to Be a Perfect Stranger, edited by Stuart M. Matlins
You Can Speak Arabic Program: Level One by Ahmed Sulieman
Understanding Speech Impediments by Gareth Weiner
Charlotte's Web by E. B. White
Everyday Life in Palestine by Nadia Mafouz
How to Disappear Completely and Never Be Found by Sara Nickerson
Christmas Cookie Recipe Round-Up by Caroline Frost

Lowering the list and lifting her eyes to meet the older woman's, Liz said softly, "Mrs. Swenson, I must ask, are you surprised by the contents of this list?"

Unwilling to speak, Olga nodded. Then she shook her head. Signaling Liz to remain seated, she stepped into the living room and then returned with a small stack of books including all but one of the books that were noted as not yet returned. The title *How to Disappear Completely and Never Be Found* seemed to describe the state of the only book from Ellen's list that remained unaccounted for.

"I found this on the floor in Veronica's room," she said, lifting the copy of *Charlotte's Web*. "The rest were on Ellen's night table," she added, pointing to the others. "Take them if you like. For now, I need to go home and collect myself." Her tone was steely.

"Please help me just a bit more," Liz begged.

But Mrs. Swenson shook her head

"Think of Ellen . . . ," Liz pleaded.

"What do you think I'm doing, *every* minute of *every* day?" Olga snapped. She stood up and extended her arm to indicate that Liz should lead the way out of the house.

"I hope you believe I mean to find your daughter."

"Please!" Olga said, slamming Ellen's front door. Striding down her daughter's front walk, she fumbled her car's lock, muttered a curse, got into her car, and drove off without a backward glance.

Standing on the sidewalk, Liz folded the list of books and tucked it into her purse. Then she stood still for a moment, regarding the piece of wallpaper in her hands. Damp and torn, it depicted twelve little girls in two perfect lines, and the last of them all was Madeline. The troublemaker. Liz knew it was time to find the Wharton Alternative School's equivalent of Miss Clavel.

It was just a few minutes past two o' clock when Liz rang the doorbell of Dr. Mayhew's Brookline home. Standing across the street from a park graced with leafless weeping willow trees, the brown-stained, wood frame house appeared to have been built during the first years of the twentieth century. Its furnishings dated from the middle of that same time period, Liz noticed, as the former headmaster ushered her through his living room into his den.

"Bachelor housekeeping," he said apologetically, as the pair passed stacks of books and papers in the living room. He spoke in the booming tones of a man who is hard of hearing.

"Looks more like scholarly housekeeping to me," Liz said, matching his volume.

"You're too kind. I wish I could call myself a scholar. When I retired from Wharton, I had great hopes of writing a truly worthwhile study, but I suppose that was just another case of 'the best-laid plans of mice and men.' Please sit down, Miss Higgs."

"I'm afraid I didn't speak clearly enough on my phone message. It's Higgins, Liz Higgins."

"Nonsense! If I'm going to be of any use to you, let's be honest. I didn't get your name right because I couldn't hear it! Now, how can I help you?"

"All right, I will be honest, then, too. I'm here for two reasons. One is to get some background for a story I'm writing on New Year's Resolutions. Later today I shall be interviewing DYS-incarcerated girls about their resolutions and how likely they think they are to see them through."

"And, I take it, you want me to tell you what I've learned along these lines with my students. It's a dull question, but I'll help you. Nevertheless, I'm no fool. You're really more excited about learning something else from me aren't you? So why don't we begin with that?" Dr. Mayhew said, smiling.

"You're right. I'm looking for a past student of yours, sir. His name is Al Leigh."

"Say again?"

Liz raised her voice and enunciated carefully. "Al Leigh. L, E, I, G, H."

"I could hear you all right. But I can't call to mind anyone named Leigh, Al or otherwise."

"I'm told he was perhaps Hispanic, despite the surname. Perhaps his full first name was Alberto or Alfredo? He would have been a student in 1973."

"No. No Albertos or Alfredos come to mind. Hmm, 1973. Just before the school closed. Al Leigh." Dr. Mayhew shook his head and said again, "Al Leigh." Then he exclaimed, "Ali! Of course you must mean Ali. Olive-skinned Ali. Oh, what was his last name? He didn't belong in the company of those troublemakers. His only problem was his tongue."

"He was outspoken, foul mouthed?"

Dr. Mayhew wore a wistful expression. "No, no, not at all. While the other lads turned the air blue with cussing if they were angry or agitated, Ali clammed up. He was tongue-tied, you see. And English was not his first language." The headmaster paused, then exclaimed, "Abdulhazar. That's it. Ali Abdulhazar. The name was enough to make him the butt of the boys' jokes. With his speech impediment and his accent, when he *did* manage to speak, he was the center of far too much negative attention from the other boys."

"He was bullied?"

"I tried to keep them from bullying him, but there was only so much I could do, I'm afraid. When my back was turned, they circled him for the kill—figuratively, of course—like a school of sharks around a juicy tidbit. Most of those boys had been mistreated themselves, you see, so it rather came naturally to them to behave like that. Mind if I . . . ?" Dr. Mayhew said, picking up a pipe.

"Not at all."

Dr. Mayhew made much of filling, tamping, and lighting his pipe. Finally, he went on: "It was no wonder he courted detention so often, usually by straying off school grounds. The other boys hated having to sit still in my office, but I think Ali rather liked it. First, he got away from the others by wandering off. Then, once he was rounded up, he had my protection for an hour or two. Even if watching me do paperwork had to be deadly dull, it beat being teased by the other boys. I hate to say it, but he may even have built his status by running off so much. The others saw him as devil-may-care, a quality they admired."

Dr. Mayhew fussed with his pipe some more. "Ali finally got them off his back when he was caught with that girl. What was her name? Of course the incident meant his days were numbered at Wharton, so he couldn't enjoy the boys' newfound esteem for him."

"What incident?"

"In the Pinetum across the way, he was caught in some kind of compromising position with a young girl. The girl's father was livid. He insisted Ali was masturbating while watching the girl dancing. Pretty girl, I remember, a strawberry blonde, dressed in some kind of scarves. Like that dancer, Isadora Duncan." Dr. Mayhew paused to reignite his pipe. "The outfit was more unusual than revealing. Innocent-looking, I thought, not sexy. But the girl's father was beside himself. Absolutely beside himself. The more he cursed and demanded explanations, the more tongue-tied Ali became."

"Did you observe this, or did the father tell you about it? And what happened to the girl?"

"Oh, I was there, all right. But not before the father was laying into Ali verbally. It was his shouting that helped me locate the boy, who had been missing for about an hour. The girl was crying, but I had the impression she was more cowed by her father's shouting than by Ali. The mother came running and whisked the girl away. The father was a big man. I remember thinking he was a big Swede when he told me his name. What was it?"

"Swenson, Karl Swenson."

"That's it! How did you know? And the girl's name was Olga."

"No, that's the wife. The girl was called Ellen."

"Yes, yes. You've got it! What makes you ask about this?"

"I've been trying to find Ellen ever since she went missing a week ago, leaving behind her own little girl, a child called Veronica."

"Has this been in the papers? I'm afraid I only take the *Times* now. For the crossword puzzle. Don't read the local papers much anymore."

"Yes, Dr. Mayhew, we've been covering it. And what you are telling me now is extremely helpful. May I ask, was Arabic Ali's first language? And what brought him to your school?"

"Right, on the Arabic. His mother brought him to the school, literally and, I suspect, figuratively, too. That is, her inability to handle him—his learning disabilities and speech impediment—and perhaps some over-severe discipline in her household administered by her or, more likely, by her husband—had made the boy unmanageable. Like all of our boys, he could not thrive in a typical public school. But his was a need for *less* rather than *more* discipline, along with lots of speech therapy and ESL."

"You mean English as a Second Language?"

"Right again. We didn't have those kinds of specialists on hand, unfortunately. And even if we had, it's unlikely they'd have been proficient in Arabic. Still, perhaps they could have put to rest my question about how tongue-tied he actually was. When he was in trouble or agitated, he sometimes hummed or sort of mumbled. I had to wonder if he was doing the Arabic equivalent of a 'Hail, Mary,' if you know what I mean. That's not a very politically correct way of putting it, but I mean sort of calling on his deity." Dr. Mayhew shook himself. "Then again, he could have been mumbling a nursery rhyme, pop lyrics, or hurling out curses, for all anyone knew. His native language was a mystery to me."

"Do you remember him saying anything when he was being hounded by Mr. Swenson?"

"Nothing specific. But it would have been typical for him to sort of clutch his hands around his knees and mumble while looking caught, like a deer in the headlights."

"What happened to him after the incident?"

"We had to expel the poor bugger. I argued to the board that we should keep him on until a case was proven against him, but they nixed that. The school was in trouble financially and the board feared Swenson's ire would be the last nail in our coffin. They thought he'd go to the press. As it turned out, Swenson went mum as soon as Ali left. It was a matter of a day or two before the boy's parents came to collect him. As for his fate after that, I'm in the dark. I wrote down the name of a colleague at another school whom I thought might consider admitting Ali to his program, but I saw the boy's dad stuff the paper I wrote it on into a trash bin before the family got into their car. All I can say is I hope Ali was able to put his ear to good use."

"His ear?"

"He had perfect pitch. And he was clever, mechanically. Strange that a boy who faltered at speaking could sing like a lark. According to the music teacher, who came round once every two weeks, he could tell you what note you were playing just by hearing it. After Ali took apart our piano and fixed a broken key, the music teacher wanted to introduce him to a piano tuner he knew. He said the man was getting old and might take on an apprentice. But Ali was expelled before that could come to pass."

"Are you still in contact with the music teacher?"

"I never see him, but his wife always sends me a Christmas card. This year was no exception. I remember noticing the address was different this year, but I didn't save it. I never send Christmas cards. I just threw out the envelope."

"Do you remember anything about the address? Was it in Massachusetts, for instance?"

Dr. Mayhew paused. "No, I don't remember a thing about where it was. But I do remember thinking, 'God forbid I ever have to live in a place called Harmony Haven. Appropriate for a music teacher, though, I suppose. You'll want to know his name, of course. It's Buxton, Clifford Buxton."

Regarding his book- and paper-strewn surroundings with an expression blending fondness and chagrin, he continued, "And that brings us to your question about resolutions and resolve. Most of my boys possessed neither. And what kind of mentor would I have been, in the unlikely event that any of them came up with resolutions? A very poor one, I'm afraid. Do you know how many times I've made the resolution to sort out this stuff? That number is on the verge of the infinite. But have I exercised any resolve? You tell me," he said with a chuckle.

As Liz stood up to leave, the doorbell rang. Embarrassed, she realized it was probably the *Banner*'s photographer. Despite having no forewarning, Dr. Mayhew cooperated in having his photo taken as Liz thanked him and rushed off to her car.

In her car, Liz used her new cell phone to call the Newton police. Their public information officer confirmed the wallpaper stripping at Fenwick Street was done on their orders. The officer would neither reveal what the police had hoped to find nor what had spurred the authorities to strip the little girl's room. Now that she thought about it, Liz realized that, while comforting Olga Swenson, she had failed to scrutinize Veronica's bare walls. That was a missed opportunity but not overly worrisome, since she knew it was her own report that had inspired the strip search. And Liz also knew that Veronica's request for the wallpaper was made only after she had asked a half-dozen Santas for every other gift she'd ever wished for.

This last thought caused Liz to pick up her cell phone one more time.

She would have to make this call quickly, since she had to get back into the heart of Boston to meet with the DYS girls.

The phone rang several times before Tom's voice—unaccompanied this time—announced, "Hi! You've reached Tip Top Paper Hangers. Leave a message and I'll get right back to you."

Until this afternoon, Liz only thought about Tom's work in regard to his predictable appearances changing the displays on her billboard. But of course, he also worked hanging wallpaper in people's homes. He would know where to find wallpaper with a Madeline motif, if anyone did. And—just perhaps—it wouldn't be such a tragedy if the same pattern could not be found. Hadn't Veronica asked Santa for new wallpaper?

"Hi, Tom. It's Liz," she said into her phone. "I've just had a brainstorm and, oh, how I hope you can help me with it. Please call me as soon as possible." She reminded him of her home phone number and announced her new cell phone number, too.

Next, she phoned Olga Swenson's residence, only to be greeted by an answering machine message there, too.

"Mrs. Swenson, it's Liz calling," she told the machine, adding both telephone numbers. "I told you I would do my best about Veronica's wallpaper and I have an idea to share with you. Please phone me at your first convenience."

As she was about to hang up, a male voice broke in on the line. It was Erik Johansson. "I'm afraid my mother-in-law is quite upset," he said. "She told me you spent some time with her this afternoon, but little more than that."

"Did she tell you about Ellen's reading list?"

"A reading list? No. What about it? She seemed most overcome by the wallpaper stripping. I felt remiss that I didn't forewarn her about the room. I never thought she'd stop by like that before I could mention it. The police said there was a report in the paper that Veronica was desperate to change her wallpaper so they came to inspect it. When they didn't find any rude words scrawled upon it or blood smears or whatever else they hoped to find, they took the next step and stripped it to see what was underneath."

"Please don't hang up when I tell you this: I have to admit, that was my report—from the time when Veronica was evaluating the Santas—that called attention to the wallpaper. I reported that she asked the seventh Santa for new wallpaper because she'd already asked the other six for every toy on her wish list. It was a cute remark, nothing more, nothing less."

"Unless there was something under the wallpaper."

Rosemary Herbert

"Was there?"

"The police thought so."

"What was it?"

They wouldn't tell me, but whatever it was caused them to haul me into the station for another hour of inquisition."

"I'm so sorry to hear that. What was the nature of their questions?"

"Are you sorry? Really? At this point, I don't know what to think about you or about anyone else for that matter. Olga almost had me convinced you were an ally in finding my wife, and then she comes home utterly distraught after spending time in your company. Now you admit you're the cause of the wallpaper fiasco."

"Please, Erik, allow me at least to lighten your load about the wallpaper problem. As you already realize, a large part of Mrs. Swenson's agitation today has to do with the destruction of your daughter's bedroom. It's bad enough that the room has been wrecked, but then, at first glance, the fact that the paper pattern may not be available makes things even worse. But the key point is Veronica *wanted* Santa to bring her new wallpaper. Don't you see, if the wallpaper is changed, she will believe it was Santa's work!"

"How would I know what paper she would like? And Veronica is going to be home in two days. Who would hang paper on New Year's Eve Day or, worse yet, New Year's Day itself, with no advance warning, in time for my daughter's return home?"

"I can't promise anything, but please trust that I'm working on it. In the meantime, Mrs. Swenson might be a terrific help, in one regard. Do you think you could ask her if I'm correct in assuming Veronica is a fan of Wilbur, the pig, in the book *Charlotte's Web*?"

"I don't need to ask her. I know the answer to that one. That is the book my wife was reading to Veronica before Ellen disappeared. Veronica fell in love with Wilbur. She made Ellen read the book to her three times."

"I know it's a long shot, but please allow me to see if we can find *Charlotte's Web* wallpaper and one of Santa's elves to hang it for your very special little girl."

"Spare no expense. It's an inspired idea."

Chapter 18

L iz was a full twenty minutes late for her appointment with the DYS girls. Since the photographer had arrived, shot pictures, and left, Liz was left with the task of coaxing good quotes from the girls the photographer had chosen to focus in upon. It was often the case, Liz knew, that a striking face was a poor indicator of its owner's talent with words. With females, especially, a less-than-stunning appearance was often a better predictor of verbal skills. With this in mind, and preoccupied with the more pressing desire to advance the Johansson investigation, Liz labored to appear enthusiastic about her subject. But then a young woman named LaShandra Washington called her on it.

"Look. Do you care about talkin' wit' us or not? We been waitin' on you to get your ass over here so we could tell you something that *matters*. You get what I'm sayin'?"

"You're being blunt with me, so I'll be straight with you. I've got a little girl missing her mother, who disappeared from Newton last week."

"Boo *hoo*! We should care about some white-bread kid from a perfect home that turns out to be not so perfect? Some people know all about things that *never* gonna be perfect. But you people in the press, you never get it, do you? This is where the real stories are, in us kids whose moms is *always* missin'."

Liz looked LaShandra in the eye. "You have a point, LaShandra," she said. "So what do you do about that? How do *you* keep going?"

"Not by making smart-ass New Year's resolutions, I can tell you."

"That's right," a couple of other girls chorused.

"Then how?"

"By kickin' ass and tellin' it like it is, that's how!"

"Kickin' ass about what kinds of things?"

"Abuse, for one thing," LaShandra said. "Sex-u-al, verbal, e-mo-*tional* abuse. Abuse in every flavor. You mess with *me*, I kick your ass."

"That's right," the girls chorused again.

What about telling it like it is? Who do you tell?"

"Depends on what you're tellin'. If your daddy mess wit' you, you don't go runnin' to him, 'cept to tell him to go fuck his*self.*"

"That's right!"

LaShandra dropped her eyes and softened her tone. "I might tell Father James somethin' like that. Get him to restrict the old man's visits, you know what I mean?"

"That sounds like a good idea. It also sounds like it would take courage," Liz said.

LaShandra paused. "It takes that. Yeah, you need courage. But you also need re*solve*. That's it. Some things you can't fix with one of your New Year's resolutions. You got to have re*solve.*"

Thanking her lucky stars that the photographer chose LaShandra as one of his subjects, Liz spoke with a few of the other girls, two of whom she recognized as contributors to the making of her afghan. On impulse, she took from her wallet a photo of Prudence preening herself on the afghan and gave it to them. Rough and tough as they were on the surface, they all dissolved into oohs and ahs as they passed the photo to one another. Only one of them seemed unmoved by the cat photo: a scrawny teen called Eleanor, a name that seemed far too big and old-fashioned for her. Liz made a mental note to seek out the reserved girl for a future report.

Saying her good-byes to the young women and to Father James, Liz knew time was tight, lines were up, and Dermott McCann would be on the warpath when she arrived late. Thanks to the cell phone, she was able to call and say she was on her way in. But that didn't do a thing to take the sting out of city editor's wrath.

"Where the hell 've you been, Higgins?" the city editor demanded as soon as Liz approached his desk. "How are we supposed to get a paper out when we don't know what you've dug up for us till after lines are up? Was it so difficult to come up with a freakin' New Year's resolution piece with a whole day to spare?"

"I've got that and more, Dermott. I managed to get inside the Johansson house with the missing woman's mother. The police have stripped . . ."

"Yeah, yeah, yeah. What else is new?" He pointed to the television screen mounted above his head, over the city desk. Its volume was low, but the picture was clear. Standing in front of the Johansson house was Channel Six newsman George Sanders, expounding on the wallpaper stripping.

"I hope, at least, you got a good look at the clue on the wall."

"What clue?"

"I wish to hell I knew. Police aren't saying. Hell, Higgins, you better wish *you* knew. You mean to tell me you were inside the house, inside the *bedroom*, and you didn't see it?"

"I saw a completely stripped room. No, I take that back. *Three* walls were stripped completely. The fourth was only partially stripped."

"Christ almighty, Higgins! Are you telling me you didn't take a good look at that number-four wall? And why the hell didn't you call for a photographer? *Say* something! Don't just give me those puppy-dog eyes! Get the hell to your desk and file that New Year's resolution story. I hope at least you're good for eight inches on that!"

As she wrote the story, Liz felt utterly deflated. It is a reality of the media wars that television journalists have a huge advantage over daily newspaper reporters. TV types could break news the same day as it happened, instead of delivering it the next morning. But Liz had lost more than the scoop here. If she had been on the ball, she literally would have gotten the inside story and had more to report than the television people did, even if it appeared in the next day's paper.

Instead, she'd let her emotions get in the way of doing her job. No matter how much her heart went out to Olga Swenson, she did the woman no service by holding her hands instead of getting to the bottom of the mystery. Dick Manning had a point when he warned her it's not a good idea to get emotionally involved with the people you meet in the course of reporting.

And would she heed this advice tonight, Liz wondered, when dining someplace "rather special" with Cormac Kinnaird? Much would depend on the unpredictable mood of the good doctor.

Although the clock was ticking towards her rendezvous with Cormac, she took the time to search the telephone database for Harmony Haven, Clifford Buxton, and Ali Abdulhazar. Finding the music teacher was as simple as whistling a happy tune. A Buxton, Clifford, was listed as residing on Liszt Lane in Bourne, Massachusetts. The street was probably one of several that composed a housing development known as Harmony Haven. But finding Ali was not so easy. Liz learned quickly that Arabic names are spelled with numerous variations, some phonetic and others reflecting the linguistic influences of those who militarily occupied, governed, or culturally influenced parts of the Arab world. Thus, Abdul might also be spelled in the French manner, Abdoul. And then there was the punctuation problem, which presented more variations, including Ab'dul and Abd'ul. Combine this with the rest of Ali's last name and you had to search through variations such as Ab'dulhazar, Ab'dul-hazar, Abdoulhazar, Abdoul-hazar, and more. Add to this the fact that Ali is an extremely common Arab name, and Liz came up with hundreds of possibilities. Narrowing the search by age still left her with eaighty-six possibilities in eastern Massachusetts alone, and Liz did not know if it was reasonable to assume Ali had remained in the area.

If she were going to make her date with Cormac, she would have to pursue this further tomorrow, so she gathered her things and prepared to leave the newsroom. Back at her desk, she noticed the light blinking on her phone, indicating a call had come in. Picking it up, she heard a recorded message from the Cape Cod Mayhew. "Hey, it's Doug Mayhew again. You planning to cover my band's gig or not?" the voice demanded. Then he changed his tone. "I sure hope so," he said.

Ah, the power of the press to raise—and shatter—hopes! Thinking of her promise to Veronica that she would find the child's mother, Liz returned to the database in the *Banner*'s library and expanded her search to business listings starting with the words "Ali," "Ali's," "Ali Abdulhazar," and "Abdulhazar's." This gave her hundreds more listings, but one was more promising than the rest. The owner of Ali's Music Shack in Randolph, Massachusetts, might be the same Ali who appeared on the list she'd narrowed to Abdulhazars of the correct age group, with a home telephone number listed in Randolph.

Watching the clock, Liz gave Dr. Mayhew a quick call and learned he had no recollection of where Ali's family had resided. He told her Randolph did not ring a bell but it was not impossible that Ali grew up there. He promised to see if he could find Ali's address record, but given that it was amongst the disorganized stacks of papers in his living room, that might take some time.

A call to Ali's Music Shack produced nothing but a recorded message indicating the store was closed until tomorrow. It did not invite a message. There was a message machine on the home number, though. The trouble was, the message was spoken in Arabic. Liz decided it would be better to keep trying the number until someone answered directly than to leave a message on that line. After all this she decided she simply did not have time to call the Buxton number.

Back at Gravesend Street, Liz struggled to shake the feeling of failure and frustration that had settled over her, and found herself looking at her wardrobe with an air of uncertainty, too. A reporter's business dress was, on the whole, far more casual than corporate style. There was rarely a call for office wear that could also serve as evening attire in a pinch. A skirt and silk blouse were about as dressy as Liz got in the course of her job. She did possess one business suit, but it screamed "office," not "dinner date." That left her with the choice between a black cocktail dress with spaghetti straps, a teal-green wool sheath, and a longer black velvet number with a rather deep V neck. Rejecting the cocktail dress as too skimpy for the season and the black velvet as too daring for the weeknight occasion, she selected the sheath. The color was not currently in fashion, but it did set off her auburn hair to good advantage. And the cut of the dress flattered her figure. Considering she did not possess a long dress coat, the street-length dress would also look better than the others with the lined raincoat she planned to wear over it. Fortunately, there was no need to wear boots—the recent rain had washed away most of the snow in the city—since none of hers would look right with this outfit. Sheer stockings and a pair of heels would look fine with both raincoat and dress.

As Liz laid out her clothes and then stepped into the shower, it seemed both strange and inappropriate that such considerations could matter so much at a time like this. Here she was, taking time to dress up for a date while Ellen Johansson might never have the opportunity to fuss over her clothing choice again. And that raised the question of what Ellen had been wearing when she went missing. Had anyone reported on that? Certainly, Liz had not. She made a mental note to find out.

As she shampooed her hair, Liz's thoughts strayed to Cormac. What kind of humor would he be in? Smiling at the thought of the dresses she had rejected, she almost laughed to think of how awful it would be to show up in an alluring outfit, only to have Cormac confine his conversation to forensics, or worse, to speak hardly at all, or ogle some other woman. He was an enigma; that was certain. Still, Liz reflected as she toweled herself dry, it would, after all, be useful if Cormac had something to report about the forensics.

Since she had skipped lunch, Liz made herself an English muffin and ate it as she dried her hair and applied makeup. She followed it with a few slices of Swiss cheese. It would not do to have a predinner drink on an empty stomach. Although she often ate lightly out of necessity, her appetite was a healthy one. She had no fear the snack would spoil it.

After her hair was dry, she slipped into her dress, put on her pearl earrings and pendant, and transferred some items from her large purse into a smaller, dressier clutch. The cell phone bulged in it, but there was no time to fuss any further, so after setting down some food for Prudence, she hurried out to her car.

It was no surprise, on a day like this, that she was settled in the driver's seat before she realized she'd forgotten something. With a large sigh of frustration, she rushed back to the house and rummaged through the mail and other items on her coffee table until she found the thin, gift-wrapped packages of guitar strings tied up with a gold ribbon, and slipped them into her purse.

As always, parking in Harvard Square was a nightmare. This time, it felt like one of those bad dreams where you cannot achieve some time-sensitive goal thanks to everything moving in slow motion. Liz circled the area for fifteen minutes before finding a parking spot alongside the quirky building that housed a used bookshop and the *Harvard Lampoon*. Sitting on its own island in the road, the brick edifice sported a small dome and some club flags, which flapped in the same stiff breeze whipping up from the Charles River, wreaking havoc with Liz's hair.

Late and disheveled, Liz walked as fast as she could in her heels over the uneven brick sidewalks. Built of the same kind of bricks that were used in most of Harvard's classic architecture, the sidewalks added charm to the area around Harvard Square, even if they caused a good number of falls and twisted ankles. As she neared the building owned by Harvard's Hasty Pudding Club, Liz slowed her pace to catch her breath, but that effort was wasted since the well-named restaurant, Upstairs at the Pudding, was located at the top of two steep staircases. By the time she'd scaled them, Liz felt not just windswept but winded.

Given the circumstances, the music she heard performed on a piano there seemed ill-chosen in the extreme: Rodgers and Hammerstein's "It Might as Well Be Spring." Across a room filled with candlelit tables, Liz saw Cormac Kinnaird gazing at her as she gave the hostess her raincoat and then crossed the room to him.

"I'm as jumpy as a puppet on a string," he said, "but now that you're here, it might as well be—" He looked up at a waiter who appeared at that moment. Then he said to Liz, "How was your day? Should we celebrate it with champagne or recover from it with something that will warm the cockles?"

"The latter, I think."

The doctor ordered. "We'd each like a dram of Lagavulin, straight up, in a brandy snifter, please."

Liz took a moment to visit the ladies' room where, as she tamed her auburn mane, she noticed her wind-burned cheeks made her look like she was blushing deeply. When she returned to the table, Cormac told her, "That was unnecessary. You looked fine with a little wind in your hair."

"And now?"

He took the opportunity to look her over slowly before delivering his verdict. "Just as fine." He raised his glass, "Here's looking at you."

Wearing an expression composed of congratulations—and some dismay—over the realization that he'd delivered the overused line with the panache of a practiced lady-killer, Liz raised her snifter in the air between them and took a sip. Meanwhile, the pianist launched into a jazzy rendition of "I've Got the World on a String."

"That says it all for me today," Cormac said waving his drink slightly in the direction of the pianist. "Some success at work and now a lovely dining companion."

As she perused the sophisticated menu, Liz remarked, "It all looks so delicious that you could almost close your eyes and point blindly to any dish on it, assured you'd have a wonderful meal."

"Then, shall I order for you?" Without waiting for a reply, he told the waiter, "The lady will have an order of brook trout encrusted with hazelnuts accompanied by stir-fried watercress and the roasted root vegetable julienne."

The waiter nodded and took down the order carefully.

"Or perhaps she'll have an order of lamb and prune cassoulet with couscous and baby carrots," the doctor said.

"I don't understand," the waiter said, looking at Liz.

"We'll choose our wine after we decide who's eating which meal," Cormac explained.

"Yes, sir," the waiter said doubtfully, winking at Liz.

"Now we have a delicious subject for debate until the dinner is delivered," Cormac said.

As they discussed the merits of trout and lamb, it occurred to Liz that her dining companion had not called her by name since she had arrived at the restaurant. She might be any reasonably attractive "lady" keeping company with the doctor. And when he took her in with his cool blue eyes, she was quite aware he'd done the same with the redhead in Tir Na Nog. As she finished her Scotch, she decided he might rely on other men's lines, but at least he did so in a manner that made them his own. Certainly, the music—now the pianist was playing Gershwin's "Embraceable You"—and the attention were intensely pleasant. By the time their dinners were served, she'd decided on the heartier meal and red wine, while he seemed pleased to take the fish and a glass of Riesling.

Seeing her pleasure in the music, he asked her if she played an instrument or sang herself. She admitted she once dreamt of becoming a cabaret singer. Instead of running with that revelation, he said he'd once studied violin, with little success.

"To hear me play it, you would never have thought I had a musical bone in my body," he admitted. "It's only thanks to a lucky chance that I found my way to world of Irish music—a woman I knew urged me to attend some of the sessions at Tir Na Nog—and now it gives me so much pleasure."

"Was that the singer we heard last week?"

"Yes, she's the one."

"It appeared you'd known her for a long time."

"What gave you that impression? No, not really. Say, didn't we decide earlier today that you would tell me about your day over dinner?"

As the two tucked into their meals, Cormac gave his attention to Liz's account of the ups and many downs of her day. "I'm impressed at all the balls you seem to have in the air," he said. "That is often the case for me, too, but at least I'm not sent out on fool's errands like that New Year's resolution goose chase."

"You know, it's not as foolish an errand as it first appears, Cormac," Liz said. "Yes, I'd love to have been trusted to handle a more obviously important assignment, especially breaking news. And in the context of longing to devote all my attention to Ellen Johansson's disappearance, it was intensely frustrating to have to interview those girls today. But I took away some real insights from what one girl told me, which I shared with our readers in my story. Even if those words do not change one moment of any other reader's life, the fact that they are reported will have an impact on the girls I quoted, who may have some pride as a result and, perhaps, one day use the article to support a job or college application. In addition, it's good for the Department of Youth Services to have such good press. It might be useful when funding time comes around, and, God knows, those girls need all the assets they can get. It's also good for the *Banner* to be a force in the community."

"I wouldn't have thought of all that. What you say makes me reconsider my attitude towards lifestyle pieces."

"There's no doubt there's much more bang in breaking news—and there's no doubt I'd rather cover it—but I like to think soft news has its own kind of impact," Liz said, pausing to savor the cassoulet. "This is wonderful," she enthused. She told Cormac about the afghan made by the DYS crocheting group. "Often when I'm frustrated about covering the community news beat, I feel better about it at the end of the day when I cover up with that afghan. It reminds me that what I do is important to somebody. In fact, it was that beat that brought me in contact with Ellen and Veronica in the first place." Liz filled in the details of the Santa and Newton City Hall hora assignments for Cormac, explaining how her report caused the wallpaper stripping and admitting she didn't examine the walls when she had a chance because she was too busy comforting Olga.

"Is it a good idea for you to become so personally involved with your sources? Of course in my forensics work, I must guard against emotional involvement. It would ruin my judgment, I'm sure."

"Well, you're right, of course. I blew it today because I was too concerned with Olga Swenson's emotional state. But it is hard, for me, at least, to separate passion for my work from passion for its 'sources,' as you call them."

"Well, if I may be considered one of your sources, does that mean you have some passion for me?"

"Ah, that depends upon many factors. Which makes me wonder, have you any news for me?"

"Not at the dinner table, my dear. Say, how about taking a look at the dessert menu? Please don't behave like all women and say you 'can't possibly.'"

"I wasn't planning to," Liz said, drinking the last of her wine.

"This time, you order for us. Don't worry, I could happily consume anything on the menu."

Liz passed over the light sorbets and flan in favor of a slice of bourbon and pecan pie and a chocolate sponge cake. "Complementary flavors, so we might share them," she said after she ordered.

Cormac ordered two more drams of single malt whisky. "Unlike the Lagavulin we consumed earlier, which, I'm sure you noticed, had a smoky, malt taste, the Macallan we are about to imbibe is a sweeter affair, with strong hints of vanilla and spice," he instructed Liz, with the air of a bon vivant.

"You spoke of remaining detached in your work. Do you ever worry that it carries over into the rest of your life?"

Cormac considered the candlelight that shone through his drink. "Touché," he said, lifting his drink to his lips.

"Good fencing makes good neighbors," Liz parried.

"I get your thrust. Or perhaps that should be *your* line."

"Hah! Do you dare risk the unkindest cut of all?"

"A woman's scorn? Not when I can cut and run at will."

Liz looked Cormac straight in the eyes. "I wonder—" she began.

"What's in this package?" Cormac finished for her, taking a gift-wrapped box from his inside jacket pocket. "The contents might be pretty to the eye of one beholder. Now, don't say, 'You shouldn't have!'"

"I wasn't planning to," Liz said again.

While the pianist played "A Foggy Day," she carefully untied the golden cloth ribbon and undid the thick wrapping paper, patterned in burgundy and cream swirls reminiscent of an old volume's endpapers. The box might have contained a bracelet or perhaps a necklace, but Cormac's choice was more original than that. The present was a Montblanc fountain pen.

"Oh, golly!"

"For the writer in my life," he said, reaching across the table to place his hand over hers.

"For the musician in mine," Liz said after a moment, taking the four little packets from her purse and passing them across the table to him.

For the first time that evening, Cormac Kinnaird displayed his true, boyish smile as—feeling with his fingers the coiled wires through the gift wrap—he realized what the packets contained. Looking up at her, and intently, if briefly, meeting her eyes, he said just two words.

"Oh, Liz!"

Then, as quickly as his eyes shied away from hers, he seemed to lose his urbane air in favor of his familiar taciturnity.

Jekyll and Hyde, Liz thought, and requested an espresso.

Only when the coffee came did Liz dare to ask about the forensic news again. At this juncture, the doctor grasped at her question as a conversational lifesaver.

"I am the bearer of some significant news," he said, lapsing into formal tones and word choice and speaking softly because of the subject matter. He leaned across the table towards Liz. "We already knew the blood type of the drop of blood found on the poinsettia does not match the blood type reported to be Ellen's in the papers. Nor does it match that of the chief suspect, Erik. But it looks like it does match the blood type of your cabdriver: B-negative."

"Does it match the DNA on the cigarette butts I retrieved from the taxi?"

"No, no, Liz. I think that test should be run, but those results will take at least eleven weeks to come back. I tested the blood I found on a scrap of tissue I found among the cigarette butts. Looks like your guy nicked himself shaving and threw the tissue in the ashtray once he was in the cab."

"That's marvelous news!"

"Not really. If—and remember, it's a big *if*—the scrap of tissue is from your cabbie, it only proves he had the same blood type as the unknown bleeder in Ellen's kitchen. We need the DNA test to prove it was the same person. For that, we can test the blood on the tissue and the saliva on the cigarette butts, too. But, as I said, that will take about eleven weeks."

"Eleven weeks? It takes that long? That's awful!"

"Actually, that's extraordinarily quick. For the police, it ordinarily takes a few months. We have an advantage in that I can run the samples in a teaching lab and don't have to wait in a line for priority."

"Wouldn't this high-priority case take precedence for the police, too?"

"Yes, and no. The violence in Ellen Johansson's kitchen suggests foul play, but if she's dead, her life is not on the line. Police labs are also at work on testing samples from death row inmates. It's usually the case that there's a bit of a backup in police labs."

"I don't like relying on a lead time of only a week or so. Fortunately, I wasn't planning to give them the information at this stage anyway." Liz set down her espresso and picked up her unfinished single malt. Raising it to her companion she took a long sip, and then blew Cormac Kinnaird a kiss across the small table.

Cormac's response was steely. "You know, you should report what you know to the police, Liz. Failure to turn over evidence that one knows might be useful to the solution of a case amounts to obstruction of justice."

"But we don't know if it's important until we get back the results. Surely, we don't have to share this information until we know if it is significant."

"That sounds like a good argument to the layperson, but are you willing to put that to test in court? You'd be up for a seven-to-fourteen–year prison sentence. And even if you got off on some remarkable technicality, no police department would ever be willing to work with you again. That would spell disaster for your career."

"Not to mention yours. Oh, Cormac, I don't want to hand this over to the police at this point."

"But you do want to know what happened to Ellen?"

"Of course, but I want to know *first*, before anybody else. Do you think the police would share information with me first if I hand over the cigarette butts?"

"You *are* green at hard news reporting, aren't you? They might, but I wouldn't count on it. Even your having the poinsettia in your possession is enough to get you in trouble. The only thing that keeps you from being in hot water on that one is that Erik apparently gave it to the aftercare teacher. I'll be interested to learn why it was not sprayed with luminol by the police. I'm afraid, Liz, you'll have to count on our advantage in getting DNA results back from the teaching lab."

Avoiding Liz's eyes, he signaled the waiter for the check, paid it with a flourish, and led Liz to the coatroom. There, he helped her into her raincoat, and allowed his hand to linger on her back as he escorted her down the stairs. On the lower landing, he pulled her around to face him and surprised her with a lingering kiss. Then, taking her hand, he led her into the cold and blustery night.

As the pair rounded the corner onto Mt. Auburn Street, Liz's cell phone interrupted their progress—in every sense of the word—with a piercing ring.

"I'm so sorry, but I think I should answer it. It might be Olga or Erik."

But it wasn't.

"Tom!" Liz exclaimed.

"I know it's late but you seemed so desperate to hear from me," Cormac heard Tom's voice say, as he leaned closer to Liz.

"I'm outside and it's freezing. Will you be findable mid-morning tomorrow?" Liz asked.

"I can be at your door at dawn if you like—or earlier," Tom said. "But I have a billboard to hang. So I'll have to leave by about 10:00 a.m."

"Tell him you'll be there," Cormac said, revealing he'd heard it all. "I won't darken your door tonight. I'm shattered."

Chapter 19

"It's not a *Banner* day," Liz told Prudence when the cat nudged her awake on December 27. As she turned over in bed, she realized she had a mild headache. Since she was not scheduled to work, the day was hers, to use as she liked. That meant she could lie in bed, at least for a little while, and nurse her headache while speculating on its source. Did it stem from too much single malt and wine? Did it result from the fact that she'd have to turn over her ace in the hole to the police? Or was it founded on frustration with Cormac Kinnaird's mixed signals?

Then again, if this was a tension headache, it might have a much more profound cause. After all, now Liz felt convinced that the New York City cabdriver had visited—and been injured in—Ellen's kitchen. And, she reminded herself, Ellen had been injured, too, as was certain from the blood found on the cookie ingredients. If she turned over the evidence to the police, the discovery she had hesitated to reveal would land her a scoop. But Kinnaird still had the bag of evidence. She wouldn't let on to the city desk until late afternoon. That would leave her free to find Cormac, follow up on some lines of inquiry, and look for Veronica's new wallpaper, too, if time allowed.

With all this in mind, Liz decided not to catch a few more winks, even though it was 6:00 a.m. Instead, she got up and threw on some jeans and a turtleneck, boots, and a jacket, and drove to Rella's Italian Bakery, where she purchased a good-sized square of crumb cake, a loaf of bread, and bacon, eggs, and milk from the dairy case. She also bought copies of the *Banner* and *World* at a newsstand. Back at home by 6:30, she took another half-hour to shower and dry her hair before phoning Tom.

"I hope you meant it when you said you'd like to come over early," she said.

"Course I meant it." Tom's groggy voice was evidence she'd woken him, but he didn't complain.

"I can offer you bacon, eggs, and crumb cake as soon as you can get here."

"Give me three-quarters of an hour."

Next, Liz phoned the Ali Abdulhazar of Randoph, hoping to catch him before the start of the business day. The woman who answered spoke only Arabic. Although Liz could not understand a word she said, the woman's anger came through loudly and unmistakably. Next, Liz phoned Erik Johansson, hoping to catch him before he set off to work. The phone answering machine picked up, this time with a recording of Erik's voice stating, "You have reached the Johansson home. Please leave as long a message as you need to. This machine will not cut you off. If you have information about my wife, Ellen Johansson, be assured I will check this machine frequently."

As Liz began to speak, Erik cut in and said, "You start your work day early! I'm not sure. . ."

"I have important news, Erik, and would like to deliver it in person before I report on it for tomorrow's paper."

"News of Ellen?" The note of desperate hopefulness in his voice was unmistakable.

"If you mean, 'Is there any sign of her?'—no. I'm terribly sorry. But I have a lead about the altercation in the kitchen."

"Can't you tell me about it now?"

"I'd rather tell you in person." Liz hoped Erik would consent to meet at his home where she might convince him to give her a peek into Veronica's room, but he insisted they meet at his workplace at 10:00 a.m.

Next, Liz called Clifford Buxton. Against background jazz, the music teacher's message announced that he and his wife were out of town but would check messages now and then. Liz left one, then filled the coffee maker and laid bacon on her frying pan. By the time Tom arrived ten minutes later, the little house beside the turnpike was filled with the smell of breakfast cooking.

"Coffee smells good," Tom said, wiping his feet on the doormat. "Bacon, too. I sure could use some."

"It'll taste even better with this crumb cake," Liz said, laying out plates and cutlery for two on a tongue of countertop that served as an eating bar. When the eggs were cooked, the pair sat on high stools and dug into the breakfast.

"Do you mind?" Tom said, as he sopped up egg yolk with the crumb cake.

"Not a bit," Liz said, doing the same. As he bent over his plate, Liz noticed with a feeling of tenderness, that Tom's freckled nose was wind-burned. Then she told him about her wallpaper fiasco and the scoop that she'd rather have kept quiet until DNA evidence was available.

"At least the scoop will rescue your reputation at the *Banner*," Tom smiled. "And I think we can rescue Veronica's bedroom situation, too. If we can get our hands on the paper you want, I could hang it over the weekend."

"You realize it's the holiday weekend?"

"Sure. But my heart goes out to that kid. Do you have a *Yellow Pages*?" He circled ads for three wallpaper outlets. "These have the largest stock around. We'll call them first. Let's have the *White Pages* for Boston." Tom flipped through the book. "We'll try this place, too. It's a kids' furniture place really, but it has a small decorating department for upholstery and wallpaper. The paper selection is small, but it's all for kids. Lot of French imported wallpaper, but it's worth a shot. If these places don't have the paper in stock, we can call the warehouse. It'll cost, but the warehouse can send paper by overnight mail if they have it. The important thing is to iden-tify the pattern and the company. I'll have to get in and measure, too."

"I was hoping that would be necessary." Liz cut Tom a second square of crumb cake and poured them both more coffee. "If you meet Erik, don't let on how well we know each other. Let's let him assume you are the first or only decorator who would consent to work on the holiday weekend."

"No problem. I'd give you the *World*, and you know it, Liz," Tom smiled, handing her a copy of the *Banner*'s competing newspaper. "This one's easier to read," Tom winked, opening the tabloid *Banner*. "You got anything in the paypuh today?"

"Yeah, my New Year's resolution piece. Nothing about Ellen, I'm sorry to say. But that doesn't mean Dick Manning hasn't gotten something on the case."

"It's too early to make those calls about the wallpaper, so how about I help you check out these papers? You need more room to spread out that paper. Come on." Tom took her hand and led her to the sofa. Once she was seated, he pushed a footstool in place for Liz's feet, turned on the Christ-mas tree lights, realized the tree needed watering and took care of that, and, finally, topped up their mugs with coffee and delivered them to the coffee table. Settling in next to Liz on the sofa, he patted her thigh before licking his thumb and turning the pages of the *Banner* with an earnest flourish. Smiling at him, Liz realized her headache was old news.

"Hey, I see the Red Sox manager resolves to win the World Series this summer," Tom laughed, reading Jared Conneely's sidebar.

"Hope springs eternal, I guess. Are you a Sox fan?"

"Yeah, sure. But I never know if that means I'm a loyal guy or a loser."

"Not a loser," Liz said, giving him a quick kiss.

"I guess not! Come spring, I'll have to take you out to a ballgame."

"'Buy me some peanuts and Cracker Jack,'" Liz sang and then broke off as the phone rang. Setting aside the *World*, she crossed the room and picked up the phone.

"Liz Higgins? This is Clifford Buxton returning your call. You have a question about my former student Ali Abdulhazar? How may I help you?"

Liz outlined her progress on the case and her reasons for finding Ali.

"I haven't kept in touch with Ali over the years. It's been a long time so there's no telling if this will be helpful, but I do remember Ali took up as an apprentice piano tuner with Jan Van Wormer after he left the alternative school. The kid had a wonderful ear. Perfect pitch. And an aptitude for fixing things. Troubled home life, though, and a speech impediment. No get-up-and-go, no initiative. I don't know if he'd stick with a job for any length of time. Van Wormer was no spring chicken all those years ago. If he's living today, he'll be in his nineties, I'd guess. But he worked out of South Boston back in the 1970s."

"This is very helpful," Liz said, picking up the *Yellow Pages*. "Do you recall anything about Ali getting in hot water with the Swenson family?"

"Those people across the road? I wasn't there the day that happened. I only worked at the Wharton School two days a week. But I was there the next day when Ali was hauled in with his parents before the director, the chairman of our board, and the faculty. Douglas Mayhew—he was the headmaster—let on he wanted to cut the kid some slack. I think he was hoping the board would buy a good explanation accompanied by an abject apology. But Ali always clammed up under pressure—and I had the impression he was terrified of his parents. All he managed to say, with lots of mumbling in Arabic and stuttering on the *d*s was, 'I'm *not* sorry because I duh-duh-duh-didn't duh-duh-duh-do that duh-duh-duh-disgusting thing.' His father shut him up with some sort of command in Arabic before the poor kid could say anything more in his own defense."

"We're in luck!" Liz said. "There's a Van Wormer Piano Workshop listed in the phone book. Thank you for your help."

Before Liz could dial the number, the phone rang again.

"I am speaking with Mizz Higgins?" an Indian-accented voice asked.

"Yes."

"I am Ali Kumar, proprietor of Ali's Music Shack. How may I be of service?"

So, the owner of Ali's Music Shack was not the right man. On the off chance that the shop owner knew Ali Abdulhazar of Randolph, Liz inquired about this, only to have the music man take offense.

"So, you are thinking every person named Ali must know every other person of the same name?" he said angrily. "You should be knowing not every Ali is an Arab!" he added, hanging up.

"Well, well, well," Liz mumbled, as she dialed the piano workshop, only to hear the elderly owner's answering machine message, backed with piano scales. When she tried to leave a message, she found the voice mail was full. She added the piano man's South Boston address to a reporter's note-book labeled "Johansson Contacts." The same notebook also held the phone number of the taxi garage in New York City. Liz was in better luck calling that number, as Jake's unmistakable voice came on the line. Liz asked if his driver, Samir Hasan, had shown up.

"Nah! Hasan's still AWOL," he said. "Sonovabitch. Hey, listen, I got my hands full here. Hang on a minute."

Liz heard him harangue a driver for being late.

"The reporter at work," Tom said, standing up and delivering her coffee mug to her. He pointed to the clock, gave her a kiss on the top of her head, and said, "I've got a job to go to. I'll make those calls about the wallpaper. You have enough to do. I'll call you later."

"I got a helluva lot to do here," Jake complained over the line. "But I took my valuable time to drive to the Brooklyn address he gave me. I already knew it was a wild goose chase, but I had to be sure. Street is there but the house numbers stop at 249. Hasan listed his address as number 270."

Liz blew a kiss to Tom as he left and asked Jake a few more questions about how long Hasan had worked for him and about the driver's work habits, scribbling all the while in her notebook. Hanging up and slapping the notebook shut, she remembered she had not phoned Florissa's Gift Emporium, so she found the number and made the call, only to have the manager confirm that she'd sold a teacup and saucer manufactured by Royal Doulton on the day in question. The manager could not identify the specific china pattern. Disappointed, Liz collected the breakfast dishes, ran water over them in the sink, put out dry food and fresh water for Prudence, and turned off the Christmas tree lights.

Snow was falling as Liz made her way to the offices of Environmental Solutions in Lexington. Housed in a brown-stained, wood-shingled building, the offices were fronted by an unusual parking lot, pocked here and there with small circular grates.

"They're to collect the runoff. Instead of pouring it down the city sewer, for three seasons, at least, we use it in the waterfall you see on that rock face," Erik explained as he showed Liz into the building. "Of course, the waterfall is not in operation during the winter, but the rest of the year it serves to aerate and help purify the water before we siphon some off to our various projects."

"Such as?"

"We're working on designing eco-friendly dishwashers and clothes washing machines. The water gets used again as we test the prototypes. Saves us plenty on our water bill, I can tell you."

Erik delivered this information with practiced ease, but his eyes told another story. They were heavy with sleeplessness. As soon as Liz was in his office and the door was closed, he urgently asked her, "What is the news you have about blood in my kitchen?"

When she told him the blood type evidence suggested a stranger had been injured there, Erik put his head down on his desk and moaned. Over his sunken shoulders, Liz noticed a family portrait pinned to the wall. It was drawn in crayon and signed "VERONICA" in the awkward printing of a very young child. Labeled with the words, "MOMMY," "DADDY," and "ME," three crayoned figures were drawn holding hands and wearing huge smiles. A slight yellowing of the paper and drawing skills that spoke of a child much younger than Veronica's current age made it clear Veronica had drawn this some years ago.

Erik lifted his head. "My God, Ellen!" he exclaimed, as if to his wife. "What happened to you?" Turning his attention to Liz he said, "I had hoped that second person was someone known to us, not a stranger. I've been praying that she cut herself cooking, that she wasn't attacked! Who would have done this?"

"I have to tell you, Erik, we know whose blood it might have been. Do you or Ellen have any connections with a New York taxi driver known as Samir Hasan?"

"Absolutely not. I never heard of the guy. Who is he? What was this guy doing in my kitchen?"

Erik was almost as mystified when Liz told him about Ellen's recent note on Veronica's emergency information card, warning the aftercare teachers not to allow her daughter to take a ride from a taxi driver. "After she came home from meeting her pen pal in New York, she mentioned something about a strange taxi ride," he said. "But at the time I didn't think it was significant. The city is full of kooks. I was more concerned about the fire she escaped in the Windows on the World Restaurant."

Erik filled Liz in on the fire and he added, "I was so relieved that turned out okay that I didn't pay much attention to the calls we received in the middle of the night. I just thought they were prank calls, so I hung up after the third one and turned the phone's ringer down so we wouldn't be bothered by any more of them."

"What did the caller say?"

"Nothing."

"Did Ellen answer any of the calls?"

"No. It's better to have a man answer, don't you think, when the phone rings unexpectedly in the night?"

"Did you often receive annoyance calls?"

"No. I can't remember when we last had any unidentified people call us. So, this was odd, to say the least. I guess because we didn't see ourselves as targets of a nut, we didn't worry. Or, at least, I didn't worry. Now I wish I'd kept the caller on the line, tried to draw him out to say something."

"You did the best you could with the information you had at the time. Have the police turned up any information about the incoming calls?"

"They aren't sharing any information with me. Unfortunately, when a woman goes missing, her husband is the most likely suspect. Before they haul me in on some trumped-up charge, give me a chance to get a hold of that cabbie. What do you know about him? Where can I find him?"

"He's gone missing, too. The last time he was seen was during the day Ellen took a ride in his car. That's why the matching blood type seems significant. But you must remember, it's not conclusive. Until DNA results come back, we cannot be sure it's the same man."

"It's a rare blood type, though, isn't it? And then the cabbie has gone missing? That's enough evidence for me!"

"I think it's significant, too. I know this is awful news. That's why I wanted to tell you in person before I report it in the paper, Erik."

"*And* so you could get a few tidbits out of me for your story, too!" Erik's tone was furious.

"I understand your impulse to blame the messenger of bad news. And I'll do you the service of admitting that everything you tell me is useful to my work. But if you think my goal is to report a story with a tragic ending, you're mistaken. There's tragedy enough here, as you well know. I'd like to make sure there's a positive outcome, Erik. I know and like your wife and I'm very fond of your daughter. I want to see all of you reunited. In the meantime, I'd like to help you make Veronica's return to her bedroom a pleasant surprise. I've located a wallpaper man who is looking for the *Charlotte's Web*-patterned paper and willing to hang it on the holiday weekend for you. He said he will have to get in and measure the room before he can order the paper. Here's his phone number."

"I'll measure it myself and call him. That would save time."

"Whatever you decide, give him a call soon so you can confirm his availability on the weekend."

As Liz walked to her car, she noticed the swiftly falling snow had blanketed the macadam and the water-collecting grates in the Environmental Solutions parking lot. Seated in the Tracer, Liz phoned Tom to tell him about this wrinkle in their plans, but had to leave the message on his answering machine. If he accepted the measurements over the phone from Erik, it would be days before he saw the writing on Veronica's wall.

Passing by the Minuteman Statue on Lexington Green, Liz found herself longing for another cup of coffee so she entered a gingerbread bakery that sported a HOT COFFEE sign in its steamy window. On impulse, Liz purchased a gingerbread man and gingerbread woman festively decorated with raisins, icing, and sprinkles. Her cell phone rang as she carried the bakery box through the snow to her car.

"I'll be measuring Veronica's room at noon," Tom told her.

"How did you manage that? Erik seemed set on doing it himself."

"I told him the truth. I have to measure and make the calculations myself. Even when customers have already bought paper, I won't take on a job without measuring first. I bought a point-and-shoot, throwaway camera, too. I can't guarantee Erik won't stand over me the whole time I'm there, but I'll do my best to get a shot for you."

"Brilliant!"

"Just call me Watson."

"My *dear* Watson."

"That's okay, too. If I can't use the camera, I'll try to draw a copy of whatever's on the wall. I should be out of there by, say, 12:30. Wanna meet for lunch?"

"Absolutely! But not in Newton. Too much chance we'll be overheard by Johansson neighbors. And I don't want to run into Erik and make it clear we're friends."

"I have another job in Newton, so I need to stay in the area, Liz."

Looking at the bakery box, Liz said, "Then how about a picnic in your van? Do you know a place they call the 'Cove'? It's in Newton but not in Erik's neighborhood. I'll meet you there at around 12:40, and I'll bring lunch."

"I know where it is. You'll see my van in the parking lot."

Wading through the slushy snow to her trunk, Liz took out a thermos, returned to the gingerbread bakery, and had it filled with hot coffee. Then she walked down the street to a deli and purchased two turkey sandwiches and dill pickle spikes. With an hour and a half to spare before she was set to meet Tom, Liz returned to her car and tried phoning Jan Van Wormer, only to get his voice-mail message again. She also got a voice-mail recording when she phoned Cormac Kinnaird. She left him a message saying she planned to report on the blood information today and turn in the cigarette butts to the police. She asked him to let her know when and where she could pick up the evidence and reminded him she'd have to tell her editor about the story no later than 3:00 p.m., in time for the afternoon news meeting. She also called René DeZona to be certain he was in, have him fetch a copy of his kitchen photo to use with the blood article, and let him know he might have a front pager if he could chase down Kinnaird and get a photo of him before the afternoon was over.

With this accomplished, Liz spent a full fifty-five minutes driving the seven and a half miles from Lexington to the "Cove" in Newton. The trip took her through well-heeled neighborhoods graced with large nineteenth-century homes; into other, more modest residential areas; and past numerous minimalls, still dolled-up with Christmas lights. Cars coming and going from the minimalls added to the traffic, which was already slowed by the heavy snowfall.

Although the lane leading to the "Cove" was poorly plowed, Liz enjoyed negotiating the hilly stretch, which led to a parking lot, playing field, and large park on the banks of the Charles River. Schoolchildren on vacation added color and activity to the wintry scene, as they pulled one another on sleds in the flat floodplain landscape or rolled huge snowballs and stacked them to build snowmen.

Opening one of her sandwiches, Liz took out two carrot sticks she'd seen the sandwich maker pack in the waxed paper. Stepping out of her car, she gave them to a girl who was making a snowman with her friends.

"We've got two noses!" the girl crowed, brandishing the carrot sticks to prove her point.

Minutes later, Tom pulled his van up beside the Tracer and led Liz to the back doors. Opening them with a flourish, he took out a hard plastic bucket, turned it upside down to make a step, and led Liz into the van. She saw he'd removed a seat, bundled his wallpapering equipment on the remaining bench seat, lined the compartment with a brightly striped Mexican blanket, and set up two more overturned plastic buckets with a board across them as a mini-table. The Beatles tune "Paperback Writer" was playing on his radio.

"You provide the picnic, I provide the picnic spot," he smiled.

Sitting beside Tom with her legs bent to one side, Liz fell into him as she tried to give him a hug. A few minutes of snuggling ensued before the two, with much steamier windows surrounding them, sat up, unwrapped their sandwiches, and poured out coffee.

"I've seen all kinds of things written or drawn on walls underneath wallpaper," Tom began. "Lots of dates with names of wallpapering crews— some cute messages, too. I remember one where some girl wrote, 'Finally, I'm getting new wallpaper for my room.' It's common to see kids' names and ages in kids' rooms. Less often, I see a drawing obviously done by a kid. But until I saw the drawing in Veronica's room, I've never seen anything upsetting on a stripped wall."

"What is in the drawing?"

"It's a drawing of a girl with long hair and her father, flying a kite. I know that, because it says 'DADDY' under the man. But—I almost hate to tell you this—the man has a big penis sticking out from his front."

"Are you sure?"

"I took a picture, so you can see it for yourself."

"Can you draw it for me?"

"I tried to copy it." Tom took a much-folded piece of paper from his pocket and spread it out on the makeshift table.

"Oh, Tom! I'll have to see the photo to be sure, but I think the thing you think looks like a penis is actually a picture of Erik's tie."

"What makes you think that? Why would it be so huge, and why would it stick out like that?"

"I've just come from Erik's office. He has a family portrait taped up, drawn some years ago by Veronica. I couldn't help noticing Veronica drew her dad wearing a huge purple tie. She drew her mother holding an oversized pocketbook, too." Liz scrutinized Tom's drawing. "See the kite in this draw-ing? Maybe she's remembering an outing with her dad on a windy day. The tie blew around in the wind."

Tom looked doubtful. "For Veronica's sake, I hope that's true. But I wouldn't count on it. What kind of guy takes his kid out kite flying dressed in a business suit?"

"I don't know," Liz admitted. "But I do know it's all too easy to vilify the husband when a wife goes missing."

"I think you'd better not get too attached to this family, Liz. You might be disappointed in them."

Liz poured more coffee and opened the bakery box. As she placed the gingerbread man and woman on napkins, she noticed how huge the raisin buttons were in proportion to their icing outfits. But she didn't point this out to Tom. Finishing off the cookies, the two sat side-by-side in silence. Inside the steamy vehicle, the homey blend of gingerbread and coffee fragrances made a sharp contrast with their worries about the Johansson family.

Chapter 20

After the gingerbread was consumed, Tom took Liz's hand and led her back to her car. As he gave her a hug, Liz realized he was never the first to end an embrace. When they broke apart, he added his drawing to a plastic bag containing the point-and-shoot camera and handed the bag to Liz. Taking it, Liz gave Tom a kiss and made sure she was the last to end it before getting into her car.

Thankful the snowfall was less intense, Liz wound her car through deep snow to the well-plowed Massachusetts Turnpike. Her route from Newton to Boston took her past her own little house. The winds of the snowstorm had formed drifts around it. They had also given the billboard—which read, "Maksoud Motors: We always go the extra mile!"—a frosty whitewash. Liz remembered Tom would be changing the billboard's advertisement soon, since Old Man Maksoud had hired the space for end-of-year car sales only. It was only a few days until January 1st.

As was usual during a daytime snowstorm, the *Banner*'s parking lot was a mess. It was nearly impossible for a plow to work there with so many employees' cars to maneuver around. Snow spilled into Liz's boots as she walked from her car to the building. Inside, she shook off her coat and went straight to the photo department. René's broad smile told her he'd snapped Kinnaird and was eager for the front-page placement of that photo.

"The doctor says he'll call you around 4:40," René said taking the point-and-shoot camera Liz handed him. "These things are a bitch to take apart," he said, "but I'll do my best. I'm on overtime in ten minutes. Will I be able to claim the overtime, or am I doing you a favor?"

"Um hm," Liz said, looking into the plastic bag the camera had been in. She saw it contained Tom's drawing *and* an airmail letter addressed to Ellen Johansson, postmarked from Heathrow Airport, London, December 18.

"What do you mean by 'um hm', Liz? Which is it, pictures for a story that will run or another of your speculative ventures?"

"It'll run," Liz said, listening to the radio that was always turned on in the photo department.

"*World* reporter Mick Lichen and Erik Johansson of Newton were both arrested after allegedly assaulting one another at the latter's home today," the announcer said. "According to jogger Sy Eliot, who witnessed the incident, Johansson shook a ladder Lichen was standing on when he discovered the reporter peeking into his daughter's bedroom. The reporter fell to the ground, breaking his left leg in the process. But that didn't stop Lichen from striking out at Johansson. According to Eliot, Lichen wrapped his arms around Johansson's leg, causing him to fall to the ground. Erik Johansson is the husband of Ellen Johansson, the librarian who went missing from her Newton home December 18. The incident raises the question of how far a reporter may go to get his story. Even before he dragged Johansson to the ground, was Mick Lichen a law-breaking trespasser and voyeur, or was he a professional going the extra mile to get a job done? For analysis, tune in tonight at ten to WLTR's *Letter of the Law* program."

Certain the *World* would report on what Lichen saw, Liz knew she had two stories on her hands, and it wasn't even an official day at work for her. Looking at the clock, she decided to postpone conferring with Dermott McCann. If she told him about the blood types and the drawing on Veronica's wall, he would surely put another reporter on one of the stories. She wanted them both. Not only that, but she was the only one who had a hope of speaking with Veronica herself to find out about the kite-flying episode. With the news meeting that would decide what stories would be given precedence in the paper just two and a half hours away, Liz decided to take a chance on covering both. Heading down the ink-stained hallway to her car, she phoned Olga Swenson and told her she wanted to see her in advance of reporting some important news. Naturally agitated after learning of her son-in-law's arrest, the older woman nonetheless consented to see Liz at her Wellesley home and gave her driving directions to the place.

Back in the Tracer, Liz headed west on the Massachusetts Turnpike, listening to news radio as she drove. The back of her billboard was still lit with "MERRY XMAS LIZ" spelled out in lights. Allowing herself a fleeting smile, she listened carefully as the radio announcer reported more breaking news in the Johansson case.

"'We have evidence two people were injured in Ellen Johansson's kitchen,' Newton police chief Anthony Warner told WLTR-News today. Two days after the Newton librarian and mother of one went missing, leaving bloodstained cookie-making ingredients on her kitchen counter, police confirmed the blood belonged to the missing woman herself. Now, Warner revealed, analysis of swabs taken from the kitchen floor area indicates another, unknown person was also injured in that kitchen."

"Shit!" Liz exclaimed, thinking she'd lost her scoop. But then she realized WLTR did not have the whole story. Only she and Kinnaird knew the probable identity of the second injured party. She had to believe the doctor would not share his information until she reported it and turned in the cigarette butts to the police. Still, the timing of the WLTR report was a disaster in the making for her. As soon as she got off the turnpike onto Route 16, she pulled over and phoned the city desk.

"I know who the unidentified bleeder may be," she told Dermott McCann without preamble.

"Then where the hell are you? I realize it's your day off, Higgins, but were you waiting to be back on the clock tomorrow to tell me?"

"What do you think?" Liz shot back. "Ask DeZona if you want proof I've been on this all day."

"Since when do you report to DeZona?"

"Look, Dermott, I don't have time to argue with you. Just trust me on this one. While I verify one more piece of information, save me a four-inch front page story with a twenty-two-inch jump and a front page teaser for a ten-inch piece on Page Three."

"Who the hell are you to tell me . . ."

"Liz Higgins, star reporter, if you want to know. I'll see you in about an hour and a half."

Liz pushed the button to cut the call on her cell phone and drove on to the Swenson residence. Thanking Providence, she caught sight of Veronica playing in the yard before she reached the house. Turning off her headlights and parking her car out of view of the house, she approached the child on foot.

When she saw Liz, Veronica flew to the reporter. "Did you do it? Did you find my mommy?" she asked.

"Not yet, Veronica, but once again, you can be a big help."

"I can?"

"Absolutely."

"Don't you need your detective pad?"

"I've got it right here," Liz said, looking around as she pulled the note-book from her bag. "Oh, Veronica. I see you've made a super snow fort. It would also make a great private eye office, if you lived in the North Pole."

Veronica smiled. "Let me show it to you."

Sitting on a block of snow that served as a chair, Liz took out a pencil and held it poised over a new notebook page. "You should hang a few pictures in your fort, Veronica. Your daddy showed me a great one you drew of your family that he has hanging in his office."

"That's a *baby* picture!" Veronica said disdainfully. "It's not very good. I drew that when I was *little*!"

"In first grade?"

"No. That was in kindergarten. I remember because we only got one box of crayons then. I used up my purple crayon before Thanksgiving and I couldn't have another one."

"You must like the color purple!"

"Oh yes. It's my favorite color, still!"

"In that picture your dad has in his office, you drew a purple tie on your daddy."

"That's because I love purple and I love my daddy. When I was little, I always used to draw him with a tie. You wanna know why? Because he used to let me pick the tie for him to wear every morning."

"*Every* day! Wow! You were such a good help to your dad. Some dads like to wear something different on weekends. Does your daddy usually wear a tie even when he's not at work?"

"No, Liz. He hardly *ever* wears a tie when he's raking leaves or things like that."

"What about if you do something fun together, like flying a kite? Would he wear his tie then?"

"One time he did wear a tie when we flew my kite. It was my purple kite!"

"Were you in kindergarten then?"

"I don't know. I remember it was funny, though. My Daddy was trying to run with the kite and his tie kept hitting him in the face."

"It must have been very windy!"

"Yes, it was!"

"Veronica, I hear you have Madeline wallpaper in your bedroom. Is that right?"

"Yes, but I'm tired of it."

"Do you remember if you were in kindergarten when it was put in your room?"

"Maybe. My mommy let me write on the wall. That was so cool."

"She was in kindergarten then," Olga Swenson interrupted. "Why are you sitting outside in the cold?"

"I was showing her my private eye . . . ," Veronica began.

"Her private, fully furnished snow castle!" Liz interrupted. "Do you know, my mother used to let me put candles in my snow forts. I could never, *ever* light candles in the house, but my mother used to light some for me in my snow forts."

"Don't give the child ideas!" Olga snapped. "Indoors or out, she might get burned." Olga hustled everyone inside. After she'd settled Veronica with hot chocolate in the den, she listened as Liz explained the blood evidence she planned to report on.

"No, I never heard Ellen talk about a taxi driver. It must be some madman. Do you think he harmed my daughter?" Grasping at straws, Olga added, "That blood they found—do they know how long it was there? Maybe someone got hurt while they were investigating the scene."

This line of conversation came to a dead stop as Veronica flew into the room announcing, "They arrested my daddy!!"

"I *told* you to watch the video, not the regular television!" Olga scolded, then changed her tone. "Oh, dear Veronica, forgive me for scolding you. It's just that I knew the police were asking your daddy questions and I wanted him to tell you about that himself. They only want him to help them find your mommy."

"But they said the police *arrested* him! When people get arrested, they go to jail! Everybody knows that!"

"Please, Liz, allow me to talk with my granddaughter," Olga said, nodding her head in the direction of the door.

"Of course. I'll let myself out," Liz said. "Goodnight." Looking over her shoulder she saw that Olga's eyes were haunted, red from crying, but she mustered a soothing voice on her granddaughter's behalf.

"Sometimes the reporters get it wrong," she heard Olga tell Veronica. "The police can come and drive someone in their car to their station to help them. That's not the same thing as being arrested."

Walking to her car, Liz thought honesty would be a better policy, but she could not fault a loving grandmother for cushioning her grandchild from these harsh realities. Before making her drive, she phoned Lucy Gray at the library and asked her if Ellen had any old drawings by Veronica pinned up at her desk. Lucy said she did, and verified that one portrayed Erik wearing an outsized tie. Lucy promised to meet Liz at the library door with the drawing.

The rush-hour traffic was terrible, but Liz made it to the library and then the newsroom by 5:30. Lines had been up for well over an hour, and McCann was edgy at setting aside significant space to be filled by an absent reporter.

At her desk, Liz found she had missed Cormac's 3:15 phone call, but at least he'd left a message. "Don't worry about fetching the evidence, Liz," he said. "I turned it in to the authorities myself."

So, he didn't trust her to do what he considered the right thing.

"From my experience, I know you will need these facts," Cormac continued on her voice mail. After providing his job title and university affiliation and some details about the bloodstain analysis, he added, "I hope this is adequate because I'm going to be out of reach this evening."

"Yeah, sure!" Liz muttered.

Reading the assignment sheet, Liz saw she'd been given slots for 24-inch and 8-inch stories. Her over-long requests had worked. McCann had cut them to the story lengths she'd hoped for. The first was assigned to run on Page One with a 20-inch jump running on Page Three, along with the 8-inch related story. But there were question marks next to it. Liz knew the only way she could erase them was to deliver the news, so she got right down to writing it.

When she'd filed the articles electronically, she found DeZona, gave him the lead story's slug, and told him to mark the photos of Kinnaird and the file photo of the bloodied kitchen with matching information. Then she handed him Veronica's drawing. "Can you scan this for me?"

"I recognize the style," DeZona said, handing Liz prints of the pictures Tom had taken. Apparently in order to fill the frame with the drawing, Tom had shot the photos at close range. Designed to be used at a distance, the cheap flash had washed out Veronica's pencil drawing in every one of the close-ups. But, apparently as an afterthought, Tom had taken a picture of the whole room.

"When I looked at that shot with a magnifying glass, I figured you'd need this," the photographer said, handing Liz an enlargement. "Not a pretty picture," he said.

"Not when you see this. Take a look at the tie. Veronica always drew her dad wearing an oversized tie. Freud might make something of that, but not me. Read all about family ties in tomorrow's *Beantown Banner!*"

"'FAMILY TIES.' Not a bad headline, and it looks like you've got the art to back your story, too. Great job, Higgins. I gotta hand it to you," Dermott McCann said, standing in the doorway to the photo department. "You made front page, with a lead and a teaser. Take the day off tomorrow. I've got Dick working on the Social Security angle. He's got the contacts. Even if it's a dead end, we've got to report what the government knows about this Hasan's work record."

Leaving the newsroom, Liz wondered if she could ever take a day off while a little girl counted on her to bring home her missing mom. Tired as she was, when she arrived home, she made another phone call to Jan Van Wormer's Workshop, only to find the voice mail still jammed. Ali just had to be found. Two mysterious Middle Easterners connected to one missing woman were two too many. Their connection to Ellen demanded explanation.

"Wait!" Liz said aloud, startling her cat. "There are not just two but three people in Ellen's life with ties to the Middle East." Pouring a glass of Chardonnay, flipping on her gas fireplace, and pulling her afghan over her lap, Liz settled down in her armchair and opened the airmail letter addressed to Ellen.

18 December 2000

My Dear Ellen,

How can I ever express how marvelous it was to meet you at last! Such a strange experience it was, don't you agree, to meet for the first time someone who has been your bosom companion for two decades? I am glad I need not struggle to describe such a feeling, because I know you, my dear friend, have experienced it, too.

Here I sit, in Heathrow Airport, wishing I could actually lie down during this tedious time they call a layover. As my English instructor would say, "I feel frightfully shattered!" I think in America you would say, "exhausted utterly." In my part of the world, I would say, "Jiddan ta ~ bana," which means, "I am very tired." (I write it down for you knowing you are making a study of my language. How pleased and surprised I was to hear you greet me in my own tongue when we met in New York.)

I suppose the strangest and most wonderful thing about meeting you in person (I keep returning to the indescribable—I just can't help myself!) was the opportunity to be looking into your eyes as you spoke. This, I think, was especially important regarding the confidences you shared with me. During my flight to this airport, I was unable to sleep, so I gave much thought to what you told me and I am of two minds about it. I have no doubt that I admire your courage, my dear friend. But I feel just as convinced that you are opening a Pandora's box. I know you have told me there is relief in putting things out in the open, but I feel in my heart some things are better left with the lid on. Particularly, if they might be monstrous.

Still, dear Ellen, you may count on me to support you no matter how you decide to proceed. Perhaps if you take the path I would not choose, you shall prove me wrong and win liberation for yourself in the process. But what will happen to your family, your mother, if you seek that liberation? You must think how they will fare when you are not in what you called the "circle" anymore.

Perhaps, even now, you have already flown that circle. I sincerely hope not. Such decisions must be considered carefully and at great length. I regret I shall be world-hopping for the UN again, with no fixed address for several months, but I shall look for your letters when I return to my home in September. I hope they shall bear the familiar postmark, "Newton, Massachusetts," on the outside—and happy news within.

With my love and friendship,
Nadia

Chapter 21

"What a fool I was!" Liz exclaimed. "Dick Manning, and even Tom, are right after all. I'm too close to this family."

She did not wish to consider the letter's implications but she knew she must. The fact was, Ellen had considered voluntarily exiting the family circle. If this were true, it would account for some circumstances Liz had chosen to gloss over. There was the blood flung with the fingertips over the cookie ingredients. And the "FORGET ME NOT" message. Now that looked like it came to mind thanks to the broken teacup's pattern name and seemed a good thing to write in the circumstances. And, of course, it accounted for Ellen's reading choices, particularly *How to Disappear Completely and Never Be Found.* Liz was furious with herself for not keeping that book title in the front of her mind. And it occurred to her that in her haste, she had forgotten to thank Lucy Gray for e-mailing the code word "Blister" to her. Well, perhaps Lucy would rather not admit she'd sent it, after all.

Haste. That was always the problem, wasn't it? Here it was, December 27. Ellen had gone missing from her home December 18. While much had been accomplished in nine days, key items had been overlooked, and Ellen's whereabouts remained unknown. The apparently perfect mother might have chosen to manufacture a scene of distress and desert her family, but that didn't mean Liz should be any less earnest about finding her. She still had her promise to Veronica to keep. But what kind of revelation would accompany locating Ellen? How would it affect Veronica?

Gazing into the flickering flames of her fireplace, Liz felt angry with herself not just for believing in Ellen, but also for wishing she could continue to believe in the picture-perfect mother. Getting up from her chair, she crossed to her kitchen, poured herself another glass of wine, turned on her radio, and peeled an apple in readiness to slice it. But she soon froze, with the apple skin curling over her fingers, as the voice of the WLTR-Radio announcer caught her ear.

"During routine towing of illegally parked, snow-covered vehicles in Boston this afternoon," the announcer said, "Boston police uncovered a car rented by Ellen Johansson, the woman who has been missing from her Newton home since December 18. According to police spokesperson Tara Foley, the vehicle was found completely buried in plowed snow near the Boston Public Library.

"Inside the car, police found paperwork indicating the car had been rented by Ellen Johansson yesterday, eight days after she went missing from her home. The woman's husband, Erik Johansson—who had been released from Newton police custody after he was questioned about assaulting *Boston World* news reporter Mick Lichen—was taken in to Boston police headquarters again this evening, where he identified the fountain pen, wedding ring, and brace-let found in the car as belonging to his wife. Under questioning, he admitted all the jewelry found in the car had been gifts to his wife from him. Lichen remains in the Newton-Wellesley Hospital with a broken leg sustained in the altercation. Boston police are holding Erik Johansson in custody overnight."

When the report was finished, Liz set down her apple, rinsed her hands, and phoned the newsroom. "We're onto it," Jared informed her. "Dick's at the car rental place now."

"Is that Higgins?" she heard Dermott McCann inquire. "Hand me the phone. Listen, Liz, are you sure that drawing is of Daddy's tie? It's looking like something was rotten in that household."

"Yeah, I'm sure. About the drawing, at least. When you print the piece, don't cut Veronica's quote about the kite-flying outing when the tie flew up and slapped Erik in the face. We really need that quote now."

"Gotcha. Hey Garamond," he called out to the copy editor. "Can you stet that kid quote I cut in 28DRAW1? By the way," he said to Liz, "forget about that day off tomorrow. I'll need you to follow up on the Social Security infor-mation for that guy Hasan. I had to pull Manning off that and put him onto the car rental place. I'll have Dick message his contacts to you."

Liz decided not to tell McCann about Nadia's letter. Knowing the reali-ties of the newsroom operation when news broke mid-evening, she knew something would get short shrift if a story on the letter was added—and a good candidate was the article about the drawing. Even if Erik had given Ellen reason to leave him, there was no sense in tarring him with the child abuse label unfairly. And an incomplete report on the drawing would make Erik look very suspicious indeed.

But in the hands of the *World*'s Mick Lichen, that is exactly what happened, as Liz learned when Tom knocked on her door in the early hours of December 28.

"Sorry to wake you, but I thought you'd want to see this. You not only scooped the *World* but got the front page, too. Take a look." Wiping his feet on the mat, he handed her two newspapers. Then he set down a bakery box and two Styrofoam cups of coffee on Liz's coffee table.

In uncharacteristic uppercase type the *World*'s front page announced, "ABUSE QUESTION RAISED IN MISSING MOTHER CASE." In the article, Mick Lichen made much of his observations through Veronica's window:

> A child's portrait of her father raises the question of sexual abuse in the Newton household that has been home to tragedy since Ellen Johansson, 34, went missing from it December 18. Ever since they stripped the wallpaper in the bedroom of Veronica Johansson, age 8, last week, police have been mum about the clue they found written on the wall. Now, based on exclusive observation of Veronica's bedroom, we can report the writing on the wall spells trouble for Erik Johansson, 37, husband of Ellen and father of Veronica.
>
> The drawing depicts a large protuberance extending outward from the chest or midriff area of a figure labeled "DADDY." According to Dr. Lesley Choate, professor of child psychiatry at the Harvard Medical School, "The huge ball-and-rod-shaped protuberance appears to be a classic depiction of the male member as seen by an abused child. The drawing is particularly disturbing in that it depicts a symbol of rape in a scene of innocent play or father-and-daughter companionship."

Lichen went on to suggest that child abuse accounted for all the problems in the household, including serving as the spur for Ellen's leaving it. However, because she didn't see Veronica's drawing as an indicator of abuse, Liz knew that notion was false. In addition, she still could not visualize Ellen leaving her daughter in danger. There must be another reason she departed.

The *World* also ran an article by Nancy Knight about developments with the rental car. Like Manning in the *Banner*, Knight read the cast-off jewelry, particularly the wedding ring, as a sign there was marital trouble, but she followed in Lichen's footsteps and based the spousal discord on the premise of child abuse. The large front page of the *World* also held room for a piece by Lichen, headlined "Blood of a Stranger," in which Lichen let on the *World* had no idea who'd been injured in the kitchen with Ellen.

In contrast, the *Banner*'s front page screamed, "POINSETTIA POINTER: Was Hackney Hacked in Mystery Kitchen?" Liz's lead article was accompanied by a file photo of the Johansson kitchen showing the poinsettia there and by a cameo shot of Cormac Kinnaird scrutinizing a poinsettia petal with a magnifying glass. Manning's article about the rental car, headed "WEDDING BAND BLUES," speculated on marital discord and showed the car rental clerk as gaga about getting her name in the paper and incapable of spitting out a sentence without several "likes" and a "whatevah." A photo of the clerk captured her in the act of chewing gum while screwing a cap on a jar of nail polish. Finally, a front-page teaser zooming in on Veronica's drawing of the wind-blown tie, was emblazoned with the words, "DADDY DEAREST: Veronica's Drawing Tells All."

"I'm sorry you had to realize the truth about Erik," Tom said. "I know you liked him. I heard on the radio, as I was driving over, that the Department of Social Services is stepping in to take temporary custody of Veronica, based on newspaper reports."

"Not mine!"

"But it says here, 'DADDY DEAREST.' Doesn't that mean you wrote about the abuse? That teaser makes me think of the movie *Mommie Dearest*, about Joan Crawford's abuse of her kid."

"No! For once the *Banner* headline writers' words can be taken literally. Sure, they tried to pique readers' interest by making it look like a parallel to that case. But that's just to get readers to turn to Page Three."

"Well, it fooled me. Especially since there's that penis drawing right there. It makes me think Erik Johansson is guilty as sin. Not everybody is going to read any further, Liz. If your story says Erik is a good guy, it's not clear from this front-page teaser."

"He is all right, at least in this regard. I talked with Veronica myself yesterday and she told me her drawing depicted a windy day when Erik's tie blew into his face while he flew a kite with her. That drawing is not evidence of sexual abuse."

"Well, I sure hope the Department of Social Services reads past Page One of the *Banner* then, because the *World* won't help them here. Maybe you should call them and inform them of what you know."

Before Liz could cross the room to it, her telephone rang.

"Liz. This is Olga. I have to thank you for your piece about Veronica's drawing. When I called it to the attention of the Department of Social Services, they said they'd release Erik later this morning, as soon as they can complete their paperwork on this. I have to question, though, the box on your front page. If you didn't know better, you would think the paper was reporting on a child molester rather than a misunderstood child's drawing. The way they enlarged that picture of the tie is utterly irresponsible."

"I see that, Olga, and I'm sorry for it, but remember, even without that drawing, the *World* got the story completely wrong. At least we printed the truth."

"Yes, and now the truth has come out about the car rental, too. I can't tell you how relieved I am. This means Ellen was alive and well enough to rent a car two days ago."

"Yes, but one has to wonder what kept her in the area and away from her family throughout the holidays."

"I know, I know. There has to be an explanation. There just has to be. It must have something to do with that taxi driver. Maybe he was a crazed man, stalking my daughter."

"I understand your impulse to blame the cabbie, but remember the book list you showed me? One of the titles on it suggested Ellen was planning to disappear."

Olga was silent. Had she forgotten about the book list?

"Must you always upset me?" she demanded at last. "I'm trying so hard to focus on the good news that my daughter is alive, and now you try to tell me she wanted to run away."

Olga hung up without another word.

After telling Tom what had ensued, Liz phoned the United Nations in New York. The central office receptionist could not confirm that Nadia had ever worked for them. "That doesn't mean much," she added, "since literally thousands of individuals do work for people who are on the official UN payroll. They may be translators, couriers, or personal assistants, but if they are paid by the UN employee instead of directly by the UN, we would have no record of them here."

"Another dead end," Liz said to Tom after hanging up the phone.

"Well, at least I have some good news. I found the *Charlotte's Web* wallpaper. Wait a minute while I get the sample book."

The big book held an eighteen- by twenty-inch sample sheet of the wallpaper. With its pink pastel tone and Garth Williams line drawings of Wilbur and a spider's web that read, "SOME PIG!" the paper introduced a much-needed moment of pleasure to the tension-packed morning.

"It's perfect! Veronica will love it."

"Since it appears Erik will be welcoming Veronica home after all, I'd better get going on picking up that wallpaper," Tom said. "Then I'll try to reach him to set up some time to hang it over the weekend."

Before he could leave, Liz wrapped her arms around Tom. This time, she was the last to release the embrace. After Tom left, she slipped out of her robe, dressed for work, fed Prudence, and drove straight to South Boston and the Van Wormer Piano Workshop.

Located in the basement of an architecturally pleasing, three-story brick row house, the workshop was accessible through an arched front entrance underneath and shaded by the first floor's front steps. A small sign with a keyboard motif identified the premises and drew Liz's attention while she waited for the proprietor to open the door. The nonagenarian piano man kept the door chained so it would open only about two inches until Liz introduced herself and showed him her I.D.

"Old habits die hard," he said in a German, or perhaps Dutch, accent. "This used to be a much more dangerous neighborhood."

"I tried to phone to make an appointment but your message machine has been filled."

"I forgot all about it! I always left the task of answering those messages to my assistant."

"You speak in the past tense. Is he no longer with you?"

"I'm not certain. Ever since last Tuesday, he has not been in."

"Was it an unplanned absence? Or might he have taken some time off for the holidays?"

"Oh, yes, it is unplanned, indeed. You see Al lives with me, in his own small unit on the third floor. Surely, he is not in some trouble?"

"First, let's be sure we are talking about the same person. I'm inquiring about Ali Abdulhazar, a man who would be just short of forty years old this year."

"That is my assistant's legal name, but he has called himself Al Hazard for many years now. He came to me as an apprentice many years ago, to learn how to tune pianos. Now he carries the lion's share of my business. I don't know what to tell my customers about when he will return. This is so terribly unlike him."

"Do you have any reason to think he's visiting family, in trouble, or perhaps run off with a woman?"

"None, except that he did not tell me he'd be away. His family returned to the Middle East before he reached age twenty, and he's hardly mentioned them since. It did occur to me that perhaps he'd received a message from them, calling him home to attend to an illness or, God forbid, a funeral. Not that they'd ever given him much in the way of family support. I took the liberty of looking in his room, but I didn't find any letter."

"Did you try his telephone answering machine?"

"He doesn't have a telephone upstairs. He always used the one in the workshop. But, of course, I never checked that! How stupid of me."

"Perhaps it holds the answer. Might we check it together?"

"That would be helpful. I'm terrible at all this technology. But first I must know why it is you are looking for him."

Liz might have said she was an old friend or offered up some other tall tale, but she opted to tell the truth. It seemed to give Van Wormer pause, until Liz added, "If you read today's newspapers, I think you might find you'd rather have me than my competitor look into the connection between Al and Ellen. I promise to tell the whole story and not to rake up dirt on your assistant just for the sake of it. Most likely, his absence is unconnected, anyway."

Van Wormer led Liz to the phone machine. The tape of recorded messages was mostly filled with several concerned—and a few angry—inquiries about upcoming and then missed piano tuning appointments. Only one of them offered anything different, and it was from a male caller with a Middle Eastern accent, suggesting that Al meet him "in the usual place" on December 19. The day Ali went missing and the day after Ellen left home.

Another dead end.

Liz asked Van Wormer if he would like her to run a check on Ali, using his Social Security number, only causing Van Wormer to draw the line on helping her any further. "You may mean well, Miss Higgins, but unless and until my employee is gone for a far longer period of time, I am not willing to share his private information with you."

"Of course, I understand," Liz said. She knew it was best to mask her frustration here. If she remained pleasant and helpful, it maximized the chances that Van Wormer would turn to her later. "I hope Al returns soon. If he does, I hope you will let me know. If he doesn't, perhaps you might turn to me for help. I know how upsetting and expensive it would be to use the services of a private investigator. I have free access to some investigative databases at the *Banner*."

Handing the keyboard expert her business card, Liz made her exit and hurried to the newsroom, where it fast became clear that Samir Hasan's Social Security number was a fake.

And that was no surprise.

Chapter 22

L iz's newsroom stature rose substantially after she topped the *World*'s incomplete and inaccurate reports about Veronica's bedroom and the taxi driver's blood. Not only did she garner numerous lead stories as 2000 came to a close and 2001 began, but she gained a demanding workload, too. Like well-placed reporters in all of the local media, she found herself absorbed in the case of a cross-dressing dermatologist from a well-heeled suburb who slaughtered his wife, and then in a mystery surrounding a woman who was killed in a Cape Cod beach house..

Liz did tell her city editor about Nadia's missive, but he had her follow up on Samir Hasan's Social Security information instead of pushing for coverage of the purloined letter. The Social Security search only proved Samir Hasan was paid for three years under that name by the cab company Jake headed. The Social Security Administration also had fallen for the fake address, and there was no information about Hasan holding any other jobs. A follow-up on the short-wave radio license also led nowhere. False identification had been used successfully here, too.

Hasan's genetic identity was easier to pin down when, eleven weeks to the day after Kinnaird submitted the cigarette butts and spots of blood on the tissue and on the poinsettia for testing, DNA results proved the cabbie had been injured in the Johansson kitchen. Liz got the scoop on this, since police DNA testing did not come back until four weeks later. Still, beyond the DNA results, the cabbie's trail was cold.

Since he had no knowledge that Liz had read Nadia's letter, Erik Johansson had no notion of how much Liz now questioned his role in Ellen's disappearance. Grateful for Liz's part in exonerating him of the child abuse charge, and for making it possible to welcome Veronica home to a beautifully wallpapered room, Erik kept in touch with Liz as winter wound its way into springtime. He shared with her Veronica's belief that Ellen was wearing her Christmas sweater with a reindeer pattern knitted into it when she went missing. Although Veronica said her mother had not been wearing her "Rudolph sweater" when she drove Veronica to school that day, the sweater was nowhere to be found in the Johansson house and it seemed likely Ellen donned it sometime before she disappeared.

Erik also showed Liz more incoming mail—all postcards—from Nadia. None of them had a word to say about the secret the pen pals had shared in New York. Nor did they indicate when Nadia expected to return to her home in Jerusalem.

In addition, Erik let Liz know he phoned Nadia's Jerusalem home twice a week, every week. Liz had been doing the same thing. There was no answering machine, so the phone just rang and rang each time either of them called. In February, while Veronica spent her school vacation with Olga, Erik made an unproductive trip to Nadia's Jerusalem address, only to have neighbors tell him they had no idea when she would return. They insisted they had no information to share about relatives or friends of Nadia.

Unwilling to trust Erik on this, Liz prevailed on the *Banner*'s travel editor, Susan Damon, to visit Nadia's address while she was on assignment there in May. Susan, too, found Nadia's neighbors less than helpful.

Once a month, Liz penned a letter to Nadia, expressing her concern for Ellen and her hope that Nadia would contact her at the first opportunity. She also phoned Jan Van Wormer on the eighteenth of every month, the anniversary of Ellen's disappearance. But there was never news of the man who called himself Al Hazard. Spring came and went as Liz, working with Erik, systematically contacted United Nations personnel who they thought might require the services of a translator with skills in English and Arabic. Not one of them knew a thing about Nadia.

Still, the pen pal's postcards kept coming. Most were sent from airports and bore messages indicating Nadia was about to leave for another destination. This had been true throughout the pen pals' correspondence, Erik said, recalling how his wife had envied the international life her correspondent enjoyed.

Veronica's June 11 birthday came and went with no word from Ellen. However, that day there was a phone call made to the Johansson home from Ellen's cell phone. The caller—was it Ellen?—said nothing. Investigation of the cell-phone records indicated no roaming charges for the call, which must have been placed from a location tantalizingly close to home. At the urging of the police, Erik continued to keep the cell phone in service, in case another call came through.

For her birthday gift to Veronica, Olga had Veronica's birthstone attached to Ellen's wedding ring circlet to make a unique pendant. "I know people think Erik did something to drive Ellen away, but I'm sure he didn't. That marriage was rock solid," Olga told Liz, "so I'm celebrating it and Veronica's birthday with that pendant."

On June 18—the six-month anniversary of Ellen's disappearance—Liz wrote a recap of the mystery for the *Banner* and included Olga's heartwarming vote of confidence in her son-in-law to balance the many unanswered questions that led many to think ill of him. Nevertheless, Erik was uncomfortable with the article and dropped his contact with Liz after it ran. The anniversary article also drew criticism from Lucy Gray, who phoned Liz in a pique when it was published.

"I didn't betray your trust . . . " Liz began, in response to the librarian's angry tone.

"You couldn't have!" Lucy said. "I never gave you access to the information."

"Well, not directly. But you did e-mail me the title of the list, if not the password."

"What e-mail? What password?"

"You didn't send all those e-mails with the word 'Blister'?"

"No, I didn't! I debated about letting you know but I just couldn't."

"Then, it must have been someone else. But who was it? I didn't talk with anyone else at the library."

Liz explained how Olga had retrieved the information. Could it have been the most unlikely person the two could imagine: Monica Phillips? In any case, Lucy seemed to relax knowing someone else had done the deed she had debated about perpetrating.

"So, you know about Ellen's reading choices then?" Lucy asked.

"*How to Disappear Completely and Never Be Found*," Liz said, naming the memorable title.

"Not that one! That's a children's book."

"With a title like that?"

"Yes. You can tell by the call number indicating the juvenile category. She probably took it out to read to Veronica along with the other children's title on the list. No, it was the title about child abuse that concerned me."

"I don't remember anything about that on the list."

"The circulation list does not provide subtitles. Perhaps that's why you didn't see *Silent Knights* as significant."

"Is it a book about child abuse? Did Ellen ever let on to you any fears that Erik might abuse Veronica?"

"Erik! No. The book Ellen was reading was more along the self-help lines. That book's full title is, *Silent Knights: Finding the Courage to Admit Aberrant Impulses*. It addresses how to overcome the impulse to behave abusively. When I told you the reading list made me doubt how well I knew Ellen, this is what I was talking about. I have to wonder if Ellen herself had a problem."

"That's why you were reluctant to share the information."

"That, and my profound belief in the right to readers' privacy. Suppose Ellen was only trying to get further support on a problem she had thus far been able to control? If the reading list were known, she might be vilified despite doing a good job of maintaining self control."

"You have a point there."

"I have to wonder, Liz, if Ellen fled in order to prevent herself from hurting Veronica."

It was an avenue no one had explored thus far, but why would a New York taxi driver be traveling that route with Ellen? Was it just a fluke that he had entered her life at that moment? Or was he some kind of stalker? There seemed no way to find out.

After Dick Manning outdid Liz by scooping a few early summer news items, Liz found herself back on the community news beat, for the most part. She was also asked to cover some home and garden items for vacationing columnists. While she sometimes ran into Cormac Kinnaird when covering breaking news, as her hard news assignments dropped off they did not cross paths. But she and Tom discovered a passion for picnicking, and when it was possible, she took Tom along on some of her garden-related assignments, where they spread out his Mexican blanket with the greatest of pleasure.

In August, another call was made from Ellen's cell phone, this time to the *World*'s Nancy Knight. The reporter made much of her scoop, even though the message was another blank one. A psychiatrist consulted by Knight told the reporter, "It's evident this model mother cannot entirely separate from her child." While Newton police duly discovered the phone call had been placed somewhere where roaming charges did not apply, the new contact seemed destined to underline Ellen's absence as voluntary, even if it was uncertain who had made the call.

Then in September 2001, everything changed. Everything.

On the second of the month, Liz returned to Gravesend Street to find in her mailbox the long-awaited letter from Nadia. Tearing it open, she stood in her tiny driveway, oblivious to the sounds of passing traffic and of Prudence meowing inside a window. Posted from Jerusalem, the letter read:

> Dear Liz Higgins,
>
> Forgive me for my delay in contacting you, which is made all the more dreadful by the fact, which I have just learned from your letters, that my dear friend Ellen is missing. I'm afraid my work keeps me world hopping, and my stays in each destination are too short to make the forwarding of letters practicable.
>
> Ellen did share some confidences with me when we met in New York City. I swore I would hold them secret for all my life, and I find it difficult to reconcile this promise to her with the needs of this investigation into her whereabouts. This is, in part, because she may, as is suggested in the news clippings you sent me, have decided to leave her home by choice.
>
> Still, I remember Ellen spoke highly of you. Thus am I willing to meet with you and discuss the matter further. Unfortunately, I depart again tomorrow morning for more travels. Would it be impossible for you to meet with me in Singapore? It is a long way to go to meet a woman who might disappoint you once you get there. I make no promises about how much I will confide, and even if I trust you wholly, the information I have to share is limited. Still, I must pass through Singapore three times during the next two months. The first time, I will be staying at the Fullerton hotel on the nights of 6–9 September. Please don't send Erik in your place, or let him know we are communicating. I will explain why, if and when I see you.
>
> Yours sincerely,
> Nadia

Without much hope of receiving an answer, Liz phoned Nadia's Jerusalem number again. It rang and rang and rang, with the strange double-ring pattern that is common outside the United States.

Certain the *Banner* would not pay for a speculative jaunt to Singapore, Liz went straight to the newsroom, looked up the Singapore Tourism Board on the Internet, and discovered there was a celebrated orchid garden in that city. If the *Banner* saw her as a garden writer, it might be to her advantage. Collaring the travel editor, Susan Damon, she pitched a story about the orchids and great ethnic shopping, while reminding Susan she had vacation time available to spend on the enterprise. Susan composed a letter to the tourism board, which Liz faxed immediately. A half-hour later, she followed up with a phone call.

"Certainly, we'd love to host you at the Fullerton hotel. It's just been renovated and the management is looking for coverage," the public relations manager said. "As long as it is midweek, we can make the arrangements."

The airfare was another story. It cost the earth. But Liz decided to go for it. She smiled to think a garden- and travel-writing assignment might provide her ticket to the front page again. Even more important, it might help her keep her promise to Veronica.

Chapter 23

Singapore, September 9, 2001

While she tried to recline in the cramped economy-class seat of a Singapore Airlines jet, Liz experienced the longest sleepless night of her life, as she traveled westward over the international dateline, and into the next day in the process. In Singapore, a city that savvy travelers dubbed "Asia Lite," Liz was whizzed from the airport to her hotel in air-conditioned ease. After leaving a message for Nadia announcing her arrival, she fell into a deep sleep.

Seven hours later, a room service meal she had not ordered was delivered to her door, along with a ticket for the cable-car ride that overlooked the city and its harbor. A small vase of orchids on the tray bore a card that read, "Let me show you Singapore! Let's meet at the cable-car station at 4:00 p.m.—Nadia"

Liz ate a leisurely meal of tropical fruits, an egg-white omelet, and coffee, then showered and dressed for tropical heat and humidity. After riding the elevator downstairs to the hotel's expansive, marble-floored lobby, she took a taxi to the cable-car station. With a picture of Nadia and Ellen in hand, Liz had no trouble recognizing Nadia. Before much could be said, the two were seated in their own cable car, which lifted off on a trip across Singapore Harbor to Sentosa Island.

Distracted by the vista of the huge Merlion statue—a half-mermaid, half-lion mythological beast that is said to guard the port of Singapore—Liz nonetheless managed to fill Nadia in on her efforts to find Ellen, and she made sure to let on that she had paid for this trip out of her own funds. "Beyond that, I'm not certain how to convince you that I care about her well-being," Liz added. "I know it appears she left of her own volition, but if that is so, I would like to know why. Yes, solving this case would be a boon to my career. But more important is my promise to Veronica. I told her I would find her mother."

"Your traveling this far is proof enough that you care, Liz. Ah, here we are on the landing station. You've come so far. Let me make your trip memorable."

Although Liz was itching to learn more about Nadia's insights into Ellen, it was clear the Palestinian woman would not talk about this in public. So Liz dutifully—and with increasing pleasure—accompanied Nadia through the interactive Singapore History Museum, then climbed the Merlion statue to get a view from the observation window that was also its mouth, and strolled through the tropical gardens on the island. As she answered many questions from her companion, Liz realized Nadia was trying to learn as much as she could about the reporter. Liz was glad to cooperate in hopes of winning the woman's trust. In return, however, the Palestinian woman revealed little about herself.

Back in the cable car, Liz mentioned how she had tried without success to reach Nadia through the United Nations and said she guessed Nadia was an international consultant with a mission other than translation.

Nadia looked her straight in the eyes and said, "Let's just say my translation skills are necessary to my work and leave it at that. There is much static these days that must be sorted out, for the good of us all."

"You mean international misunderstanding?"

"Worse than that." Nadia turned her attention to the panoramic view until the cable car reached its station. "Now, let me take you along to the Raffles Hotel. The bar there is quite famous, you know." Nadia waved a cab away and signaled for a rickshaw instead. "I always promised Ellen I'd take her on a rickshaw ride here when Veronica is grown up and Ellen has the time to travel."

The British-built, white colonial edifice that was the Raffles Hotel screamed "Raj," and there was no denying it was elegant. Fronted by a circular drive lined with traveler's palms—so-named, Nadia explained, because they held water cupped in the base of their fan-like display of leaves—the hotel looked like an imperialist's dream come true. At sunset, the long bar was mostly populated by Japanese tourists, the men in white suits and Panama hats and the women well coiffed and dressed in long, sleeveless frocks.

Nadia steered Liz to a pair of plush-cushioned rattan chairs with high backs that curved over their heads. Then she ordered two Singapore Slings, sweet alcoholic drinks that arrived in martini glasses. Only after the waiter stepped away did Nadia lean forward and say, "I have debated at length about this, and I hope I am making the right decision. I do not break confidences easily and I hope you won't break mine without serious cause, either."

"Are you saying I cannot report what you tell me?"

"Yes, Liz, I am saying that. Unless it will help to save Ellen's life."

"You have my word."

"Good. Then I will tell you. While we were in New York, Ellen confided that she had been experiencing some frightening flashbacks to an incident from her girlhood."

"When a boy exposed himself to her? Yes, I know about that."

"It was not a boy."

"Perhaps it was a different incident then."

"Perhaps. She said the flashbacks began after she received a phone call, a year ago just before Christmas, and the speaker hummed some unknown but oddly familiar gibberish to her. 'A tuneless hum,' she called it. The caller never phoned again until just before she met me in Manhattan, but the flashbacks kept coming nevertheless. They always began the same way, with the tuneless hum and a visual image of a topiary garden she loved, a place with trees pruned into marvelous shapes. But although she loved that place, the hum made her extremely uneasy. She told me that when she remembered it, she said she broke out into a cold sweat.

"The flashbacks seemed to have something to do with tea, she said, because after Veronica broke a teacup, she started to experience them more frequently and at greater length. Each time they overtook her, more was revealed.

"First there was the hum and the sculpted trees and the uneasiness. Then the hum and the trees and the uneasiness and a kind of umbrella of pine needles. Then, she said, there was the humming and the sculpted trees and a shadowed figure under an umbrella of pine needles. Then there was all of this and the dark figure was revealed to be a man. Then there was the humming and the shaped trees and the needles and the man in the shadows stroking himself. He was forming a word, Ellen said, the 'f-word.'"

"'Fuck.'"

"These flashbacks were disturbing enough in themselves, but what worried Ellen most was a certainty that the identity of the man would inevitably be revealed to her. She did not want to know who it was. And yet she did. To protect her daughter. After she received the phone call, she felt the man was targeting her home. She was afraid for Veronica. You see now why I must consider that Ellen might have had good reason to flee from her home? She was protecting her child by drawing the perverted man's attention to herself."

"Why didn't she tell her husband about this?"

"She planned to do that. Just as soon as the man's face was revealed to her. Until then, she thought it sounded mad, crazy."

"The tuneless hum, did she repeat it for you?"

"No, but she told me that something in her cab ride in New York City called it to mind. The driver was an Arab, as you discovered. He made her uneasy, she said, talking on his short-wave radio in salacious tones about a girl named Tina. I told her, in Arabic *teena* is a word for fig, as well as a rather improper euphemism for a female. Ellen had good instincts. She knew the driver was talking about her in, let us say, over-familiar terms."

"Then it makes sense that he followed her home? She walked straight into the path of a classic stalker."

"That seems likely, but then what about the phone call she received a year ago and then again before she met me in New York, before she met the taxi driver? Doesn't it seem extremely unlikely that two men were stalking our friend?"

"Yes, but it's slightly more believable than the notion that the taxi driver and the man who called are one and the same. How could a taxi driver plant himself in the position to pick up a particular woman at Penn Station? It's just too impossible to engineer. But the caller could well have been Ali, the tongue-tied boy from her past who, I learned, exposed himself to her in the incident she is calling to mind in her flashbacks. Olga told me someone mumbling a tuneless hum phoned her at the same time every year until last year. She feared he'd turned his attentions to Ellen instead. I discovered where Ali lives and works, but he went missing two days after Ellen did. Now *there's* a coincidence I know is real."

"The fact that both men are Arabs is suggestive. I wonder if a common expression, or simply words spoken in the flowing Arabic language, might have been used by both."

"The tuneless hum! That might be it!" Thinking about tones of voices led Liz to ask, "Did you, by any chance, phone the Johansson house on December 18, the day after you parted with Ellen?"

"As a matter of fact, I did. But I only left a message. I felt terrible about losing a roll of film I'd taken of us in New York."

"Do you recall saying, 'It's all my fault'?"

"I might have said something like that. I knew she'd be disappointed because it was a standing joke between us about how dreadful a photographer she was. We both used our cameras while we were in Manhattan, and she was sure my photos would be far better than hers."

"In your letter to Ellen, you advised her not to open a Pandora's box. What did you mean by that?"

Nadia's expression changed to one of shock.

"I'm sorry, Nadia," Liz said. "I must admit, I read your last letter to Ellen. It was given to me by a workman who had access to her house."

Nadia was quiet for some minutes.

"Ellen told me she was going to find a hypnotist to help her unveil the figure in her flashbacks," she said at last. "It made me terribly uneasy for her. It's one thing for a repressed memory to reveal itself, don't you think? It might be monstrous, but at least it's pure. It seems to me a hypnotist might manipulate things, twist the truth. Then you never know the actual truth of the matter."

While Nadia engaged in "urgent work" in unidentified offices in Singapore, Liz toured the extensive orchid gardens there, marveling at their quantity and variety. She also located and interviewed the horticulturist for her travel article and arranged for photographs to be sent to her at the *Banner* newsroom. Later, Liz shopped in Chinatown and Little India, ethnic enclaves where beautifully crafted items were plentiful and cheap, and browsed without buying anything in the opulent Japanese department store on Orchard Road, a thoroughfare known as the "Fifth Avenue of Singapore."

In the evening, the two met at a hot pot restaurant decorated with Mao Zedong and Chinese Communist memorabilia. After ordering their fare from waiters dressed in classic comrades' garb, they collected tofu, pieces of raw fish, several varieties of mushrooms, and a half-dozen varieties of Asian greens and took them back to their table. In the center of it, a waiter installed a steaming pot of broth, which was kept bubbling on an electric burner. Using chopsticks to drop in the food they had collected, they watched it cook and then ladled the soup into bowls. As the two dined, Liz enthused about the orchids she'd seen.

"Then you must come along with me to Fiji," Nadia said. "There's a marvelous orchid garden there established by the actor Raymond Burr."

"It sounds wonderful, but I've already broken my bank by paying for my airfare to get here."

"Use some of my frequent-flyer miles. I have more than I can ever spend. And you can join me in my lodgings. I travel alone so much it will be a pleasure to have your company during this little holiday. I shan't be working in Fiji, so I will have more time to converse with you. We will have more opportunity to put our heads together about Ellen, too."

On the morning of September 10, the two made their way to Fiji's main island and installed themselves in the aptly named Shangri-La's Fijian Resort. After freshening up, they toured Raymond Burr's Garden of the Sleeping Giant orchid plantation, so-named for the long mountain, shaped like a reclining titan, which stretches out above and beyond the garden. Liz took photographs and copious notes for another travel article. And then she and Nadia returned to the resort, in time to attend a fire-walking demonstration and outdoor banquet.

"I had thought fire walkers would skitter quickly across the stones," Liz said. "But they seemed to linger on them."

"Like you with your work and me with mine."

"I'm not so sure that's true. Here we are, behaving as tourists and making little progress at all."

"If you think so, you are mistaken. The more I get to know you, the more I feel I can say about Ellen. You see, she has been my friend for two decades. I have known you only for a matter of days."

"You haven't, however, spent much time with Ellen, have you?"

"Not in person. In fact, I have now spent more time in your physical company than I have in hers. But that doesn't matter. Since we were girls, we have shared our lives through writing. I can say, without hesitation, that Ellen was one of my dearest . . ."

Liz met Nadia's eyes. "You feel she is gone, don't you?" Liz asked.

"My mind tells me there are questions enough about her circumstances to suggest she chose to leave, but my tongue betrays me." Nadia paused. "Yes, I already think of her in the past tense."

Liz placed her hand over Nadia's. "We will find the truth, Nadia. That's all we can do now," she said.

Chapter 24

The following day, the pair took a deHavilland Beaver to one of Fiji's three hundred islands, where Nadia had a reservation at a rustic-style resort.

"This makes me think of the film *Cast Away*," Liz remarked, as the two installed themselves in a grass hut with a thatched roof just steps away from the water. The beach hut, or *burrah*, would have been charming enough from the outside, but it was even more delightful inside. Brightly colored batik spreads covered two beds, and intricate, hand-painted patterns in black and cream adorned the deeply peaked ceiling above them.

Obviously designed for barefoot visitors, the hut's concrete slab entryway was fitted with a hand-woven straw mat. A dishpan of fresh water sat in front of a small bench there, so visitors might remove sand from their feet with ease before entering the hut.

"Do you see that island there?" Nadia said, pointing to a small mound or rock across the blue water.

"Um hm."

"That is where the movie you mentioned was filmed. I gather the bar and restaurant at this resort were favored by cast and crew during the filming."

After changing into bikinis, the pair stepped out of their hut and settled in the shade of a palm tree. Nadia, who knew the resort well, seemed set on reading. Liz, however, took out her book and only laid it on her lap. She found it hard to settle her eyes on a book when she could gaze instead at the expanse of aquamarine water, dotted with distant islands, that was laid out before her. But her book caught Nadia's eye, nonetheless.

"You carried a library book halfway around the world!" Nadia exclaimed, noticing the call numbers pasted on the book's spine.

"It's one Ellen was reading before she disappeared," Liz said, and explained to Nadia how she gained access to Ellen's library record.

"You and Mrs. Swenson have missed your callings," Nadia chuckled. "You should have taken up my line of work. But that's a children's book, isn't it?"

"Yes. I suppose Ellen might have been reading it to Veronica."

"May I take a look?"

"Of course."

Nadia read aloud the blurb on the back of the paperback. "'Margaret's father died in a mysterious drowning accident when she was eight years old.'" She stopped and looked hard at Liz. "When did Ellen take out this book? Do you know?"

"Sometime last November, I think. I've got my folder about the case in my suitcase. I could check on it." Liz retrieved the folder from the grass hut and returned to the chaise lounge under the palms. "Here's Ellen's borrowing record." She spread it out on her knees. *How to Disappear Completely and Never Be Found* was borrowed November 16 and returned the next day."

"Then that may well be the book she wrote to me about. She never mentioned the title, but in a letter she wrote in mid-November, Ellen said little things, even picking up a children's book, were stimulating flashbacks. This book perhaps reminded her of her father. He died in a drowning accident when she was eight years old, you know. She always referred to him as her hero, her 'Rock of Gibraltar.' She was a—how do you say it?—'father's girl.'"

"'Daddy's girl.' I suppose reminders of his death stirred her up emotionally, leaving her more vulnerable to those flashbacks."

"That is how she saw it. I imagine she never read that book to Veronica. That's why she returned it the next day."

"Seems sensible. Look at this," Liz said, handing to Nadia the library record.

"There are shadowed lines here and here on the paper."

"I asked Olga to make a copy of the reading list for me. I wonder if she did a little cutting and pasting of a longer list. Ellen's friend Lucy Gray told me she had seen Ellen's library record and it worried Lucy to know Ellen had been reading about child abuse."

"Why would Mrs. Swenson wish to hide that from you?"

"The book in question was a self-help book. Look, it's this one: *Silent Knights*. Olga must not have realized the nature of the book from its title, since the subtitle is not listed here. It has to do with having the courage to address one's propensity for engaging in aberrant behavior. Although I had the impression from Ellen's librarian friend that there was just a single book in question on this topic, maybe that was not the case. Perhaps Ellen had taken out another book along those lines and Olga did not wish for me to know it."

"You mean it looked like Ellen was a child abuser? Ridiculous!" As if to wash away that foul notion, Nadia leapt up from her chaise lounge and strode into the sea.

It was nighttime before the two women addressed the topic of Ellen again. Lying on their backs in their beds, neither could settle down immediately. For Liz, it was a case of overexcitement at the unexpected visit to Fiji. Nadia seemed unsettled after making radio contact with her colleagues.

"It seems you do not wish to tell me about the specifics of your job, Nadia," Liz said.

"It's not a question of wishing to tell you or not. I *cannot* tell you."

"Can you tell me, at least, if I'm correct in assuming that you are working in intelligence?"

"You are correct about that."

"For whom are you working?"

"I will tell you what I tell everyone who asks: I am an interpreter working on various United Nations projects."

"Is the U.N. actually your employer?"

"Please, Liz. Understand I have told you all I can regarding my job."

"Can you tell me something about Ellen, then? Was she also engaged in espionage?"

Nadia laughed. After a pause, she said, "I'm sorry to make light of your question. If you think our correspondence contained some sort of coded messages, you are mistaken. In fact, Ellen lost a briefcase full of old letters from me, and her purse, when we were in New York."

"I was thinking more about the book she had in her possession—some sort of phrase book for intelligence officers."

"Such books are not top secret and, while they are not sold in Barnes & Noble, they sometimes turn up in used-book shops. You might get in touch with the Brattle Book Shop in Boston and see if they have any record of selling it to her. I remember the shop name because I looked up the word *brattle* in my dictionary to see what it means. It wasn't in the dictionary, so I assumed it's the owner's name. In one of her last letters, Ellen was most enthusiastic about a purchase she said she made in the Brattle, saying it would enrich our meeting. Since she never did give me a book when we met in New York, I now ask myself if it is possible that purchase was the phrase book that enabled her to greet me in Arabic."

"I will check with the Brattle, of course. It does seem likely she was preparing to meet you. But then, I'm troubled, too, about her interaction with the cabdriver."

"You mean he might have been an intelligence contact? You should know, Liz, that those kinds of machinations—a certain cab collecting a certain woman at a major train station—only happen in the movies, not in the life of actual espionage agents. It's actually much more likely, unfortunately, that a certain woman would become the victim of a random psychopath encountered when she gets into the wrong cab."

"What did she tell you about that cab ride?"

"Not a lot, Liz. We were so focused on meeting one another for the first time. She did tell me she surprised the driver by thanking him in his own language. When she did so, she said, the color drained from his face. That's not an expression I've heard before, and it was very memorable. But it was even more memorable because Ellen seemed so—how do you say it?—shook by the encounter."

"Could she have overheard anything significant in his radio conversation?"

"From what she said, it sounds to me like the driver was talking about her or another woman in sexual terms. You mentioned he used the word *teena* several times. As I told you, that is the word for *fig*, but it also refers to a woman as a sort of tasty dish."

Suddenly, a sharp, shrill chirp pierced the air. Liz sat up and turned on the bedside light.

"Is there a bird in here?"

Nadia burst out laughing. "No, no! It's just a lizard."

"What do you mean 'just a lizard'?" Liz said, hopping out of bed and shaking out her sheets.

"Take a look at the ceiling."

Liz looked up and saw that part of the pattern painted there seemed to move. It was a lizard scurrying directly above her head. Then she saw another one, closer to the peak of the ceiling.

"Will they drop down on us?" Liz asked.

"I hope not. If they do, I believe they are harmless."

"Startling, though," Liz said, returning to her bed.

"Certainly. Think about it, Liz. A lizard in the night would make great fodder for a postcard message."

"Let's write one for Ellen."

"If we post it, Erik will know we've been together."

"That's true. And, before we met, you told me you had something to say about him. I had the impression that the 'something' might have been a reason for Ellen to leave him."

"She wrote that Erik had a problem with outflow at work. There was dirty business, money laundering. There was no doubt she loved her husband, but I thought she might separate herself from him to retain power over her own resources."

"She wrote this? Did you discuss it further in New York?"

"Yes, she told me in a letter. And I asked her about it in New York. She said he'd found a way to recirculate the flow, so the outgo problem was not so serious. I felt she rather brushed off my concern, which, of course, was magnified once again when she went missing."

"Oh Nadia! I think you've misunderstood. I've been to Erik's workplace. He was working on designing an environmentally friendly washing machine. The costs of refining it were running high, largely due to his water bills, so he found a way to use recirculated runoff from his parking area to test the machine."

"No wonder Ellen seemed unconcerned in New York! All these years I have prided myself on my English comprehension, but most certainly I read that letter all wrong!"

"You can't blame yourself. The best linguists can get stumped on slang and jargon about machines."

"But now you've come all this way, and my information is worth less than nothing."

"Is that what you were writing about when you advised Ellen to be careful about leaving the family circle?"

Nadia seemed to weigh her reply.

"It's little wonder you sought me out," she finally said "Yes, I did advise Ellen to think carefully about shattering the family circle. I did not think it was worth doing for financial reasons. And, as I mentioned, I worried that the hypnotist she considered consulting would lead her to think a family member was the figure in her flashbacks."

"I, too, would have questioned her involving a hypnotist. But we're still left with the fact that Ellen was overcome by the flashbacks. If she could not prevent them happening, she may have felt she was not in control of herself. And if she had an impulse to abuse, it would account for her leaving Veronica. By leaving her, she would be protecting her. The flashbacks you tell me about indicate a woman who felt out of control, overwhelmed."

"Well, yes, the flashbacks seemed to overtake her. But when she spoke of them in New York, she was more worried than frantic. Even if they did make her feel as though she was losing control, it was not regarding handling herself with her child. She did not have it in her to abuse. I'm certain of it. No, Liz, I must say, it struck me that she wanted to face the flashbacks head-on and eliminate the source from which they sprang."

"But didn't you tell me she was reluctant to discover who the figure in the shadows was?"

Nadia did not reply. The two women stared up at the ceiling in silence. Liz wondered, could we have found a reasonable motive for suicide? Or, for the murder of the figure in the shadows?

"Ayeeeeeee!" Nadia shrieked, jumping from her bed and shaking a lizard from her sheets. Liz jumped up, too. Laughing, Nadia said, "Do you happen to have an extra postcard?"

"Eleven September 2001," Nadia said aloud as she wrote the date on the postcard. "Someday, we hope, we will all sit down together and we will tell you how we came this far to find you," she added and handed the card to Liz.

"The occasion for this postcard is easier to sum up," Liz wrote. "Just call it 'The Curious Incident of the Lizard in the Nighttime.'"

After signing their names on the postcard, the two women got into their beds and, pulling their sheets completely over their heads to shield themselves from falling wildlife, attempted to drop off to sleep.

September 12 dawned pink as the inside of a seashell. Liz looked at it, bleary-eyed from lack of sleep, through the lens of her camera. She had not slept well with the lizards chirping above her through the night. While she headed down the beach to photograph the Fijian sunrise, Nadia had gone in search of coffee at the island's tiny shop and outdoor dining complex. Liz was zooming in on the "Cast Away" island when Nadia signaled her from the front of their grass hut.

"Come here right now," she ordered.

There's a side of Nadia I've never seen! Liz thought, impressed with the woman's bossiness. Liz raised a finger to indicate, "Just a minute." She wanted to catch in a photo the sun's arc rising over the horizon, like the edge of a fabulous doubloon.

Nadia strode down the beach with a purposeful air that only made her look comical, dressed as she was in a sarong and flip-flops. "It's very bad in the States," she declared. "You must come immediately."

"What? What are you talking about?"

"Manhattan is under attack."

Liz stood stock-still.

Nadia repeated the news. "Manhattan is under attack."

"By what? By whom? And Boston?"

"Not Boston. My contacts tell me Boston is not yet hit."

"Not *yet*?"

"I hope it will not be. But it's not just New York. The Pentagon has been hit."

There was just one television in reach and it was not quite on the island. Nadia outlined the unbelievable as the two made their way to it. Housed on a luxurious yacht anchored offshore, the television was only accessible via boat. Unfortunately, all of the island's kayaks were already tethered to the yacht. Stripping to reveal bikinis, Liz and Nadia grabbed Styrofoam boards fitted with plastic windows, designed to be used by leisurely swimmers to look at life on the coral reef below.

"Normally, I could swim this distance," Nadia said, "but under the circumstances, I don't trust myself." It was the first time she indicated her own agitation over the news.

The swim was anything but leisurely. Once on the yacht, they strained to see, on a miniscule television screen surrounded by some half-dozen tourists, the media coverage of the terrorist attacks on New York City. One viewer expressed confusion.

"I don't get it," he said. "Why are we finding out about this a day later? They keep saying this happened yesterday."

"We're eighteen hours ahead of New York time," the yacht owner explained. "In real time, the planes flew into those buildings while we were sleeping, at around three in the morning here. But it was around eight in the morning yesterday in New York City."

Nadia prevailed on the yacht owner to let her use his radio. Liz stood transfixed in front of the television. Despite the tropical heat, she shivered. Nadia pulled her aside.

"My contacts say U.S. airspace is closed and is likely to remain so for days. I must move urgently. I cannot tell you where. It is best that you do not accompany me. I shall take the next Piper Cub to the main island."

"I'll help you pack."

"There's no need."

"Yes, there is. It will steady me."

With the images of the attack in her mind, Liz was grateful for the swim board as the two made their way back to the island. As Nadia strode toward their hut, Liz rushed to the outdoor dining area, which was open an hour earlier than normal. On the blackboard that usually announced the day's specials, someone had written, "Breakfast on the house. We pray for the USA."

Liz accepted two coffees, two bananas, and two slices of pineapple bread and carried them back to the grass hut. "Please eat some of this. You don't know when you'll have another meal."

Nadia waved her hand toward a single-engine plane in the sky. It was headed for their island. "No time now," she said.

Liz removed a notebook from the Ziploc bag she kept it in and stuffed the pineapple bread in its place. She zipped up the bag. "At least take this," she said.

"And you take these," Nadia said, handing Liz the postcard they had written during the night and a wooden bangle bracelet. "For Ellen."

"Then you still have hope for her?"

"In times like these, hope may be all we have."

As Nadia slogged through the sand, Liz stood before their hut, gazing at the extraordinary beauty of the sea spread out before her. Islands that she knew were surrounded by fabulous coral reefs thrust themselves up from the water, looking as remote and unspoiled as any place in the world could be.

Ravenous for this peacefulness, ravenous, even, for breakfast, Liz fetched the fruit and coffee and downed every sip and morsel of the meal for two, sitting cross-legged in the sand. Every so often she pressed her hand into the sand, as if to get a literal grip on the world.

Then she went to the boat dock, which was the hub for both boat and plane rides to and from the island. Learning she could not even leave for the main island until the following day, she signed up for a midnight fishing expedition. Then she swam to the yacht again and watched, as did people around the world, the relentlessly repeating images of planes slamming into New York City's Twin Towers.

Finally, the day came to an end and, long after night fell, Liz made her way to the boat dock. No one else had signed up for the fishing expedition. Nonetheless, the guide was eager to take her out in his small motorboat.

"It will help you to sleep, the fishing," he told her as he steered the boat out onto the black water.

"It's so strange," she said, "not to be in my newsroom when news like this is breaking. Here I am, a world away, in paradise."

"The world is smaller than you think. When it comes to World War III, no one on Earth is a world away. And nowhere on the planet is paradise."

Feeling stripped of the one illusion that had helped her get through the day, Liz tried to steady herself by looking at the sea. When the boatman turned off the motor, the vessel settled on water so still that the stars shimmered on the surface. Looking up, Liz realized the points of light were arranged in unfamiliar constellations. She was so far from home that even the stars offered her nothing to steer by.

The boatman brought her back to earth by handing her a drop line. "I'm sorry for the children tonight," he said, as Liz dropped the lead-weighted line, with a small plunk, into the water. "This is a time for nightmares."

They sat in silence, mulling over that thought for a long time, the serenity of the scene quietly protesting, "It can't be so." Then, Liz felt a strong pull on her line. With much ado, she hauled in a twenty-inch fish, the largest she had ever caught anywhere in the world. Under the boatman's flashlight, it was revealed to be bright blue.

"That one is very good eating. You must have it for breakfast."

"I couldn't cook it. Please, take it for your family."

"No, they will cook it for you at your place. Taste your good fortune before you return to the States."

"Yes, all right."

With enhanced sensitivity, born of the day's trauma, to every small thing, Liz shuddered at the sound of the boat's motor starting up again. It seemed to thunder the fact that she must return to a very changed world. She was grateful, at least, that the noise covered the sound of the beautiful blue fish's last gasp.

Newton, Massachusetts, December 18, 2000

Having traveled by train from New York City, Samir Hasan stepped off the Green Line trolley at the Newton Highlands T stop and pulled a sheet of paper from his small backpack that contained Ellen's purse. He scrutinized the map he had printed on a computer in the New York Public Library. Then he set out in the direction of Fenwick Street near Newton City Hall. While making the half-mile walk along sidewalks banked with shoveled snow and crunchy with rock salt, he reflected that he was ill dressed once again. In the World Trade Center, it had been a question of style. Now the problem was fabric. His thin jacket, which was more than adequate for his work driving a heated taxi, was hardly hefty enough to fight the chill breeze that sent sheets of snow flying from piles all around him.

At least here, in a town of many Volvos and top-of-the line SUVs but few pedestrians, it was easy to tell no one was following him. Why did that provide him with a sense of relief? He wanted to believe he still had a chance to get the woman and himself out of danger. But how?

Why should such thoughts cross his mind? What was it about the shaqra that caused him to question the mission he had been assigned? Just because she moved to help him in the restaurant, just because she asked him about his son, were these enough to stop him from carrying out his promise?

What promise? He had never pledged to end this woman's life. Not with his own hands. In the New York City mosque, when he'd been asked to transmit the list of code words, he knew the cause justified killing. Killing on a large scale, perhaps. But he himself was only a—what was it called in English?—a cog. A cog in the turning of a bigger machine. Now he was called upon to be the wheel that crushes. Was he man enough to do this deed? Or, was he strong enough to listen to his heart, to save this woman from the danger in which he had placed her?

Every time he considered warning her of the danger she was in, the thought was paired with panic about the practical aftermath of such an action. His own life would then be threatened, too. How would the two of them—together or singly—elude Fa'ud for any length of time? Perhaps the only course was to kill her.

A gust of wind whipped icy crystals into his face. Samir Hasan squared his shoulders and picked up his pace.

With the cookie-making ingredients set out in the kitchen, Ellen decided to make herself a cup of tea. Taking out the china she had bought in New York City to replace the cup Veronica had broken recently, she realized she now owned an extra saucer, since the shop would sell her only the cup-and-saucer set. Turning the saucer over, she looked again at the name of the china pattern: Forget Me Not.

And then it happened again. A strangely unsettling feeling washed over her like a wave breaking on the side of her head, spilling down her arms and torso, producing a cold sweat. Gripping the saucer in one hand and the kitchen counter with the other, she saw again the marvelous shapes of topiary trees. And then, like a relentless lens trained on a reluctant subject targeted by paparazzi, her mind's eye zoomed in on a sort of umbrella of pine needles. And, yes, there was the tuneless hum again. And more sounds came to her too. The moan of a man, the man seated stroking himself under the tree. After he moaned, he formed a word, a word starting with the sound of the letter F, and this time he finished the word. With horror, Ellen heard two all-too-familiar syllables, Flicka.

Swedish for "Pretty Girl." Her father's pet name for her.

"Forget me not!" Ellen cried out, shocked into a state of mind that was no longer dreamlike in the least. Keenly aware of the saucer in one hand, of the counter edge she gripped with the other, of the shriek of the teakettle, Ellen recalled, with a kind of exhilaration, the sound of a zipper in the shadows, her father standing up, emerging from the shadows, taking her in his arms. Then he pointed, thrusting out his finger as if to stab the air, and he bellowed, in an unfamiliar, throaty voice, "Forget me not, young man! I will not let you get away with this."

Loosening her grip on the countertop, Ellen picked up a piece of chalk and wrote the words "FORGET ME NOT" on her blackboard. Her hand was shaky, but the writing seemed to settle her. She turned off the teakettle, and without washing the new cup, prepared herself a cup of tea in it.

Marveling at her mastery of these ordinary things, she carried the cup of tea into the living room, sat down in her chair, and then realized she had carried the extra saucer along without realizing it. She set the teacup with its own saucer on the side table and picked up her Arabic phrase book. Still holding the orphaned saucer in her left hand, she found herself tapping it on her thigh as, all at once, the flow of words, words in any language, seemed marvelous to her. So did the sound of her own voice. She sat and tapped the saucer against her thigh and read phrase after Arabic phrase with a facility that had heretofore always eluded her.

Meanwhile, Hasan had made his way to the Johanssons' front steps.

Hearing Ellen through the door, he found himself astonished again at this woman's ability to surprise him. Perhaps her conversational Arabic was rather good, as he'd originally thought, even though she seemed perplexingly unfamiliar with the word for coffee and the names of some fruits. How could he be certain about the shaqra's failure or success at understanding the code words? It was all too much for him. Utterly unmanned by the consternation he felt, Hasan did the only thing left to him.

He whispered a fervent prayer for guidance.

Only then did he reach out and ring the doorbell.

Startled, Ellen stood up, and set down her book. She was not expecting anyone. Still holding the saucer, she crossed the room and opened the door.

Hasan could take no chances. Even as he greeted her politely, he strode past her directly into the house, knocking her arm and causing the saucer she was holding to crash to the floor.

Allah be praised! This gave Hasan an excuse to bend down and assist in the cleanup, hiding his face while he continued to deliver the complicated greeting that he hoped would buy him entrée into the home.

"Dear lady," he said, "I have news of vital importance, which I beg of you to hear."

"Please, I'll take care of that," Ellen said, glancing at the shattered saucer. But she remained standing, afraid to squat near this intruder. "I must ask you to leave."

"Please, it is for your good that I have come to say . . ."

"I will call the police!"

Hasan clenched the shard, cutting himself. "Ayah!" He cried out, dropping his backpack and the china and standing up suddenly, clutching his bleeding hand.

Alarm overcame Ellen's instinct to help but Hasan cut short her effort to shove him toward the front door. Holding his uninjured hand over her mouth, he pushed her toward the back of the house, through the dining room and into the kitchen.

"Please, lady!" he urged, as Ellen squirmed free and rushed toward a block of wood holding a set of knives. To prevent her grasping a knife, he grabbed her hands with both of his, including his injured hand, dripping blood. Ellen slipped her left hand from his slippery grip. Disgusted, she shook her bloodied hand over the countertop.

"You!" she cried recognizing him fully now. "What are you doing here? What do you want with me?"

"Hamdu-lillah! I only want to—"

Ellen opened her mouth to scream.

Lunging, Hasan clamped his hand over Ellen's mouth. But her panic gave her cleverness he did not expect. She relaxed all of her muscles, dropping in a quick movement toward the floor.

Just then, a gunshot rang out.

And Ellen finished her journey to the floor—arriving dead at the cab-driver's feet.

Chapter 25

September 16, 2001

Unable to fly via Singapore, thanks to impossible flight delays in that hub of international travel, Liz decided to travel eastward from Fiji to Los Angeles. Entailing daylong waits in Fiji's airport and then again in Los Angeles, the journey was a fruitful one for *Banner* articles on passenger frustration and airport security.

Liz finally arrived in Boston's Logan Airport late in the afternoon of September 17. Taking a cab directly to Banner Square, she filed her stories and collected her messages before she returned to Gravesend Street. Pausing only to greet and feed a jubilant Prudence, she fell into bed and slept for twelve hours straight.

Only when Tom arrived at daybreak to feed Prudence did Liz awake. She began to apologize for her failure to phone and save him the trouble of feeding the cat, but then she broke off in the middle of the effort and said, "Oh Tom! I'm *not* sorry you've come. I'm so glad to see you!" And she threw herself into his outstretched arms. Exhausted from her trip and weary of holding herself together for days without emotional release, she simply sobbed.

After awhile, Tom left to pick up some groceries for Liz while she showered and made herself some coffee. Only then did she look over the telephone messages she had noted in the newsroom the day before. There was one from Doug Mayhew, the would-be rock star of Cape Cod, announcing he had written a "cool new ballad" in response to the terrorist attacks. There were two more from book publicists pushing authors of books about the Middle East as experts to be quoted in the *Banner*. And there was a call from a man with a Middle Eastern–accented voice, too

"Hello, M-Ms. Higgins. This is Al Hazard. Mr. V-V-V-Vee said I should c-c-c-call." He left a phone number Liz recognized as that of the Van Wormer workshop. "Mr. Vee" must be Jan Van Wormer.

When Liz dialed, the man picked up. Thanks to the stuttering and another more general hesitancy that was evident even over the phone, Liz realized it would be best to talk with Al in person. She arranged to meet him at the workshop within the hour. After cursorily drying her hair and leaving a note for Tom, she set out immediately for South Boston.

Along the way, she was startled to find American flags had materialized everywhere, especially as stickers in car windows, on bumpers, and even on car bodies. Flags waved from car antennae, too, and she saw Old Glory plastered on fences, porch railings, and automobile overpasses. At Van Wormer's South Boston address, the flag was in evidence, too, hanging stripes downward, like a curtain, from the little archway leading to the workshop entrance.

"I put it there for Al's sake," the elderly piano builder said as he opened the door for Liz. "Personally, I don't see how hanging the flag will achieve much, but it might make Al look like a patriot—and in a time like this, that's not a bad thing."

"When did he return, Mr. Van Wormer?"

"September the thirteenth. He said he was kicked out of his rented room because he is an Arab. Sadly, that may be true. In any case, I'm sure he feels safer here. He's ready to talk with you, too."

"That surprises me somewhat, grateful as I am for it. Why—if he's nervous about having the spotlight on him—is he ready to talk with the press now?"

"He's still not very comfortable about this, but he knows another man of Middle Eastern background is implicated in Mrs. Johansson's disappearance. Al says he fled from my house when he heard on the news that a Middle Easterner might have had something to do with her troubles. Now that that man has been identified, he's willing to tell you what he knows."

As Jan Van Wormer finished speaking, a timid figure slunk into the room. Lingering in the shadows near a grand piano, he spoke up.

"That's r-right," he said. "Mr. V-V-Vee? Would you p-p-please stay with me?"

"Sure, Al," the piano man said, motioning for Al to be seated on a worn settee while he and Liz took chairs facing him. Saving Al the struggle of spitting out his entire story, Jan Van Wormer told Liz, "Al here has told me he was falsely accused of some lewd behavior regarding Ellen Johansson, back when he was a student at the Wharton School out in Wellesley. Of course, Mrs. Johansson was just a girl then." Looking at Al, he said, gently, "That right, Al?"

"Y-yes, Mr. Vee," Al managed to say, while he brought his knees up to his chest and visibly struggled not to hug them to himself.

"It's all right, Al," Liz said encouragingly. "I'm here to tell the truth, not to get you in trouble for something you didn't do. I already know Dr. Mayhew doubted you had done anything wrong."

Al unfolded his knees and set his feet on the floor again. "He d-d-did? *Hamdu-lillah!*"

"Yes, Al. Mr. Buxton, your music teacher, told me he thought you were scared because Mr. Swenson was so angry. Dr. Mayhew said the board members at the Wharton School wouldn't give you a chance to tell the whole story. Now you can tell us everything, Al."

"I d-d-d-didn't do it," Al said.

"But you saw something that shocked you, is that right? Something that made you say 'Rah, rah. Shock-rah, shock-rah.'"

"How do you know that?" Al managed to spit out.

"Dr. Mayhew remembered you said that."

"I was d-disgusted."

"Not shocked? Then why did you keep saying 'Shock rah'?"

"*Shaqra,*" he said. "It means 'yellow hair'."

"Blonde? The word '*shaqra*' means 'blonde'?"

Al nodded. "I was d-d-disgusted, and sad, too. I was sorry for the *shaqra*. I was sorry for what Ellen maybe saw."

"What did Ellen see, Al?"

"It is d-d-difficult for me to tell this to a lady," he said, drawing his knees up and wrapping his arms around them this time.

"You saw a man behaving badly, didn't you, Al?" Jan Van Wormer said in a low tone. "The man was masturbating, wasn't he, Al? It's all right to tell the truth," he said, reaching across and placing his gnarled hand on Al's wrist.

"Allah help me, it is the truth. M-M-Mister Swenson. He was d-d-doing this thing."

"Did Ellen see what he was doing, Al?"

Al nodded and then shook his head in a contradictory motion. He seemed unable to speak.

"Al told me he was not sure how much Ellen saw," Jan Van Wormer said. "She ran to her father and then fled towards the house where she lived. Then Mr. Swenson began to shout at Al."

"F-F-F . . . ," Al began.

"Al told me Mr. Swenson was mumbling the word '*flicka.*' I think it's a Swedish endearment. But that was earlier, while the man was masturbating."

Tongue-tied, Al nodded exaggeratedly, then he moved his hand in a rolling motion as if performing a charade to indicate moving ahead.

"When he became angry, Ali," Ellen pressed, using his boyhood name, "did he say 'fuck' then?"

Al shook his head violently. 'F-F-F-FORGET ME NOT!'" he bellowed, and then fled from the room.

Liz had every intention of confronting Olga Swenson with her knowledge as she drove out to Wellesley from South Boston. Fatigue, hunger, and finally traffic gave her pause, however. Unwilling to face Olga on an empty stomach, she stopped at a lunch place in Newton Lower Falls and purchased a take-out container of clam chowder, a tuna sandwich, and potato chips. The September skies, whose beauty was so remarkable on the day of the terrorist attacks, remained as blue as any on a picture postcard. And, as Liz took her sandwich outdoors to a picnic table overlooking a fast-flowing stream that she knew was the Charles River, nearby trees with leaves just beginning to change color looked like harbingers of autumn.

It was nine months since Ellen had gone missing. Observing water splashing over a dam as brightly as if Ellen's disappearance or the pain of terrorists' victims had never occurred, Liz felt keenly alone with her thoughts. What did this new piece of the puzzle augur? Could one assume Ellen had called to mind her father's words at last—perhaps reminded by the name of the broken teacup's china pattern? If so, would that have given her relief from her flashbacks, or only endowed her with more pain?

If the shakily written words "FORGET ME NOT" on the blackboard were any indication, she was certainly agitated. But surely, Liz hoped, Ellen must have realized she now had the upper hand over the flashbacks. Even if it was painful to know her father had behaved appallingly, a woman like Ellen, a woman who knew how to turn to books for information about her worries, must have known she could get help overcoming this painful knowledge. She must have experienced some sense of relief as she wrote those words on her blackboard.

Why then, did she go missing? Tilting her head to look up at the gloriously blue sky, Liz thought again about Nadia's account of Ellen's strange cab ride and the events at the World Trade Center. The night before the attacks, Nadia, who was herself an intelligence operative, had not seen anything significant in the cabdriver's radio talk. The terrorist attacks put everything in a different light. What would Nadia think now? Had Ellen overheard something she shouldn't in the two-way radio conversation?

Finishing her sandwich, Liz returned to her car and phoned Faisal al-Turkait. He sounded far more reserved than he had been during their earlier encounter. But he consented to meet her later that day in his shop. Unsure what she wanted to say to Olga at this stage, Ellen nearly turned her car eastward towards Boston. What point was there in dredging up the ugly fact of her husband's behavior, except to see if Olga was aware of it? But, even so, on impulse she turned west and drove to the Swenson house.

If Olga was perplexed to see Liz, she hardly showed it. Instead, she seemed relieved to have company and to share her thoughts about the terrorist attacks.

"It personalizes things, doesn't it, when you have a loved one who has been on the scene where a tragedy later occurs? Only months earlier, Ellen was having such a memorable meeting with her pen pal on the top floor of one of those towers," Olga said as she poured hot water into a china teapot.

"Yes," Liz said. "It makes the unimaginable all-too-imaginable, unfortunately."

"Shall we take the tea outside and enjoy the weather?"

"Good idea. Let me help."

Liz welcomed the chance to be occupied with the tea things, since she remained uncertain about sharing Ali's revelation. The walk through the house, down the stairs, and through the mudroom bought her a few minutes to think. In the mudroom, Liz noticed Olga's aluminum vases were filled with fresh-cut flowers, and an incomplete flower arrangement stood on the potting table.

"Did I interrupt you in your arranging?"

"Yes, but it doesn't matter. Just as I felt strange taking up old hobbies although my daughter remains missing, I now find myself feeling odd about arranging flowers while the world is in such a state. It feels rather like fiddling while Rome burns." Olga seemed to shake herself as she stood poised to exit the mudroom.

Meanwhile, Liz took a scarf from her purse. "I seem to have picked this up accidentally during an earlier visit. Shall I hang it here?" she asked.

Olga nodded. As Liz tried to drape the scarf on an overloaded coat hook, she knocked a coat to the floor. Picking it up, she tucked the scarf into its pocket and hung the coat on the hook again by the little chain sewn to its collar.

Burdened with the tea tray, Olga signaled Liz to make haste into the fresh air. "That is one of Ellen's favorite old scarves," she said, her eyes brightening with tears. Thrusting the door open with her shoulder, she added, "It's stuffy in here, don't you think?"

"I'd call it 'close,' thanks to the mixed fragrances of the flowers."

Liz contented herself with making small talk, until she realized it was time to head for her appointment with Faisal al-Turkait in Cambridge.

"Was there a particular reason for your visit, Liz?" Olga asked.

"I thought I'd let you know, 'shaqra' means 'blonde' in Arabic."

"'Shock-rah!' Then that Al Leigh was not so tongue-tied!" Olga said, her eyes widening. "It's dreadful, don't you think, the assumptions we make about foreigners? No wonder they hate us! What will become of us, Liz?"

Faisal al-Turkait greeted Liz with polite formality at the door of Turkoman Books. Moving a stack of volumes off his sofa, he invited her to take a seat and join him in drinking coffee.

"This time I was expecting you, you see," he said as he poured. "I hope you will understand if I am reticent in other regards, though," he said. "At this time, I would not like to have my name in the paper or even to discuss much of anything over the phone."

Liz was shocked. "Do you think you are under some kind of surveillance?"

"Certainly. This country is under attack by enemies of Middle Eastern extraction. As an American citizen, I applaud this vigilance."

"As a person of Middle Eastern extraction, surely you feel uncomfortable about it as well?"

"I understand it."

"I can only express my admiration! I'm not so sure I would feel similarly understanding if the nation were under attack by women with auburn hair and I was hounded as a result."

"When I walk down a city street at night and a woman is the only other pedestrian, should I blame her if she crosses the street to ensure her safety from a male stranger? I am no assailant, yet I am not offended to see a woman exercise such caution. The same is true now. In the interests of our nation's security, I am not offended to see our government scrutinize me. But let us talk of other matters. You have some more words for me to translate, I assume?"

"Actually, it is the same list of words that concerns me," Liz said, taking out the grocery list. "Do any of these words have double meanings? I mean, could they refer to some sort of terrorist activity, meeting, delivery, or anything of that sort?"

"No, I think not. These are the most ordinary of words. Truly, they look like a simple grocery list of fruits."

"I guess I'm searching for significance in Ellen's interaction with the cabdriver, even trying to connect it to the terrorist attacks. That's a pretty big leap, though, isn't it?"

"That's understandable, particularly after the events of September eleventh. Didn't you show me, last time you were here, a photo of a book she had that was written for intelligence experts?"

"Yes, and I still don't know where she acquired that. I plan to see if they have any record of selling it to her at the Brattle Book Shop in Boston, where, I understand, she purchased something in order to prepare to meet her pen pal."

"I know the owner there and I know he now records his book sales on the computer. Most book dealers do, these days, because so many of us also sell on-line. We need to keep track of individual volumes. He might be reluctant to tell you who bought the book, but if I ask him for the book, as though I wish to acquire it, he might tell me if and when it was sold."

Putting through a call to the store, the book dealer discovered the book in question had been sold there on October 13, 2000. There was no credit card or check information, since the purchase had been made in cash. But the Brattle's owner did let on he'd thought the customer was surprising. Most of the time, he told his colleague, he sold odd books like that to professors or students. This customer looked like a suburban housewife.

The likelihood of Ellen serving as an intelligence operative seemed unlikely now. Surely, if Ellen were a spy, she would be supplied with such books, not reduced to finding one in a used-book shop. Liz returned to the question of the cabbie's grocery list.

"Are any of these words also used euphemistically, as sexual slang, I mean?"

"This is not easy for me to discuss with a lady," the book dealer said, echoing a similar statement by Ali. "But the answer is yes. *Teena*, the word for fig, can also be used—man-to-man only, of course—to refer to a woman." He blushed.

"What about the other fruits? Here in America a man might say of a woman, 'Look at them apples,' for instance," Liz said.

Faisal's complexion reddened further. "No, I wouldn't say the other words on this grocery list would be used in that way. More coffee?" he said, ducking into the kitchen.

"I ask because we know that the cabdriver who drove Ellen Johansson in New York, and who also visited her house on the day she disappeared, made her uncomfortable by using that word in a sleazy tone in a two-way radio conversation with another male. She wondered if the cabbie was talking graphically about her, and then, when she heard him continue to use the word, she relaxed a little, thinking he was talking in sexual terms about a woman called Tina."

Returning to the room, Faisal underlined Nadia's view. "I think she was correct in feeling uncomfortable. I think perhaps the driver was talking in a most improper manner about his passenger."

Chapter 26

After leaving the book dealer, Liz drove the Tracer to the *Banner* parking lot and stopped in at the city desk, only to learn that she'd been put on another mall story. This time the assignment was to interview store managers about the drop in customer numbers in response to terrorist-inspired fears of gathering in public spaces. Liz drove to the closest mall she could think of, the CambridgeSide Galleria, a snazzy shopping complex in Cambridge, across the Charles River from Boston.

Inside the mall she met *Banner* photographer Jim Collins, who shot photos of the unpopulated place from the top of an escalator. This turned out to be a good spot to get comments from a sampling of the few who had decided to shop, terrorist threat or not.

"I'm getting married next week," one young woman told Liz defiantly. "I'm not letting al-Qaeda prevent me from buying my bridesmaids their gifts!"

"Let 'em try to shoot me!" a belligerent older man wearing a Veterans of Foreign Wars baseball cap declared. "They'll regret it!"

Despite the small number of shoppers, excellent quotes were easy to get. With time to spare, Liz and Jim decided to cover two more shopping venues, Boston's upscale Newbury Street and then more humble Washington Street, also known as "Downtown Crossing." Thanks to the dearth of shoppers, it was unusually easy to find parking spaces on Newbury Street. They decided to walk a block over to Boylston Street, where the very posh toy emporium FAO Schwarz seemed a great choice to represent this shopping district. What did well-heeled parents think about spending big bucks on playthings now?

"You can't buy security, I know," one mother said, "but you *can* buy together time. I'm purchasing this horribly complicated Taj Mahal model to show my son the beauty of another culture's architecture and to give our family something to do together. I'm uneasy about taking my kids to public places at the moment, so I figure we'll be spending more time together at home."

With answers like this, Liz knew she had the makings of a sidebar, if hard news about the terrorist attack aftermath didn't grab all the space in the paper. Thinking ahead, she got contact information from the woman for a possible family page piece about family time as an antidote to terror. The toy store interviews were so productive and time-consuming that Jim Collins had to leave her so he could cover another story. Outside the store, feeding the parking meter, Liz realized she did not have enough time to walk to Downtown Crossing after all, a pedestrian mall where parking was nonexistent.

Instead, she returned to Newbury Street and strolled along it for several blocks. Rejecting a ladies' hat shop, several beauty salons, and some art galleries that were all too posh to provide contrast with FAO Schwarz, she made her way on foot back to Boylston Street. Running parallel to Newbury Street, this thoroughfare offered a mix of shopping, from the posh toy shop and elegant Shops at Prudential Center mall to discount pharmacies. Scanning the stores, she made her way to a place bearing the sign "Puttin' on the Ritz: Off-Price Remainders." The customers here were all female, and the well-heeled matrons and homeless women seeking warmth in the chill of the autumn afternoon represented two extreme ends of the economic scale. None of them seemed eager to talk with Liz, so she killed fifteen minutes by pushing designer leather jackets around on their rack, while trying to over-hear shoppers' chatter about what was on their minds. The effort was fruit-less for the purposes of Liz's article, since the bargain hunters were mostly shopping solo and those who spoke to one another seemed absorbed in talk-ing about the fact that the shop stamped the word "Ritz" in hot pink on the trendy designer labels, but she *did* get a great buy on a leather jacket.

If anyone were to interview me about this expenditure, she thought, *I'd say it is an indulgence along the lines of comfort food. A guilty pleasure.*

Before Liz could return to the Tracer, her cell phone rang. It was Cormac Kinnaird.

"Where are you, Liz?" he demanded. "Have you heard the news?"

"Has there been another attack?"

"No, thank God, no. But some hikers in a state park out near Plymouth have turned up the remains of two bodies in a wooded area. I'm surprised your editor hasn't called you."

"Someone else might be assigned to this. When and how did you hear about this?"

"Just now, on the radio. I know I won't have access to the heart of the scene, but I'm heading out there anyway. You might be able to barge in on it better as a reporter."

"What do you know about the scene?"

"Two sets of skeletal remains, that's all the police are saying."

"Let me contact the newsroom and I'll call you right back."

Liz was in luck. Thanks to the fact that Dick Manning was following up on a bomb scare, Dermott okayed her heading out to Forges Field Recreational Area in Plymouth County, where the remains had been found.

It was midafternoon as she drove southeast from Boston, leaving the urban scene behind and entering a sandy landscape of scrub pines, blueberry bushes, and cranberry bogs. Ordinarily, a visit to such a scene would provide welcome recreation, but that was not the case now. Grateful that this was not happening a few weeks later, when the change from daylight-savings to standard time would plunge the area into darkness within an hour, Liz nevertheless made haste to arrive while a reasonable amount of daylight remained.

The recreational area was well named. Home to a playground, two baseball diamonds, and a few soccer or football fields, it looked like a regional gathering place for team practices and intramural sports. Extensive parking lots were filled with vehicles that spoke of school sports and the suburban lifestyle: bright yellow school buses, minivans, and SUVs. Parents, team coaches, and uniform-clad kids were now clustered in the playground area, the children's faces rosy with excitement. Unable to approach the scene of the crime, they focused their attention on the access road to the recreational area. It was lined with police and rescue vehicles, the latter sadly useless in the circumstances. Flashing lights and radioed conversation kept the scene lively.

Pulling on her new jacket against the afternoon chill, Liz clipped her *Banner* I.D. card on her chest pocket, grabbed a reporter's notebook, and strode into the underbrush far to the left of the obvious path to the crime scene: Liz knew it was unlikely she would get very close to the scene before being barred by the police, but at least she might get a sense of the lay of the land.

And, covered with white pines, pitch pines, and tangled underbrush, the landscape could only be described as undulating. Visible chiefly because of bright lights set up in advance of dusk, the center of police activity was located at the bottom of a depression. Liz shivered to think it was walking distance from a center of kids' activity and wondered if the hikers who had come across the skeletons were young people—and if they remained in the vicinity.

"Hey, you!" a policeman bellowed at her just then. "This is a crime scene. You can't walk in here."

"I know, detective," she said, looking at his badge. "I'm Liz Higgins from the *Beantown Banner* and I was trying to get a sense of the lay of the land here."

"I'm not in charge of talking with the press. You'll have to talk with the sergeant."

"Can you just confirm a few things that are already reported, like who found the remains?"

"I guess so, but don't use my name. It was a pair of bird nuts and their daughter."

"Are they still here? Do you know their names and the girl's age?"

"You'll have to ask them. They're sitting in a cruiser back there." He nodded toward the line of police cars along the access road. "You'd better get out of here, now."

Thanking the detective, Liz made her way to the last cruiser in the line of police cars. Leaning on its trunk, Mick Lichen was haranguing a police officer about getting access to the trio of hikers. Clad in jeans, hiking boots, and fleece jackets in complementary colors, and wearing horrified facial expressions, the family looked like an L.L. Bean ad gone wrong. The red-eyed daughter, who clung to her father, looked to be about fourteen years old.

"It's a free country. You can't prevent them from commenting on what they saw," Lichen argued loudly.

"No, I can't, Mr. Lichen. But I can make a request, and these good people can choose to honor it in the interest of seeing this crime solved."

"Is that what you want? To be silenced?" Lichen said to the family.

"Leave us alone, please," the mother said.

Lichen stalked off too soon. His challenge seemed to stir the fourteen-year-old.

"Why are you letting the police shut us up?" she demanded, wrenching herself free of her father's embrace and getting out of the cruiser.

"If the criminal doesn't know everything the police have discovered, it may make it easier to catch him," her father began.

"But it's too late for the dead people, anyway, isn't it?" the teen cried. "I want to tell what I saw. It was gross stepping on those bones. Really gross!"

"You can tell me," Liz said, stepping in to introduce herself.

"My name is Jessica Sobel," the girl announced, thrusting away the hand her father raised to signal her to keep quiet.

"Maybe it's better that she talks, John," said the woman. "I'm Joy Sobel and this is my husband, John," she said to Liz.

"My dad's a science teacher," Jessica said. "He's always dragging us along on nature hikes."

"In preparation for my classes at Plymouth High School," John explained. "We were looking for birds that migrate and birds that remain here through the winter. Down in that protected hollow we found plenty of chickadees— that's our state bird you know—as I expected we would."

"Why would the chickadees favor that hollow?"

"It's the site of an ef—"

"Of f-ing corpses!" Jessica interrupted. "Cut the lecture, Dad! Those birds were flying around landing on the bushes and trees, probably eating bugs from the bodies." Jessica shivered.

"No, no, Jessica," John said. "Any insect life associated with the deceased was long gone. There were only bones there, Honey."

"'The deceased'!" the teen mimicked her father. "Always the professor! Can't you just say 'dead guys'?"

"Jessie, Jessie!" her mother soothed. "Try not to upset yourself." She turned to Liz. "It seemed so idyllic at first," she said. "John was just point- ing out the tall grass all pressed down where the deer had slept on it, and then my daughter stumbled on the bones."

"Did you see anything else, Mr. Sobel?"

"If you mean did I see a murder weapon, the answer is no. Naturally, we were trying to rush our daughter away from the area."

"What about clothing, shoes, a handbag—anything like that?"

"Nothing. I'm no expert, but I thought the bones looked very old. They were very brown, as if they were tea- or coffee-stained. I guess they looked so old, I didn't expect to see any clothes or shoes with them."

As more reporters discovered the family's location, René DeZona arrived and joined the crush of press focusing in on the family. Liz lingered long enough to take down her sources' ages, as told to a television anchor, and then returned to the Tracer to phone in her story. Dusk was falling when she arrived back at her car, where she found Cormac Kinnaird tying his shoe with his foot up on her bumper.

"Any luck viewing the scene?" he asked.

Rosemary Herbert

"No. You?"

"No access either, but I talked with one of the officers. The ME for Plymouth is in Manhattan helping out at Ground Zero. They've got a new guy covering this. He'll likely keep information close to his chest, hoping to make a name for himself here."

"That's not good news."

"You're right about that. But the weather report is. With a downpour predicted for tomorrow afternoon, he'll make haste to move those bones. We'll have to be ready to reconnoiter as soon as the police finish scouring the area."

"Won't that leave us without the hope of finding any evidence? They will have grabbed it all."

"Take a look around you. It's a tall order to thoroughly scrutinize this place, and remember, it's a green medical examiner on this case. By the way, did you find out what took those hikers to this particular spot?"

"The man's a high-school science teacher. He was making a dry run for a school nature walk, with his wife and reluctant daughter in tow."

"If he knows the area, he might be useful to us. See if you can get him to join us when we come back here."

"Good idea. Why are you so interested in these remains, Cormac? Do you think they could belong to Ellen and the cabbie?"

"From what we know, the bones sound older than nine months old. That would seem to eliminate Ellen. Let's just say, I'm eager to see a certain reporter at work."

Before calling in her story, Liz made an effort to get a comment from the police spokesman and to talk with Stu Simmons, the assistant medical examiner on the scene. The former offered, "No comment," and the latter remained with the remains. After Jared Conneely took her information over the phone, Liz made the hour-and-a-half drive back to Gravesend Street while listening avidly to the radio all along the way. Amid much focus on September eleventh aftermath stories—especially interviews of New Englanders whose kin had been killed in the hijacked jets or in the Twin Towers—little attention was paid to the discovery of human remains in the Forges Field Recreational Area. Brief reports added little to the facts Liz had already gleaned at the scene. Liz did learn, however, that police planned to scour the woods around Forges Field at dawn.

Back at Gravesend Street, she found her refrigerator stocked with milk, orange juice, fresh eggs, and an unfamiliar bowl containing homemade fruit salad. On the kitchen counter, weighed down with six cans of cat food and a package of English muffins, she found a note from Tom.

"See you tomorrow? I'll be changing the billboard here," it read.

Liz gave him her answer by phone. "I'm planning to be in Plymouth County at sunrise," she said, "so I don't think I'll be here. But thank you for all the goodies! Now, I've got to call the science teacher who discovered the remains, to see if he can meet me."

John Sobel was eager to meet Liz at dawn, but warned that he'd have to leave the recreational area by 7:45 in order to get to school. The science teacher knew just when the sun was slated to rise and set a time for them to meet.

Hungry, Liz served some fruit salad into a bowl, sliced an English muffin in two, and placed the halves in her toaster. She pushed the toaster handle and the button on her phone answering machine down simultaneously. What she heard on the answering machine was somewhat surprising, since the caller had avoided her for some months.

"Liz, it's Erik. I'm sorry I haven't been in touch. I hope you can help me. The police won't tell me anything. Could it be Ellen and that cabdriver they've found out near Plymouth? Oh . . ." The call was cut off as Erik was distracted by something.

Liz froze in the act of hanging up her receiver and stared at the telephone number on her machine's caller-I.D. display. She had memorized it nine months ago. The call had been made from Ellen's cell phone—a phone that had been unaccounted for since Ellen's disappearance. What was Erik doing with that phone? Had he placed the calls that came through from that phone in June and in August? The only reason to do that would be to make it look as if his wife was in the vicinity—alive and well enough to phone on Veronica's birthday and again in August. Up till now, the calls from Ellen's cell phone had provided hope. But if Erik had been making them, then another conclusion seemed chillingly likely: Erik had reason to toss red herrings on the path of the investigation, leading police astray as they sought the truth about his wife.

Liz knew she should inform the police immediately. Instead, she unplugged her answering machine, locked it in the car's trunk, drove straight to Fenwick Street, and surprised Erik by knocking on his door. Finding that Veronica had a friend visiting, she convinced Erik to take a walk to the Newton City Hall Common. Noting that he carried a receiver for his portable phone with him as he left the house, she asked, "Do you also carry your cell phone with you at all times?"

"Absolutely," he said, taking his phone from his pocket. "If Ellen gets in touch, I want to be available."

"Do you know what time it is?" Liz asked. "I'm on tight deadline today," she fibbed.

Erik turned on the cell phone and showed its small screen to Liz. The time and date were shown there.

"Thanks, Erik. What are your thoughts on the phone calls from Ellen's cell?"

"My thoughts? I can hardly separate them from my emotions on this. Intellectually, I know someone other than Ellen might be making these calls, just to suggest she is somewhere near us. If that's the case, and Ellen is the victim of foul play, her victimizer has added cruel insult to injury."

Liz noted an odd formality in Erik's speech. Was this his way of feeling some sense of sanity in a situation he could not control, or was it an indication of guilt?

"I don't really believe that the calls are from Ellen," Erik went on, "but I can't help hoping that they are, especially the attempt to reach me on August eighteenth. I haven't pointed this out to anyone else, but Ellen and I first met eleven years ago on that date. In any case, the calls have been an unbearable tease, especially for Veronica." Erik paused. "I'm surprised you're asking me about the cell phone calls on this day of all days. I had hoped you might have something to tell me that would shed light on the bodies found near Plymouth. Tell me the bones can't be hers," he pleaded.

"Observers say the bones seem too old. But there's nothing conclusive. Erik, I have to ask you, why did you pick up Ellen's cell phone today and call me? Was it because, in your distress about the discovery of the bones, you grabbed the wrong cell phone? Where have you hidden it all this time?"

"What? I don't know what you're talking about! Are you suggesting I have Ellen's cell? That's madness!"

"Her cell number came up on my caller I.D. when you called to ask about—"

"That's impossible! Look, here's the number of my cell." He pushed a button on his cell phone, revealing its telephone number. "It's a digit off from Ellen's. The last part of mine is 4441; hers is 4440."

"4440 came up on my caller I.D. And you were the speaker."

"That's inexplicable! I tell you, I don't have Ellen's phone." At the sound of sirens, Erik looked toward Commonwealth Avenue frantically. "Did you report this to the police?" he cried out.

"Not yet, Erik. I wanted to see what you had to say first."

"Then why are they here?" he said, turning distraught eyes on the reporter as several officers arrived.

"The line was bugged with your permission, sir," an officer said. "Come along with us now."

"Stay with Veronica until my mother-in-law arrives, would you?" Erik pleaded. "She's on her way with groceries for us."

"Of course, Erik," Liz said.

Turning towards Fenwick Street, Liz ran across the common. Fortunately, it seemed Veronica had not heard the commotion. Liz could see her through the window engrossed in a video cartoon on the television. Liz waited on the front steps, a quiet guardian for Veronica, until the grandmother arrived. Grateful it was not her report but rather the traced call that had summoned the police, she nevertheless ached for the child whose father was now under arrest.

Liz called in her story to the city desk and then drove to Newton Police Headquarters, where she volunteered to answer questions and turned over her answering machine to authorities. Only after all this did she return home to get some food and rest.

Chapter 27

Too soon, Liz's alarm announced it was 4:00 a.m. Time to swallow down some breakfast and get on the road to Plymouth. Coverage of 9/11–related stories still dominated television news. But on the radio, as Liz drove east, newscasters found time to vilify Erik as a jealous husband who most likely had known his wife was involved with a "Middle Eastern stranger." They implied he must have done his wife and "her lover" in, and then placed calls from her phone to make it look like she was alive and well during the ensuing months.

Stopping for coffee, Liz bought a copy of the *Banner*. Under the headline, "CELL TO CELL," her own report outlined the facts of the phone call and Erik's arrest, while Dick Manning's piece, headed "MYSTERY MAILS," used a quote from Newton mail carrier Len Fenster to suggest that Erik pursued strange passions: "Imagine those ladybugs crawling all over a nice lady like that? Wouldn't that give anybody the creeps? And she was always getting letters from the Middle East. Coulda' been from that Arab guy who bled in her kitchen."

Arriving at Forges Field just at sunrise, Liz found René DeZona already on the scene, strapped to the top section of a telephone pole and armed with a very long lens. Apparently the police who had been guarding the scene had not looked up: They seemed unaware the photographer was there. Following DeZona's hand signals, Liz drew one police officer aside and loudly fired questions about the case at him, covering with her voice the sound of DeZona's camera work. After a few minutes, DeZona pointed to a Porta-Potty nearby. As Liz approached the unit, she heard the sound of two small items dropping to the ground near her feet. Film cans. Stooping to tie a lace on her hiking boot, Liz pocketed the film. Minutes later, the police noticed the photographer and confiscated the film that was then in DeZona's camera.

Just then John Sobel and Cormac Kinnaird arrived in separate vehicles. When Liz told them she needed to pass the film to René, Kinnaird surprised her by producing a pipe from his pocket. Taking the film, he approached the photographer and asked for a light. As the photographer fumbled for matches, Kinnaird passed the film to him. Film in hand, DeZona drove off, presumably headed for the newsroom.

As expected, the police prevented the reporter, teacher, and forensics man from entering the area they'd surrounded with crime scene tape. The trio hiked into the woods and then circled toward the vicinity of the crime scene.

"They've closed off a wide area around the remains," the science teacher said.

"But that doesn't mean they'll find everything," Cormac said. "That ME is green. And he's rushing. I wonder if he'll realize skeletal remains that have been there over time may have been disarticulated."

"You mean taken apart?"

"That's right, Liz. Scattered or even carried away into burrows by animals back when there was meat on those bones."

Liz grimaced.

"It concerns me for another reason that this Stu Simmons seems in such haste to remove the bones. If they are kept in their position and context, it will be easier to evaluate the shower of organic material to which they have been exposed. In an area like this, we can tell quite a bit about the time of death—or at least the time when the bodies were placed here—by cataloging that organic material. Pollen found on the bones will tell us during which seasons they were exposed to the elements. Working back from that, and using insect evidence, we can make a remarkably accurate guess as to how long the body lay here before it was stripped of tissue by maggots and animals. These bones have been here for quite some time. Simmons is a fool if he thinks one more rainstorm will destroy the evidence they hold."

Liz recalled the doctor's scolding her about withholding the cigarette butt evidence months ago. "Even if we found a disarticulated bone or two, Cormac," she asked, "wouldn't you insist on turning it in to the police? What kind of advantage would that give us?"

"As much as I'm eager to see you get a scoop, we have to keep in mind that the search for the truth takes precedence."

"But it sounds as if you're better qualified to handle this scene, this evidence anyway. Doesn't it look like the police will bungle this?"

"I'm not saying I wouldn't take a good look at anything we turn up before handing it over, but I *would* absolutely hand the evidence over. Even to a bungler. That's the law."

"Look here, Liz," the science teacher said. "Here's the opening to a fox den. No, I don't see any human bones conveniently sticking out of it. But you should take a look anyway to help you find more animal abodes in the landscape. Do you see how the fox has taken advantage of the protection afforded by the tree stump? From the other side, the opening to its den is invisible."

"That's not very encouraging. Does this mean we'll have to walk in circles around every tree stump?"

"It wouldn't be a bad idea."

"We shouldn't overestimate the likelihood of finding bones this far from the bodies, in any case," Cormac cautioned.

The trio combed the woods for some forty minutes in silence. Then, the science teacher announced he would have to head for his classroom. Liz looked up to watch him as he trod reluctantly up the hill, leaving behind the most exciting nature scene he was likely to see in his lifetime.

"Yesterday, you said you expected to see chickadees in the hollow," Liz called out to him. "Why there and not right here, for instance?"

The bird-lover turned his head and looked at her over his shoulder. "The hollow is the site of an ephemeral pond or vernal pool. Dry now, of course, but a few feet deep after the snow melts in springtime."

Cormac Kinnaird stood stock still. "That changes everything," he said. "If your photographer has been able to zoom in on that scene, or if I can get into that scene soon, we've got an advantage, Liz," he said. "A big one." With that, he took Liz's hand and led her up the hill to their parked cars, whistling an Irish reel all the way.

Since the police on the crime scene would not offer comments, Liz drove to Plymouth Police Headquarters to see if she could get an official state-ment on the case. It was early in the day and things might change before her afternoon deadline, but it didn't hurt to be thorough. Plymouth Police Chief Martin Oliver curtailed repeated inquiries by promising a midafter-noon press conference. Returning to Forges Field, Liz found police personnel adamant that nothing would be revealed until the press conference, so she drove to the newsroom to find DeZona.

"Your friend the forensics guy said he'd appreciate having copies of these," the photographer said. "Not that they show much of anything." The eight-by-ten photos taken from the telephone pole perch showed the bent backs of police officers gathered around what looked like some dark sticks. Presumably, they were pieces of the discolored skeleton. Much was obscured by branches of trees located between the photographer and his quarry.

DeZona slipped the photos into a manila envelope and handed them to Liz. "See you in Plymouth later?" he asked. "I hear we're to cover the press conference."

"You bet," Liz said. Then, she returned to her desk, called a courier, and arranged for the photos to be delivered to Dr. Kinnaird's university office.

With hours to kill before the press conference, Liz gave Tom a call, leaving a message on his answering machine. Then, she decided to drive out to the Wellesley College campus, which seemed an ideal place to think things through. Parking her car at the Faculty Club, she took a leisurely walk along Lake Waban in the direction of the Pinetum. This time, she was not alone. About twenty yards ahead of her, two young women walked along, lost in animated conversation about a "hot" professor. As she followed them through the Pinetum and the students emerged into the more open area of the topiary garden, one of the young women turned around to face Liz.

"Would you take a photo of Florrie and I, please?"

Can these be the nation's best and brightest? Liz asked herself, cringing at the grammar. "'Of Florrie and *me*,'" she said, realizing even as she said it how schoolmarmish she must sound to them.

But Florrie and her friend were not annoyed.

"My English Comp prof is always telling me the same thing," the poor grammarian said.

Liz cringed again when the girls arranged themselves on the grass between two topiary trees.

"Don't you see the sign?" she asked. "It says to stay off the grass."

"It's only for a photo," Florrie said as Liz stepped back into the shade at the edge of the Pinetum to shoot a backlit picture without having direct sunlight on the lens.

Liz heard one of the young women exclaim delightedly, "Look, Ellen! A chocolate Lab, just like my dog at home."

Liz followed Florrie's gaze. At the far end of the topiary garden, Olga Swenson froze in the act of throwing a toy to her dog, Hershey. At the sound of her daughter's name on another's lips, her face collapsed into an expression of excruciating pain. Deciding that Olga did not need the intrusion of a reporter at that moment, Liz handed back the camera, turned around in the shade of the conifer collection, and walked back to her car.

At Plymouth Police Headquarters later that afternoon, the press conference offered little new information. Police Chief Martin Oliver reiterated how the remains had been found and declared that the skeletons appeared to be those of a male and a female whose bones had lain in the hollow for some years. Although no flesh remained on the bones, strands of hair found there indicated both victims were dark-haired. Pressed by Liz and her colleagues, he said there was dentition under examination, but it did not match any dental records for unsolved crimes currently in the database. Asked specifically if the remains could be those of the missing Newton mom, he said the apparent age of the bones, the hair color, and the lack of a dental match made it look extremely unlikely.

After the press conference, Liz decided to heed her hunger pangs, but not before purchasing a postcard for Nadia. Fortunately, in this vacation haven "gifte shoppes" were located cheek-by-jowl with restaurants. After buying a postcard picturing a cranberry bog in a shop called "Plymouth Rocks!", she took a window seat in a waterfront eatery called the Mayflower Café. There, she ordered a special called Pilgrim's Progress: a turkey and cranberry sauce sandwich followed by a bowl of Indian pudding à la mode. While looking out the window at the tourist-magnet *Mayflower II* sailing ship, she took out the postcard.

"Dear Nadia," she wrote on it. "Here I am in Plymouth, Massachusetts, covering a crime in cranberry bog country. There are two victims, but the age of the remains seems to eliminate Ellen."

What a strange thing to write on a postcard! Liz shook her head.

She changed the period at the end of the second sentence to a comma and added, "fortunately, your pen pal remains much on my mind." She turned over the card and examined it, then turned it over again. "On this card," she continued, "you can see the bright red cranberries, as well as the colored leaves typical of an autumn landscape in eastern Massachu— "

Abruptly, Liz stopped writing. She wished she had not sent DeZona's photos to Cormac Kinnaird before studying them better, for suddenly she called to mind something in the wrong color family that appeared in the foreground of a couple of the photographs. Now she realized that when she had scrutinized the pictures to get a glimpse of the remains, she had not looked carefully at the out-of-focus elements in the photos' foregrounds.

Signaling the waitress, Liz paid her bill and made haste to Forges Field

Recreational Area. By the time she arrived there, she had to phone in the press conference story to the city desk, cursing the fading afternoon light all the while. With the story filed, she strode over to DeZona's telephone pole. Standing at the base of it, she realized she needed to climb the pole to get the correct angle on the scene. The pole must be climbable if DeZona had managed it. But Liz was not so skilled, nor did she have the telephone company–issue climbing belt that had helped DeZona clamber up the pole. Giving up on scaling the pole, she moved her car next to it and stood on its roof. She saw nothing out of place in the scene. That was not surprising, since the car's roof was nowhere near as high as DeZona's perch had been.

If she could not look down on the scene from above, there was one more option: walk into the scene and look up. But how would she ensure that she did not get lost as dusk fell completely while she was in the hollow? Returning to the car, Liz grabbed an extra reporter's notebook and a flashlight. Then, she stepped into the woods. When her car was nearly out of sight, she attached a page from the notebook to the branch of a tree at eye level. She marked more trees and shrubs this way as she worked her way into the depression from which the police had so recently removed the remains.

Liz made it to the base of the hollow—the place where the deer had taken their rest so close to those human bones—without seeing anything out of the ordinary on the way down. In the heart of the hollow, she paused and shivered. It seemed only right to do something to honor the pair who'd met their ends here, whoever they were. But the light was fading and there was a hint of pink in the sky, signaling sunset. There was no time to linger. Very quietly humming the hymn "Amazing Grace," Liz stood quite still as she regarded the reddening sky. She asked herself which way felt right for retracing her steps and pointed her arm in that direction. Dropping her eyes to look, she saw that, without her paper markers, she would have walked into the woods in a direction that was about thirty degrees off from the correct one.

Thanking herself for marking the path, Liz made her way up the slope again. It was an easier task to remove than to attach the papers to the trees, so Liz was able to concentrate better on examining the branches above her. When she came to the end of "Amazing Grace," she hummed it again, a little more loudly. This time, she was humming it as much for reassurance as to honor the dead. She longed to share the intensely lonely scene with something living, even a chickadee. But there was no sign of the little birds, not even the sound of their distinctive call, *chicka-dee-dee-dee*.

But it soon became evident that Liz was not alone in the darkening hollow. Suddenly, the silent woods did produce a noise sounding, for all the world, like an old biddy shrieking, "Drink your tea!" There it was again, "Drink your tea!"

As a branch moved off to her left, Liz realized the noise had been a bird-call. She could not call to mind the name of the bird, which she now saw possessed an iridescent black body and a brown head. The bird dropped to the ground, poking its beak at the underbrush. Liz looked away from the bird, scanning the landscape.

And then she saw it. The same metallic red color she'd seen in the blurry foreground of DeZona's photo. A synthetic strand of knitting material, worked into a bird's nest on the ground. But it was the tree branches, not the ground, that must have formed the foreground to DeZona's photos. Had the nest fallen from a tree? No, it looked as though it had been built where it lay, nestled into the twigs and leaves there. Liz shone her flashlight on the nest. It also contained some finer strands of strawberry-blonde human hair.

Grasping the sap-covered trunk of a young pitch pine for support, Liz heard a sound she recognized. The same kind of keening she'd heard from Veronica when the child flew across the Newton City Hall Common and threw herself into Liz's arms. This time, however, the sound came from Liz's own throat.

She turned her eyes to a sky that had turned the color of flame. And as she did, she saw the glint of another piece of synthetic yarn snagged on a tree branch, the kind of yarn that might well be knitted into the nose of a reindeer in a Christmas-patterned sweater.

Chapter 28

Although it was in easy reach, Liz did not remove the bird's nest from its place. Instead, with delicate movements born of respect for the dead, she pinched a few strands of hair between her fingernails and pulled them gently from the nest. She also used the scissors on the small Swiss Army knife she carried on her key chain to snip off a tiny segment of the synthetic yarn. Carefully folding the evidence into another sheet of paper taken from her reporter's notebook, she put the little packet into the pocket of her leather jacket.

Next, Liz looked around at the increasingly dim scene. The only outstanding landscape feature was a boulder, looking like a ghostly white mound in the falling light. She would have loved to measure the nest's distance from the boulder but had nothing except her feet or her notebook to use as a ruler. She was reluctant to pace the distance without having another landmark to find it by in the future. In her mind's eye, she drew a line from the boulder through the bird's nest to the first tree beyond the nest. It was the same pitch pine she grasped for support earlier. But, amongst so many other pines, how would she recognize this one later? She could tag the tree with paper but paper is not weatherproof and she did not want to call anyone else's attention to the spot. Looking fruitlessly for something to mark it with—even a pile of pebbles to place by its trunk—she realized she could bend and break some branches on the tree to mark it. Only after breaking three of them did she pace out the distance to the boulder. Then she used her flashlight to help her find and remove one piece of paper after another until she left the hollow behind her.

As she approached her car, which stood alone in the parking lot, she reproached herself for failing to comb the scene for any dark hairs the police might have left behind. Kinnaird would wish to compare them with the paler strands, she was certain.

In her car, she placed a call to her answering machine in the newsroom, hoping she would find a message on it from Cormac. There was no word from him. Instead, a message from Jan Van Wormer prompted her to phone him immediately.

"Al told me he returned to the topiary garden in Wellesley today," the piano builder said. "He said it was the first time, since that long-ago incident, that he could bring himself to visit a place he had once loved. When he was there, he saw an older woman tossing things to her dog. She didn't look particularly familiar, he said, but when he heard the sound of her voice he took another look. It was Ellen's mother, Olga Swenson."

"Yes, I know she was there today. I saw her there myself. But I didn't see Ali. What time of day was this?"

"Around one-thirty."

"That's when I was there."

"You wouldn't have seen my apprentice anyway. You see, after he looked into the little hidey-hole, he hid."

"What hidey-hole?"

"The place where he and Ellen—they were friends, you know—used to hide little toys and treasures. It's in the summerhouse, under a loose board in the floor."

"What did he find in the hidey-hole?"

"A toy horn I think. He said he blew it, but then, after spitting this much out, he went all tongue-tied on me."

"Perhaps I can get him to tell me more."

"I'm afraid that's impossible. The poor fellow has run off again."

Overtired from her day and confused in the darkness, Liz made a wrong turn as she attempted to drive back home. The mistake cost her almost an hour, as she found herself winding through sand-edged roads and past several small ponds in Myles Standish State Forest. But the long drive also gave her time to think. Teased by the fact that she and Ali had both been on the edges of the topiary garden at the same time but had not seen one another, she recalled René DeZona's remark, "My lens often sees things the eyes don't."

She recalled how, earlier that day, two students had posed on the hillside leading up to the summerhouse. Liz remembered framing them in the larger scene. Did her photo include the summerhouse, too? Perhaps. It was a long shot, but what if the photo revealed Ali holding the object that had upset him?

Pulling off the road, she dialed the operator and asked for the telephone number for Wellesley College information and then dialed it. She was in luck. The person on information line duty at Wellesley College was a student. Although at first the student told Liz she was not supposed to give out telephone numbers unless the caller knew both first and last names, she relaxed when Liz said, "You know that hot prof Florrie's nuts about? Well, I'm his TA. He asked me to get in touch with her for him."

"Oh, well, if you're his teaching assistant. . ." She supplied the number.

Fortunately, Florrie was thrilled to be contacted by a news reporter. Although the camera was not hers, she knew it was a digital model. She said she'd get in touch with her friend Ellen and ask her to e-mail the image to Liz as soon as possible.

It took almost an hour for Liz to reach the newsroom, where she accessed her e-mail. Sure enough, the Wellesley student had come through. There was the image of the two attractive young women in the topiary garden. Unfortunately, though, the camera angle did not take in the summerhouse. Liz should have remembered this, because when she stood in the shade at the edge of the Pinetum to take a backlit shot, she would have had to point the camera westward, not northward, up the slope. The wider scene Liz had framed included Lake Waban and the balustrade that defined the shore. Exhausted, Liz printed out the image on ordinary paper, folded it into her pocket, and drove home.

Too tired to fuss with the window shades, Liz left them open and went straight to bed. That meant she had a great view of Tom's legs through her kitchen window when she awoke in the morning. She invited him in and, ruefully, he agreed to give Cormac Kinnaird the packet of evidence Liz had prepared, if the doctor came by to collect it while Tom was still there. Standing at her kitchen counter and gazing at the photo she'd taken in the topiary garden, she left a telephone message for Cormac, telling him about the bird's nest find and adding, "I'm off to inform Olga about what I've discovered. I'd tell Erik in person, too—it seems the civilized thing to do to inform the family personally—but he's in police custody. Perhaps we can do that together, later," she added, as Tom's expression darkened.

Chapter 29

Liz drove to Wellesley and parked on the college campus. She wanted to make her way to Olga's through the Pinetum and topiary garden. The walk would give her time to consider how to break the news.

Liz's beautiful legs felt leaden as she left the topiary garden behind and rounded the lake to Olga's house. And yet she strode on purposefully. Approaching the house from the lakeshore, she walked directly toward the door of the mudroom. Standing slightly ajar, the door was caught by a gust of wind as she neared it, affording her the chance to look inside while remaining unobserved. Olga could be seen standing with her back to the door. For the first time, Liz thought how odd it was for Olga to work with her back to that view. Then, she thought, perhaps it was explicable after all, since the woman's husband had died in those waters.

On Olga's potting bench stood not one but three flower arrangements. On the floor to the left and right of Olga stood still more. As Liz ran her eyes over the arrangements, she realized Olga had executed eight different designs representing as many schools of flower-design technique. There was a formal French arrangement, strong on big, blowsy blooms, in a gilt pedestal-style container. It would have looked at home in a French château. At the opposite extreme was a minimalist Ikebana design. Dependent on one bamboo stalk, one striking bloom of *Heliconia*, and a spear-like leaf Liz could not name, this was a study in proportion and balance. Olga's technically perfect but disparate arrangements looked unlikely to be useful in any single venue.

Olga turned. She seemed unsurprised to see Liz standing there.

"I'm missing Ellen," was all she said. She waved an arm towards the arrangements. In her hand was a pair of florist's scissors designed for rose cutting.

Entering the mudroom, Liz removed a coat from one of the hooks near the door and held it, her arms extended, displaying to Olga the manufacturer's label, marred with the word "Ritz" stamped on it in hot pink ink.

"I see we shop in the same place," Liz said. "Puttin' on the Ritz. Excellent bargains there, don't you think? Even during the week before Christmas, one can buy a new coat, even a complete new outfit, on sale."

Olga said nothing.

"You didn't care about the price, though, did you, when you purchased this coat in that shop last December? It was more the convenience that attracted you. Money would have been no object in covering up what you did. No, it was the convenience that attracted you, wasn't it, Olga? The shop is right around the corner from your hairdresser."

Olga shifted the scissors from one hand to the other. She said nothing.

"The neighborhood around your hairdresser is one you know well, isn't it? You could almost call it a 'haunt.' You've had the same hairdresser for years, even decades, haven't you? You usually park your car under the Prudential Center, where Lord & Taylor is. Or, on occasion, you park it in Newton and travel into town on the Green Line with your daughter—the wife of an environmentalist, after all.

"Yes, you know the area well, in every season. Not far from Lord & Taylor are the Boston Public Library and the Copley Square T stop for the Green Line. A quick taxi ride would deliver you to Back Bay Station and the commuter rail that runs all the way out to Wellesley: a convenient route to Wellesley if you go into the city by train—let's say, to rent a car after an accident. There's a car rental place on Boylston Street, just doors away from Puttin' on the Ritz.

"You also know that, in the winter when there is a snowstorm, snow gets thrown up on cars so that they are entirely covered with the stuff. Sometimes vehicles sit there for days or weeks before the city digs them out and tows them away."

Olga set down her scissors and picked up a rose from the potting bench. Peering at Liz over its tightly closed bud she tore off a blood-red petal and cast it on the floor at her feet.

Still, she said nothing.

"You knew if you rented a car in Ellen's name some days after she disappeared, it would suggest she was still living, that she had exited her kitchen, if not voluntarily, at least alive. And covered with snow, the car might take some time to be found. You had your daughter's purse, Olga, didn't you? Her credit card, her driver's license, even her fountain pen. You must have been bundled up when you rented the car, wearing a hood, perhaps. It was an awful risk to take but you were in luck, with a clerk who was more interested in painting her nails than in taking a good look at you. Perhaps she was lax, too, in providing you with a pen. You didn't want her to look up from her manicure so you used Ellen's fountain pen to sign the car rental agreement. The pen Erik gave Ellen to celebrate their anniversary. Not the anniversary of their wedding, but the anniversary of their meeting: August eighteenth."

Olga tore another petal off the rose and dropped it to the floor. And another. Then another.

"The earlier phone call, on Veronica's birthday, in June: Anyone could have made that call. Even a cabbie might draw that date out of a passenger while making small talk. Erik hardly dared hope it was Ellen who made the birthday phone call. But a call on August 18? Well, that was different. It had to be significant that a call arrived from Ellen's cell phone on that date!

"But Erik and Ellen are not the only people who know that date's import. You know it, too, Olga, don't you?"

Olga raised the rose before her eyes and scrutinized it. Without a word, she tore off two more petals, dropping each to the floor.

"Then panic set in and you became sloppy. After you guessed I'd spoken to Ali and after you accidentally revealed that you knew his Middle Eastern background, you had to suggest Ellen was still living, didn't you, Olga? And after you saw me looking at your coat collar, with its label stamped by a cheap discount store, you had to throw the suspicion on someone else, didn't you?

"How convenient for you that Ellen's husband had a cell phone that was identical in appearance to your daughter's. One that doesn't even reveal the phone's own number when you consult it to find out the time. If you substituted it briefly for Erik's, he'd never realize it was not his. And then, with your entrée to his house, you could easily retrieve the phone after you knew he'd made a call on it."

Olga peeled another petal from the rose. She held the petal out before her on the palm of her hand and blew it off. It fell to the floor slowly, without a sound.

"You couldn't know the bodies would be found while he had the phone in hand, though, could you? If you'd known they would be found then, you'd have made another wordless call yourself, wouldn't you? The idea was to suggest she was alive, after all.

"And you couldn't know he would phone me, of all people, could you? He might have called anyone, even perhaps the police. How bizarre *that* would have been! The most likely suspect in the murder of his wife phones the police on his wife's cell phone—the very phone that has been used for months to suggest she is alive—to request information about the scene of the crime.

"But, in any event, he did not phone the police from Ellen's phone. It was the trace on his line that led the police directly to the most likely suspect: the missing woman's husband.

"You had to know the press would have a heyday with this, the perfect target. How could anyone help but think Erik had sought out the man with whom his wife presumably disappeared, and done him in? And after September eleventh, it is so easy to vilify anyone of Middle Eastern extraction. The public would support Erik's wrath even as he was condemned for it legally."

Removing the last three petals from the rose, Olga looked Liz directly in the eye with an expression that could only be read as challenging. Still, she said nothing.

"You don't think I can produce any evidence, do you? Well, you're wrong there. Remember, Erik phoned me—the one journalist who's more concerned with the truth than with a sensational headline about a jealous husband, the one reporter who knows and cares about your daughter. When you found out he was on the line with me, you interrupted him, didn't you? I heard him say 'Oh!' as if he'd been distracted. But it was the start of your name, wasn't it? He was beginning to say 'Olga'."

Olga's face came alive as she made a disdainful snort.

"You're right, Olga. That would never convince anyone in a court of law. But, you see, there's something else to worry about. After I received that cell-phone call from Erik, I went to see him. He showed me his cell phone. Yes, *his* cell phone, not your daughter's. Sure, he might have hidden hers. But I know he didn't, because when Ali came out to the summerhouse yesterday to revisit it after all those years, he found it in the hiding place there. He started to make a call on it—later, when he realized he'd nearly used an important piece of evidence to make a call to his boss, he said he "almost blew it." But he stopped dialing when he recognized your voice calling to the dog.

"He replaced the phone and hid up there, behind the summerhouse. And he saw you retrieve the phone and heave it, like a dog's toy, into the lake. Only this time you had Hershey on a leash, didn't you? The dog strained to leap into the lake, but you did not let him."

Olga picked up the pair of rose cutters. Centering the rose stem between two small bites in the blades, she closed the scissors and pulled the flowerless stem between them, shearing off the thorns, one by one. With little sounds like time ticking away, they hit the cold slate floor between Olga and her challenger.

"With Erik in police custody and the convincing suggestion made that he had been using the phone all along, that phone had no more usefulness to you. You're counting on a jury to find such ramblings mere speculation. But that's not all, Olga. I, too, was there yesterday afternoon, photographing two young women you would call 'coeds' in the topiary garden. You didn't see me? Well, I saw you. And my heart went out to you when one of the young women called out the name 'Ellen.' But the photograph I took of those girls tells another story. You see, you and Hershey appear in that photo, too. Hershey is straining at the leash as the 'toy'—no, Olga, the cell phone you had just tossed—is frozen by the camera in its trajectory into Lake Waban. I have no doubt police divers will be able to find it there."

Olga considered the rose stem. Placing it between the flattened fingers of her two hands, she rolled it back and forth. A bit of thorn must have remained on it to prick her. At long last, the flower arranger flinched. And her blood flowed.

"The place where the bodies are, near Plymouth, that's not the scene of the murder, is it? You killed your daughter in her own kitchen when you came upon her with the swarthy-skinned man. You feared Ellen would confront you—even broadcast to others—the secret you'd hidden for decades: Her father and your husband—Karl Swenson—was a pervert. When you saw the cabbie, you thought he was the boy, all grown up now, who witnessed your husband's masturbating over his own daughter. The same boy who phoned you on the anniversary of that awful day, year after year after year after year in December. So you killed them both, Olga.

"I wouldn't have thought you capable of murder, Olga. Not until I realized you were cruelly capable of feeding Veronica false hope by making that call on her birthday. And not until I saw that you would stoop to implicate the only parent Veronica has left. Not until I saw you cared more about your husband's reputation and your own freedom than about the well-being of your granddaughter. I thought you loved your granddaughter."

In a sudden movement, and with a sound like a snarl, Olga shoved Liz into the doorjamb and reached past the several coats that were hanging on the wall. She wheeled around, training a rifle on Liz.

"Veronica!" she cried out. "Don't you *dare* tell me I don't love Veronica.

That's not true! I did what I did to be here for Veronica. You think you're clever, don't you? But you're wrong about Karl. He would never behave like that. Never!"

"You may deny it and you may kill me, as I think you did your daughter, but there are still two more people who know what happened that day by this lake: Ali himself, and Ellen's pen pal, Nadia. The police will know you murdered to hide your family secret. Count on it."

The gun moved in Olga's shaking hands. "I believed my husband when he told me the tongue-tied boy had exposed himself to Ellen. I still believe it! When I arrived at Ellen's house and saw through the window a man clapping a hand over my daughter's mouth, I knew it was that boy grown up. He was saying the same strange words, like a tuneless hum. It had to be the same person! I went out to the garden shed, where I'd hidden the skeet shooter I'd bought for Veronica for Christmas, and I loaded it. When I came back to the house the man had my daughter pinned to his side, with his bloody hand over her mouth. I wanted to stop him but I'm no killer. I aimed for his legs and pulled the trigger. I closed my eyes on what I'd done." Olga shuddered and hugged the rifle to herself, barrel pointed upward. "But when I opened them, there was Ellen, on the floor. She was dead."

Heedless of the rifle butt, which was now pressed against the underside of her chin, Olga sobbed. Liz stepped forward, reached for the weapon, and very slowly put her hand around the barrel. Relinquishing the gun, Olga sat down hard on the cold slate floor. She picked up some thorns and rolled them in her palms, bloodying her hands as she spoke.

"I must have killed her. It was inexplicable but I must have! The man kept up that awful humming. I had no idea what to do. I wanted to shoot the man, just to stop him humming. I wanted to run and run and run.

"Then the cookie ingredients caught my eye and I thought of Veronica. I couldn't let her come home to this kitchen. I just couldn't. I still had the gun. I could make the man clean the place up. First, we had to—to do something about Ellen. I looked around and saw the tree bag, the kind you use to wrap up a Christmas tree before you put it out for the trash. I made him put Ellen inside it. And I made him put the bag outside the back door. It was cold out there; it was beginning to snow. But how else could we clean up for Veronica? We came back inside the house then. I directed him to put on the rubber gloves that Ellen always keeps around. I told him to fill the dishpan on the side of the sink with water and some floor cleaner. I made him put the bottle of floor cleaner back under the sink. I made him use a sponge to wipe the floor and the wall behind where Ellen had—had been. While he was mopping, he knocked over one of the poinsettias. After it looked like he had done a pretty good job cleaning up, I made him carry the poinsettia into the living room. I wanted to keep his hands busy. I had to keep that man with me everywhere so I could point the gun at him.

"That's when I saw Ellen's purse in the man's open backpack. There was no time to wonder what it was doing there. I pulled the purse out of the backpack and took Ellen's keys out of it. Something fell out of her purse and when I bent down to pick it up, the Arab set down the poinsettia suddenly and flew across the room at me. He was reaching for the gun when the doorbell rang. Instead of grabbing the gun, he fled the room! You would have thought the man would have welcomed what we glimpsed through the window. It was two foreign-looking men, maybe Middle Eastern.

"I was afraid he would lunge at me again; I had to keep him under control. I followed him into the kitchen and kept the gun pointed at him. I wanted to stay in the kitchen and clean the counter where the cookie ingredients were, but he's rattled me so! I was shaken. I put on my coat and grabbed Ellen's jacket, too. I don't know why I took the jacket. It just seemed like a good idea. Later I found Ellen's purse and mine, and the Arab's backpack, in the car, but I hardly remember putting them there.

"After we heard the two men drive away in their car, I made the man put the Christmas tree bag into the trunk of Ellen's car. My head was spinning and I couldn't think straight. I wanted it to be my car but it was too far away. Because of the snow storm, I had parked it in the City Hall parking lot, which is always kept plowed. We got into Ellen's Honda. I made him drive. I sat in the back seat so I could keep the gun pointed at him. It was not easy to do in the car.

"At first, I didn't care where we drove, as long as it was away from Ellen's house. Then I thought of Plymouth. I had picnicked there when I was a girl. I knew there were some isolated woods there.

"The drive was a blur. I was so shattered and it was snowing so hard. By the time we got to some deserted recreational area, the snow was quite deep, but not deep enough to make it easy to slide the—the Christmas tree bag into the woods. There was a lot of underbrush, and stumps, and even holes in the ground that you couldn't see in the snow. I hung back, gesturing with the gun at him every time he seemed likely to turn on me, and made him put her in a hollow. Then I told him to cover her up with snow. I didn't want to kill him but I was sure I must. All I could think was Veronica would not have a woman in her life—not a mother, not a grandmother—if I were turned in for what I'd done.

"When he bent over to cover Ellen with snow, I shot him. He fell down on top of the plastic bag. On top of my daughter.

"Up until then, I was a person in a daze. But that seemed to wake me up. Suddenly I realized I needn't have done this thing. Surely, I could have explained to the police that I'd tried to protect my daughter from an attacker. After all, shooting my daughter was an accident. But then I thought, how could Veronica love the person who had killed her mother, even if I shot her unintentionally?

"There was something else. I did not *feel* innocent. I felt guilty about him. I told you before, I'm no killer, so I aimed at his legs, but I didn't *want* to aim at his legs. I wanted to kill him point blank for exposing himself to Ellen and for all those phone calls and for putting his bloody hand over her mouth in her kitchen. I *wanted* him to die. And I wanted to be the one to kill him."

Olga looked up at Liz with an expression of relief on her haggard face.

"So when those two men arrived at Ellen's house and startled us, I felt like a guilty woman who has no choice but to flee. And I fled.

"There in the woods, in the snow, I had to move that man off my daughter. I went down into the hollow and pushed him off her. It was not so hard to slide him across the plastic. But as I pushed him, my hand encountered his belt. I realized someone might figure out who he was from his clothes, and then they would connect the boy from the Wharton School with our family. So I removed his boots, and an awful gaudy ring he was wearing, and his belt. I took his wallet, too. It fell open as I held it, and I saw a taxi driver's I.D. card in the wallet's plastic window. The picture matched the man's face, but the name was not Al Leigh. It was something foreign. Seeing this, I felt I couldn't breathe. But I could see my breath in the air, big clouds of it. I must have been gasping.

"I opened the bag and took off Ellen's wedding ring, and her earrings, and her shoes. It was much harder to take off her sweater, but I did that, too. I think it tore as I took it off of her. I was glad she was lying on her face. I covered her up with snow then and walked back up the hill. I put the sweater, the shoes and boots, and the gun and things in the trunk, but I kept Ellen's jewelry in my coat pocket.

"I got into the car and turned on the engine. When the heat came on I realized how chilled I was. I didn't know where I was exactly, so I just drove. I would have loved to drive around mindlessly forever, but I knew I had to get back to Ellen's to wipe off the counter. Silly of me, I know. It was already too late in the day for that. Veronica would have come home by then. But that's what I thought. It was the only thought in my mind. I didn't even think about what I would do with the car.

"Then I saw the pond and it occurred to me that I could just drive the car right into it. But there was a kind of metal edging there to prevent cars running off the road. I kept driving. Then I saw the second pond. It was set back farther from the road but there was nothing stopping me from driving in. I got out of the car first and traded my coat for Ellen's jacket. It had a hood and it was cleaner and much drier than my coat. I took the jewelry out of the coat and put it into my purse. I also added some things from Ellen's purse to mine. Then I put my coat and Ellen's purse into the trunk and locked it. I got in the car and positioned it on a slope that leads toward the pond, leaving the engine running. I put on the handbrake and got out.

"I took a plastic shopping bag that was in the car and filled it with snow—I don't know what made me think of this—and I put the bag on the gas pedal. Then I reached in and released the hand brake. The bag of snow wasn't very heavy, so the car only edged forward, but it kept going, right into the pond. I watched until it sank out of sight.

"I walked along the road for awhile. It seemed a long time but I don't think it could have been. Then, in a little pull-off, I saw a car idling with no one in it. I suppose someone was walking a dog there. There were dog tracks and boot prints leading away from the car. I got in and drove the car to Boston. The radio was playing 'God Rest Ye Merry Gentlemen.' I listened to the carol all the way through. Then the announcer told the time. I turned off the radio then.

"I realized it was too late to clean up the kitchen, but there was time to keep my hairdresser's appointment. I don't know how I remembered that appointment. But I knew if I kept it, it would make it look like I'd had a normal day's outing. I parked on Boylston Street, where I saw the off-price clothing outlet. There were homeless people in there sheltering from the snowstorm. If I appeared disheveled, I looked no worse than they did. I bought the coat, new slacks, and a sweater. Then, in a Dunkin' Donuts bathroom a few doors down, I changed my clothes. I stuffed the shopping bag of old clothes in a trash can on Boylston Street by the car rental place and went straight to the hairdresser. After that, I went to FAO Schwarz and bought a teddy bear for Veronica. I knew the Christmas shopping would help make my day look normal, but that isn't why I bought it. I bought the bear because *I love that child*," she said. She lifted her thorn-torn hands and gazed at them, perplexed, as though she had no idea how they'd been bloodied.

Sitting on the chilly slate floor, amid the rose petals and thorns, Olga said no more.

Liz was silent, too, as she mentally calculated the time it would have taken Olga to take the Green Line to Newton Highlands, pick up her car at Newton City Hall, and drive to Wellesley in the snow. She must have had to turn around immediately upon arriving at her house and drive back to Newton through the storm to collect Veronica from the Johansson house.

But it was difficult to keep her mind on matters of timing as she stood in the doorway between the distraught woman and the view of the lakeshore. So much had happened in the landscape Olga refused to look at from her home. Looking down at Olga as the woman sat, mute now, on the slate, Liz slumped against the doorjamb, staggered with pity.

"You don't have to report what you know," a voice told Liz, expressing the thought that was running through her mind. "You should think it through before you do. What do the police have on Erik, anyway? Just circumstantial evidence. You are in the position to let a little girl who's lost her mom keep her grandma *and* her dad."

Liz looked down at Olga. The older woman seemed utterly unmoved.

Perhaps Liz was hearing things. She moved to sit on the floor herself.

But strong hands and arms reached out and supported her. She turned and relinquished herself to Tom's embrace.

"I followed you," he explained, "to surprise you with a picnic lunch." He pointed to the Mexican blanket and a small backpack from which a baguette and bottle of wine protruded. "I didn't want you to go off with that guy Kinnaird. When you went inside, I waited out of sight here." He pointed to a spot behind the open mudroom door. "When I heard you confront Olga, I was afraid she'd hurt you."

"Exactly!" Liz said, stepping back from Tom's arms—and from the temptation to let Olga go free—in one movement. "That's just it, Tom! You see, there's no telling how many times she would kill in order to remain a loving grandmother, in order to stay in Veronica's life."

"But if you don't report it, Liz, she'll have nothing to fear. She's not attacking you now, even when you might still report her! Think of Veronica more than your career, Liz! She needs a loving woman in her life. Look," he said, striding into the mudroom and picking up a framed photo of Veronica blowing out nine candles on her birthday cake, with her grandmother smiling over her shoulder.

Liz stared at Tom, stunned he would support Olga. Then she remembered that Tom had been brought up by his own grandmother in the absence of his mother.

Liz turned her attention to the photo. Hanging around Veronica's neck was the wedding ring Olga had ornamented with a stone for Veronica—the wedding ring that she had stripped from her daughter's lifeless finger. It was one thing to do everything possible—even to cover up a killing—to remain in a beloved child's life. It was another thing entirely to hang a memento of that horror around that child's neck. As Tom looked on aghast, Liz took out her cell phone and dialed the police.

Chapter 30

Even with television and radio reporters covering the arrest of Olga Swenson in the evening news, Liz's full solution to the crime, set to run in the next day's *Beantown Banner*, was a scoop.

"That's star-spangled reporting for you," Dermott McCann admitted, lifting a drink to Liz at J.J. Foley's, a Boston bar frequented by news reporters. "Great legwork," he added, slapping her on the back and looking down at her legs.

Esther O'Faolin winced. Then she said, "Good job, Liz."

"Nice that you had that forensics guy in your back pocket," Dick Manning admitted. "How'd you get ahold of him?"

"That was thanks to Esther, actually. And Dermott, too. They insisted I cover a mystery writer's conference at the Worcester Public Library." Liz smiled as Cormac Kinnaird walked in and crossed the barroom where no Irish music played. "I was so fascinated by his bite marks presentation that the rest is history," she said, winking, as Kinnaird arrived at her side and put an arm around her shoulder. "Here's the good doctor himself."

"Liz wrote about your assessment of the crime scene in Plymouth," Esther said. "Because Olga Swenson confessed, we cut some of it to put the focus on the confession. But I'd like to hear more about it. I gather from what Liz wrote that if the Swenson woman hadn't confessed and you hadn't realized there was an ephemeral pond there, the identities of the skeletons might never have been discovered. The police would have thought the bones were too old to have anything to do with the case."

"Possibly," Kinnaird said, "although, under ordinary circumstances, the dental work should have been matched to Ellen Johansson's in a matter of minutes on the police databases."

"The guy who didn't enter them into the system is in deep shit, I'll bet," the city editor said.

"Not as deep as it might have been if the Johansson case didn't look like a possible voluntary absence," Kinnaird said. "Remember, it was not clear murder was done. I think the error would have been caught more quickly once the bones were found if the ME had not been in Manhattan helping out with the remains from Ground Zero."

"What about the cabbie's teeth? Didn't they have dental records for him on the database, too?" Jared asked.

"No one filed dental records for him. The only person who seems to have missed Samir Hasan was the manager of the taxi garage," Liz said. "And he soon discovered Hasan had given him false information. Hasan was so successful in hiding his true identity that we still don't know who he was. Ironically, he was killed based on mistaken identity, too. I wonder if somebody, somewhere, cared about him," she added, running her fingers through her hair and looking across the barroom distractedly.

"Did Mrs. Swenson have any notion why the cabbie was in her daughter's kitchen?" Jared asked Liz. "Or did she kill him before she could find out?"

"She told me she believed he was the same person who had masturbated at the sight of her scantily dressed daughter when Ellen was just eight years old. She said she shot him, not just because he had a bloody hand over her daughter's mouth, but because he used an Arabic expression that made her think he was that person come back to threaten Ellen again. She would have liked me to think Ellen never knew about Karl's perversions. Perhaps she didn't, but it's just as likely she killed to keep the family secret."

"If it wasn't the same guy, then why was the taxi driver in the kitchen?" Jared asked.

"I'm not sure we'll ever know," Liz said. "Ellen told her pen pal, Nadia, she'd taken a strange cab ride during which the driver communicated in Arabic on the two-way radio with another Arabic speaker. We know the word *teena*—the Arabic word for 'fig'—was used in that conversation and it appeared in a list of words found in the cab's glove compartment. Was this a code word used for some illegal operation, even a terrorist plot? Was the driver simply talking salaciously about a woman named Tina? We can't be sure."

"I'll bet he had a terrorist connection," Manning put in. "Probably he was sent to do Ellen in after she overheard something he said. Didn't you say she spoke some Arabic?"

"Just a few words and phrases. If Hasan sought to eliminate Ellen," Liz said, "why would he panic when the car dealers arrived at the Johansson house? Shouldn't they have appeared to be welcome allies? It's just as likely the cabbie came to warn her that something she'd overheard had put her in danger."

"In any case, Ellen's own mother did her in," Esther said, apparently satisfied with that incontrovertible fact. Turning to Dr. Kinnaird, she added, "Tell us more about the ephemeral pond."

"I worked under a great disadvantage, of course," Kinnaird obliged, "since I didn't have access to the police evidence from the scene of the crime until the department took me on as a consultant today. But while the police had the physical evidence, they did not know the crime scene was submerged with water a few months after the bodies were placed there. Ordinarily, this would make the remains appear less old than they are. Even if an expert had examined the bones with the organic shower in mind, he or she might think the bones had arrived there relatively recently, since pollen that had fallen during the wet season would not cover the bones in the ordinary way. Those bones would have been shielded from the rain of organic material by the water."

"But surely not entirely?" Jared Conneely piped in.

"That's right. Some pollen from all of the seasons during which the remains had been outdoors would potentially show up after careful analysis. But it would not be obvious on preliminary examination."

"Why, then, did the bones seem older than they were?" René DeZona asked.

"For the reason this young man suggests," Kinnaird said, pointing to Jared. "There was, indeed, organic material in that pond. Remember, the area is surrounded by white and pitch pines. Stewing in that pond each year is pitch from those trees, loading that water with tannin. Bathed in a sort of acidic tea, the remains were immersed in a kind of natural preservative. To some extent, those bones were on the road to mummification. Think of the bog people archeologists have discovered."

"Wasn't the ME getting a grip on this, now that he's back from New York? He told me today he thought the bones must have been placed there more recently," Dick Manning said.

"Yes, but it was the hair found with the bones that still gave him pause. I discussed that with him this afternoon. He was puzzled at how the bones could appear so old and stained while rather well-preserved hair was found under the skulls. If he'd known a seasonal pond was there, he might have figured it out. I told him about the pond and the preservative effects of tannin. The tannin not only stained the bones. It also acted as a dye when it was absorbed into Ellen Johansson's hair. Samir Hasan's hair was already black. That's why initial reports indicated the two victims were dark-haired."

"The bog people all had dark hair, too," Jared volunteered. "I've seen pictures of them. But they were preserved, skin and all. Their skin looked like leather! But there was no skin on the bones in Plymouth."

"Unlike the bog people, our two victims were not immediately plunged into water. Remember, they lay out in the elements, where animals could strip those bones. Water only covered the bones after the snow melt formed the ephemeral pond—some would call it a vernal pool—in the spring."

Dick Manning was not convinced. "How can you be so sure about the pond?" he asked. "There might be some ponds in there, but that's a big woods. What if the science teacher is wrong about that pond's location? Isn't it dry there now?"

"I examined the area myself, after the police were through with restricting the scene. Even in this dry season, I know that depression holds water in the spring. I can tell from the signature species—plant and animal life that exists only under specific conditions. I found certain salamanders, sedges, white-bracted boneset, and bladderwort there. These are signatures of a vernal pool. Even that tall grass, where the deer lay down, is evidence that standing water prevented the encroachment of other shrubs and ground cover there. Yes, there is no doubt this is the site of an ephemeral pond."

To his credit, Dick heard Kinnaird out. Then he said, "Another round to celebrate Liz's success? It's on me."

Liz embraced her rival.

"I'm wondering why that Christmas plant you tested was never sprayed with luminol," Dick said.

"Olga had Hasan carry it out of the kitchen," Liz said. "She wanted to 'keep his hands busy.'"

"But wasn't it in my photo, which was taken after that?" DeZona asked.

"The poinsettia labeled for the aftercare teacher did remain in the kitchen. Veronica gave her teacher the unlabeled plant that Hasan had carried into the living room."

Just then, ever-helpful editorial assistant E.A. Tenley entered the bar. "I saw your story for tomorrow's paper, Liz," she enthused. "What a scoop!"

"A front-pager if I ever saw one!" Jared said.

"Actually, *not*," the editorial assistant said. "I'm sorry to tell you, Liz. I saw the edition."

"We had to lead with breaking news out of Ground Zero," Dermott told Liz. "But don't worry. We gave you a front-page teaser."

Dick returned with a pint of ale for Liz. "Have a whole pint, not just half. You're in the big time now, kiddo," he said and walked off to deliver another drink to Esther O'Faolin.

Over the pint, Liz asked Kinnaird, "Was it inevitable that this case would be solved, Cormac? I mean, it looks like the bodies would have been identified in any case and the timing established, but do you think there was any chance Olga Swenson might not have been identified as the perpetrator?"

"Not with the information you assembled—the photo of her tossing the cell phone into the lake, for instance."

"But what if I didn't . . . ."

"Didn't report what you know? It might have been pinned on someone innocent, like Erik."

"But if the evidence was only circumstantial . . ."

"Look, Liz," the doctor said, taking her elbow and leading her across the room. As the two seated themselves at a small table across from each other on tall stools, Kinnaird leaned forward. "That way leads to disaster."

"What way?"

"Second-guessing yourself. It's never a good idea. It's morally incumbent upon us as professionals to report what we know. We can't let misguided emotions get in our way. That's all there is to it."

Liz looked doubtful.

"Remember, you had the guts to phone the police, despite Tom's urging you not to."

"It was more than guts, Cormac. There was that photograph of the wedding ring necklace on Veronica. But there was something else, too."

She shuddered as her companion waited patiently for her to continue.

"It was the lake," Liz said. "She never faced the lake. I had to wonder if she protected her daughter from Karl's perversion by pushing him through the ice. But there's no evidence to support . . . ." She broke off and raised her hands to her temples.

"I'll say it again. You can't afford to let your emotions take over."

The doctor held out his hands, palms up, hands that had opened countless cadavers. Slowly, he moved his right hand to grip his own pint glass of lager. Silently, he held open his left hand and regarded the calloused fingertips his companion had once kissed, one by one. His face and his voice softened.

"Actually," the doctor added, "that's not all there is to it, as we both know. Like me, you'll have to find a way to make peace with what you've set in motion. You've got to find a way to live with it." Standing up, he took her hand in his calloused grip. "Now, let's get out of this place and find some music."